The Black Gigolo

A Novel

Denzil Devarro

The Black Gigolo

A Novel

Denzil Devarro

LILBURN   TRUTH OF LIFE PUBLISHING   GEORGIA

Copyright © 2006 by Denzil Devarro
Lilburn, Georgia
All rights reserved
Printed and Bound in the United States of America

Published and Distributed by:
Truths of Life Publishing

Cover Design/Photography
Cover Layout Formatting by Milligan Books

First Printing, January 2007

ISBN 978-0-9791087-4-7

The text book is composed in 12 pt. inch Franklin Gothic
he text book is composed in 12 pt. inch Franklin Gothic
1. Fiction—2. Mystery

───

Truths of Life Publishing
Lilburn, GA 30274
Email: denzilandrews328@yahoo.com
(404) 438-8674

Chapter 1

MICHAEL ALEXANDER WAS A FORMER professional basketball player that played overseas for a couple of years. At age 27, he left pro sports and became an insurance salesman, working his way to the top of a leading insurance company. He was always successful at everything he'd put his mind to and found the insurance business to be no different. But little did he know his life would soon be spiraling out of control into a dark world of sex and drugs. In an attempt to find his true self, Michael would travel the world in search of his true inner being. The one thing that kept Michael above ground was the love women seem to instantly have for him.

But will that love be a blessing or a curse? This is the story of Michael Alexander. His story begins at the Shark Club, downtown Los Angeles. The occasion, Progress Insurance is about to introduce their first-ever African-American national president. Over 700 people have gathered together for this festive occasion.

"Baby, be careful," said Sheila Alexander. "That's the third shot of Hennessey you've had already."

"Ah, baby," said Michael to his wife, "it's not every day that you become national president of the largest insurance company in America. You know, baby," he continued, "a million dollar salary, a mansion in Bel Air, a beautiful sister by my side, a beautiful four-year-old daughter—what more can a man ask for?"

Michael's friend, Kenneth Bolling, listened with his wife, Cheryl, as he reflected on the events of the evening.

Michael began to kiss Sheila as Kenneth approached.

"I'm jealous," Kenneth said as Michael kissed his wife, "and I'm also going to tell your wife that some strange woman is kissing all over you." Sheila looked up from the kiss.

"Oh, Sheila," Kenneth said, "I didn't know that was you."

"Yea, right," she replied, hugging Kenneth while Michael greeted and kissed Cheryl. Michael and Kenneth had been friends since childhood, and the girls were best friends in college, where they all met.

"Mike, let's walk over here for some male bonding," suggested Kenneth.

"Male bonding, huh?" said Cheryl. "Don't bond too much and leave us over here by ourselves."

"Don't worry," said Michael, "we wouldn't leave the two most beautiful sisters in the house by yourselves. Besides, we wouldn't want any other brothers in tuxedos taking our women from us."

Michael stood 6 foot 4 and weighed 235 lbs with a muscular frame. A strikingly handsome black man with natural curly locks, he had beautiful skin and a nice, dark complexion and a "I'm in charge" type of swagger that men envied and women swooned over. Sheila was a drop-dead gorgeous, almond-skin sister, with a 5 foot 9 beautiful frame. She was Michael's high school sweetheart, who had been with him through thick and thin, good times and bad. Kenneth and

Michael had been best friends since age five and were best men at each other's wedding. Sheila and Cheryl were best friends since college. They were a close-knit bunch.

"No one could ever take me from you," Sheila said to Michael. "You are the love of my life."

"Ah, I think I'm gonna cry ..." Kenneth playfully commented. They all laughed as the two men walked off.

"Congratulations, Michael," a co-worker said as he walked by, extending his hand.

"Thanks," replied Michael.

"Yeah, congratulations," said a gorgeous black female co-worker with a low-cut formal skirt on, trying to grope Michael as Sheila watched from a distance.

"The nerve of that heifer trying to feel on my man!" Sheila grumbled. "And I thought this was a formal party anyway. What's she doing with that on?"

"Ah, girl, that's Wanda Davis," said Cheryl. "She has no class. And besides, I'll bet she's made a few visits to the men's room tonight already."

The two women laughed. Michael pulled away from the woman, and he and Ken went a little further to stop and talk.

"Here, brother," Ken said, handing Michael a glass of Hennessey. "A toast to Michael Alexander, national president of Progress Insurance."

The two men raised their glasses to toast. Ken held a small glass of champagne.

"Take it to the head," says Ken.

Michael vowed this would be his last drink as the two men finished. He was not much of a drinker, but was totally enjoying "his" night.

"I just want you to know how proud I am of you," added Kenneth. "We've been friends for 22 years, and you've accomplished everything you set your mind to—basketball, school, and the finest wife in America. I just want you to know how much I admire you, and that I will always love you as a brother. You know, I live my life vicariously through you."

Michael was speechless and hugged Ken as they made their way back and the ceremony was about to begin.

"Places, everyone!" the Master of Ceremony yelled. "Let's get started."

⋆⟫ ⋆⟫ ⋆⟫

Two hours later, at about 11 p.m., the ceremony began breaking up and Michael and Sheila headed towards the exit. Michael was feeling somewhat funny, but still reveling in the adulation of the night.

"Good night, Mr. President," said a co-worker as he left.

"Yea, congratulations, Michael," said another group of people.

"You alright?" asked Ken. Michael smiled, but seemed a bit woosy.

"I'm fine," he replied. "Maybe it was those Hennesseys you've been bringing me all night."

"It was only three," replied Ken. "There was a time when we would start out with three."

"Yea, that was a long time ago. Besides, they didn't hire me to be a drunk president. I've got huge plans for the company. I've got to validate my promotion."

Michael had made it to the top of the company in only five years based on huge sales numbers and his tremendous leadership qualities.

"You sure you're alright? You need me to drive you home?" Kenneth asked.

"No, brother, I'm good. Besides, Sheila and I have a surprise. We're going to have a son. After all, we want to give our little Brittany a baby brother, so we tried it again. You know, she's almost five now."

"We're not sure it's a boy," said Sheila.

"It's a boy!" said Michael, rubbing his wife's stomach.

"Congratulations!" said Cheryl, hugging Sheila. "And you didn't even tell me!"

"We wanted it to be a surprise," Sheila replied.

At that moment, the valet brought Michael's brand-new gold V-12 Mercedes 560 sedan.

"Mr. President, you're not riding in a limo?" asked Ken.

"I don't like people to be subservient," Michael responded.

"Well, your car should be gold, 'cause, brother, you've got the Midas touch."

Sheila told her friend Cheryl good-bye. Cheryl took a long look at Sheila. Michael escorted his wife to the passenger side and tipped the valet as he drove out of the driveway. He shook his head as if he were dizzy, but continued driving.

"Mike looked a little unsteady," observed Cheryl. "Maybe we should follow him to make sure he's OK."

"He's cool," said Ken. "Besides, we need to get home. I want to work on a son of my own."

Cheryl smiled and they gave the valet their ticket.

Michael and Sheila continued down Wilshire Boulevard toward their Bel Air home.

"Are you alright, baby?" she asked.

"Yea, I'm good, baby girl," he replied with a smile.

On the other side of the road, a truck approached at about 100 yards. Michael swerved slightly and then blacked out, losing control of his car and heading directly into the oncoming truck.

"Michael!" screamed Sheila as the new Mercedes collided head-on into the truck.

Sheila was killed instantly and Michael was knocked unconscious. He awakened two days later in a hospital bed, heavily sedated with multiple contusions, and handcuffed to his bed. He soon discovered that he was charged with one count of vehicular homicide and driving under the influence. Toxicology reports, however, showed that Michael's blood alcohol level was below the legal limit and the case was ruled an accident. The DA was forced to drop all charges based upon Michael's clean record and no priors.

Michael was so despondent over Sheila's death that he couldn't bring himself to attend his own wife's funeral. He viewed his wife's body at the initial viewing and fell into a deep state of depression. In an effort to erase the horror of this event, he decided to withdraw all his funds from the bank, left his mansion in Bel Air, and simply disappeared with his young daughter, Brittany. People attending Sheila's funeral were outraged and called Michael all kinds of names, but he was nowhere to be found. The day of the funeral, it rained heavily in Los Angeles. After the crowd left the burial site, Michael came to his wife's plot, just to work out his own emotional struggles at her grave. Grieving in his own way, Michael cried painful tears and just lay down at his wife's grave. He curled up across the grave as if he were in bed with her. Michael's tears were endless and with the rain, they seemed to go on forever. It was cold and wet, but Michael was unconcerned for his own health. He simply grieved for the woman he had loved his whole adult life, the woman he would always love. At this moment, he realized that life and death were one.

Chapter 2

ONE YEAR LATER, KEN FIRED up the engine on his 4-wheel drive Jeep and headed towards downtown Los Angeles. He had hired a private detective that had finally located Michael and his daughter, Brittany, at the Downtowner Hotel in the heart of the garment district of downtown Los Angeles. Kenneth couldn't believe that Michael had been so close for a year and yet, had not been found, and also that he went from living in the lap of luxury in a Bel Air mansion to the crack-infested slums of downtown Los Angeles. He was excited at the prospect of seeing his friend, but also very unsure of what kind of man he would find. Kenneth pulled up to Adams Avenue, where the hotel was, and was quickly propositioned.

"What you need, brother?" asked a man with a hood pulled over his head.

"Nothing from you," Ken answered sarcastically.

"Fuck you, ole sidity ass nigger," said the man in the hood.

"I can make you feel *real* good," said a black woman weighing about 100 lbs, wearing a miniskirt and her chest out, but her breasts sagging. She was also missing a few teeth.

"No, thanks," he replied.

"Well, how 'bout a dollar?" replied the woman.

Ken just kept on walking to the entrance of the hotel. As he entered the hotel lobby, he noticed a bunch of brothers sitting around, playing spades, while another group sat around watching *Soul Train*.

"You reneged," said one of the card players. "You cut diamonds a minute ago, and now you're playing the queen of diamonds."

"Man, these bitches be super fine on *Soul Train*," another man said, watching TV.

The hotel was very dirty, with the smell of urine everywhere and the stench of bodies needing to take a shower. Kenneth approached the front desk and spoke to the attendant, a middle-age white man.

"Sir, what room is Michael Alexander in?" he asked.

"I don't know any Michael Alexander," said the attendant. "This is a welfare-sponsored hotel, and I know very few faces or names that live here. They get their key and go directly to their rooms."

"Well, you have to know who they are to hand them a key," Ken persisted.

"Look, man, I told you, I don't know him."

A middle-age black woman stood by and listened to Ken argue with the attendant. She began to speak.

"Give me five dollars and I'll tell you where he is," said the woman.

As Kenneth reached into his pocket, a man approached from the side. "Frances, what are you doing?" he asked the lady. "She doesn't even know who she is, let alone anyone else. Who are you looking for, brother?" asked the man addressing Kenneth.

"I'm looking for this man," he said, holding a picture of Michael.

"I've never seen him before" replied the man.

"He's about 6 foot 4 and has a little girl with him. His name is Michael," added Kenneth.

"There is a guy that lives in room 340 that has a pretty little curly head daughter," said the man. "We get high together. You ain't 5-0, are you?"

Kenneth shook his head as if to say no.

"Okay," said the man. "He sits down here and plays cards with us, but he doesn't look that good. He doesn't look nearly that good. Come to think of it, his name is Mike."

"Room 340?" asked Kenneth.

"Yea, 340, right off the elevator on the third floor."

As the man finished telling Kenneth the information, he extended his hand in anticipation of money. "Give me a couple of dollars to get me a beer and a cigarette," he said.

"A pack of cigarettes cost five dollars by itself," said Kenneth.

"My man on the corner sells Double Deuce beers for ninety-nine cents and sells cigarettes for a quarter a piece."

Kenneth gave the man a five-dollar bill and the man pointed him to the elevator. As they came closer, Ken grabbed his nose because of the stench coming from the man and the hotel. He never thought in his wildest dreams that he would ever find Mike in a place like this. Michael was always a health nut, a neat freak. Kenneth only wondered what he would see next. There were only three floors in the hotel, but the elevator took what seemed like an eternity to come down. When it arrived, Kenneth hesitated briefly about getting on. Then a large, older brother got on first.

"You getting on or not?" asked the man. "I don't have all day."

Kenneth reluctantly stepped into the elevator and began the slow ride to the third floor.

"What floor you live on?" asked the stranger.

"I don't live on any floor," answered Ken. "I live in Bel Air."

"That's how it is with you high-society ass people. You live uptown, but you come downtown to do your dirty work."

Kenneth simply ignored the man and continued to ride the elevator, hoping that it wouldn't malfunction.

"This elevator used to be real slow before they speeded it up ..."

Kenneth couldn't imagine the elevator being any slower and after what seemed like forever, they finally reached the third floor. He was in mental anguish the entire ride and gladly got off the elevator and looked about for room 340, which was situated directly across from the elevator.

Room 340 of the Downtowner Hotel had a wooden door with a fist-sized hole in it, no doorknob, and no means to lock the door. Kenneth expected the worst, and the worst is what he saw. The tall, handsome man who Kenneth had toasted on the night of his promotion no longer existed. Michael was now very frail and smelled very badly. As Kenneth opened the door, Michael sat on the floor, trying to light a pipe and didn't even realize that Kenneth had entered the room. Potato chip wrappers and candy wrappers were strewn all over the floor and in the corner on a small little cot was a very pretty little girl trying to sleep. Kenneth was initially happy to see Michael, but his happiness turned to rage as he saw the condition of Brittany, Michael's daughter.

"Come on, bitch," said Michael, talking to his pipe. "Show me how much you love me, girl."

As Michael went to light the pipe, Kenneth slapped it away from him in anger. Michael arose from the floor and spoke.

"Man, how the fuck did you get in my room?" he yelled, while reaching in the corner for an iron pipe. "Man, get the fuck out of my room."

Michael continued to rant and rave, more because Kenneth had knocked his pipe out of his hand than anything else.

"How can you smoke that shit in front of your daughter?" yelled Ken. "How can you allow Brit to live like this?"

At that moment, a light went off in Michael's head and he realized who he was talking to.

"Ken!" yelled Michael, moving forward to hug Kenneth.

But as Michael tried to hug his friend, Kenneth refused to come in contact with him. Michael's 235 lb frame was now 165 or 170, at best. His eyes were bloodshot red and sunken, but he still had his trademark smile and his handsome face.

Kenneth walked over towards Brittany and began to rub her hair. She was simply a pretty little girl trying to sleep and was immune to her father's problems. Kenneth picked Brittany up and threw her across his shoulders as he walked towards the door. Michael stepped in front of Kenneth, who was tall and a rock-solid 210 lbs., and began to speak.

"Where are you going with my baby?" he demanded angrily.

"I'm taking her out of here," Ken shot back. "If you want to sit here and kill yourself, that's your business. But from this day forward, Brittany is going to be with me and Cheryl."

"You're not taking my baby anywhere," said Mike. "She's with me wherever I am."

"Step aside," said Ken, putting Brittany on her feet as she began to awaken. "I don't think you want any part of me."

Michael lunged at Ken, who simply sidestepped Michael and pushed him to the floor.

"Daddy!" Brittany screamed as Michael hit the floor and began to cry, releasing a year's worth of pain.

"I didn't mean for her to die," cried Michael. "I just blacked out. I don't know what happened. I made by daughter motherless, and I killed my son. I have nothing to live for. I just wish that I would die."

"You can live for me, Daddy," said Brittany, breaking the tension of the moment.

"You're right, baby," he replied, wiping his eyes and hugging his daughter. "Daddy will live for you."

"Well, brother, you're welcome to come too," said Ken. "We've been best friends since we were as small as Brit, and we are best friends no matter what."

"Thanks, brother," Michael sobbed as he embraced Kenneth.

He walked around the room, trying to gather odds and ends for himself and Brittany.

"Forget that stuff," said Kenneth. "We'll get more stuff for you guys."

Michael reached for his pipe.

"*Definitely* forget that thing," ordered Ken.

"You sure, brother?" asked Mike.

"Definitely," replied Ken, turning his nose away from the filthy clothes and especially the crack pipe.

With that, the three of them headed towards the elevator and Ken remembered how slow it was.

"Let's take the stairs," he suggested, carrying Brittany in his arms.

"I'm with you, brother," added Mike.

Michael, Ken, and Brittany left the hotel and walked towards Ken's jeep, when the attendant stopped Mike.

"You know you have to leave your key," said the attendant.

"Here, keep it. I won't be needing it any-more."

As they continued towards Kenneth's jeep, another street woman came up to proposition Kenneth. "I bet you can't handle this good stuff," said a heavyset sister with a short miniskirt on and her breasts hanging out.

"Get your fat ass on," replied Michael as the three got into the Jeep.

"I wasn't speaking to you anyway" retorted the woman, "and besides, I'm not fat. I'm just big-boned."

"Well, you've got some of the biggest bones I've seen in a long time," Michael responded.

"Well, I'll have you know that I just lost 100 lbs," she said.

"Hooooey," yelled Ken.

"Well," said Michael, standing behind the woman after jumping from the jeep and pointing to her butt, "I just found the 100 lbs you lost, plus another 50 lbs hiding over here on the side."

"Fuck you … ole skinny ass nigger," huffed the woman. "I bet you have to run around the shower to get wet."

Ken laughed at Michael and the woman as he drove off after Michael jumped back into the Jeep, with the woman still slinging insults.

"Boney motherfucker," she said. "I knew your mama when she was hoeing in the street. The bitch was so hoeish, they called her deep freezer because so many niggers packed meat in her."

"Damn!" yelled Ken.

"Ah, you big, fat, jelly, donut-eating bitch," said Michael. "You can't go to the zoo 'cause they won't let your big ass out. You got to stay with the rest of the hippos."

Ken drove faster as the woman continued to talk badly about Michael.

"I never heard you cuss like this before," said Ken. "You always talk like this in front of your daughter?"

Michael replied, "I never lived like this before, so I don't have anything to compare it against."

Ken traveled towards Wilshire Boulevard and the Bel Air district. Michael hugged Brittany and let his hair blow in the wind.

After 25 minutes, Kenneth pulled up in front of his 2-story Bel Air mansion and accessed the gate code. As the gate opened, he drove through and opened the garage. In it were matching BMWs for Ken and his wife, Cheryl. Ken was a high-level executive for Progress Insurance. He was promoted by Michael to his lofty position, and his wife, Cheryl, was a successful Los Angeles real estate attorney. Also in the garage was parked a 1970 white Cadillac convertible in mint condition.

"Living good these days," said Michael.

"I'm blessed," replied Kenneth. "The Bible says, 'Ask and it shall be given, seek and ye shall find, knock and the door shall be opened onto you.' I knocked, brother."

"When did you become a religious man?" asked Michael.

"Cheryl got me going to church, and you know pops was head deacon in the church back in the day, so I know a little something."

The house was a beautiful design with eight bedrooms on the golf course, with marble floors from the entrance through the kitchen and a basketball court in the backyard.

"You see, I got the court back there," said Ken. "I owe you a good whupping."

"In your dreams, brother," said Michael. "You know you could never handle me."

Michael thought about his beautiful house which he abandoned and simply allowed to go into foreclosure after his wife's death. He was still high from smoking crack and for the first time, was somewhat embarrassed about his situation.

Cheryl screamed, "Brit! Michael! I'm so glad to see you both."

She rushed forward to hug and kiss Brittany and Michael with tears in her eyes. Brittany didn't remember Ken or Cheryl, but was seemingly glad to be out of that drug-infested hotel.

"Brittany, do you remember me?" asked Cheryl. "I'm your godmother. I was your mother's best friend."

Brittany didn't remember, but embraced Cheryl as though she did. Cheryl looked at Michael and was amazed at all the weight he had lost, but the amazement turned to anger at the condition Michael had allowed his daughter to exist in. But Cheryl remembered Michael's fragile state and how it must feel to lose someone that you shared so much with, so she composed herself and made a suggestion, just being glad that they were both alive.

"Why don't you both get cleaned up and then we can all sit down and have some dinner? Would you like that, Brittany?"

"I'd like some potato chips and maybe a candy bar," replied Brittany.

Cheryl realized that Brittany hadn't had a good meal in a while and it brought to light how potentially fragile the situation might be.

"No candy bars or chips, sweetie. You're going to have some real food."

"Yeah, Cheryl is on this no-red-meat thing, and all we eat around here is fish and turkey and vegetables and fruit," said Ken. "What I wouldn't do for a big, juicy, filet mignon and some Popeye's chicken."

"No chicken either?" asked Mike. "Y'all the only black people in America that don't eat chicken. What's wrong with the yard bird and the T-bone or porterhouse? What about prime rib and pork chops?"

"Beef clogs the arteries, causing heart attacks. Chickens are shot up with steroids to make them grow, and pork has too many diseases. You do remember the story in the Bible where the demon was cast into the swine by Jesus?" said Cheryl.

"That's too deep for me," said Mike, "besides, I'm not hungry. I want to smoke a joint."

"We definitely won't be having that with dinner," stated Cheryl sarcastically.

"I love you, Mike," added Ken, "but we don't do any kind of drugs in this house. That behavior will get you an instant eviction notice. Besides, why don't you guys get cleaned up for dinner?"

Michael and Brittany both seem a little overwhelmed by the situation, so Ken gestured to Mike and Brittany to follow him down the hall.

"Brittany, after dinner, I'm going to do your hair and have you looking so beautiful that the men won't even recognize you," Cheryl added.

Kenneth showed Michael and Brittany adjoining rooms down the hallway. "The rooms connect directly, so you can go in and out at your leisure."

"Thank you, but Brittany and I can use the same room," said Michael.

"No, Daddy," replied Brittany, who, though only five, was conscious of her femininity. "A lady needs to have facilities of her own."

They all laughed at that statement.

"A lady, huh?" replied Michael. "Okay, well, I guess my little woman is too big to share a room with her father."

"Come on, Mike," said Ken, "I'll show you to your room."

Kenneth escorted Michael to his room and showed him where everything was. Michael began to take off his filthy clothes as Ken walked in with some toiletries. He grabbed Michael's clothes and turned up his nose at the foul odor.

"If you don't mind, I'm going to throw this stuff away," he said.

"But I don't have anything else to put on," Michael protested.

"I'll get you something," he replied. "Just go ahead and shower."

Michael turned the water on, and Ken threw his filthy clothes in the outside dumpster, replacing them with one of his old outfits. Cheryl worked with Brittany to get her cleaned up. After a 30-minute shower, Michael emerged and found an outfit on the bed. It was now about 7 p.m. and Cheryl, Kenneth, and Brittany sat down for dinner. Kenneth yelled for Michael to join them because Cheryl won't start her meal until everyone prays together.

Michael quickly oiled down and looked on the bed to see a pair of pants and shirt. The shirt was a perfect fit, and the pants fit perfectly in the waist, but only came down to the top of Michael's ankles.

Michael laughed out loud. "Look at these high-water pants," he said. "I guess it does rain in Southern California."

Michael realized that he had no choice but to wear the short pants to the dinner table. He and Ken were the best of friends. Ken and Cheryl loved to clown. As Michael entered the kitchen, Ken and Cheryl immediately broke out into a chorus of the old gospel tune, "It's Gonna Rain."

"Very funny," laughed Michael. "I can't help it if you're a midget, Ken."

"And you're a bean pole," he came back. "And you can hula hoop through a cheerio."

"Ah, brother, that's a real old one," said Michael. "Robin Harris you are not."

As Michael sat down, Cheryl began to speak seriously. "Michael and Brittany, I can't tell you how happy I am to have … I mean … *we* are to have you safe in our home. This is the answer to many prayers. You are home," she continued, "for as long as you need to be home."

"Definitely," added Ken.

"And Brittany," said Cheryl, "after dinner, I'm going to tackle that hair because your father is no hair stylist."

"I did the best I could, but I must admit that I'm glad you're able to take over. I want my baby to look beautiful again," added Michael, while holding his daughter's hand.

At no time did anyone mention Michael's wife, Sheila, as the whole situation was too tough for everyone, especially with Brittany being so young.

"Brittany, tomorrow, we are going to see about getting you in school," said Cheryl, gesturing towards the child.

"Let's eat," said Ken. "I'm about to starve."

With that, he led the blessing, and then they enjoyed a fabulous home cooked meal.

At 10, everyone wound down and Brit had a fresh hairdo. Michael tucked his daughter into bed.

"Okay, baby, get under the cover. Did you say your prayers?"

"Yea, Daddy, I prayed for you and my new Uncle Ken and Aunt Cheryl, but God already answered my biggest prayer."

"He did?" Michael responded.

"Sure, Daddy," said Brittany, "I prayed to God to bring you out of that bad area because I want you to be happy, Daddy." Brittany never spoke of herself.

"Thank you, baby," he said as he gave his daughter a kiss. "God blessed me with such a beautiful, intelligent child, and I'm so thankful for you, and I promise you, baby, that I'll never let you suffer again."

"I know you won't, Daddy."

"Okay, baby, good night," Michael said as he started to leave the room.

"Daddy?" asked Brittany as Michael reached the door. "Is God watching out for Mommy?"

"Yea, baby," he said sincerely. "God is watching out for Mommy, now go to sleep, baby."

Chapter 3

IN THE MASTER BEDROOM, KEN and Cheryl talked and listened to the news broadcast. "And LA police found the body of little April Woods in a wooded section of Orange County." Ken turned off the television.

"They need to catch that guy soon. That's 15 kids already," he added. "I pray every night that they catch him."

"Yea," Cheryl agreed, "we have to keep an eye on Brittany, a close eye."

"I will," said Ken. "I'll watch her real close."

Meanwhile, Michael tossed and turned in the bed for several hours before he finally went to sleep. He began to dream about the car accident. He remembered laughing and joking with his wife and suddenly, he headed down an embankment and tried to slow down, but the brakes went out. "Oh, no," Michael yelled, "I can't stop!" A truck approached driving fast, riding on the wrong side of the road. Michael's Mercedes jumped the curve to avoid the truck. As this happened, he woke up in a cold sweat.

"Nooooo!" Michael yelled, waking up in a cold sweat. "No." He slowly recognized his surroundings and readjusted his body in the bed. Reaching out, he caressed a pillow as if he were holding onto his wife and softly laid his head across it and fell asleep for the night.

For the next few weeks, Michael stayed exclusively in the guest bedroom, emerging only to check on Brittany or go to the gym downstairs. He seemed totally depressed and embarrassed over the conditions he existed in over the last year. After several weeks passed, Ken called his wife's office to speak to her during his lunch hour.

"Attorney Bolling's office," Cheryl's secretary answered.

"Is my wife free?" Ken asked.

"Hold on, Mr. Bolling, I'll patch you through," she informed him.

"This is Attorney Bolling."

"Hey, baby, how is your day going?"

"Surprisingly light," Cheryl replied. "And yours?"

"I'm swamped. Listen, honey, I'm real worried about Mike. It's been days since he's come out of that room, and the last time I did see him, he looked pretty bad."

"Yea, I know," she agreed. "Maybe we should try to get him some form of therapy or counseling."

Upon hearing that statement, an idea immediately flashed into Ken's head. "I think I know just the therapy he needs," he said. "I'll talk to you later, baby."

He rushed to hang up the phone even as Cheryl tried to ask him what he meant.

⇥ ⇥ ⇥

KEN ROSE EARLY the next morning, which was Saturday, and left the house. He stayed gone most of the day without so much as a word to his wife. Brittany and Cheryl ate breakfast while Michael continued to stay secluded in his room. Brittany took a breakfast tray to her father, who was so depressed that he almost didn't want to see his own daughter.

"Daddy, I've got your food," Brittany said to her nonresponsive father. "Daddy, Daddy."

After a few moments, she began to sob and finally, Michael opened the door.

"Here, Daddy," she sobbed as she passed her father his breakfast. "Daddy, what's wrong?"

"Nothing, Brit, Daddy's just a little tired," he responded.

Michael was in better physical health than when he came, but emotionally, he still hurt. He put the food down and lay across the bed while Brittany retreated to her room. Cheryl watched and felt helpless to do anything about the situation. She went to console Brittany, while Michael stayed wrapped up in his gloom.

About 6 p.m., Kenneth returned home, carrying several packages. Cheryl and Brittany were in the kitchen and Michael, as usual, remained in his room. As Kenneth entered the house, Cheryl saw the packages and was naturally curious.

"What's all that?"

"You'll see," he replied, going towards Michael's room. Reaching it, he simply walked in. The room was dark. He turned on the light, pulled back the drapes, and opened the blinds as Brittany and Cheryl watched.

"Hey, man, what's going on?" said Michael.

"It's time for you to get up and take a look at this stuff I bought for you," said Kenneth.

"What stuff?" said a dazed Michael.

"I had to drive all over town just to get the right outfit," said Kenneth. He opened one bag and pulled out a powder-blue suit from M2 of downtown Los Angeles, with a designer shirt and shoes to match. "I even got you designer drawers," he said, pulling out the expensive silk underwear.

"That's some nice stuff, Ken, but what am I going to do with it?"

"You're going to wear it out tonight. It's ladies' night at the Beverly Club on Beverly Boulevard, and from what I hear, the clientele is very nice."

"Who did you hear that from?" asked Cheryl, making Ken squirm.

"I heard it through the grapevine … at the job, baby," he said apologetically.

"Uh-huh, I bet," she replied sarcastically.

"I don't want to go anywhere," said Michael, "and besides, what about Brittany?"

"We've got Brittany so get in the shower. I've got you some Right Guard and some Hugo Boss body oil … everything you need is in one of these bags."

"Yea, Daddy, get ready and go out," Brittany chimed in.

"Yea, Michael, go for it," Cheryl encouraged him.

"Now, it's unanimous. Get dressed, brother."

"Wait a minute, brother," Michael protested as Ken attempted to shut the door. "Silk drawers make me itch."

"There are some Fruit of the Loom briefs and some boxers in there too. Now go ahead and shower, brother."

Ken left the room and closed the door as Michael sat on the bed and hesitated for a moment, staring in the mirror.

"I'm not ready for this," he said to himself. After sitting and staring at himself for a few moments, Michael reluctantly turned on the shower while three interested people outside his door listened intently to the sound of the shower coming on.

"You think this will work?" asked Cheryl.

"I hope so," her husband replied.

After a 30-minute shower, Michael emerged from the bathroom and looked through the bag of toiletries. He saw the Hugo Boss body oil and rubbed it across his frame. Next, he unwrapped the suit and designer shirt. He handled them expertly because he always spared no expense on his outfits before and during his life in the corporate world. As he continued to dress, Michael saw a different side of himself, a side he hadn't seen in a very long time. After putting on the final touches, he left the room and headed towards the family room, where everyone was sitting, watching television.

As Michael appeared from seemingly out of nowhere, all eyes focused on the man in the designer suit that appeared to be a ghost from the past. In the background, the television focused on the continued disappearance of little girls, but everything stopped when Michael appeared and they all stared.

"Well?" he said. "What do you think?"

"You look very handsome," said Cheryl.

"Yea, Daddy, you look good," repeated Brittany, rushing to hold her father.

"I don't know. I think I'd better call the police because there's a stranger in this house," said Kenneth.

"Funny. How do I look, brother?"

"Michael, you're sharper than a Track 2 razor blade and cleaner than the board of health."

"Old and corny," said Michael.

"Come here, Michael," said Cheryl, pulling Michael toward her to adjust his shirt. "There you go," she said as she finished.

"Well, brother, I guess it's about time for you to get going," said Ken.

"It's only seven o'clock," said Michael. "It's too early to go out."

"No, it's not. I hear that they have an early evening crowd there. And there's an all-you-can-eat buffet, and the ladies arrive early for happy hour."

"And who did you hear this from, Ken?" asked Cheryl.

"Ahhhhh, just a buddy at the job," he replied, trying to wiggle out of it.

"Yea, I'll bet. When Mike leaves, I want you to tell me more about this Beverly Club."

Ken took Michael's arm to lead him out of the room as Michael kissed his daughter and told her to be good and Cheryl told him to have a good time.

They went to the garage, "Here, you can drive the Cadi," Ken said, referring to the convertible Cadillac parked in the garage. "And here's some spending money." Ken gave Michael two one hundred dollar bills.

"Brother, you thought of everything. What did I do to deserve a friend like you?"

"Yea, I am straight," said Kenneth.

"I'm going to pay you back, I promise," said Michael.

"You paid me back when you came out of the room with your daughter," said Ken. "Tonight is going to be a new beginning for you. I truly believe that. Man, that Hugo Boss is smelling good."

Michael embraced Ken with a brotherly hug and sat in the Cadi, inquiring about the directions to the Beverly Club.

"It's straight down Beverly Boulevard, on the corner of Beverly and Melrose. It's on the left side, so you can't miss it. And oh, the honeys over there are off the hook—beautiful. And they love to have a good time."

"You know a lot about this place from hearing about it 'through the grapevine,'" Michael added as Ken pushed the button to the garage door and he headed out to the Beverly Club.

Chapter 4

MICHAEL STOPPED AT A GAS station to get some mints, stared at himself in the mirror, and began to feel very confident about his appearance.

"Michael Alexander, back to life," he said as he exited the car.

He purchased some Clorets and walked towards the door, where two women complemented him on his suit.

"Hey, sexy," one of them said. "Where's the party?"

"I'm on my way to the Beverly Club," he answered.

He took a closer look at the woman in the short miniskirt with long, beautiful legs and made a suggestion. "Why don't you meet me there later? By the way, my name is Michael. What's yours?"

"My name is Terri, and this is my friend, Peaches."

"This suit is working for you," said Peaches. "Not everyone can wear the color blue. We're gonna be at the club in a little while. Why don't you save us a dance?"

"I will," he promised. "Here, take my phone number in case you get too tied up. Call me anytime."

With that, Michael jumped in the Cadi and drove off. After arriving at the Beverly Club, he valet-parked the car, took a deep breath, and made his grand entrance.

"Well, here goes," he said to himself in a whisper.

Although it was early evening, the Saturday happy hour crowd made the house already jam-packed. There was no cover charge before 9 p.m., and no cover for ladies at all. He worked his way through the crowd and found a vacant table to the left of the dance floor not too far from the bar. The crowd was buzzing and the oldies played until 9. The dance floor was already packed. The crowd was mixed, about 60 percent black, the rest white, Spanish, and a few Orientals.

"What a nice turnout," he said to himself. "Honeys everywhere."

The crowd was about 70 percent female, and the club was very classy with an exotic décor and some very attractive waitresses. After sitting, a beautiful Nubian waitress approached his table and asked for his order.

"What can I get for you, sir?"

Michael looked over toward the waitress and stared at her from head to toe. He tripped on her incredible body and face.

"Shit, she's fine," he said appreciatively to himself. "What's your name, honey?"

"Jasmine," the waitress said.

"Well, Jasmine, I'd like to have some legs on the rocks," said Michael playfully, hoping for a response.

The waitress smiled, "I'm sorry, sir, we don't serve legs on the rocks."

"Oh, really?" Michael replied, looking the waitress up and down again. "Well, I think you should tell your owner to add it to the menu. But seriously, give me a shot of Hennessey with a coke back."

He added, "And write your phone number down also."

Jasmine smiled and left to retrieve Michael's drink as he took another look at her walking off.

"Ummm," he said, "man, I got a lot of catching up to do."

Michael continued to groove to the music and vibe with the crowd. Across the way, he noticed a young lady sitting at the bar and jumped up to meet her. As he started to leave, the waitress returned with his drink.

"Here's your drink, sir. That's seven dollars."

"Seven dollars? I thought this was happy hour."

"It is. They're normally fourteen."

Michael looked at the woefully small drink barely touching the bottom of the glass, but not wanting to seem cheap, he pulled out a one hundred dollar bill and handed it to the waitress, who gave him his change. He tipped her and watched as she stuck a piece of paper in his pocket.

"We're not supposed to fraternize with the customers, but call me anytime," Jasmine told him with a smile, turning and walking away.

Michael was happy about Jasmine's number, but he couldn't take his eyes off the young lady sitting at the bar. He approached her with his drink in hand.

"Can I have this dance?" asked Michael, extending his hand.

"Yes," she said and Michael took her hand and walked her towards the dance floor.

A medley of oldies was playing. Michael and his new dance partner worked good on the floor together. A Prince song was on and Michael began to converse.

"Do you like Prince?"

"Yes, I love Prince," answered the woman.

"I don't like all his music, but this is my favorite Prince song."

The song was "I Wanna Be Your Lover."

"My name is Michael."

"I'm Michelle."

Michael's conversation was interrupted as some people formed a Soul Train line to Michael Jackson's "Don't Stop Till You Get Enough."

"You want to get in that Soul Train line?" she asked.

"I'm game if you are."

The crowd was really hyped for the oldies so the Soul Train line was very long with everyone yelling, "go 'head, go 'head" each time a new person went down the line. Michael and Michelle were grooving and finally they headed down the line with Michelle doing her thing and Michael coming down behind her mimicking Michael Jackson's robot. Everyone started to laugh, and Michelle turned around and laughed herself. They continued having fun. The DJ played a slow song next, giving those who wanted to a chance to get close while others took time to relax and catch their breath.

"You want to keep going?"

"Yes," said Michelle.

As they embraced and began their dance, Michael was being watched from across the room. At that time, a beautiful woman summoned Jasmine, the waitress.

"Yes, Ms. James?" answered Jasmine.

"You see that man on the dance floor with that powder-blue suit on?" said Ms. James, pointing to Michael.

"Yes, ma'am."

"Send a bottle of Don Perignon to his table and tell him the only stipulation is that I join him."

"Okay, Ms. James," Jasmine replied, remembering that she had given Michael her phone number.

"So where are you from, Michelle?"

"I'm originally from New Orleans, but I live here off and on whenever I do shows in the area."

"Are you an actress?"

"No. I model internationally, so I work everywhere. I'll be here for about a month this time on assignment."

At that point, the record ended and Michelle excused herself to go to the ladies' room.

"Okay, but I'll be back to get you on the next good song."

Michelle acknowledged the invitation and walked off to the restroom while Michael retrieved his drink and returned to his table to find a full bottle of Don Perignon Champagne and two empty glasses. Michael beckoned Jasmine to come over to his table.

"Sweetheart, I didn't order this champagne," he said.

"No, Ms. James sent it," she replied, gesturing to Ms. James, "but the only catch is that she wants to come over and have a drink with you."

"You mean that beautiful chocolate thing right there?" Michael asked. "Tell her she can come over whether she sent champagne or not."

Jasmine gave Michael a smile and went back to deliver the message to Ms. James. She immediately walked over to Michael's table, escorted by a huge Oriental man, Manu, who had stood up to acknowledge her.

"Hello, I'm Coretta James," she introduced herself, "and this is my confidant, Manu."

Michael extended his hand, but Manu only gave him a little scowl.

"You have to excuse Manu," she said. "He's not the social type."

"Maybe you should have brought a leash for his big ass," Michael said softly under his breath.

"What was that?" she asked.

"Nothing, I'm Michael Alexander," he replied. "Please have a seat."

Michael attempted to pull back Coretta's chair, but Manu pushed him back and did it himself.

"Did you feed him today?"

"Manu is just very loyal to a fault," she replied, "and extremely protective."

"Is he house-trained?" asked Michael as Manu scowled.

"Manu is a seventh-degree black belt with a very low tolerance for fun," said Coretta. "I've only got so much control over him, so bridle your tongue."

Michael had a few more comments, but thought better of them and addressed the rest of his comments to Coretta. Across the way, Michelle returned from the ladies' room and noticed Michael sitting with Coretta. She simply took it in stride and returned to her perch at the bar.

"Why the champagne?" asked Michael.

"I noticed you on the dance floor," Coretta answered. "I saw how sleek you look in that suit and how you handled yourself with that woman. I was quite impressed. I've been looking for a man with your looks and flair for a while."

"Oh, you need a man, huh?" he questioned playfully.

"Yes, but not for personal fulfillment—well, maybe just a little personal fulfillment. Tell me, Michael, what kind of work are you presently involved in?"

Michael motioned to open the champagne, but Manu stopped him and opened the bottle himself and quickly poured Coretta a glass while leaving Michael's glass empty.

"Okaaay," said Michael.

At that time, Coretta took out a cigarette. Michael wanted to light it for her, but thought better of it as Manu quickly lit it.

"Me, currently? I'm unemployed. Why do you ask?"

"I would like you to work for me," she replied. "It's a job that can pay you six figures a month. You could go anywhere and purchase anything your little heart desires."

"And what are the qualifications for this job? You haven't even checked my references."

"Actually, I checked your references while you were on the dance floor. You're highly qualified."

Michael didn't think much of the offer and believed Coretta was playing some silly game with him, but with the potential money so big, he continued to inquire.

"So what exactly does this job entitle? And how can you tell from just looking at me that I'm so qualified?" Michael had gained a lot of his weight back from lifting weights in Ken's gym and also from Cheryl's good cooking, and at 6 foot 4, he was a dark, mysterious, and handsome man.

"The job is in human services," Coretta replied.

"Human services? What kind of human services?"

"The kind of human services that can make you a rich man. I can make all your material dreams come true. Are you interested?" asked Coretta.

Michael pondered the offer for a second. "Nope, sorry, lady, I don't sell drugs."

"My dear, you won't have to sell drugs," she replied. "You just have to sell yourself. I'll tell you what, why don't I take you to my office right now where you can fill out the application and then I can tell you more about the job. Then if you decide it's not what you want, we can both move on. Fair enough?"

Michael thought for a second and felt there was nothing to lose. What could it hurt to listen? "Okay," he said reluctantly, "but first I need to do something. I'll be right back."

Coretta watched Michael as he walked off, then instructed Manu. "Tell Stephen to pull the car around," she said.

Manu didn't say a word, but left immediately to follow her instructions.

Michael made his way over to the bar where Michelle was sitting and tried to start a conversation with her.

"May I?" he asked, pointing to the empty seat.

"I don't know," Michelle replied. "You think your girlfriend will mind?"

"She's not my girlfriend," said Michael. "Believe it or not, she was offering me a job."

"Yea, I'll bet she was," Michelle stated sarcastically. "What kind of job is someone offering in the club? Does she know you from somewhere?"

"No, I don't know her," Michael said. "I met her when I got off the dance floor with you, but she offered me a job in human services. Anyway, enough about her. Let's get together tomorrow and have some dinner," he suggested.

"Just like that, huh?" asked Michelle.

"Why not? Are you committed to someone?"

"No, men seem to be intimidated by my stature."

"Well, you know they don't make brothers like they used to," he laughed jokingly, "but I don't see how a man can be intimidated by a beautiful lady like you."

"You'd be surprised," said Michelle, taking a pen from the bar and writing down her number. "I'm at the Hotel Nikko. They reserve the same suite for me each time I'm in town."

"Who is they?" asked Michael.

"The agency I work through."

As Michael took the number, he stood and gave Michelle a kiss on the cheek as Coretta approached and let it be known that Michael was leaving with her.

"Are you ready, Michael?" Coretta said, making her way between the two.

"Yea, I'm ready," Michael replied. "I'll call you tomorrow," he said to Michelle.

As Michael walked off, Coretta leaned over and whispered to Michelle, "It will definitely be tomorrow, bitch, because he won't make it home tonight." Then she walked off under Manu's protection.

Michelle sat at the bar somewhat in a daze, not believing what just happened to her. But she didn't attempt to cause a commotion. She just gave Coretta a blank stare. Michael walked away, unaware of Coretta's little encounter with Michelle. Manu and Coretta were close behind.

"Michael, where is your valet ticket?" Coretta asked, approaching the exit.

"It's right here," he replied.

As Michael stood outside, waiting, he was shooting the breeze with the guy working at the door.

"Man, I saw you all over those honeys," said the doorman to Michael. "Now that you're leaving, maybe the rest of us will have a chance."

"It's not like that, my brother," responded Michael.

"It's not?" said the doorman. "Look at that queen you're leaving with now."

"Naw, man," said Michael, "she's got some kind of job for me."

"I bet," he smirked. "Tell her I need some work too."

While Michael joked, Coretta instructed the valet to deliver Michael's car to her house later and handed him some money.

"How will he know where you live?" asked Michael.

"I'm majority owner of this club," Coretta said. "They all work for me."

As they stood there, Coretta watched Michael as he gazed at every woman passing by.

"Yes, my brother," she said, "you're gonna love this job."

At that moment, a long gold and black stretch limo pulled up in front of the club. Manu opened the door and stepped aside as Michael opened his own door.

"Charming fellow," Michael said to Manu. "I see you and I are gonna be the best of friends."

Manu never said a word, but his dislike for Michael was obvious.

Coretta and Michael sat in the privacy of the back of the limo and she flipped a switch, causing a fully stocked bar to appear. Michael gazed at the bar and Coretta gestured for him to help himself. He fixed a stiff Hennessy XO as he checked out the black and gold interior of the super long stretch Mercedes limo.

"Whoever you work for must be super rich to afford a car like this," he said in amazement. "The interior is off the hook. I mean, you have a bar, a large screen TV, an entertainment center of sorts, CD and DVD player," he remarked, looking around. "The only thing missing is a Jacuzzi."

Coretta pushed a button on the control panel and a small Jacuzzi was uncovered from the center panel.

"Real good for long trips," she stated, referring to the Jacuzzi, "and just for future references, *I* own this limo. *I* am the boss."

"What kind of business are you into that can allow you to own the hottest club in the city and a stretch limo from heaven? Does my job require me to take the limo sometimes?"

"Don't ask so many questions," Coretta replied. "Just sit back and enjoy yourself."

With that, Michael switched on the TV, sipped on his XO, listened to a Sam Cooke CD, and just enjoyed the ride.

Chapter 5

BACK AT KENNETH'S HOUSE, BRITTANY was getting ready for bed and Ken offered to take her to the room, but Cheryl insisted on doing it. They also spoke about Michael.

"I wonder how Michael is doing," Cheryl said aloud. "You know, this could backfire with Michael being around all that alcohol and nightlife."

"We can't babysit him," said Kenneth. "He was about to rot in that room. There are risks, yea, but Mike needs to have some fun, and what could be more fun than the Beverly Club on Saturday night?"

"You seem to know a lot about the Beverly Club," Cheryl said drily.

At that moment, Brittany wanted to be read a story.

"Saved by the bell again," said Cheryl. "Let's go read you that story, honey."

⇥ ⇥ ⇥

AFTER A TWENTY to thirty-minute drive, Coretta's limo pulled up in front of a three-story mansion in Beverly Hills. Manu stepped out to help Coretta from the limo and almost closed the door on Michael.

"Damn, that's an ignorant chink," he grumbled as Coretta and Manu approached the front door of the Gothic-style mansion.

"Man, this shit is off the hook," Michael said admiringly as he stared at Coretta's mansion.

Coretta spoke into the voice-controlled security gate directly adjacent to the front door, and the door opened instantly. She entered, followed by Michael, while Manu turned and headed back to the car after giving Michael a nasty look.

Coretta led Michael down a long corridor leading to a den located next to her super huge master bedroom. Stephen, the driver of the limo, was a 6 foot 2, 210 lb black man from Cleveland, Ohio, who was Coretta's right-hand man and a jack-of-all-trades. His trades included money laundering, drug trafficking, and many other small and large crimes, including murder. Stephen was not the typical limo driver, and between him and the fierce Manu, Coretta had enough protection to stop a small army.

"I don't like that pretty nigger," Stephen complained to Manu, who just looked at him and frowned. "There's just something about him. Let's go make the pickup."

They drove off in a black Range Rover while Coretta and Michael began to unwind.

"Now, what kind of work do you do to afford such luxury?" asked Michael, marveling at the huge mansion with the exotic paintings and the state-of-the-art everything.

Coretta didn't respond at first.

"Do you mind if I use your restroom?" he asked.

"Go right ahead. It's right through that door," she said, pointing.

Michael walked into the huge restroom and released some pressure. "Damn, this bathroom is as big as some apartments."

He washed his hands and returned to the den, where Coretta had already removed her shoes and was quite relaxed. About this time, he wondered what he may have gotten himself into but was distracted by the beautiful Coretta.

Coretta was a shrewd businesswoman, but she was as gorgeous as any sister you want to see—with her light chocolate complexion, long, slender legs, and a body that Cleopatra would die for. And she also had pretty feet.

"You want to massage my feet?" she asked.

"No, thanks, I'm not into feet."

Coretta was not used to being told no and was puzzled by her prospective employee.

"I thought you wanted me to fill out some sort of application," he said.

"As a matter of fact, I do, but fix yourself a drink and try this," Coretta said, pulling out a tray of coke. "It's the best powder that money can buy."

Michael was very tempted, but didn't want to toot in front of her.

"I'm going to get your application. Make yourself at home, and I'll be right back."

Michael tried to fight the temptation, but did a line with each nostril, then drained it with some water. Then he tried to position the cocaine back to appear that he hadn't done any. After that, he walked around the room and admired the luxurious furniture, and paintings, and the design of the room and the floors. Obviously, no expenses spared. As Michael admired the lavish house, Coretta reappeared from the other room and stood and stared at him for a moment. Michael looked at one of the beautiful mirrors and saw Coretta's reflection on the other side. His mouth flew open and he turned around quickly, dropping his glass of Hennessey. In front of Michael stood a totally nude Coretta with a flawless body. He was speechless for a moment. Any objections that he might have had vanished at the sight of the gorgeous, naked Coretta. Michael was stunned at first, but quickly regained his composure.

"All applications should look like this," he said admiringly, "and if they did, I would be job hunting every day."

"Well, usually I leave the training process up to my ladies, but in this case, I wanted to take a hands-on approach."

Michael started to undo his shirt at that statement. "Well, come on, baby, and put your hands on me," he said.

Coretta approached Michael and took off his coat, his shirt, and undershirt. He had lost a lot of weight from his one-year binge on alcohol and drugs, but for the few weeks he had been spending at Ken and Cheryl's, he ate well and worked out twice a day, even though he seldom mixed in with the others in the house. The food and workouts had added much definition to his body and since Coretta didn't know him before, she had no complaints. She began to caress Michael's chest and kissed up and down his upper torso. He slid his hands up and down Coretta's luscious body.

"No hair on your chest," she said. "I usually love a hairy chest, but yours is so smooth, it doesn't matter."

Coretta kissed Michael's nipples as he caressed hers. Then he lifted her up into the air. She straddled her legs around his waist as he sucked her breasts. Michael placed her on top of the bar, and she unzipped his pants. Then he lifted her again and she wrapped her legs around his waist. They began to kiss wildly and Michael, without any thoughts regarding consequences, penetrated her and began to violently thrust his pelvis back and forth as she moaned in pleasure.

"Oh, yeah, baby, give it to me," shouted Coretta. "Work that dick, baby, work that dick!"

Coretta licked Michael's fingers and licked him everywhere else as he gave it to her. He was so ready that he pretty much skipped the foreplay and went right into the main action. But it didn't matter. Their sex started in the den, moved to the bathroom, and then to the bedroom and back again to the den, on the table, on the sofa, and on the floor. Mike and Coretta made love all night long like two animals starved for something they had never experienced. The two connected physically, but they never connected any other way.

Chapter 6

WHILE MICHAEL AND CORETTA TURNED her mansion into a wild sex palace, Stephen, Manu, and another member of Coretta's entourage named Carlos, a Mexican American and Coretta's tie to a Miami business connection, went downtown to meet with another business connection set up by Carlos. They pulled into a deserted warehouse. Carlos spoke to Manu and Stephen.

"Just wait here," he said, checking his 9mm Glock for ammunition. "I'll handle everything. They don't like strangers."

Carlos then stepped from the car and talked to the men who emerged from a black limo while Manu and Stephen watched intensely, their guns cocked. Carlos stopped talking for a moment and returned to the car. He gestured for Stephen to roll down the window.

"They've got the stuff," he said. "Give me the money."

Stephen reached down and handed Carlos a briefcase, and Carlos immediately returned to the men and opened the briefcase while the men opened the case they were carrying. Both sides nodded and exchanged briefcases, then Carlos returned to the Range Rover.

However, before he did so, Stephen noticed one of the men putting something in Carlos' hands.

"Aw, this motherfucker is up to something," Stephen said quietly as Carlos approached the car and got in. Both cars then left the warehouse.

"Did I see that man give you something?" asked Stephen suspiciously.

"No," replied Carlos, "we just shook hands."

As the three drove off, Stephen and Manu made eye contact, but didn't say anything. They went to Coretta's mansion. Stephen took the briefcase and entered his quarters on the compound while Carlos and Manu went to their own separate living quarters. Then Stephen called Manu on his Nextel phone.

"Manu, that bitch is on the take," he said, referring to Carlos. "We're gonna set his ass up."

Manu didn't speak, but Stephen knew he understood.

⇥ ⇥ ⇥

AT 7 A.M., MICHAEL woke up in Coretta's super king-size bed and rolled over to find that she was not there. Instead, she was outside, standing by her Olympic-size pool, talking to Stephen on the phone.

"Boss lady," he said, "we've got to take this motherfucker out. He's working both sides."

"Test the stuff to see how pure it is first, and before we take him out, we need to know who he's working with."

As they talked, Michael approached from behind. Coretta heard his footsteps as Manu stood silently by the pool. As

Manu watched Michael approached, he moved toward him in an offensive manner. But Coretta spotted Manu's movement, hung up the phone quickly, and called her protector.

"Manu," Coretta yelled.

The burly Chinese man stopped in his tracks, his face showing total disdain for Michael.

"Manu is usually overprotective," said Coretta. "But he is not normally this aggressive about anyone I deal with. There is something about you he seriously doesn't like."

"Maybe he's a big Chinese faggot," Michael said aloud. "Hopefully he realizes I'm not his type."

Coretta knew that Manu would love to kill anyone he felt threatened by and Michael's flippant attitude was not good for his well-being.

"Let's go back inside," Coretta said.

"Michael, tell me a little something about yourself."

"Do you usually question your men after you have sex with them?" he inquired.

"Don't be so temperamental."

Michael hesitated for a moment. "Well, there's not much to tell. There's only me and my daughter, Brittany. Her mother, my wife, is dead."

"Did you kill her?" asked Coretta matter-of-factly.

Michael hesitated.

"You *did* kill her," Coretta said as Michael was reminded of the accident.

"Yes, I guess I did, sort of. It was a car accident one night while celebrating a promotion on my job. Can we talk about something else?"

"Okay. I watched you intently as you danced and interacted with the women in the club. I've been looking for a man with your looks and your style for a long time. And that was the best fuck I've had in forever, so all the job qualifications I had, you've fulfilled."

"So what exactly do you want me to do?" he asked.

"I want you to do what you did to me to many, many lonely, rich, beautiful clients, women that will take one look at you and become instantly generous. I have many women that work for me, but I've been looking for just the right man to branch my business out."

"So you want me to be a male hooker?" he asked.

"I don't employ hookers. I employ people that give high-class service to their clients, whatever service they need," she added.

Michael did not respond to Coretta's statement and simply walked over to retrieve his pants, taking off the expensive terrycloth robe that she had left on the bed for him.

"Look, Michael," said Coretta, "this can make you rich beyond your wildest dreams. You can go anywhere and do anything that you want to do."

"I don't want to be running around with a bunch of ugly, fat women who are desperate for some dick," he replied flatly.

"I guarantee you that there won't be any unattractive women in the bunch," promised Coretta, "and the way your pockets are gonna be lined, you won't even care."

"I gotta go," Michael said abruptly. "Where is my car?"

"It's parked out front," she replied. "You a mean little ole pretty thing," she added. "I bet what we did last night didn't mean anything to you. That's good."

Michael continued to put on his suit hurriedly as Coretta continued talking. "If you don't do it for yourself, then do it for your daughter."

"My daughter?"

"Yes, your daughter. You know black men sometimes fail in the fatherhood department, and this will give you the opportunity to be a strong male role model in the eyes of your child."

"First of all, that's a very stereotypical statement about black men," he countered. "Second, how's my daughter gonna respect me if she knows how I make my money?"

"How will she find out? All she'll know is that you're providing for her."

Coretta touched a nerve with Michael because he had put Brittany through so much over the last year. But Michael was a stubborn man and very sensitive when it came to Brittany, probably because he felt guilty.

"I can take care of my daughter just fine, thank you."

He grabbed his coat and headed towards the door. Coretta stopped him and put a large envelope in his coat pocket, along with her card.

"This is a little something for a job well done," she purred, "along with a card that has all my numbers. And even if you don't take the job, come back over and give me some more of what I got last night."

Michael didn't answer. Instead, he merely jumped into Ken's car and drove to his house. As he was traveling, he checked the cell phone mounted in the car for a dial tone and called Ken's house. The phone rang.

"Hello," answered Ken.

"Hey, man," said Michael, "what's going on?"

"What's going on with you?" Kenneth replied. "We got kind of worried about you. Where did you spend the night?"

"I'll tell you the story shortly," Michael said. "Where's Brit?"

"Cheryl took her to church, and I waited around to hear from you," Kenneth replied. "She asked about you, but I assured her you were okay."

"Thanks, Ken. Hey, man, is it okay to have a guest for dinner? You think Cheryl will mind?"

"I wear the pants around here," Kenneth answered, "and if I say it's okay, it's okay," he said jokingly.

"Yeah, right," Michael replied with a grin.

"I'll ask her, but I'm sure it will be okay," Ken said.

"Okay, brother, I'll see you shortly," Michael said, then hung up the phone and found Michelle's number and called her. She answered the phone, and he began his mack.

"How you doing, baby?" he asked. "This is Michael Alexander from the club last night."

"Where's your girlfriend?" she replied. "How did the job interview at night go?"

"Everything went well, I guess," he said, not wanting to go into details.

"What was her job offer about?" Michelle pursued.

"Let's not talk about that. What are you doing later?"

"How much later? I've got a meeting with my agent at three and then after that, I'm done."

"How would you like to come over for dinner?"

Michelle was somewhat leery and questioned Mike about who else was coming to dinner and more importantly, who was not. "Will your friend from last night be there?"

"No, of course not," he said. "It would be my buddy, his wife, and my daughter, Brittany."

Michael was extremely attracted to the caramel-colored beauty and looked forward to seeing her again. At that moment, he remembered the envelope that Coretta had placed in his pocket. He took it out and felt it, temporarily ignoring Michelle's conversation.

"I wonder what's in the envelope ..." he mused aloud while feeling it.

"What envelope?"

"Nothing. Can you be at my friends' house by six?"

Michelle never agreed to Michael's initial invitation, but said she would be at Ken's house after her meeting. He gave her directions and inquired about her diet.

Michelle was a fish vegetarian. She loved salmon. Michael hoped that Cheryl and Kenneth had salmon, and although his finances were low, he remembered the change left over from the two hundred dollars Ken gave him to go out. He hung up the phone with Michelle and about ten minutes later, pulled into Ken and Cheryl's driveway. Cheryl and Brittany had just returned from church, and Brittany screamed with joy when she saw her father.

"Daddy!" she yelled as she ran to hug him.

"Hey, baby, you look so pretty in this dress Cheryl got for you."

"Daddy, I went to church with Aunt Cheryl."

"Oh, yeah? Why didn't Uncle Ken go to church with you?"

"Uncle Ken won't miss next week," Cheryl said drily.

Michael laughed as Ken looked embarrassed.

"Thanks a lot," said Ken as Michael continued to laugh.

After that, Michael went back to his room to shower and Brittany went with Cheryl to change and relax. After Michael showered, Kenneth walked into his room and surprised him.

"Starting to get back in shape?" Kenneth asked, noticing Michael had regained some of his weight. He startled Michael.

"Where did you come from?" asked Michael surprised.

Ken didn't answer, but instead, asked Michael about his night.

"Man, the honeys were superfine," Michael stated, "but I didn't get a chance to make my rounds because I ran into this beautiful sister, who is at least a millionaire, and come to think of it—"

Michael stopped mid sentence and remembered the envelope again that he put back in his pocket while talking to Michelle. Quickly, he retrieved it from his pocket as Ken looked on.

"What's that?" asked Ken.

Michael didn't answer but opened the envelope to find a bunch of one hundred dollar bills. Michael excitedly began to count until the dollar amount went up to ten thousand dollars.

"Ten thousand dollars!" yelled Ken. "Where did you get that?"

"From the lady I spent the night with," Michael answered. "Oh, and there's a note with it."

He opened the note and read, "This is just an example of what you can make if you accept my offer."

"What offer?"

"She offered me a job making six figures a month," said Michael.

"Doing what? Did you have sex with her?"

"Yeah, I knocked it out," said Michael. "You should have seen that body. It was incredible."

"Big tits?" asked Ken.

"Yea, they were nice," came the response.

"You *did* use a condom?"

Michael paused and didn't speak momentarily. Ken switched his temperment and immediately went off on Michael.

"I can't believe you didn't use a condom with a strange woman. I don't care how fine or rich she was," said Ken matter-of-factly. "I guess you want your daughter to be an orphan after spending a year living like a vagabond."

At that point, he walked out and closed the door, obviously upset with Michael. Michael realized had Ken changed a lot. Never before had Ken been so self-righteous towards Michael, no matter what he had done. However, Michael put his spat with Kenneth aside for a moment and called to Cheryl on the house intercom to inquire whether Ken had mentioned his dinner guest. Ken hadn't mentioned the guest, but Cheryl was a very sweet and sociable sister and told him it was no problem.

"I guess last night went well," she said.

"Not bad," he answered. "Her name is Michelle, and I told her I would get her some salmon. I'll get dressed and go to the market."

"I love salmon," Cheryl said, "I already have some in the fridge. "I'll grill it with some vegetables."

"Thanks, Cheryl," said Michael. Then Kenneth entered the room with Cheryl so Michael ended his conversation on the intercom.

"Looks like your idea worked," she said to her husband. "Michael is bringing a guest for dinner."

"Oh, yeah?" Ken replied sarcastically. "And what did King Michael request?"

"Nothing, Ken, nothing."

After a few moments, Michael called Coretta to thank her for the money. He pulled her card from his pocket and dialed her number.

"Coretta James speaking."

"Coretta, this is Michael Alexander."

"I was expecting, rather, I was hoping for your call," she said.

"Thanks for the money."

"That's only a small amount of what you can make. The sky's the limit in your line of work."

"I've still got to give it some thought. I'll be in touch anyway."

He hung up the phone and lay down to take a nap. Though it was only 3 in the afternoon, he was quite exhausted. Brittany came down the hall, saw her father sleeping, and climbed in the bed to join him. Cheryl and Kenneth began to prepare the food for what would be an eventful evening. Around 5, Michael arose from his nap and realized that he didn't possess any nice clothes to wear for the evening, so he asked Ken if he could borrow a car and run up to the mall to get a couple of outfits with some of the money from Coretta. Ken was a bit moody but allowed Michael to go.

Brittany was still asleep so Michael went alone to the Beverly Center, where he picked up a couple of outfits and returned in time to change clothes right before Michelle arrived for dinner. Ken heard the doorbell ring and went to answer the door to see the statuesque Michelle standing there. He gasped before speaking.

"Hi, I'm Michelle Davis. Michael invited me over for dinner."

"Hello, I'm Kenneth Bolling, and this is my wife, Cheryl."

"Come in," said Cheryl. "Make yourself at home."

Ken wiped the drool off his face.

"Brit," yelled Cheryl, "come on. Get ready to eat."

"OK," yelled Brittany, putting away her dolls.

"Daddy, come on, let's eat," said Brittany.

Michael put on the peach slacks and almost see-through white shirt with his new, comfortable, tan shoes.

"Where is your bathroom?" asked Michelle. "I'd like to wash up."

"It's right through there," pointed Cheryl.

Michelle washed up and returned from the bathroom, and Cheryl handed her a plate with utensils.

"Make yourself at home home and dig in," said Cheryl.

"Everything looks and smells so good," Michelle replied. "I don't know where to start."

"Need some help with anything?" Ken asked, flirting.

"She'll be okay," Cheryl replied wryly.

Michelle introduced herself to the beautiful 5-year-old Brittany and offered to help her with her food. Brittany was agreeable, so Michelle prepared her plate.

"There you go, sweetie," Michelle said. "Come over here and sit by me."

"Are you my daddy's girlfriend?"

"No, actually your father and I just met," came the reply.

At that moment, Michael entered the kitchen with his usual fanfare and flair. "Sounds like somebody's talking about me," he said, making his grand entrance.

"Hey, Michael," said Cheryl, "that's a smooth outfit."

"Thank you." He embraced Brittany and then embraced Michelle before grabbing a plate to fix some food.

"Would you like me to do that for you?" asked Michelle.

"Sure, if you don't mind," he replied.

"No, not at all."

She took the plate from Michael, asked what he wanted, and filled the plate with food. Ken began an evening of nitpicking.

"Did you tell your new friend about your moniterial gain?" he inquired.

Michael frowned angrily, but didn't respond to Kenneth's comments.

"What money?" asked Cheryl innocently. "Michael, you've been working and not telling anyone?" she said with a smile.

"Oh, yeah, he's been working," reported her husband, "real late-night work."

"Drop that shit, man," said Michael. "What I did last night is my business."

"Yeah, well, maybe you can pay us back for the room and board that you've abused," he said with attitude, "or do you want to freeload the entire time you're here?"

Kenneth's statement caught everyone by surprise, and Michael fired back angrily, "I'll pay you anything you feel like I owe you. Just name the price."

Cheryl was shocked by Kenneth's bluntness and was very upset not only at the statement, but also at the timing. She pulled her husband aside and chastised him for the way he brought his unprovoked tirade over dinner.

"What the hell are you doing?" she demanded. "Why are you bringing up this mess now? We told Michael and Brittany they could stay here as long as they needed to. We've got more money than we could ever spend, so why all of a sudden are you making money an issue?"

"I'm just tired of Prince Michael being put on a pedestal by everyone. He's a deadbeat drug addict who can't even take care of his own daughter."

"Where is this coming from? That man has been your best friend your entire life, and he is also my friend. His wife was my best friend, and that is my goddaughter in there. That child has lost her mother, her home, and almost lost her father in the last year. We're going to make her life as comfortable as possible. So whatever you have against Michael, keep it to yourself."

"He slept with a woman last night without a condom," said Kenneth, "then he invites this girl over for dinner the very next day."

"That's Michael's business, Kenneth, not yours. It sounds to me like you're jealous. Now let's go back in there and have dinner and any beef you have with Michael, you bring it up *later*, to Michael, *alone*, if you have to, but not now."

Kenneth didn't answer but went back in with a frown and reluctantly continued his meal. Michelle was very attracted to Michael and Brittany and ignored Kenneth's statement. She continued to play with Brittany and speak with Michael. Michelle was not the scandalous type, but felt a mysterious connection with Michael. After the main course was consumed, Cheryl brought out the banana pudding with whipped cream that she had made and offered it to everyone.

"Still making that banana pudding, huh, Cheryl?" asked Michael.

"You know it," she answered.

"Well, I'll definitely take some," he said. "What about you, Michelle?"

"I don't think so," she replied. "I'm watching my figure. The way I look writes my paycheck."

"Well, in that case, baby girl, you must be rich," said Michael, "because you're about as beautiful and fine as a woman can be."

Kenneth listened to the talk between Michael and Michelle and almost went off into a jealous rage. The two of them continued flirting in the midst of this potential hostility.

"Flattery will get you everywhere, my handsome brother," she said, "*everywhere.*"

"I guess you had a lot of flattery last night," Kenneth said, interrupting, "because you didn't make it here until this afternoon."

At this point, Michael was more upset than he had ever been in his life. It took everything he had to keep from lunging at Ken.

"Oh, did you tell your girl you're broke?" Kenneth taunted. "I bet you didn't tell her that we found your deadbeat ass living on skid row with the rest of those deadbeat bums."

Michael moved toward Ken, but Michelle stopped him.

"No!" she said, putting her hand in front of Michael. "Let's leave."

"How's he gonna leave?" laughed Ken. "He doesn't even have a car."

"*I* have a car," said Michelle. "Come on, Michael."

"Go ahead, Michael," said Cheryl, "I'll take care of Brittany."

Cheryl was also furious with Ken, who showed her a side she had never seen before. Michael and Michelle took off in Michelle's convertible Mercedes 560 SL.

"Where are we going?" asked Michael.

"For now, we are just going to ride," she answered. "That man is not your friend, I hope you know that."

"Ken and I have been friends since we were boys, since we were five," said Michael, "but sometimes he acts like a little bitch. He's always done everything exactly as I've done it. I played basketball, he wanted to play basketball. The only difference was that I was a star and he sat on the end of the bench. I won a national dunk contest and played overseas, while he never went anywhere. I go into the insurance business, and he follows me there. I married my Sheila, and right after that, he marries Cheryl. He once told me that he lives his life vicariously through me."

"He's got a problem," said Michelle. "The way he attacked you tonight was no coincidence. He's got some serious hatred built up for you. Something tonight pushed him over the edge and his true feelings came out."

"No way," Michael protested. "He loves me like a brother. We've been best friends for years."

"Sounds to me like he's been riding your coattail," said Michelle. "Anyway, brothers who care about each other don't hate on their friends like that. If he does love you, he has a funny way of showing it."

Michael paused for a moment to think back over his friendship with Ken and realized that Michelle possibly had a point about Kenneth's obsession with him. But he refused to give up that quickly on his childhood friend and asked Michelle for the use of her cell phone.

"Let me call and check on Brittany and make sure Ken is okay," he said naively.

Chapter 7

BACK AT KEN AND CHERYL'S place, the two of them were in a heated argument over Ken's actions.

"Why are you acting like this?" Cheryl demanded. "You made a fool out of yourself in front of our guest."

"She wasn't my guest," he replied, "and I don't care what she thinks. I don't know that bitch."

"Oh, yeah?" Cheryl said. "Well, you sure acted like you wanted to know her. I thought you cared about Michael."

"I never really cared about that punk," he said coldly, referring to Michael.

Cheryl was as shocked as Michael at Ken's actions and realized these feelings couldn't be isolated. As they continued to argue, the phone rang. Michael was on the line.

"Ken, can we talk for a second, brother? What's your problem?"

"You're my problem," said Kenneth. "I want you to collect your shit and get out of here."

"Why, man? Why you tripping like this?"

Cheryl tried to take the phone and talk to Michael, but Kenneth quickly hung up. Mike called back, but only got a busy signal.

"That fool won't answer the phone," Michael told Michelle, "and he told me to get out."

"Just like that?" asked Michelle.

"Just like that. Take me back to get my stuff and my daughter."

"Not now," said Michelle. "In your frame of mind, who knows what will happen. Cheryl won't let anything happen to Brittany and besides, where will you go?"

Michael looked away with despair written on his face. He couldn't believe Ken changed up on him so fast and didn't have a clue as to where he would go or what he would do. Michelle saw the look on Michael's face.

"Well, tonight, you can hang out with me," she said.

"But I don't have anything to offer you. I'm broke, and I'm homeless."

"Life is not all about material things," said Michelle. "You have a lot to offer, I can see it in your eyes. And I believe you have a good heart."

Michelle pulled up to a grocery store to go inside. "You want to come in with me?" she asked.

"No, I'll wait for you to get back, but may I use your phone again?"

Michelle handed him the phone and went in the store to buy her favorite bottle of wine. Michael stared at the phone and dialed the only number that he knew may offer assistance.

"Is this Coretta?" he said to the voice on the line.

"Yes, it is. Who am I speaking with?"

"This is Michael, Michael Alexander."

"Two calls in one day, Mr. Alexander. To what do I owe this unexpected pleasure?"

"I really don't know what I'm doing, but I want to take you up on your offer," Michael explained.

"Which offer, the one where we have sex again or the job offer?"

"The job offer."

"That was fast. Why the quick switch?"

"Let's just say I don't have anywhere else to turn right now," he replied. "But I need you to do something for me. I need a place to stay right away."

"Is tomorrow soon enough? Also, tomorrow, I would like to have a little get together at the house in your honor, introduce you to some people. Come around eight p.m. and please feel free to bring a friend. Michael, do you have a number that I can reach you on?"

"No, I don't have a phone."

"Don't worry, I will have you one by tomorrow morning. Call me early so you can pick it up."

"I gotta go, later," said Michael because Michelle was approaching, so he hung up.

"Come on, let's go to my suite," suggested Michelle, driving off in the car.

She had an adjoining two-room suite at the Hotel Nikko, complete with a fully stocked bar, a beautiful entertainment center, and all the luxuries of home.

"I was out of Chardonnay," she said. "Would you open the wine for me?"

Michael spotted some Remy Martin at the bar and began to pour himself a drink. "I hope you don't mind," he said. "Cognac is my favorite."

"Help yourself to anything you see."

"Oh, yeah?" he said, looking at Michelle seductively.

"Well, almost anything," she laughed.

"So how did you get into that situation you're in with that pretty little girl?" asked Michelle.

"Let's not talk about that, please. Let's just sit back and enjoy each other's company."

Michael and Michelle sat back and conversed and shared about each other's dreams and desires and before you knew it, Michelle finished off the whole bottle of wine. She didn't hold her liquor well and went over to the bar to pour Michael his third shot of Remy.

"I'm sorry, baby," said a tipsy Michelle, "let me pour another one."

"No, no," said Michael. "That's alright, I've had enough anyway."

"Oh, yeah, well, how 'bout I do a little dance for you?" Michelle suggested. She began to dance seductively and started to remove her blouse.

Michael ran up and stopped her. "I want you, baby, but not like this."

He kissed Michelle's pretty lips. She playfully dove for Michael, but missed him and landed on the plush couch in her suite. As he approached, she pulled him down on top of her, but still Michael resisted. They delicately kissed, but Michael was adamant about not wanting to take advantage of her while she was intoxicated.

"Do you have any oil?" he asked.

"Yes, in the cabinet in the bathroom."

"Well, I'll tell you what. You lay across the bed, and I'll give you a massage," he said.

"Alright, hurry back, baby," replied Michelle.

Michael popped her bra and laid her face down across the bed. As he looked at her smooth skin and the shape of her beautiful butt, he wondered how he could resist throughout the night without taking advantage of her. He went into the bathroom to retrieve the oil, but couldn't find it.

"You did say in the cabinet, right? Oh, yeah, here it is, baby oil. This will work."

Walking back to the bedroom, Michael found Michelle sound asleep lying across the bed. He lay down on the bed and gently took Michelle's head, placing it across his chest. It had been a long day and soon, Michael fell asleep. Tomorrow surely wouldn't be as eventful for Michael as today, would it?

Around seven a.m., Michelle's cell phone rang. She scrambled around to find it, bumping her head against the headboard. Finally, she located her phone on the nightstand.

"Hello," she barely uttered, still half asleep.

"May I speak to Michael Alexander?" a voice requested.

"Who is this?"

"It's Coretta James," said the voice coolly.

Michelle woke Michael. "Coretta James for you."

"How did she get your number?"

"It's called caller ID," she replied.

"This is Michael."

"You got a pen?" asked Coretta.

"Good morning to you too," he responded.

"Good morning, Mr. Alexander. I conduct my most important business first thing in the morning. And now, sir, do you have a pen?"

"Michelle, do you have a pen?"

Michelle had a bewildered look on her face, but reached in her purse and handed him a pen.

"Okay, go," he said.

"You can pick up your Nextel phone from the Nextel store on Wilshire across from the mall. Ask for Tom. He's expecting you. They open at 10. Next, you can pick up your car from Edwin at Edwin's imports in Glendale and inside the car will be directions to your new condo. Edwin is expecting you at noon."

"Are you serious?" he asked in disbelief.

"Very," said Coretta. "Call me when you get into the condo. And don't forget, I'm expecting you at 8 tonight. I'll have my driver pick up you and yours at 7:30. Oh, I forgot, my tailor is expecting you at 8 this morning. The shop is called Men's Fine Designs. David Devarro is my tailor. The store is on Magnolia and Cahuenga in North Hollywood. Don't be late, chow."

"Wait a minute, I don't have a—" Michael suddenly realized that he'd been hung up on.

"I guess you've got quite a day ahead of you," said Michelle.

"What's your calender like for today?" he asked.

"What time do you need to be there?" she answered.

"By 8 a.m. We've got only 50 minutes to get to North Hollywood."

"What do you mean, 'we'?"

"I mean, do you mind?" Michael asked politely.

"No, I don't mind, but next time, don't call another woman on my cell phone. Everything done in the dark always comes to light."

Michelle and Michael washed up and drove out to Men's Fine Designs in North Hollywood. They arrived at 7:57 a.m. and found the doors already open. Walking inside, they were greeted by a black man dressed in a designer suit, all white, with a white shirt and red tie, accented by a small amount of lip gloss and a white scarf. The man was very gay.

"Come on in, honey," said David Devarro. "You must be Michael Alexander. Coretta said you were fine, and she wasn't lying."

David's eyes traveled up and down Michael's body, while Michael and Michelle looked on in amazement.

"Oh, it's going to be a *pleasure* taking your measurements and getting your wardrobe together. I'm going to make you look delicious."

Michael was speechless. David called him over to take his measurements. Looking at Michael's complexion, David commented, "They say the blacker the berry, the sweeter the juice. Bring your tall, chocolate, fine ass over here."

Michelle began to laugh and joined in on the conversation. "Girl, I know what you mean," she snickered. "He's fine, isn't he?"

"Yeah, girl," said David, "if I were you, I would take every last drip drop of Mr. Nestle Quick Chocolate."

"Be still, honey," said David to a squirming Michael, "I'm trying to get your measurements." As David said that, he was giving close scrutiny to Michael's groin area.

"Looks like about a ten," said David. Michelle fell over laughing as David continued to compliment Michael on *all* his features. Looking at Michael's size 13 shoe, he spoke again.

"Is it true what they say about big feet and big hands?" David asked.

Michael leaned over and David touched his wavy locks. "And curly hair too."

"Hey, man, cut that shit out," Michael said as Michelle laughed.

Coretta planned to get the measurements by phone from Michael and have several items off the rack for him until his wardrobe was ready. Finishing up, Michael hurriedly exited the store after being measured by David. Michelle was overwhelmed with laughter as they headed for the Nextel dealership.

"I bet you thought that shit was real funny, huh?" he asked.

"You should have seen the look on your face," said Michelle. "Looks like I'm going to have some competition."

"Funny, you should join the comedy tour."

"Michael, do you know anything about this woman, Coretta?"

"I met her the same night I met you, remember? I know she can make things happen. It's a blessing that she's getting me everything that I need right now."

"Material things are not always a blessing," Michelle replied. "There's nothing free in life. She'll want something in return."

"You know, you speak with a lot of sense, sista," said Michael. "Where did you get your wisdom from?"

"My father always told me to beware of strangers bearing gifts. I don't like it when people to try to win me over. I want a man to simply give me the gift of love, and everything else already comes along with that."

"That's a deep statement, but you do need money to survive."

"I agree you need things," said Michelle, "but you need faith more than anything."

Michelle thought about last night and felt somewhat remorseful about what happened.

"Michael, I hope I didn't get carried away last night," she said. "That Chardonnay kinda went to work on me."

"You were a lady all night long," he said, "a perfect lady."

Chapter 8

KENNETH DECIDED TO CALL CHERYL at her law practice to apologize for his rude behavior. Cheryl's assistant answered the phone.

"Donna, let me speak to Cheryl, please," said Kenneth.

"Sure, Mr. Bolling, please hold on," Donna replied.

"Cheryl, it's your husband on line one."

"Thanks, Donna," said Cheryl.

At that moment, a large bouquet of red roses arrived at Cheryl's office.

"Flowers for Mrs. Bolling," said the deliveryman.

"How did you time it so well?" Cheryl asked Kenneth.

"I spoke to the driver on his cell phone as he pulled up. Would you please accept my apology?"

"Michael is the one you should apologize to."

"One step at a time," he said.

"I can't talk right now," said Cheryl. "I'm due in court shortly, and then I need to pick up Brit. After that, I'll see you at home and we'll talk."

⇥⊙ ⇥⊙ ⇥⊙

AFTER MICHAEL PICKED up his cell phone, he arrived at Edwin's Mercedes Benz dealership at 12:15 p.m., after stopping first for breakfast with Michelle.

"Do you want me to wait for you until you're done?" she asked.

"You got a 2 o'clock appointment, right?" asked Michael. "I'll be fine. Everything else today has been a breeze."

"Will I see you later?" wondered Michelle.

"Call me and we'll talk. Here's my number: (310) 770-8747. Call me when you finish your meeting and we can go from there."

Michelle gave Michael a kiss and drove off. Michael entered the dealership, where he met Edwin, who was upset that Michael was eighteen minutes late. Edwin was an Iranian man, with a medium build, dark black hair, and was a stickler for time.

"Hi, are you Edwin? I'm Michael Alexander. Coretta James sent me to pick up a car."

"You were supposed to be here 18 minutes and 55 seconds ago," he answered. "Now you just fucked my whole day."

Michael was caught off guard by Edwin's remarks and apologized for his tardiness.

"'I apologize' my ass," the irrate Iranian said. "Now I have to replan my whole day."

Edwin continued to rant and rave until Michael finally got fed up. "Okay, I get the message, Saddam Hussein."

"Who you call Saddam Hussein?" he demanded to know. "What if Saddam Hussein put his foot in your tall ass?"

Michael laughed.

"Here, sign right here," said Edwin.

"What am I signing?"

"You're signing for your car. The address to the condo is on the dash, and your tags will come as soon as the state gets around to it."

"How much are my payments?" asked Michael.

"What are you, an idiot?" Edwin asked in disbelief. "There are no payments. Coretta paid for this car in full. Neither you nor Ms. James have to do anything. It's that convertible 320 pulled up in the front."

Michael signed the papers, and Edwin threw him the keys.

"You must want me to put my foot deep in your Iranian ass," said Michael.

"This ain't the Gulf War," yelled Edwin. "You don't want me to pull out a can of whup ass from this drawer."

"You'll get *your* ass whupped," yelled Michael, entering his car. The two men continued to argue as Michael drove off. Michael was so busy quarreling that he didn't pay much attention to the stylish convertible that Coretta had given him. Out of nowhere, the words of Michelle came back to him as he drove towards his new abode. The words were, "Nothing in this world is free."

The address on the dash directed Michael to a somewhat new subdivision in Sherman Oaks called the Plaza at Sherman Oaks, a four-story luxury condominium with an extensive security system located across from the five-star Plaza Hotel. Michael parked in the hotel parking and walked into the condominium, going to the Concierge Desk, where he was expected.

"Mr. Alexander, 4th floor, number 435, right off the elevator," said the concierge. "Whenever you come in, you need to show your ID in order to be buzzed in. There's always someone at the front desk. Someone will be up to explain how to work your security system. Here are your keys. The silver one's for the top lock, the gold for the bottom, and the third, smaller key is for your storage unit. Welcome to the Plaza Condominium, Mr. Alexander, and please let us know if we can be of any service."

Then Michael was buzzed through the door and rode the elevator to the fourth floor. Apt 435 was off the elevator. He turned the lock and entered. Once inside the door, he was surprised to find a tall, light-skinned, perfectly gorgeous, young black woman standing next to the door.

"And who may I ask are you?" he said. "Do you come with the room?"

"No, my name is Myra Irvin. I'm a student at UCLA. Coretta is a good friend of my sister, and she knew I needed a job so I could continue to work my way through grad school," said Myra. "She said you had a daughter and I could take care of her for you until you made other arrangements."

"UCLA, huh? What's your major?"

"Child psychology. I want to work with children in some capacity. I love children and look forward to some day being a mom."

Myra had a very pleasant personality and was instantly attracted to Michael.

"The fridge is full. What would you like to eat?"

By now, it was about 4 p.m. and Michael still needed to get his daughter from Ken's house. Myra showed Mike to the master bedroom and the other master bedroom for Brittany. There was a third, large bedroom where she would bunk. In all, the condo had 3000 square feet, 3 bedrooms, 3 baths, a den and a deck.

"So you're going to live here?" Michael asked.

"Yes, if it's okay with you," she replied.

"Yeah, it's okay. Coretta thought of everything."

"Maybe one day you can join me for service at my church," Myra said. "I go to Friendship Baptist in Yorba Linda."

"That's all the way in Orange County," he stated.

"Yeah, I've gone there since I was a little girl."

Michael's closet was fully stocked with clothes, the condo was fully furnished, and Michael began to wonder what he had gotten himself into. Then his cell phone rang.

"Mr. Alexander, we need you to come down and sign the title on your condo," requested the concierge.

"Myra, if you don't mind, you can prepare something for my daughter," said Michael. "I'm going to pick her up now. Myra, how much do you know about Coretta?"

"I've known her my whole life," replied Myra. "She's a sweetheart."

"Yeah, a sweetheart that gives away four hundred thousand dollar condos, convertible sports cars, and full wardrobes," he said.

"Actually, these condos are appraised at well over a million," Myra said. "She's quite smitten by you. She's a very wealthy woman and can afford to give, but I've never seen her anywhere near this generous. She pays me two thousand dollars a month and room and board. She can be very frugal at times."

Michael ended his conversation and went downstairs to the concierge, where a document was waiting to be signed.

"Ms. James quick claimed the condo over to you," said the concierge. "All you have to do is sign right here."

Michael reluctantly signed the quick claim deed to the condo and drove off to pick up his daughter.

Chapter 9

KENNETH WAS ON HIS WAY home and Cheryl and Brittany were having a snack. Cheryl saw Michael on the other side of the door and told Brittany that her father was at the door. Brittany clapped her hands and jumped up and down in joy at the thought of her father.

Cheryl opened the door, greeting her old friend. "Hello, Michael."

"Hey, pie face," Michael said, lifting his daughter.

Cheryl looked outside and saw the new convertible in the driveway. "New car?"

"Something like that," he answered evasively. "I came to get Brittany."

"Michael, she can stay here until you get it together," said Cheryl.

"I got it together."

"But where will you take her?" asked Cheryl.

"I've got a place."

"Michael, don't do this because of what Kenneth did. You know how he gets sometimes," she pleaded.

"He told me to come and get my shit," Michael responded. "Well, Brittany is the only thing I have, so I guess he meant her."

"Michael, he didn't mean Brittany," Cheryl said. "You know she can stay here forever, if necessary."

"Well, thank God, it's not necessary," he stated.

Michael and Cheryl went back and forth for a few moments. Cheryl realized that Michael would take his daughter, so she packed up the child's clothes and toys that she had purchased for Brittany over the past several weeks. Michael put the stuff in the car, including his few remaining items, took his daughter, and headed toward the door.

"You can see her anytime, Cheryl," he added. "You know that."

Cheryl began to sob and hugged and kissed Brittany and her father. Then he got into the convertible to drive off, but at that exact moment, Ken pulled into the driveway and blocked Michael's car in.

"Move your car," said Michael.

"Not until you talk to me," replied Kenneth.

"We have nothing to talk about," flatly stated Michael.

"Where are you taking Brittany?" Kenneth demanded.

"Ain't none of your damn business where I take my child, now move your car, man. I gotta go."

"Go where?" Kenneth challenged. "I'm not moving until you tell me where you're going."

"Nigger, either you move that car, or I going to run that motherfucker over. You choose," said Michael.

"Ken, just move the car," urged Cheryl. "You can't make him stay against his will."

"Yeah, especially since you're the one that asked me to go," said Michael.

Kenneth reluctantly moved his car and Michael sped out

of the driveway. It had been a very long day, and Michael still had a very long night ahead.

"Daddy, where are we going?" asked Brittany.

"To our new home," he replied. "To our new home."

Michael pulled into the lobby past the concierge desk and with the evening shift change, the heavyset woman at the desk asked him for his ID. He showed it to her, then was buzzed through the door.

"When did he move in?" the new attendant asked.

"Today," said the outgoing attendant. "He moved into Ms. James' suite. In fact, she signed it over to him."

"I see why. He's cute."

Michael took Brittany up the elevator to their condo to find Myra preparing dinner for everyone.

"Brittany, this is Myra, and she's going to be living with us for the time being," said Michael. "Myra, this is my daughter, Brittany."

"Hello, beautiful," said Myra to Brittany. "I'm making some dinner. Are you hungry?"

Brittany looked at Myra, but didn't speak.

"I know," said Myra, "how would you like to go on the playground and get on the swing?" Brittany looked at her father to get his approval, and he nodded that it was okay, so Brittany and Myra walked outside.

"Everything is turned off," said Myra. "I'll take her around the corner to the playground."

Chapter 10

Michael was resting on the couch to kind of catch his breath from the last couple of days when the doorbell suddenly rang. It was about 6:45 in the evening and he was exhausted.

"Who is it?" he yelled. Then he opened the door, assuming that Myra had come back for something, but there standing in the doorway was Stephen and the burly Manu.

"What's going on?" he asked.

"Boss lady sent us over here to pick you up," Stephen stated.

"I'm not ready yet," Michael replied.

"Well, get ready. You've got a closet full of brand-new suits," said Stephen, "and remember, this is black-tie."

"I'll drive myself," said Michael, trying to close the door on the men. Manu kicked the door open.

"Look, get ready, punk," Stephen stated. "You see, your dumb ass is into boss lady for a million dollars a day. Didn't your mama tell you not to sign anything without considering the consequences? Boss lady likes to have all her employees there early for special occasions, and since this party is especially for you, she wants you there *real* early."

"What if I don't want to go?" asked Michael.

"Then that means you don't want to work for boss lady and in that case, we have to collect a million dollars and since your broke ass probably can't rub two nickels together, that means we have to let Manu do what he does best. Give him an example of what you do best, Manu."

The burly Chinese man grabbed a steel rod from Stephen and bent it across his head without flinching. Michael could see in Manu's eyes that he would love to kill him and realized that he had no choice but to get ready and go. Besides, he wanted to leave before Brittany returned.

"Besides," Stephen continued, pulling a 9mm from his pants, "if necessary, I would just pop your ass. Now get dressed, bitch. I don't like your bitch ass no way. I can't wait for you to fuck up so I can have an excuse to kill your ass."

That said, Stephen relaxed on the sofa and kicked his legs up on the table as Michael changed.

"Let's see what this bitch has in his refrigerator," Stephen said to Manu. "Boss lady's got the place stocked. I've never seen her go out for anybody like this, and she just met this fool. Well, he don't have no room for error. One mistake and he's gonna pay for it with his life."

Michael showered quickly and tried to get dressed before Myra and Brittany returned. He took a quick look through the closet and put on a black tuxedo which Coretta provided with a white French-cut shirt and white tie. Coretta purchased various colognes for him and although Michael felt the pressure of being totally indebted to someone, he was truly impressed with how thorough Coretta was for details. He had diamond cuff links and stylish shoes of all colors. Michael put on a pair of beautiful black shoes size 13 and some Diesel cologne.

"This shit smells good," he said. He put some waves in his hair and checked himself out in the mirror one final time. Then he walked out into the living room and spoke to his escorts.

"Alright, let's roll, man," he said.

"The pretty bitch is ready," smirked Stephen.

"I got your bitch, you punk motherfucker," Michael retorted.

"Oh, the bitch got some balls," said Stephen.

"Don't you forget who's running the show," Michael replied. "See, you ain't nothing but a punk ass errand boy. Stephen, get this, Stephen, get that. But I got to fuck the boss. I get to live in the boss's condo. I get whatever I want, and I've only known her for two days. You ain't nothing but her dog—fetch, boy!"

Michael took a big chance speaking to the short-tempered Stephen this way, but he just didn't know how to back down. Stephen wanted to terminate him badly, but realized that Coretta was taken by Michael and this whole night was for him. She would die if anything happened to him.

"You gonna fuck up, somehow, somewhere," said Stephen, "and when you do, your ass is grass and Manu and I are the lawnmowers."

"Why do you need Manu, that big, hairy ape, every time you want to handle your business?" asked Michael. "Without Manu and that gun, I'd beat your fucking ass."

Stephen had never been spoken to like that by anyone working with Coretta. He had worked with her for years and had always been in charge of everything. Michael's arrogance was too much to bear, but he couldn't do anything about it at the time. Stephen had been a street hustler, robbing and poaching in downtown LA. Coretta brought him from the streets and gave him a good life in return for his services. Stephen would never cross Coretta, for any reason, but he just couldn't understand her obsession with Michael. Coretta was gorgeous, filthy rich, and had been involved with royalty and all types. He couldn't understand what was so special about Michael that intrigued her. This was the first time Stephen had ever considered going against Coretta and it took everything in his power not to just shoot Michael in the head. But Michael wasn't through. He would only make it worse.

"I'm leaving with you, but I'm driving my own car," he flatly stated. "I'll follow you there."

He walked away from Stephen and Manu and went to the Mercedes Coretta had purchased for him, fired up the engine, and waited on Stephen and Manu.

"Don't worry, Manu," Stephen said. "We'll get his ass yet, don't worry."

Coretta's mansion had been decorated lavishly, befitting a king. All of her influential friends turned out to enjoy the evening. Coretta owned extensive real estate across the South and combine that with all her illegal business, she was worth millions of dollars. But her girls were her most cherished possessions. They were exquisitely beautiful girls, servicing the wealthy, the influential, and the powerful. Her clientele list is a who's who of the city of Los Angeles, the nation, and the world. Her powerful ties kept her above the law and at 29 years old, she planned to stay above the law. Michael didn't realize the magnitude of the woman he signed his life over to, but he was about to find out.

Just as Michael was leaving for the festivities, Brittany and Myra arrived back at the condo, laughing and enjoying the moment.

"That was fun, huh, Brittany?" asked Myra.

"Yeah, let's tell Daddy about it."

"OK," agreed Myra. "Let's tell Daddy."

They searched for Michael, but he had already left. All the two ladies found were his underwear thrown across the bed.

"Typical man," said Myra.

"Yeah, typical man," repeated Brittany.

Myra laughed and brought Brit in the kitchen so that they could enjoy the dinner she had prepared. Brittany was a very contented child. Even as a baby, she never cried much, so she was very easy to keep, even for those she didn't know. Myra loved children, even those considered to be bad, so she felt quite privileged to be around Brittany. Brittany instinctively clung to her, almost as she had clung to her mother. The two really enjoyed each other.

⋅→⊫◎ ⋅→⊫◎ ⋅→⊫◎

MEANWHILE, KEN'S TRUE hatred for Michael had finally surfaced. He had envied Michael his whole life, although you wouldn't think that. Ken would have been happy had Michael not been alive. He truly felt nothing but animosity for Michael for a very long time. He couldn't even concentrate for thinking of Michael.

As 8 o'clock approached, Brittany wanted to call Cheryl to say good-night and let her know that she was okay. Myra was surprised that Brittany remembered Cheryl's phone number so well, but after all, Brittany was a very enlightened child. Also, Cheryl had gone over the number with Brittany until she was sure she had it in case anything happened to her or her father. Myra and Brittany dialed up Cheryl as she sat at home at the kitchen table with a brooding Kenneth.

"That fucking Michael," said Kenneth. "There's no telling where he has that girl right now."

At that moment, the phone rang.

"Aunt Cheryl," said a cheery little girl, "this is Brittany."

"Brittany!" yelled Cheryl, "how are you doing, baby?"

"Fine," said Brittany, "how are you?"

"Fine," Cheryl replied. "Where are you?"

"I'm at my daddy's new house," she said.

Ken jumped up to listen to the conversation and grabbed the phone from Cheryl. "Brittany, this is Uncle Ken. Let me speak to your daddy."

"My daddy's not here."

"Your daddy's not there? You mean you're there by yourself?" he asked.

"No, Myra's with me," she answered.

"Who's Myra?"

"Sweetie, let me take the phone for a minute," Myra said to Brittany.

"Hello," said Myra.

"Who are you?" asked Ken.

"I was hired to look after Brittany while Mr. Alexander works," explained Myra.

"Are you living in the house with Michael and Brittany and sharing a bed right under that little girl?" Ken demanded.

Cheryl tried to snatch the phone away from Ken, but he pulled it back.

Ken blew up. "Y'all fucking right there with that little girl in the house?"

"We're not fucking!" yelled Myra, almost forgetting Brittany was there. "You should talk to Mr. Alexander because I'm not getting into this."

"Where is Michael?" he asked.

"He's at a party at Coretta's house," Myra answered. "I guess he left before we got back."

Ken instantly switched up to try to get some information. "Oh, he told me about that party. I've been waiting for him to call with directions, but he didn't get back to me yet. Where's it at again?"

"It's at Coretta's mansion in Bel Air," Myra informed him.

"You have the address? I think I'll go ahead and go."

Myra gave Ken the address, and he immediately handed Cheryl the phone and rushed into the restroom to shower and change. Cheryl and Myra conversed. Myra thought that Ken was a strange bird, but didn't tell Cheryl that.

→▷ →▷ →▷

Michael arrived at Coretta's mansion at 7:55 on the tail of the limo driven by Stephen and Manu. Inside, Carlos and Coretta were conversing. "So what's up with this guy you're throwing the party for?" he asked.

"I'm introducing him to some of my friends and colleagues," Coretta explained. "He's going to be my first male hooker."

"Why didn't you allow me to get the market started?" Carlos wanted to know.

"I've been with you," she said. "You're not that good."

Carlos was a very handsome man of Spanish descent who had worked with Coretta for a couple of years. They occasionally had slept together whenever Coretta felt the need, however, Coretta didn't like being questioned by anyone.

"So what are you planning to do with this guy and where does it leave me?" asked Carlos.

"Look, just because I let you jump up and down on me a few times doesn't mean you have the right to ask me any questions," explained Coretta.

At that moment, Michael got out of his car and walked to the front entrance of Coretta's mansion.

"Hello, Michael," said Coretta. "How was your trip over here?"

"It was fine, all except for your two brutes trying to strong-arm me to try to get me to ride in the limo," he complained.

"I asked them to bring you, Michael. I wanted you to be on time."

While they spoke, Carlos stood there, not being acknowledged at all by Coretta.

"Where are the valets?" asked Michael, "or do you want me to leave the car there?"

"No, I'll get you a valet," she replied. "Carlos, please park Mr. Alexander's car."

Carlos looked sideways in disgust, but took Michael's keys and drove the car off to park it.

"What's wrong with him?"

"He's having a bad day," Coretta replied. "I hope this party is up to your standards. Fix yourself a drink while I check on my girls. I want to make this a night you'll never forget."

Michael fixed himself a stiff shot of Remy Martin and just stood there, not knowing what to do. After a few moments, 10 beautiful women of all nationalities came up to him to meet him and engage him in conversation.

"There they are, Michael," said Coretta, "the best paid, most professional women in the business, and also the most beautiful, don't you agree? Their job tonight is to satisfy your every need, from getting you a drink, to giving you good loving. Anything your heart desires, they will do for you. Now, Mr. Alexander, this way, if you please."

Michael walked arm in arm with these exquisite escorts into Coretta's ballroom. There, hundreds of people were gathered, having a good time, drinking, and celebrating. There were many high-profile guests, including a long list of Coretta's clients in her escort service.

"Isn't that Mayor Allison?" Michael asked Coretta.

"Yes, that's Mayor Allison, one of my greatest customers."

"Where's his wife?"

"Anywhere but here, I'm sure," replied Coretta.

"Isn't that Shaq?" he asked in awe.

"Yes, Shaquille O'Neal is another client, but only in my real estate ventures. He has no idea about my other endeavors."

"Call him over," Michael requested. "He looks just like baby Huey."

"Shaquille," Coretta called, "I have someone I want you to meet."

Shaquille came over and kissed Coretta on the cheek. She introduced Michael.

"Shaquille, this is my newest employee, the one who will break the bank for me," she smiled. "This is Michael Alexander. Michael, this is—"

Michael cut her off in mid sentence. "Everybody knows who Shaq is," he said, "especially in LA."

The two acknowledged each other and Michael began to talk "stuff."

"You've got to be the biggest human being in the world," he said to Shaq. "If I had a ball, I'd dunk on your big ass."

"Only in your dreams," Shaq smiled.

Coretta continued to take Michael around, introducing him to dignitaries and the wealthy and giving him access to anything that was at her disposal. Michael was quite impressed, but still leery about the situation. Carlos stood close by like a puppy dog all night long while Stephen and Manu watched from a distance with venom in their hearts. After about an hour of partying, an unexpected person entered. Kenneth had invited himself to the festivities. Manu and Stephen moved towards Kenneth, but at that moment, Kenneth spotted Michael on Coretta's arm and walked over.

"Very nice party," Kenneth said to Michael. "Nice of you to invite me."

"I didn't invite you," replied Michael. "How did you know where I was?"

"Your new live-in told me," he answered. "Aren't you going to introduce me to your friend?"

"My name is Coretta James, and I don't remember inviting you to this party."

Kenneth was taken by Coretta's beauty, but Coretta did not like strangers inviting themselves to her gatherings.

"Kenneth, was it? Let me repeat myself, I don't like uninvited guests."

"You did invite me," Kenneth said flippantly. "You probably invited me in your dreams."

"I would never invite you in or out of my dreams," replied Coretta, "but you have two choices. You can leave voluntarily, or I can have my friends escort you out."

At that moment, Manu stepped up with Stephen and cast a very distinct frown towards Kenneth.

"The choice is yours, sir," said Coretta to Kenneth, "but you don't have much time to think about it."

Kenneth quickly headed towards the exit, watched closely by Manu and Stephen. He wisely rushed to his car, jumped in, and took off. Michael found it quite humorous at the manner in which Coretta handled him.

"I like that," said Michael. "He's been a real pain lately."

"Do you need me to take care of him for you?" Coretta asked, looking serious.

"No, no, no," Michael quickly said. "He's just a temporary problem. And as of today, he's part of my past. By the way, thank you for the car and the clothes, and the condo. I kinda feel like I've signed my life away."

"Nonsense," said Coretta. "By the way, I know of a wonderful school we can put your daughter in starting tomorrow and when you get back Wednesday, you can check it out for yourself. I'll have Myra register her in the morning."

"Get back from where?" asked Michael.

"From Chicago. I'm sure you've heard of Barbara Brown."

"Yeah, she's the talk-show host from Chicago. I've seen her in many magazines. She's beautiful. What about her?"

"She's being honored at a black-tie function in Chicago, The Black Achievers of Illinois, I think it's called. It's tomorrow, and she needs an escort," said Coretta. "She's in her early 40s, but she loves younger men. I've already told her about you, and she can't wait to meet you. Take a condom. She's very sexual. Here's your itinerary and your round-trip ticket. You fly out at 12 noon and arrive at O'Hare Airport at 5:17 p.m. I'll have the limo at your condo at 10 a.m."

"Please do me a favor," said Michael. "Have someone other than the monster twins to drive me to the airport."

"Stephen can be a bit intense," said Coretta, "but he's very loyal."

"Who's that chick right there?" asked Michael.

"That's Toni Jones," said Coretta. "She's the writer of that series about men having good D.I.C."

"Oh, yeah, good dick," said Michael.

"Yeah, D.I.C.," repeated Coretta. "I had forgotton what the initials stood for. It's one of those relationship books. I have it but never read it. Would you like to meet her?"

"No," said Michael, "I don't need to meet any sister with a preconceived notion of what a man should do for her. I bet she doesn't even have a man."

"As a matter of fact, she doesn't."

"Then how can she write about relationships?" Michael asked.

"Maybe she's talking about past experiences that she's been through," suggested Coretta.

"A woman can't tell a man how to be a man no matter what she's been through," stated Michael, "especially a black man. No man has been through what we've been through."

"You're getting a little deep on me, my brother," said Coretta, "besides, a woman knows the difference between good dick and a man that doesn't know how to handle his business."

"*That's* the problem right there," Michael said. "If sisters didn't sleep with so many men, they wouldn't know the difference."

"Men sleep with many, many more women than we would even consider," Coretta stated, "and some brothers, no matter how much we love them, just don't have the right equipment."

"It's not that we don't have the right equipment, but it's a thing of chemistry. You see, some brothers are just freaks and can perform no matter who the woman is and what she's about, but brothers like me have to have to have chemistry with the woman to put out. That's why brothers have to eat pussy now because they settle for anything. Sisters have been with white boys that do anything, and they expect us to do anything, and so brothers eat coochie now like it's going out of style."

"You don't eat," she pointed out.

"No, ma'am," Michael firmly stated. "No hairy hamburgers. You can't go to club 69 with me."

Coretta wanted to continue the conversation with Michael, but so many guests were coming by and Michael's voice carried so she discontinued that conversation. After all, this was a party. She whispered into Michael's ear. "I don't care what you feel, Mr. Man. I want some dick tonight."

Michael just looked at her, then turned towards the bar to get another Remy. As he neared the bar, he crossed paths with Stephen.

"Hey, boy, get me a drink," said Michael. "This is *my* night and *my* party and you better do what *I* ask."

Michael had had a few too many Remys and was talking too much stuff.

"I'm gonna get you, motherfucker," said Stephen. "You don't like living too well, do you?"

One of Coretta's girls came up and poured Michael another drink and walked him away from Stephen. Her name was Bernadette, a sister from Panama. She offered to take Michael to a private room and get him away from the festivities for a while. Coretta told the girls to take care of Michael's every need, but she later decided that she wanted to be with Michael herself tonight, so no one was supposed to have sex with him but Coretta, at least in Coretta's mind. Michael began to feel the pressure of the evening and wanted to get away for a little while. As he and Bernadette were walking, he saw a heavyset white woman.

"How did she get her big pale ass in here?" he wanted to know. "If I had a harpoon, I'd throw it at her."

Bernadette realized that he was drunk and led him to her room. Michael took her hand and passed by a fully intoxicated David Devarro, just like himself.

"Oh, yeah, you wear that suit so well," said David. "I told you I could make you a star."

Michael thought back to his uncomfortable encounter with David while he was being measured earlier that day and went off even as Stephen, Manu, and Coretta looked on.

"Man, get your faggot ass away from me," said Michael. "You put on a show today, but I'm not going to let you clown me tonight like did today in front of my girl. I would kick you in your punk ass, but you'd probably like it, gay bastard."

"Come on, baby," said Bernadette as Michael was embarrassing himself. As she led Michael to her room, Stephen said, "You sure you want to put yourself out like this, boss lady, with this pretty boy? He obviously can't hold his liquor and doesn't know when to bridle his tongue."

"Yeah," said Carlos out of nowhere, "you know I would never disrespect you at a function like this."

"No," said Coretta, "you would only disrespect yourself chasing behind me."

"Come on, boss lady," said Stephen, "I don't trust this nigger."

"Yeah, honey," chipped in a hurt David Devarro, stung by Michael's comments. "Who does he think he's talking to like that?"

Coretta didn't want to hear any more, so she walked away to greet some of her guests. Michael and Bernadette went upstairs to her room, and he had another Remy in his hand.

"You know, Coretta said I could have anything that I want," said Michael, "and I'm sure that that includes you."

"Normally, I would agree, but Coretta told us that she wanted you for herself tonight," Bernadette said, "and I don't want to cross her because she's been good to me."

Michael took a look at Bernadette's big legs and began to

think quickly on his feet. "She changed her mind," he lied. "She wants me just to enjoy myself with whoever."

"Are you sure?" said Bernadette naively.

Michael took a long look at her ravishing body and beautiful face. "Very sure."

About twenty minutes later, Coretta found herself looking for Michael.

"Guest of honor got a little drunk?" asked a male guest.

Coretta asked one of her girls where Michael had gone and was told that Bernie took him upstairs with her. She asked Coretta if she should get him.

"No, honey," Coretta replied. "I'll go check. You just stay with my guests."

Coretta went upstairs to Bernadette's room, opened the door and walked to the bedroom area. There she saw Bernadette's legs on Michael's shoulders and Michael was busy pumping up and down. She didn't say anything, just turned around and exited. Immediately, she summoned Stephen upstairs.

"I want everybody out of here! The party's over," she said.

"But, boss lady, the party's just starting to pop," he protested.

"I said, everybody out," Coretta screamed.

Without another word, Stephen went down to the valet station and told the valets to start bringing cars around to the front, then he went back in to announce to the crowd that the party was over. He took the microphone.

"I'm sorry, everyone, but due to circumstances beyond our control, we must end the party this evening. The valets are ready to bring your cars around so please exit in an orderly fashion."

The whole dance floor was full at the time, dancing to Sir Mix-A-Lot's song, "Baby Got Back."

"Give me a sista, I can't resist her, red beans and rice didn't miss her," sang a thin white guy dancing with a black woman, "'cause baby got back."

"Sit your little white ass down," ordered Stephen. "You wouldn't know what to do with all that ass no way."

"Coretta always carries herself with class," replied the white guy, "and with you being in her employment, you should do likewise."

"Get the fuck out of here," ordered Stephen, "before I put my foot in your anorexic ass."

The white man and the rest of the guests started to work their way towards the exit as everyone speculated about what could have made the party end so abruptly. Meanwhile, Coretta went to her room and slammed the door behind her. No one in her employment dared to go anywhere near her.

It was midnight and Myra had put Brittany to bed in her new room. Brittany had asked about when her father would be home, but fell asleep waiting. At 1 a.m., Michael emerged from Bernadette's room to find Coretta standing right outside the door in a gold negligee, looking directly at him. He was still somewhat intoxicated and had a real scruffy look.

"Was it good?" she asked as Michael looked surprised.

"Very good. That was worth the trip over here."

"I thought *we* were going to be together tonight," she said.

"Let's go do it," he replied arrogantly.

"I don't take sloppy seconds from anyone. When you tell me you're going to do something, I expect you to follow through. I thought you would be a man of your word."

"Well, I need practice, don't I? That's what I was doing, practicing. And what a practice partner! I got to hand it to you, Coretta, you pick your people well—very well."

By then, Bernadette had gotten out of bed to go to the restroom and overheard the conversation. She knew Coretta didn't like to be disobeyed.

"Hey, look, I've got to get home. I don't want to miss my flight to Chicago. What happened to the party?"

"The party's over," said Coretta.

Walking away, Michael thought of a question. "Hey, I forgot to ask. What's my cut?"

"You get 50 percent of the fee from the client," answered Coretta, "and any extra they give you, you keep for yourself."

"Fifty percent?"

"Yes, 50 percent. Don't worry, that will be more than enough to take care of your every need. Speaking of needs, do you need me to have Stephen drive you home?"

"No way," Michael replied. "I don't want to be in the car with those two gorillas of yours anytime soon."

Michael asked Coretta instructions on how to get out, then he headed for the entrance. As he did so, Coretta walked into Bernadette's room to have a talk with her. As Michael reached the front, Stephen was still coordinating the exit and cleanup. Stephen was a sharply dressed man with a four-carat diamond earring in each ear. Michael took another opportunity to crack on him.

"You know, where I come from, only gay men wear two earrings. Is that why you and big Manu are always together?"

"Times have changed," Stephen retorted angrily. "Men wear two earrings all the time now. Every NBA press conference has a brother just like me—rich, bald, and two big diamonds in their ears."

"Yeah, and they look gay too. By the way, that girl, Bernadette, has the best pussy in the world. I just spent the last couple of hours waxing that ass."

Michael didn't realize that Bernadette was someone Stephen had been trying to get with for a long time. The mere thought of arrogant Michael being with her put Stephen in a rage. He pulled his 9mm from his pocket and stuck it to Michael's head.

"If boss lady didn't want you right now for her own purposes, I'd splatter your brains all over the parking lot," he said coldly.

Without another word, Michael jumped in his car and drove away. Stephen watched the car, dreaming of the day he would kill Michael. He was extremely upset about Bernadette because he felt he was making headway. Michael called Michelle on his cell phone.

"Hey, baby girl, I told you I would call you tonight."

"Yeah, but I expected it to be before 2 a.m.," she responded sleepily. "I'm in bed, now. I've got an early day tomorrow."

"I need to see you," he said, still shaken by having a gun to his head. "Please let me come by for a minute."

"Okay, but just for a minute."

He drove to Michelle's hotel, just needing to see somebody. Arriving, he knocked on the door. Michelle answered the door, and Michael immediately grabbed her around the waist and began sobbing in her arms.

"What's wrong, baby?" she asked, surprised, caressing him like a baby. Michael didn't answer, but just held onto her tighter. He never did say anything, but just fell asleep in her arms. The two spent the night lying on her couch. Michelle awakened at 7 and ordered breakfast for two. She had a 9 o'clock appointment. When the food arrived, she awakened Michael.

"I know you don't eat too many things for breakfast," she said, "so I got you some rolls with juice. I'm eating my morning bagel. Got to watch my waistline. So, you ready to talk about what was bothering you?"

"No, I've got to get out of here. I've got a 12 noon flight to Chicago."

"What's in Chicago?"

"Business," he said evasively. "My new job starts today, and I need to get Brittany situated."

Taking a roll and some juice, he walked towards the door, kissing Michelle good-bye, but didn't tell her about his night. After a short drive, he arrived at his condo. Arriving at 7:45, he found Brittany and Myra already up, having breakfast. He walked in, asking, "What you eating, Brit?"

"Cereal, Daddy."

"Good morning, Myra," he said. "How was your night? I didn't mean to stay out all night, but I had been drinking and didn't want to drive home."

"Coretta is known to throw some killa parties," she replied. "I know there was a lot of everything."

"You can say that again. That party was crack-a-lacking."

"Daddy, I called Aunt Cheryl and Uncle Kenneth last night to tell them about our new house," said Brittany.

"I hope you don't mind, sir," said Myra. "She wanted to speak to them before she went to bed."

"Stop calling me 'sir.' I'm not much older than you. Call me Michael."

"Okay, Michael. Cheryl really was nice, but Kenneth was a bit forceful. He told me he was invited to the party too, so I told him how to get there."

Michael started thinking about the night's festivities, especially the gun to his head.

"Michael, Michael, are you okay?" asked Myra.

"We need to get Brittany into kindergarten. Do you know the area?"

"Ms. James said that Kiddy Care down the street offered advanced skills training," Myra said. "It's supposed to be the best in the country. I'll call her and see if she can set it up."

"Okay," he said, "I've got to take a shower and you can let me know about it when I get out. Oh, I've got to be in Chicago today. Last-minute thing. Do you think you guys will be okay without me?"

"Sure, Michael. Coretta already told me that you would have to travel a lot. Brittany and I will be fine."

Michael went to shower, and Myra called Coretta to get information on the school for Brittany but there was no answer. Inside the bedroom, Michael threw his smelly clothes on the king-size bed and wrapped a towel around his waist, but at that moment, his cell phone rang. It was Coretta.

"Hello," he said.

"Be ready to leave at 10," she said. "We don't want to be late for our first appointment."

"I'll be ready, but I'd rather drive myself to the airport. That fool, Stephen, put a gun to my head last night."

"You must have antagonized him," she replied, already knowing of Stephen's actions. "Stephen doesn't like disrespect. Besides, I'd rather he pick you up. When it comes to business, I like to make sure everything is handled properly."

Michael reluctantly agreed and was about to hang up when he remembered that Myra needed to speak to her.

"Hang on, Coretta. Myra wanted to talk to you about that school for Brittany. Hold on."

"That Myra is a beautiful young lady," said Coretta. "You're not going to sow your wild oats with her, too, are you?"

Michael didn't even bother to answer, but instead, called Myra to the phone. Myra couldn't help but notice Michael's body in the towel and definitely liked what she saw, but had no intentions on making a move on him.

"It's Coretta," Michael said. "When you finish, just put the phone on the table and I'll get it later."

"Hello, Myra," said Coretta. "I told you he was fine, didn't I?"

Myra didn't respond to the comment, but asked Coretta about the school.

"Yeah, ask for Mrs. Jackson. They have a long waiting list but when you tell her who I am, I'm sure she will make an exception. Get all her vital information from Michael, like her shot record, birth certificate, and Social Security card, then we shouldn't have a problem. Call me on the cell phone if there is a problem. I've got to run now."

Chapter 11

MYRA HUNG UP THE PHONE and got Brittany ready to go down to the school. Michael finished his shower and still had a little over an hour before Coretta's limo would be by. He was standing naked, putting on his body lotion and looking for underwear with his door slightly ajar when Myra looked in. Turning around and walking away quickly, she called out to him, asking where he kept Brittany's vital information. Michael had it in his bag in the room. He told Myra he would bring it out in a moment. She made a mental note to call out to Michael before coming near his room again. He threw on his robe and grabbed the bag where he kept his vital and personal information.

"I put the bag right outside the door," he yelled. "Just leave it there when you finish." This time, he closed the door.

Myra took the bag and saw many pictures of Michael, Sheila, and Brittany inside. There were wedding pictures, Brittany's birth pictures, pictures of happy times. Myra saw the beautiful Sheila and thought what a beautiful family they were. She looked at the photos and memorabilia for several minutes, then Michael walked out, this time with his shirt and slacks on.

"Did you find what you were looking for?" he asked.

Myra jumped and Michael noticed that she was looking through his photos and personal stuff.

"Sorry," she said, "I kinda got carried away. You had a beautiful wife, a beautiful family."

"Yeah," he said, "she was special. I don't think they make sisters like that anymore. I forget sometimes how much I miss her, but I miss her more for Brittany. I can't teach my baby how to be a woman."

Michael momentarily stared off in space, reminiscing, but caught himself and walked to the kitchen for some water.

"When you finish, just throw the bag back on the bed, OK?" he said.

Then he went back to his room to finish packing his bag and dress. Myra fixed him a snack before he left for Chicago. She and Brittany got ready, then knocked on Michael's door to say good-bye.

"We're gonna take off and try to get your daughter in school. Afterwards, we'll go shopping for some new clothes."

"Hang on. Let me give you some money for her clothes," said Michael.

"Don't worry about it. Ms. James told me to put it on her account. We're going to get Ms. Brit all pretty."

Brittany stood in the doorway and smiled at Myra.

"Give Daddy some sugar, baby. I've got to go out of town, but just for the day. I'll be back sometime tonight or early in the morning. Myra, did you find everything you were looking for?"

"I think so. I'll take all her personal stuff with me just in case they ask for something I didn't remember. Okay, we're gonna take off."

Michael said good-bye to his daughter and Myra, put the finishing touches to his packing, brought out his two bags, and threw them on the sofa. Then he walked into the kitchen for the food Myra left him, especially the fruit and juice. He thought about how very special that Myra was to be so caring, especially when it came to his daughter.

At 9:55, the buzzer rang, and the concierge informed him that his limo was out front. He thanked the concierge, finished eating, grabbed his bags, and left. Standing at the curb was Carlos.

"You're about the last person I expected to see," said Michael. "What happened to Heckel and Jeckel?"

"They had more important business to attend to," Carlos replied. "Besides, Coretta likes to humiliate me by making me do menial tasks. Do you need help with your bags?"

Carlos wasn't the normal driver of the limo, but he had been sent to make sure Michael made his flight on time.

"So what's your story?" Michael asked as they took off. "What's up with you and Coretta?"

"Nothing really," Carlos answered. "I love her and would do anything for her. I'm hoping someday that she'll realize that she loves me too. Together, we can do great things."

"I hate to say this, but she seems to go out of her way to embarrass you. That doesn't seem like love to me."

"She's a brilliant woman," said Carlos. "She's only 29 years old and worth hundreds of millions, maybe a billion. A black billionaire. Doesn't it make you excited to be a part of her organization?"

"If she were spending her money on her people," Michael replied, "helping the homeless and getting drugs off the streets, then I would be behind her. You see, having the money means nothing if you don't use it to help the less fortunate."

Carlos thought Michael sounded kind of preachy and came to Coretta's defense. "What are *you* doing for *your* people? Are you playing your part to bring a better way of life to the less fortunate, or are you contributing to the problem?"

"Well, I don't have her money," said Michael.

"It doesn't matter whether you have her money or not," said Carlos. "You must give all you can, no matter how much you have."

At first, Michael thought Carlos was a very weak man, but now he wondered if he were truly in love with Coretta or just lusting after her.

"How long have you been with Coretta?" Michael asked.

"For a while now. Why?"

"No reason. I just get the feeling that you want to know something, so I figured I'd ask you questions first."

Carlos ignored Michael and went on with his questioning. "You do realize that Coretta and I are lovers, don't you? And all of us in her employment are totally loyal to her. We would do anything and take out anyone who meant to do Coretta harm."

Michael realized that Carlos was giving him a subtle threat, and he also realized that in the last few days, threats had become the norm. He didn't respond and Carlos continued to probe about Michael's intentions.

"Have you slept with Coretta?" Carlos asked. "What do you expect out of her?"

"Which question do you want me to answer first?" asked Michael.

"Have you slept with her?" asked Carlos.

Just then, the limo pulled up to the curb at LAX.

"Why don't you ask Coretta? See what she tells you. I guess you guys know what time to pick me up tonight, right?

"Tell your sweetheart, Coretta, that I will call her from Chicago, and if you beg hard enough, maybe she will treat you like a house-trained puppy and let you stay inside the mansion."

It was now 10:45. Michael thought about how different Carlos was from Stephen and Manu. He was lovesick over Coretta and, thus, a serious threat to Michael's well-being. Carlos was enraged because Michael did not answer his questions. Before he drove away, he said, "Have a safe trip, Michael," not meaning a word of it.

⇥ ⇥ ⇥

EARLIER, MYRA AND Brittany arrived at Kiddie Care and Myra asked for Mrs. Jackson, the director.

"Mrs. Jackson is no longer with us," said the attractive white woman in her mid-30s. "I'm the new director, Mrs. Atkinson."

"Well, Mrs. Atkinson," said Myra, "Mrs. Jackson was expecting us today. She had worked with Coretta James in an effort to get Brittany Alexander enrolled in school."

"Mrs. Jackson didn't leave me any information," said Mrs. Atkinson, "and besides, we are totally booked and have a long waiting list. There is no way she can be admitted at this time."

"Are you sure?" asked Myra. "I'm sure Ms. James told me that everything was already set."

"I don't see how," says Mrs. Atkinson, "unless Mrs. Jackson was doing something fraudulent to get her in early."

"No, of course not," replied Myra. "Let me call Ms. James. Maybe she can shed some light on the situation."

Mrs. Atkinson walked away for a moment while Myra called Coretta to see if something could be done. Coretta answered the phone and Myra explained the situation. Coretta was in a meeting at that moment.

"Coretta, Mrs. Jackson no longer works here and the new director, Mrs. Atkinson, says there is no way that Brittany can get in at this time."

"Mrs. Atkinson? Who is Mrs. Atkinson?" said Coretta. "Put the bitch on the phone."

Coretta had exited the meeting and was talking in the hallway. Myra called Mrs. Atkinson, who reluctantly came to the phone.

"Karen Atkinson," she said.

"Karen, may I call you Karen?" asked Coretta.

"You can call me Mrs. Atkinson," came the cool response.

"Okay, Mrs. Atkinson," said Coretta, "this is Coretta James. I'm sure you've heard of me."

"Yes, I have. You're buying a lot of real estate in Los Angeles."

"Among other things," said Coretta. "Brittany Alexander has already been confirmed to be added to the curriculum and if you don't mind, I wish you would put her paperwork together so the child can get used to her surroundings this morning."

"There is no way I'm going to enroll her without going through the proper channels," said Mrs. Atkinson. "We have a waiting list of over 500 children. How can I explain putting her at the head of the list?"

"Mrs. Atkinson," came the calculated reply, "I can make it worth your while if you just put us ahead of the list and allow Brittany to become part of your wonderful school. Mrs. Atkinson, anyone that knows me will tell you that I take care of my friends. I promise you, you will never regret helping us out today."

"Ms. James," said an offended Mrs. Atkinson, "am I to assume that you are trying to bribe me? Maybe I should hang up this phone and call the police. Now get this straight, Ms. James, there's no way she getting in here ahead of any of the other 500 or so children on our waiting list. Now I suggest you go back to your day before I call the news-papers and tell them that you are calling a kindergarten, trying to bribe this child's way ahead of other children. I'm sure publicity like that won't enhance your business."

"Before the day is over, you *will* regret disrespecting me like this," Coretta said coldly.

With that, Coretta hung up the phone and instantly dialed Stephen.

"Steve, drop what you're doing and meet me at home in an hour. I've got a problem that needs taking care of right now."

Coretta hung up the phone and went back to her meeting, but she called Myra first and told her that she would take care of the situation and to take Brit shopping.

"Myra, go to Macy's in Burbank and ask for Farzana in the children's department. She will find Ms. Brittany all the clothes she needs. Myra, is Brittany beautiful?"

"She's gorgeous," said Myra, "and sweet as can be. She's the spitting image of Michael."

"You mean Mr. Alexander, don't you?" asked Coretta.

"I'm sorry, Coretta, Mr. Alexander," she replied.

"OK, girl," said Coretta, "take care of my child and I'll take care of that school situation."

Coretta hung up the phone and Myra felt offended by the way Coretta spoke to her in the end, but she brushed it off and went about her task of making sure Brittany was properly taken care of. The one universal theme among everyone concerned the care of Brittany. Michael was blessed with people in his life that truly cared for his daughter.

At 12 noon, Coretta arrived home and found Stephen waiting for her at the mansion in Bel Air.

"I've got a problem I need taken care of," she said. "Michael's daughter needs to get in school, and I'm going to get her in school."

"What's that have to do with us?" he asked.

"Mrs. Atkinson at Kiddie Care threatened to call the police and newspapers on me. She needs to find out who I am and who she's dealing with."

"Say no more, boss lady. Just tell me how to get in touch with Mrs. Atkinson."

"She's the new director at Kiddie Care about 5 miles up the road," said Coretta. "I don't know when she leaves, I don't know what she looks like, but I do know I want Brittany in school, and I don't want her to ever threaten me again."

Coretta had a look on her face that could kill. She was not just a billionaire, she was a ruthless, black, female billionaire who didn't believe in being told no by anyone, especially someone she thought was beneath her.

Stephen grabbed Manu and headed for Kiddie Care in Bel Air. They had handled much tougher assignments in the past, but they truly loved a job they considered no threat, one where they could thoroughly intimidate if need be and take out anyone that challenged them. They arrived at the school and went about the process of locating Mrs. Atkinson. Stephen immediately went into his routine.

"Excuse me, ma'am," he said, "I just moved to town, and I want to get my little girl in school. Who's in charge? I want to see about getting my baby in."

"Well, I know we don't have any openings right now," said the attendant. "We have a waiting list of at least 500 children. I would let you talk to Mrs. Atkinson, but she's outside talking to the police."

Stephen looked outside to see the LA County Police Department talking to Mrs. Atkinson, who had obviously taken Coretta's threat seriously. Stephen went back to the car in anger.

"That bitch called the police," he said furiously. "I don't believe this shit."

They sat in the black 2000 Honda Accord and waited for the police to leave. Stephen realized that Mrs. Atkinson was already a problem.

"We'll check it out," said the police sergeant. "In the meantime, do you need us to follow you home?"

"No," she replied. "I'll be fine. I just want to let it be known that people, no matter how rich, can't go around making idle threats."

Coretta James doesn't make idle threats.

Chapter 12

AT 4:25 CENTRAL TIME, MICHAEL arrived at Chicago's O'Hare. He had an itinerary, but didn't know who was supposed to pick him up. Barbara Brown's limo was parked at the curb with a sign that read "Michael Alexander." Michael saw his name and a tall black man weighing 170 lbs, but a down-to-earth, real brother.

"Michael Alexander?" asked the limo driver as he approached.

"I'm Michael. How you doing, my brother?"

"How you do, Michael?" said the driver. "My name is Gary Woodward, and I'll be your driver."

"Oh, yeah," said Michael. "Where is Barbara Brown?"

"She's out of town," replied Gary. "She's getting ready for the award show tomorrow, but she has business today."

"What do you mean 'tomorrow'?" asked Michael. "I thought the show was today."

"Not today. You're supposed to be here today to get ready for tomorrow. But the show isn't until tomorrow, so there must have been a misunderstanding somewhere."

"Hold on, brother," said Michael. "Let me make a phone call."

He quickly called Coretta, but left a message since she didn't answer. "Hey, Coretta, give me a call. I think we have a mix-up on the time of the event, and I need to know if you want me to stay an extra day."

"So where you from, brother?" he asked Gary.

"I'm originally from Chicago. I've been here my whole life."

"Oh, yeah?" said Michael. "So what's the game plan?"

"Well," answered Gary, "why don't you fix yourself a drink? The bar is fully stocked."

"You got Cognac?" inquired Michael.

"Why don't you see for yourself," replied Gary, smiling.

Michael looked in the fully stocked bar and any kind of Cognac he wanted was there. He poured himself a Remy XO and sat back to catch his breath.

"Brother, relax," said the friendly driver. "Enjoy yourself and make the best out of the situation. When you see Barbara, you will understand that she is worth the wait."

"So what am I supposed to do with the rest of my day?"

"Whatever you want to do. I'm about to take you to Barbara's plush mansion on Lake Shore. I know Chicago like the back of my hand, so anything you want to do, I'm sure I can find it for you. Barbara Brown lives alone, so the house is yours. What you want to do?"

"What's around here?" asked Michael. "What do they do on a Tuesday night?"

"Poetically speaking," said Gary, "that's what they call Tuesday night, Poetry night. And the honeys are out. They are everywhere, but that's probably not down your alley."

"That's right down my alley," said Michael. "I'm a poet, I'm a scholar."

"Alright, my brother," said the affable driver, "I'm gonna drop you off at the mansion after I show you around a little bit, and I'll be back to pick you up at 8:30. The poetry reading starts at 9:00 pm, so you need to be there early to sign up. You gonna go on the Internet to find a poem off poetry.com?"

"Now, do I look like a fake brother?" said an injured-sounding Michael. "I'll make sure I write something original, just for you to understand the skills that a brother possesses. So tell me, Gary, how did you end up driving this limo? You seem like an intelligent brother."

"I lost 3 million in the stock market," he explained. "I lost my house, my BMW, and all I have now is an old Infiniti with a bar across the front and a four hundred thousand dollar house that I'm behind on my mortgage. Barbara and I go way back and she offered to pay my house off, but I wanted to get myself out of this mess. You know a man makes his own trouble and needs to find his own way out."

"I respect that," said Michael. "I thought you lost your house."

"I owned two," said Gary.

They pulled up to Barbara Brown's beautiful mansion on Lake Shore with an awesome view of the lake. Michael was impressed but tired.

"Show me to my room, please, and pick me up at 8:30. But you can't just be a driver. You've got to hang out with me."

"I'm with you," said Gary, "but I can't drink because Barbara is true to the game, true to me, so I have to be sober any time I drive her limo. You'll understand when you meet her. She's down for me like 4 flat tires. She'll die for her friends."

Gary showed Michael to his room in Barbara's house and went to take care of his other business. Michael unwound and instantly lay across the bed and fell asleep. He was exhausted from the trip and the busyness of the past couple of days, and he needed some rest so he could be ready at 8:30.

Chapter 13

AT AROUND 4:30 IN LA, Mrs. Atkinson decided to leave Kiddie Care for the day. This particular day had been very eventful and mentally draining on her. By then, she just wanted to go home and lie down. Karen Atkinson lived about 15 minutes away in a small condominium complex in North Hollywood. As she drove off in her 1989 black Porsche 944, her dream car, she never noticed the car that followed her as she left. Mrs. Atkinson loved music, mostly gospel, but she would listen to oldies. She was white, but loved black music, Tupac, Michael Jackson—you name it. On this day, she played her gospel real loud and never looked in her rearview mirror.

Stephen was more an "anything" than an "anyone." He had killed many people, men and women, but he loved to rape his women before he killed them. He followed Mrs. Atkinson with dual intentions.

After a twenty-minute drive, Karen Atkinson arrived at her condominium complex at approximately 5 in the afternoon. At that point, she noticed the black Honda behind her, but didn't get overly concerned. The condo had a gated entrance in front and a gated parking garage. Cars frequently tailgated through the front entrance and Karen Atkinson didn't think it strange when they also tailgated through the parking structure. Besides, she was too much in the spirit since the gospel music had her going.

Her assigned parking was close to the entrance so she had to walk to the staircase to get to her condo. Manu and Stephen parked directly behind her to block her in. Stephen immediately jumped out of his car and pulled out his 9mm and broke her window. Karen Atkinson shrieked loudly in paralyzing fear. Not only was Stephen bold to break her window, but he did it in broad daylight.

"Get out of the car, you white bitch!" he screamed at her. "Get out of the car *now!*"

Mrs. Atkinson wasn't moving fast enough, so Stephen reached in and dragged her from the car by her hair. She started screaming again, but Manu came over and threw his hand around her mouth and pushed her to the ground.

"This snow bunny has got a body like a sister," said Stephen. "I've got to get me some of this."

He slapped her and pulled up her dress and began to penetrate her right in the garage in broad daylight. As he was getting his rocks off, he said savagely, "Hey, white bitch, you ever heard of Coretta James?"

Manu continued to hold her mouth as Stephen talked. She couldn't answer. "I asked you a question, bitch," he said. "Coretta James, you ever heard of her?"

Mrs. Atkinson's eyes bulged in fear, and she nodded her head up and down.

"Well, Ms. James asked me to pay you a little visit. Turns out you made a few threats, something about calling the police, which you did, and said you were going to the newspapers. Well, Ms. James doesn't respond well to threats. Manu, move your hand so the lady can talk."

Manu removed his hand, and Stephen put his finger over his lips to let Mrs. Atkinson know it wasn't advisable to scream.

"All we wanted was to get a little girl in school," he continued, "but you wanted to play hard. Manu, show the lady how we play hard."

At that point, Manu snapped Mrs. Atkinson's neck and she fell back, instantly dead.

A young woman had been walking to her car, but stopped, stunned as she watched Mrs. Atkinson die. She froze. Stephen pulled his 9mm and pointed it towards her. His first instinct was to kill the witness, but he didn't pull the trigger. He motioned for the woman to come to him. She did so, terrified and crying wildly.

"Shut up," he said. "Do you see her?"

He pointed to the dead Mrs. Atkinson. "You say a word to anyone, and you die, far worse than this, in fact. And I'll come back and burn this whole damn building down, you understand?"

The woman nodded in fear, and Stephen, amazingly, let her go.

"Oh, by the way," he added, "can you buzz us out?"

The woman buzzed the pair out of the two gates and ran to her room in fear, shaking and crying. Stephen and Manu drove slowly down the road as if nothing happened.

"I'm going to stop and get me a burrito," Stephen said. "You want anything?"

Manu simply shook his head no and Stephen continued to drive down Magnolia, looking for the nearest taco place.

A few moments later, a woman on her way to work spotted Mrs. Atkinson's lifeless body and screamed aloud. Hysterical, she ran to get the manager. They called the North Hollywood Police Department. Within minutes, the place was swarming with police and detectives. Detective Dana Andrews was the lead detective on the case. He crossed the yellow crime tape to take a look at the crime scene, then talked to one of the forensic people on the scene. Detective Andrews was a 6 foot tall black man, a very muscular ex-marine who was a 20-year veteran on the force. His partner, Lashara Gentry, was a 30-year-old black female graduate of the police academy and on her first murder case.

"Looks like she died from a broken neck," said Detective Andrews, looking at the murder victim, her eyes wide open. "There doesn't look like there was much of a struggle. Make sure you guys check for skin under her fingernails. Maybe she got a swipe at one of them."

"We found some prints on the car," reported Detective Gentry. "We'll take them downtown and see if we can get a positive ID."

"This lady stumbled onto the body," said one police officer. "She says she didn't see anyone leaving."

"Looks like she was blocked in," said Detective Andrews, "and from the sliding marks on the pavement, looks like she was dragged from the car."

"Probably by her hair," said one detective. "We found a chunk of hair that appears to have been ripped from her head."

"I just came back from interviewing all the tenants that were home," stated a white male detective. "No one seems to have heard or seen anything. However, a Ms. Jasmine Reese says she didn't see anything, but appears to be extremely shaken by something. She was crying and pleading that she didn't know anything."

"Detective Gentry," said Detective Andrews, "talk to her and see if she might feel more comfortable with you. Seems like she may be terrified of something. Maybe she stumbled on the murderers and was persuaded not to talk."

"I wonder why she was spared," said Detective Gentry. "Whoever these people are, they don't seem like the kind to leave witnesses behind."

"Who knows," added Detective Andrews. "Maybe they just had a fleeting moment of compassion."

"I doubt it," said Detective Gentry. "I doubt it."

The police continued their investigation into the murder and in Chicago, 8:30 p.m. had arrived.

Chapter 14

MICHAEL HAD WRITTEN A NEW poem and was working on a second one as Barbara Brown's limo pulled up out front and Gary, the driver, opened the door to pick up Michael. He had on a black suit, no tie, and a red shirt pulled over the collar to give it his own style. Gary came to the door, and Michael greeted him, ready to go.

"Get you a nap, brother?" asked Gary.

"Yeah, I slept for a while, but I had to get up and write a couple of poems because I definitely want to be a part of the festivities."

"I like that red shirt," said Gary. "That blood red, that's fat, brother."

"Well, I try to stay sharp," joked an arrogant Michael.

"I see you're real modest," added Gary with a broad smile.

"I try to be humble," Michael said. "Let's roll, brother, and check out some of these honeys."

Michael jumped in the car and poured himself a Remy XO and tried to finish his second poem.

"You gonna let me check out the poems?" asked Gary. "I want to see your skills."

"Nah, brother, you got to wait to hear them like everybody else."

"So you got enough nerve to get up there. I admire that 'cause I could never speak in front of a crowd."

"I love the spotlight, brother," admitted Michael.

Gary and Michael conversed until they arrived at the club and Gary parked the limo and went inside with Michael. Michael arrived at 8:45 and signed in just in time to read with the first set of poets. The club had a house band that played along with the poets. About ten poets come up in the first set, some sounding like they were auditioning for a Broadway play, while others were more militant than Malcolm X. Michael kept knocking back drinks, but still got a few butterflies as the ninth reader finished up his set and Michael was next.

"Well, you're next, my man," announced Gary. "How do you feel?"

"I feel good, man," replied Michael, "just a few butterflies. Hey, Gary, anybody ever tell you, you look exactly like Richard Pryor?"

"Oh, you got jokes, huh?" came back Gary.

At that moment, the ninth poet ended his set and Michael was next. The Mistress of Ceremony was a local DJ named Paula Rice, a tall, light-skinned, 5 foot 11 black woman and very attractive.

"Our next poet hails from the City of Angels, Los Angeles," proclaimed Paula, "and ladies, he's tall, dark, and handsome. Give it up for Michael Alexander!"

Michael slowly approached the stage and pulled over a stool to sit on. "Thank you," he said, acknowledging the cheers. "I just came from LA on business this evening, and I wrote two poems especially for this set. If you like the first, I'll read the second. I can't explain either poem. I just wrote what was on my heart. The first poem is entitled 'P-U-S-S-Y.'"

The crowd cheered as Michael gave the name of the poem and said it over and over.

"I will try to go along with the beat of the band, but forgive me if I get a little bit off track. This poem is kinda long, so please bear with me." He had the crowd totally into him and began to confidently read.

P-U-S-SY

My partner Sam and I used to
hang out at the bar
Trying to meet the prettiest woman, always looking
for a star
Sam and I both were really a trip
Neither one of us looking
for a relationship
We both had missions that
often came true
We were for sisters to lay the "pipe" to
But sometime when your
intentions are to do people wrong
Your ride in passion doesn't last too long

As Michael read his first stanza of the poem, the crowd made comments, brothers called him wild, while the women cheered but waited to see where he was going. He had to stop periodically to allow the crowd to moan and cheer. He continued:

One night Sam met a tall,
long-legged friend
You were putting her down
to call her a ten
Sam threw his "mack game"
 aiming to please
It worked like a charm,
she responded with ease
She propositioned Sam,
do you want to go home
I don't have a man, I live alone
I just wish I could have said good-bye
We never knew the power of P-U-S-S-Y
Sam walked in, she grabbed
him by the head
They hugged and they kissed
and they jumped into bed
Sam thought he was lucky
without a doubt
Little did he know his luck
was about to run out
This woman just wanted
to make her man cry
By giving up the P-U-S-S-Y
She played my friend like
a sacrificial lamb
P-U-S-S-Y took my buddy Sam

The man walked in already a grouch
Sam and his wife were still on the couch
When the lights came on,
Sam began to stare
He had her legs bucked high in the air
Sam saw the light and thought
it was a joke
He didn't miss a beat,
he continued to stroke
He had no idea he was about to die
A victim of the P-U-S-S-Y
I wonder if Sam realized he was dead
As the man pulled the gun
and shot him in the head
When I found out, I didn't
know what to say
I couldn't eat or drink I was sick all day
We had many condoms,
bought them when we got paid
Thinking that our biggest
danger was AIDS
We thought only diseases
could cause us to die
We thought that was the
problem with P-U-S-S-Y

~MICHAEL ALEXANDER~

As soon as Michael finished, he got a very loud ovation and the DJ had questions for him, along with the rest of the crowd.

"So what inspired that poem and who is Sam?" asked Paula.

"Sam doesn't really exist," he explained. "That poem was on my heart, but I can't explain where it came from. It somehow seems spiritual, but I really can't explain it."

"Well, if you could, we would love for you to bless us with another poem," said Paula, "right crowd?"

The crowd cheered their approval, and Michael, basking in the love, went right into his next selection.

"This poem is called 'I WALK IN THE VALLEY,'" he said.

I WALK IN THE VALLEY

I walk in the valley, but he's already here
I walk in the valley, but I have no fear
Hoping that God will set me free
Praying that He will somehow save me
I see the blood that's on my hand
I see the salvation of a righteous man
There are so many things
God wants me to know
I can't stop myself, I have to go
Like a sacrificial lamb, I walk up the hill
With no comprehension
of what it means to kill
They lie in wait to kill my soul
To engulf my body and eat me whole
I try to get away, but I cannot run
Just hoping to see the setting sun
I call to the Lord, but He does not hear
I know not what to do, I lie in fear
The evil one wants to find me dead
To pierce my soul, to shatter my head
I sometimes wake up in a cold sweat
And I see that God hasn't taken me yet

"That's it," said Michael, "I didn't get a chance to finish that one."

The audience again gave Michael a large ovation as he left the podium. The DJ, Paula Rice, called his name again.

"Michael Alexander, give him another hand, ladies and gentlemen," she encouraged everyone. "I hate that the poem ended because I wanted to see where you were going with it. Well, ladies and gentlemen, that ends our first set and we're going to take a 15-minute break and start with our next group of poets. How 'bout a hand for the band?"

Everyone cheered the band and all the poets that had spoken so far and they all took a break. Michael walked over to Gary, who shook his hand.

"That was some deep stuff, brother," said Gary. "You got skillz, man. You should consider writing full-time and selling those poems."

"I've got hundreds of them at home," he said, "some a lot deeper than that. I sometimes look at them and ask myself, did I *really* write them?"

"That's deep, brother," said Gary. "I'm going to the bar to grab a cranberry orange juice. Can I get you anything?"

"Yea, I'll take a Remy or Hennessey or Courvoisier. I can handle all the Cognac. Here's a twenty."

"Your money is no good tonight, so put that dub back in your pocket," replied Gary. "Everything is taken care of. Ms. Brown is first class all the way."

"I can't wait to meet her," said Michael. "Anyway, I'm going outside to call and check on my daughter. I'll be right back."

He walked outside to call Myra and Brittany on his cell phone while Gary went to get the drinks. Myra answered and was glad to hear from him.

"Hi, Michael. How is your day going?"

"It's all good except I won't be home tonight," he told her. "My appointment that I had tonight is really for tomorrow night, so I got a whole night to kill. Where's Brittany?"

"She's right here," said Myra. "We got a whole new set of clothes today, compliments of Coretta. Brittany is so excited."

Michael wondered to himself if he'd ever be able to repay Coretta for the things that she was doing for him and what her real motivation was in helping him. He asked to speak to Brittany. Brittany was very excited about her clothes and her day. She described some of the clothes to her father and Michael was equally happy for his excited daughter. After Michael shared his love for Brittany, Myra took the phone and told him about what happened at school.

"Oh, Michael," she said, "we weren't able to get Brittany into that school today. Coretta had things arranged with a woman who is no longer there. The new director, Mrs. Atkinson, made a really big issue about her not being able to get in any time soon, but Coretta said she would handle it and she would call soon and let me know what to do."

"I hate that," said Michael. "She needs to get into school as soon as possible."

"Don't worry," replied Myra, "Coretta will take care of it."

Little did they know that Coretta had already taken care of it. Michael said his good-byes and turned to head back in the club. As he did so, he noticed a dark-skinned beauty standing in front of him.

"You are a very spiritual person," said the woman, "a very enlightened man. Those poems you recited spoke to my soul. I'm Sister Maxwell."

Sister Maxwell was attractive, her head was covered with a scarf, and she had on an African robe. Michael reached out to shake her hand and thank her. She acknowledged his gesture and continued to talk.

"The Lord spoke to me about you," she said. "Tonight, you will have a chance to go a different way. The choice you make could cost you your life. You see, my brother, those weren't just idle poems you wrote. They were symbolic, speaking of places you are about to go."

Michael shrugged off her conversation and tried to make his way back inside.

"Remember, my brother," said Sister Maxwell, "sometimes it's good to say NO."

She walked away and Michael just stood there and shook his head, then went back inside where Gary had his drink.

"Sister throwing you some rhythm outside?" he asked. "Those poems really work."

"That sister out there," said Michael, "she was telling me about some spiritual connection to my poetry. It was too deep for me. Anyway, what else is going on tonight? Where do the rest of the sisters hang out?"

"Club Vision," came the response. "They party on Tuesday like it's 1999. The finest sisters in the city hang out there. I can take you there if you want to go, but you can always say no."

"Brother," said Michael, "the word NO is not in my vocabulary. Let's roll."

Michael finished his drink and he and Gary headed downtown to Club Vision, the spot to be in Chicago on a Tuesday night. The two men were like lifelong friends, even though they just met. It's as if they've known each other forever. As they got into the limo, Michael sat in the front seat so that Gary didn't have to chauffer him, at least technically.

"Hey, Michael," Gary said, "how do you please a woman? No matter what you do, they never seem satisfied."

"You can't please a woman. Women have to look within themselves to find contentment," explained Michael. "Check this out. I know this seems a little off track, but it goes all the way back to the Garden of Eden. All they had to do was eat and live in peace and do whatever God said, but the woman was tempted and gave in to the serpent, and ole sorry ass Adam followed her instead of trying to follow God. He tried to please her. You can't please no woman. You can have a 12-inch dick, and she won't be satisfied. You eat more coochie than a white boy, you can buy them diamonds and pearls, and they still won't be satisfied. They have to find contentment in themselves no matter what you do for them."

"I hear you," agreed Gary. "I use to wine them and dine them. I don't eat much coochie, only my main lady, and I definitely don't have no 12-inch dick."

"Shit, me either," confessed Michael, "and I never ate coochie."

"Never?" asked Gary.

"Never," avowed Michael, "but women don't realize that it's not about us—it's about them. Check this out. Has a lady ever said that you didn't please her sexually?"

"I hate to admit, but yeah," Gary confessed.

"Why do you hate to admit it? It has happened to everybody, but it has no bearing on your ability to make love. I have some women that I really get up for and some that I can barely even get hard for. It's the woman, the chemistry that you have with her that dictates whether you and she will be good together. Think about it."

"You know, now that you mention it, that does seem right," said Gary. "I definitely perform better with some women than I do with others. But, sisters, they try to clown you, saying you can't fuck and you this and you that."

"They're talking about *themselves*," responded Michael. "If they weren't fucking so many guys, they wouldn't know the difference. Like we got our penis from the dick factory, like you can walk in and just tell a guy, give me that ten-inch one over there with the hanging nuts."

Gary laughed. "You date white girls?" he asked.

"No, brother, I'm strictly about the sisters. I know they're a handful, I know they talk shit, want to fight, whatever, but if you find a real sister that's true to the game, one that doesn't mind being a woman and doesn't want to be a man, there is no better woman on God's green earth."

"I don't discriminate," said Gary. "Red, white, yellow or brown, as long as they like to get down. I almost gave up on sisters at one time because they were so much trouble. Sisters will call you everything but a child of God, get all in your face, try to hit you and if you respond, you're the one that gets locked up. I've been in confrontations with plenty of sisters, and never once did I start it."

"I hear you," concurred Michael, "I just don't mess with no white girls. They feel different, and they definitely smell different. Give me a sister any day. But one thing I can say about a white boy, when he does date a sister, he'll date the finest sister in the world. A brother will find the biggest, fattest, nastiest white girl in Southern California. And they're some pretty white girls out there, but he would walk around the club holding hands with the worst one and kissing her in the mouth."

Gary liked to hear Michael talk and just asked him questions to see how he responded. "Malcolm X or Martin Luther King?"

"Malcolm X," answered Michael.

"Why?"

"I don't believe in civil rights," stated Michael. "I believe segregation was a good thing. We're so worried about walking hand in hand with whites that we don't show each other love. You can't love anybody else until you love yourself. It's kinda like we tricked ourselves. We are further behind now than ever before."

"You think so? There are black billionaires now, blacks in all walks of life doing amazing things," said Gary.

"Black billionaires ain't no better than a white billionaire if he's not uplifting his people," said Michael. "A nation full of Uncle Toms ain't doing us no good."

"Halle Berry or Nia Long?" asked Gary.

"Now you're talking, my brother," said Michael. "Nia Long. Halle doesn't do much for me. Nia Long. Those legs, that body. She's gorgeous. You see her in *Big Mama's House*, in that see-through short set. *That's* my speed."

"I like Halle," said Gary, "but I like Nia too."

Michael and Gary talked the whole trip and arrived at the club around midnight. Club Vision downtown had beautiful neon lights and an upscale design.

"Look at that long ass line," remarked Michael, "and on a Tuesday night."

"Yeah, man, you should see it on the weekend," said Gary.

"I don't think I want to wait in that line," said Michael.

"Hold on," replied Gary, who then walked to the entrance and spoke to the doorman. Then he returned to Michael.

"I told him you were an NBA free agent and that you are about to sign with the Bulls."

They walked to the door and were greeted excitedly by the doorman, who escorted them into the club. Once inside, they walked around the club to check out the atmosphere.

Michael hasn't had a friend to hang out with in a while and enjoyed the comradery. He ordered a drink while Gary looked on.

"I don't like drinking by myself," he said. "You need to at least have one with me."

"I drink Grand Marnier," Gary agreed. "I'll take a shot of that."

"Grand Marnier—that's a girl's drink. That's too sweet for me. I'll take another 'Yak.'"

Gary opened a tab with Barbara Brown's business American Express and went about enjoying himself with Michael.

Chapter 15

EARLIER THAT EVENING, DETECTIVE ANDREWS and Detective Gentry were investigating the murder of Karen Atkinson. It was brought to their attention that she had filed a police report stating that Coretta James had threatened her.

"Coretta James," said Detective Andrews, "that's the woman that has been buying up half the real estate in the city."

"Yes," replied Detective Gentry, "but supposedly, she has her hand in a lot more pots than just real estate. Allegedly, she's a madam, and she also dabbles in drugs."

"Sounds like a real woman," said Detective Andrews. "First thing in the morning, we're going to pay Ms. James a visit. Do we have any concrete evidence that definitely ties her into drugs or to running a high-class whore house?"

"Nothing," replied his partner. "Her record is as clean as a whistle. Not even jaywalking. I hear she's got a lot of friends in high places. Maybe they do a good job of keeping her record clean."

"We'll see what we can get out of her in the morning," said Detective Andrews. "What about that witness?"

"She's terrified. They took her to the hospital for observation."

"Go home and get some rest," ordered Detective Andrews. "We'll definitely pay Ms. James a visit tomorrow."

"Yea. I keep seeing that poor girl in my head. We've got to catch that monster who did this," said Detective Gentry.

At that moment, an officer came in with some vital information.

"Detectives, the prints on the car all belong to the victim," explained the officer. "All but one, that is. It belongs to a petty thief named Stephen Ray Johnson, a 30-year-old black man, AKA Lawrence Futrell, AKA Stephen Watson. He has a long rap sheet, petty robbery, assault with a deadly weapon. He was a suspect in several rapes, but he has never been convicted."

"Let's put out an All-Points Bulletin for this Stephen Johnson or Lawrence Futrell or whatever his name is. I'm willing to bet that the semen found in the victim belongs to him," stated Detective Andrews.

⇢▷ ⇢▷ ⇢▷

THE NORTH HOLLYWOOD Police continued to work on their case while Michael partied it up at Club Vision. He and Gary were about 3 drinks down each at the club and talked to or about everyone that passed by.

"You'll hit that," said Gary to Michael as a fine woman passed by.

"Hell, yea," Michael replied.

"What about that?" asked Gary.

"Yea, man," said Michael.

This went on for a while until Michael got tired of it. "Man, will you stop asking me that crazy shit?" he said. "I'll fuck a snake if I can hold his head where he won't bite me."

"What about fat women?" suggested Gary. "You get down with fat women?"

"If they pay like they weigh."

Michael was feeling good, dancing in the aisles with women walking by and flirting with everyone. Soon a heavyset woman passed by and came up to Michael.

"You know, I've been watching you," she said. "You're a womanizer."

"Why do you say that?" he inquired.

"Because you check out every woman that passes by," came the reply. "Why do you treat women like a piece of meat?"

"I don't treat women like a piece of meat," he protested, steadily dancing and looking at women. "Why do you jump to conclusions?"

"I'm just going by what you show me," the woman answered. "They say action speaks louder than words."

"What's your name, sister?" asked Michael. "And why did you come over here to antagonize me?"

"My name is Renita, and I'm not trying to antagonize you, but it's niggers like you that give black women a bad name, treating us like sluts and whores."

"Renita, I'm just in here enjoying myself," protested Michael. "Why aren't you attacking any other brothers in the club?"

"Because you are getting attention because of your height," she replied. "You know that tall, dark, and handsome nonsense."

Michael and Gary looked at the woman who wanted to continue to antagonize Michael. His patience was wearing thin as the woman continued to berate him.

"Will you leave me the fuck alone?" Michael growled. "Go over there and buy yourself a chili dog or something. You're talking a lot and spitting. You're spitting so much, I thought it was raining."

"Fuck you, nigga," said Renita. "You ain't shit no way."

"Fuck you, fat bitch," he came back.

"Why do brothers always want to call sisters bitches?" asked Renita. "Do I look like a female dog to you?"

"You're right," said Michael. "I apologize for calling you a bitch, but why don't you leave me alone?"

Gary laughed at Michael going back and forth with the woman and continued to watch in amazement. A tall, pretty sister with shoulder-length hair grabbed Michael and pulled him away from the woman onto the dance floor.

"I saw you sparring with that woman and thought I'd save you," she said. "Is that your girl?"

"Hell, no," he replied. "I never met her until a few minutes ago, when she walked up and started going off on me out of the blue."

"She might have a fatal attraction or may be a stalker."

"She didn't come on to me," he said. "She just wanted to vent on someone and picked me."

"Well, I would have picked you too," said the woman. "You're the tallest brother in here, and you stand out. Oh, by the way, my name is Sherri Coleman, and I'm just out to have a good time."

"Well, I'm Michael, Michael Alexander," he said. "I'm in town for a day on business, and I'm really enjoying Chicago a lot, except for that woman grilling me a minute ago."

"First time here?" asked Sherri. "I mean, in Chicago."

"No, but it's been awhile. But I always have a good time here."

Michael and Sherri continued to dance until Renita stopped looking at Michael and walked away.

"She's gone," said Sherri. "Let me buy you a drink."

"I drink Remy," he responded.

"No problem."

The two of them walked over to the bar. Gary was close by and came over.

"Gary, this is Sherri," Michael said, introducing them. "Hey, that rhymes—Gary and Sherri. We're getting ready to have a drink. You want one?"

"Yeah, I'll take one more," Gary replied.

Michael reached in his pocket to pay for Gary's drink, but Sherri stopped him.

"I got it," she said. "Does he drink Remy too?"

"No, he drinks that sweet Grand Marnier," said Michael.

Michael, Gary, and Sherri consumed their drinks and shot the breeze for a while. A slow song came on and Sherri asked Michael to dance. As their bodies moved in sync, she took a hard look at Michael.

"You know, I've never had a one-night stand before, but I would definitely consider you. You're one of the cutest brothers I've seen in this club since I've been coming here. But let me be quiet. I don't want you to think I do this all the time. You're just so sexy."

"Who you with?" asked Michael.

"Me and my girl came together," she replied. "What about you?"

"I'm with my boy, Gary," he said. "We just met today, but it seems as if we've been boys for years.

"Where do you live?" he inquired.

"Right around the corner," she replied, "and yes, I live alone."

"Well, what do you want to do?" Michael asked.

"I want to be bad," she responded. "Let me go talk to my girl."

Sherri walked over to talk to her friend on the other side of the club, and Michael talked to Gary.

"Man, you might not believe this, but she told me she wants to give me some," said Michael. "She said she lives around the corner by herself."

"You going?" asked Gary. "If not, I'll take your spot."

"I can handle it," grinned Michael. "You don't mind waiting for me a little while do you?"

"Not at all," said Gary.

The two women came over, and Sherri asked Michael if he was ready.

"I was born ready," he said with a smirk.

"This is my girl, Keisha," said Sherri. "You guys can follow us because we never leave the club separately."

"Yeah, and I want your driver's license number, address, and all your vital information," added Keisha.

"Blood type, too," said Michael.

"If you know it," Keisha came back.

Michael, Keisha, Sherri, and Gary headed for the exit. Standing at the front door was Renita, the woman who gave Michael a hard time. Michael was hand in hand with Sherri. Renita spotted Michael and went off.

"See, I knew you were shit," she said. "Don't take you no time to find one to go home with. He ain't no good, sister. I can tell by looking at him."

She continued to rant and rave until Michael was out of sight.

"What's her problem?" asked Keisha.

"She's in love," said Sherri. "Michael's her secret lover."

"Yea, right," he said.

"Where're you parked? We're right here in this limo."

"What do you do to afford this?" asked Kisha.

"It's not mine," Michael said simply.

"We're in this blue Jaguar," Keisha said.

"What do you do for a living?" asked Michael.

Keisha just laughed and got in the car and drove off. Michael and Gary followed closely behind.

"Does that happen to you all the time?" asked Gary.

"Not like that. You got any condoms in the car?"

"I'm fully equipped," Gary shot back. He reached in a compartment next to the seat and pulled out a pack of Life Styles.

"Man, these things have a tendency to break," Michael remarked.

"Just make sure it don't," said Gary.

They only drove a few miles and pulled into a housing complex called the Butler. It was a gated housing complex. The men parked behind the girls on the main strip. Michael waited for Sherri to come out of her friend's car but she spent several minutes in the car talking to her friend first.

"I wonder what they're talking so intensely about," wondered Gary.

"Maybe she's having second thoughts," questioned Michael.

"I doubt it," said Gary. "She looks at you like she wants to eat you. Maybe her girl is jealous and wants to make it a threesome."

"Wouldn't that be a trip?" laughed Michael.

Finally, Sherri emerged from the car and Keisha skidded off out of the complex. Michael followed suit and exited the limo.

"Everything alright?" he asked.

"Yea, everything is okay," she answered.

"I might ride back around to the club," said Gary. "I'll be right back. What's the code to get back in the gate?"

"Press key, key, 5252," said Sherri.

"Key, key, 5252," repeated Gary. "Okay."

He cranked up the limo and turned on the CD as he looked for a particular CD and Michael disappeared into the house. Then he decided that he didn't want to go back to the club. He would just wait for Michael to come out of the house.

Michael and Sherri walked into the house. He took a seat while Sherri went in the back. Passing time, Michael grabbed the remote and turned to ESPN Sports Center while noticing how plush the place was. He made sure he had the condom in his pocket as he waited patiently for Sherri to return. Shortly, she came back and sat on the couch next to him.

"Do you do this a lot?" she asked.

"No."

"Yea, I bet," she replied. "Do you have a condom?"

"Definitely."

He kissed her and started to rub across her body. She had taken off her panty hose and Michael felt her big, smooth legs. Then he reached under her dress and his pulse quickened as he felt no panties. He forgot the foreplay, pulled her dress up, laid her back on the couch, pulled his pants down to his knees, put on the condom and began to pump up and down. Sherri began to moan and scratch Michael across the back, enjoying the pleasure of him inside of her.

Outside, thirty minutes passed and Gary fell asleep at the wheel. Cars came and went in the complex without Gary even moving. A black Escalade truck pulled into the complex and parked right next to the limo. Then a muscular man emerged from the truck and slammed the door shut, the force of the door slamming awakening Gary from his sleep. He looked in the rear mirror and saw the man looking in the limo.

Who the fuck is this? Gary wondered. *Oh, shit.*

He panicked because the large man walked to the house where Michael was, unlocked the door, and immediately heard the sound of a woman moaning loudly. He pulled a 357 magnum from inside his coat and didn't even bother to shut the front door, then walked into the living room area, where all the lights were off. Carefully, he turned on the lights and saw Michael with his wife's legs over the back of the couch. Michael noticed the lights come on, but didn't miss a stroke. The man put the gun to Michael's head and was about to pull the trigger.

"Drop it, motherfucker!" yelled Gary at the man.

At that moment, Michael and Sherri jumped up.

"What's going on here?" demanded Michael.

"You're fucking my wife," stated the man coldly.

Gary always carried a handgun and had placed it against the man's head. Michael quickly picked up the gun the man had dropped on the floor.

"Your *wife*?" he repeated.

"Let's go, Michael," said Gary.

Michael pulled his pants up and didn't even bother to take off the condom. Gary kept the gun on the man as the two of them ran to the door and jumped in the car. The man didn't follow them, but they could hear him screaming at his wife. A car pulled up and the gate opened. Gary cut in front of the car and sped away from the complex toward Barbara Brown's house. Michael covered his face with his hands in total shock at the events that just happened. He couldn't speak for several minutes.

"You alright, brother?" asked Gary.

Michael didn't answer. He made the ride to Barbara Brown's house without saying a word. They pulled up to the house, but Michael just sat in the car silently, with one tear in his eye as he silently looked at Gary.

"I don't even know how to thank you," he said. "I'm so glad you were there. I thought you were going back to the club."

"I was, but that Grand Marnier got to me so I tried to sleep it off," said Gary. "I didn't see him drive up. Thank God he slammed the door as hard as he did. If he didn't, I wouldn't have woken up. Besides, it wasn't me. God spared you."

"No doubt," said Michael. "No doubt. You know, I thought that girl at the poetry reading was crazy, but she was trying to tell me to turn something down tonight."

"Why would that bitch bring you to her house, to her couch that she shares with her husband?" said Gary. "He was a big linebacker-looking motherfucker."

"Women are a trip," said Michael. "He and his wife are probably having major problems, and she just wanted to go out and fuck somebody no matter whether she put his life in danger or not."

"No doubt," agreed Gary. "That's a sick bitch."

They paused for a few moments and then Gary tried to break the intensity of the moment.

"Just for the record," stated Gary, "you was tearing that pussy up. I walked in to save your life, and I almost stopped to look at what you were doing. You had them legs all over the back of the couch."

Michael paused for a moment and then laughed to release the strain of what just happened to him. "Yea, I was wearing it out, wasn't I? They should put my dick in the Hall of Fame."

He exited the car, still in shock, but feeling better because of Gary.

"You know, brother, you're my man for life," said Michael. "We will always be boys, no matter what."

"No doubt, brother."

Michael walked towards the house.

"Hey, Mike," yelled Gary. "If you're gonna live the lifestyle you live, you better get a gun. I can see you being caught up again."

"That's a good idea," Michael replied.

As he walked in the house, he was still in a daze over what happened. He looked in the air and talked to God. "Thank you, my friend. You always bless me like You do. I don't know why, but whatever the reason is, I thank You."

Michael undressed and took a shower in the plush bathroom in his room. After a long, hot shower, he put on the terry cloth robe that had been set aside for him, lay across the bed, and fell asleep.

"Hello, Michael," said Sheila, his wife. "I've missed you."

"I've missed you too," Michael replied, kissing his wife. "Where have you been?"

"I had to go away," she said, "but I came back for you."

"For me?"

"Yes, Michael, I came back to take you with me. I know you've been lonely without me. Soon, you, Brittany, and I will be a family again. Wouldn't you like that, baby?"

"I would like nothing more than that," he stated. "I could never love another woman the way I love you, Sheila," he said softly. "Baby, can I ask you a question?"

"Yes, Michael," answered Sheila.

"Why did you go away and leave us all alone?"

"You've never been alone," said Sheila. "I've always been with you. Michael, I've got to go now, but I'll be back for you soon, real soon."

As the words faded, so did Sheila.

"Come back! Come back! Come back!" he yelled. "No!" shouted Michael as he awakened from his sleep.

He was in a cold sweat but wondered aloud what the dream meant. Soon, he was able to find a comfortable spot in his spirit and fell deeply asleep.

Chapter 16

AT 7 A.M., CORETTA CALLED MYRA to speak about Brittany. She had set Brittany up in another school in Hollywood a little further out and not as exclusive as the previous school, but nevertheless, a very good school. Brittany could enroll at the school immediately and start her transformation into the everyday school setting. Coretta gave Myra the directions and answered any questions she had. At that moment, Coretta's butler came in and announced that she had guests.

"I've got to go," Coretta told Myra. "Call me and let me know how everything works out."

Going downstairs, Coretta found Detective Andrews and Detective Gentry standing in her parlor.

"Ms. James," said Detective Andrews, "I'm Detective Andrews, and this is Detective Gentry. How are you this morning?"

"I'm well," she replied. "How can I assist you today?"

"We're investigating a rape and murder that happened yesterday afternoon at a condominium complex in North Hollywood," said Detective Andrews. "A Mrs. Karen

Atkinson was brutally raped and murdered in broad daylight."

"And what would such a tragic incident have to do with me, Detective? Certainly you don't think I murdered and raped another female."

"Of course not. There was male sperm inside the woman and the way her neck was snapped required the kind of brute strength a woman such as yourself doesn't appear to have," added Detective Gentry, "but the victim called in a complaint against you to the Los Angeles Police Department, claiming you verbally threatened her. Then within a few hours of that complaint, the woman was dead. That's quite a coincidence, wouldn't you agree, Ms. James?"

"Sure, if you're looking for sensationalism, but if you're looking for reality, you have to look much further than me."

"Did you have an argument with her, Ms. James?" asked Detective Gentry, perturbed by her attitude. "Did you threaten her in any way?"

"Please watch your tone, Detective," Coretta responded. "Are you always so high-strung?"

Detective Andrews motioned for his partner to calm down.

"Did you have an argument with her?" repeated Detective Andrews. "Did you threaten her in any way?"

"I wouldn't call it an argument," she replied.

"What would you call it?" Gentry inquired.

"A simple difference of opinion. Of course, I never threatened. I would never do such a thing."

Coretta's sarcasm stung Detective Gentry. She appeared quite eager to continue the interrogation.

"Do you know this man?" Detective Gentry asked, holding a picture of Stephen. "Word around is that he works for you. We found his print on the dead woman's car, and we would love to ask how it got there."

Coretta looked at the picture of Stephen, but of course, said nothing incriminating.

"I have no such man in my employment. I'll have my attorney contact you and that way, you can address any more questions to him."

Dismissing the officers, she put her hand out, asking for a card from them, and then opened the door to show the detectives out.

"Good day, officers." Coretta closed the door then went upstairs to call Stephen.

"You idiot," she said to him icily. "Why did you rape that woman and kill her in broad daylight?"

"You asked me to make her understand who she was dealing with," he responded. "I'm very thorough in the way I handle my business."

"Well, Mr. Thorough," she said angrily, "you left a fingerprint and the police showed me one of your old arrest photos and asked if I employed you. You need to have a real low-profile for a while. Is there anything else I need to know?

"And another thing, did anyone see you," she demanded, "anyone that could recognize you?"

Stephen was silent, and Coretta judged that silence to be a potential problem.

"No, don't tell me," she lamented. "*Somebody* saw you. Who was it?"

"It was some girl, a tenant," said Stephen. "We scared her almost to death, so I'm positive she won't be talking."

"Oh, you are?" Coretta said sarcastically. "I can't believe you would be so sloppy, and why do you have to have sex with all the women you've taken out? They've got your fingerprint, they've got your sperm, and now I find out they've got a witness. Why don't you just deliver our necks to them on a silver platter? That witness needs to forget—permanently. Work it out."

As Coretta abruptly hung up the phone and promptly threw it to the floor, Stephen and Manu drove back to the condo to find the witness.

At the same time, detectives Andrews and Gentry arrived back at Kiddie Care and found the employees in shock over the gruesome death of their new director. Ms. Williams at the front desk acknowledged the detectives but was in tears over her colleague.

"Mrs. Williams, can you answer a few questions?" asked Detective Gentry. "Did this man by any chance show up around here yesterday?"

The woman looked at the picture of Stephen and immediately remembered the incident. "He was looking for Mrs. Atkinson yesterday. I pointed her out to him as she spoke to the police about the woman who threatened her. Is this the man who killed her?"

"We think it may be," she answered, "but we're not quite sure yet."

"That means, *I* killed her," said Ms. Williams. "I showed him who she was and that's like killing her myself."

The woman started to wail. Detective Gentry tried to console her and called another employee over to help. Meanwhile, Detective Andrews had been outside, talking with businesses across the street.

"The owner of the restaurant remembers seeing a black Honda Accord parked over here yesterday afternoon," he reported. "He says it caught his attention because the men inside seemed to focus on the school, and they didn't leave the vehicle. And a man that lives across from Mrs. Atkinson noticed a black Honda Accord slowly leave her complex yesterday, roughly around the time of the murder."

"Well, at least now we know the car that they used," said Gentry.

"We know more than that," her partner stated. "Guess who owns a black 2000 Honda Accord?"

"Lemme guess," Detective Gentry replied. "Coretta James?"

"That's right. I had her DMV record checked. She owns many cars, including a black 2000 Honda Accord. Looks like this Stephen guy, along with some other man, stalked and killed Mrs. Atkinson, but why?"

"Did you see how she looked at me today when I got cross with her?" asked Detective Gentry. "Maybe the lady doesn't like being told no."

"Let's see if we've got enough evidence to search her home," said Detective Andrews. "Maybe we can come up with something to tell us where this Stephen is hiding."

Finishing up there, the detectives returned to their headquarters. Meanwhile, Stephen began putting on one of his many disguises. Coretta had instructed him to leave her compound and remove all his belongings.

"Take everything that's yours," she had said. "I'm having all the cars cleaned and also the compound. Take any incriminating merchandise that we may have here and put it away in case we have more visitors—and don't forget to take care of our little witness."

"That's in motion as we speak," he replied.

Stephen put all his belongings in an SUV and headed towards North Hollywood with Manu. Coretta's maids gave her mansion and all the guest houses a thorough cleaning, trying to cover any tracks that could lead to Stephen.

At 9 a.m., a 6-foot-2-inch white man pulled up to Karen Atkinson's complex in North Hollywood, wearing a black suit. The police were canvassing the parking garage area, searching for clues as others checked the perimeter of the buildings. The white man pulled up to the front of the condo and looked intently at the board outside, then he rang the manager, who looked in the monitor outside, but didn't recognize him.

"May I help you?" the manager said.

The white man held up a fake badge. "Detective Jones," he replied through the intercom. "I want to ask you a few more questions about the murder."

The manager buzzed in the fake officer, although he thought it odd that the policeman would come through the front of the building when several of them were in the parking garage with access to the back area that leads directly into the building. Nevertheless, the manager talked to the counterfeit officer in the hallway.

"I need a list of all your female tenants," said Officer Jones. "We need to make sure they take all the necessary precautions to protect themselves."

"That's easy," answered the manager. "There's Kate Johnson upstairs in the corner, the two dyke girls in 21, there's Jasmine in 11, but I would go easy on her because she has been so terrified that she had to be taken to the hospital or something yesterday. She just got back a few hours ago, and then there's—"

The fake cop cut off the manager, knowing he had what he came for and slightly smiled.

"Thank you, sir, you've been a big help. I'm just going to check out the building one more time."

He walked away, as if to exit the building, and as soon as the manager walked back inside his condo, the bogus cop headed downstairs to number 11. He knocked on the door, but there was no answer. He started to look around nervously, hoping not to be seen. Then he knocked again on the door. Finally, he heard a whisper.

"Who is it?"

"Police, ma'am," he replied, holding his badge in the peephole. "I just need to ask you a few questions."

She refused to open the door.

"I know you've had a bad experience," he said. "I just want to make sure that you're safe."

The woman reluctantly opened the door. He came in, keeping his back turned to the woman, and pulled out a semi-automatic gun with a silencer, turned, and shot the woman at point-blank range in the head. Then he walked away, not bothering to shut the woman's door.

He moved quickly out of the front entrance and rushed across the street. The manager, looking through the monitor, saw the bogus officer leave. He emerged from his room to see if anything unusual happened. Walking about, he looked from room to room. Seeing Jasmine's door slightly ajar, he rushed over and cautiously opened it while calling her name. Then he stared in horror at the bloody sight that greeted his eyes, threw his hands over his mouth, and ran hysterically to the parking garage to grab the nearest policeman, screaming that Jasmine had been shot in the head.

Ten minutes later, Detective Andrews received a call from the crime scene as he and Detective Gentry pressed for a search warrant for Coretta James' mansion.

"Okay, we're on our way," he said tersely. "Gentry, we've got to go."

"Where?"

"There's been another murder at the condo in North Hollywood, a Ms. Jasmine Reese."

"Who is Jasmine Reese?" asked Detective Gentry.

"She was the woman too terrified to talk," said Detective Andrews. "I guess somebody decided against leaving any witnesses.

"These are very dangerous people. Not only do they rape and kill a woman in broad daylight, but they come back the very next day and kill a witness with police swarming all around."

"That's the boldest crime I've ever heard of," said Gentry.

Meanwhile, the bogus cop had arrived back at the parked car, jumped in, and the driver sped off.

The driver was Manu, and the fake cop was Stephen, who used chemicals to make himself look white.

"Worked like a charm, baby," said Stephen, filled with pride. "There are no more eyewitnesses to worry about. Let's go to the suite. I need to blaze me up a joint and relax. Let me call boss lady and tell her the good news. This should make her happy."

Coretta had commissioned several cleaners to do a thorough job on the huge compound, not leaving any stone unturned in her effort to eliminate the presence of Stephen from ever being there. She always tried to think ahead. For all her class and style, she not only had a mean streak, but a total disrespect for any form of authority other than her own. Coretta came from money, a stable home environment, a mother and a father that loved her and supported her in all her endeavors. She had always deceived her parents with her innocence and would go to any extreme to get her way.

Chapter 17

AT 9 A.M. CENTRAL TIME, BARBARA Brown arrived at her mansion on Lake Shore Drive in Chicago. She was a statuesque woman in her early 40s, had a creamy brown skin, and was as beautiful and spicy as any black woman could be. Ms. Brown was worth millions, and although she had her own television show, she had nowhere near the following of Oprah Winfrey. But she had a huge following on syndicated TV stations.

Barbara was originally from Mississippi and was far more outspoken than Oprah for black America. In fact, she was too outspoken to be mainstream, but she had an incredible following amongst blacks and was surprisingly strong in white households also. Barbara was single, no children, who considered Coretta James a confidant, a girlfriend, and a woman in control of her own destiny.

Coretta had called Barbara and spoken so highly of Michael that Barbara was willing to pay to spend some time with him. But unlike Coretta, Barbara had no thirst for power. She only wanted to be a voice for the community.

She condemned the war in Iraq and the reasons for it and was adamant about her beliefs. She had no idea what she would do with Michael, but was totally intrigued at the thought of him.

She walked into her beautiful mansion and put her bags on the table. Michael had been awake for several hours and was feeling the difference in the time zone. He had only slept a few hours because of the eventful night he had. He had on a pair of blue stretch boxer underwear and a wife beater T-shirt. At that moment, he strolled through the front of the mansion looking lost and reflecting on a life that he felt was very unfulfilled. Then he walked right into Barbara, who saw him coming.

"So you're Michael Alexander," she said. "Do you usually parade around half naked through strange women's houses?"

Michael tried to cover up, but Barbara quickly made him feel comfortable.

"Don't cover up on my account," she said. "Not a bad view for first thing in the morning."

"Sorry, I didn't know you were here," he replied. "I'm definitely not trying to flash you early in the morning."

"So come, Michael, tell me about yourself."

"Let me put my robe on."

"Don't do me any favors," she said suggestively.

Michael slyly smiled, went to his room, and returned wearing his robe. Barbara was tired, but feeling some energy returning, took off her shoes and sat back on the sofa, waiting for him.

"Come, sit over here with me, honey," she said. "Let's be friends."

Michael walked over to the sofa and sat beside her, then fell back on the couch, looking exhausted.

"Poor baby," she said. "Lie back."

He was obedient and lay back on the sofa while Barbara came behind him and began to massage his neck.

"Ahhh, that feels good," he said. "That's just what I needed."

He got so relaxed, he fell asleep and began to snore. Hearing himself, he jumped up, not realizing he was sleeping.

"My fault," he admitted sheepishly. "I was almost out."

"You *were* out," she stated. "These magic hands did the trick."

Michael didn't say much, but tried to sit upright up on the couch.

"So Michael, tell me about your childhood. Have you been this mack daddy, lady-killer your whole life?"

"Not at all," he replied. "I was as skinny as a toothpick my whole school years. I was tall, 6 foot 4, and weighed in at 165 lbs when I graduated from high school. I couldn't even get a girl all the way to my junior year in school, then all of a sudden, I went from everybody's joke to this guy everybody called handsome. I couldn't understand it. To me, I was the same man, but I guess others saw me differently. All the guys that had clowned me so bad suddenly wanted to be my friend. But you know what? It never went to my head. I wouldn't let it. I was so humbled about being laughed at that I didn't have time to pat myself on the back."

"Really?" said Barbara. "I can't see anyone clowning you."

"I got clowned bad. I went to an all-black high school, and they had no mercy. But I learned to clown back, 'cause if you're weak and go to a school like that, you're through. It took a long time for me to grow into my features, but my saving grace was that I was so good at sports. Basketball, baseball, football and track—I did it all, so that eased the load for me tremendously."

"Have you ever been married?"

"Yea, up until a little over a year ago. My wife went to school across town. I had known her for years, and she always thought highly of me. She always told me I would be successful and conquer the world."

"You're speaking in the past tense."

"Yea, she's, um, no longer with us."

"Sorry to hear that."

"You've got me out here answering questions like a guest on one of your shows. What's your story?"

"My story, honey, is that I need to take a nap," she replied. "We don't have to tape the show today, and I want to be cute for my evening at the Essence. Have your accommodations been to your liking?"

"Everything is wonderful, and your driver, Gary, is a lifesaver, literally."

"Gary is a lot more than my driver. He's a real friend. There's nothing I wouldn't do for that man."

"I definitely understand that," agreed Michael.

"I'm really enjoying this conversation," said his hostess, "but I need to wind down. I guess you already know to make yourself at home?"

With that, she exited the room and went to her large master bedroom to unwind after the long, tiring trip. Michael remained sitting, thinking about all the things he had to be thankful for.

→►══◉   →►══◉   →►══◉

A few hours have passed on the West Coast and the detectives were still questioning Dennis Smith, manager of the condominium complex where Karen Atkinson and

Jasmine were killed. Others were examining the room where Jasmine had been shot.

"So, was there anything distinctive about this man?" asked Detective Andrews. "Did he have blonde hair, black hair, was he tall, short?"

"I don't think he was quite 6 feet," said Dennis. "Maybe medium build, black hair."

"Was his nose pointed?" asked Detective Andrews.

"No, it was fleshy. It wasn't big, but it was somewhat broad."

"Anything else stand out?" asked the detective.

"Yea, I noticed he had very brown eyes."

"Brown? You sure?"

"Yeah, not that I was staring into them or anything. I guess they just stood out."

Detective Andrews gave Dennis his card, then he and Detective Gentry walked off and talked.

"The first question I have is, why wasn't there a guard at the door?" asked Detective Andrews. "A man just walks in here amongst all the police and executes a potential witness."

"Yeah, somebody should go down for this," frowned Detective Gentry.

"White people have brown eyes," said Detective Andrews, "and all of them don't have pointed noses."

"I guess not," agreed Detective Gentry, "but where are you going with this?"

"Well, what if this white man isn't white at all ..." said Andrews.

"What do you mean, not white at all?"

"Scott, come here. Take this picture to our artist and tell him to make him a white man," said Detective Andrews. "Tell him to give him black hair, like a white person, and then show it to our witness and see if this man is the police officer that killed this young lady. Get back to me immediately."

Once the photo of Stephen was passed to the officer, Detective Andrews motioned for his partner.

"What about the little girl?" said Detective Andrews. "Do we know who the little girl is that Coretta wanted to get in school so badly?"

"We're still working on that," said Detective Gentry.

"This little girl may hold the key somehow. We need to find her. Also, how many properties does this woman own?"

"At least 40," said Detective Gentry. "Investment properties are how she made her fortune."

"Check them out," ordered Andrews. "Give me a list of the people that rent from her, what they pay—whatever you can find. I'm going back to work on that search warrant."

Detective Andrews left the crime scene while Detective Gentry stayed behind to work on more clues and conduct other inquiries from the deceased's cell phone. As another dead woman was wheeled out to the morgue, the detective experienced a wave of helplessness pass through her body, knowing that the dead woman could be her, that she could be under that sheet. Detective Gentry was determined to find this killer.

◦→▐◉ ◦→▐◉ ◦→▐◉

AT 2 P.M., MICHAEL WAS RELAXING, not having anything to do until the show. Barbara Brown was conducting business by phone and knocked on his door. He still had on his robe and acknowledged Barbara's knock.

"What are you wearing?" she said.

Michael walked to the closet. "This black tux."

"No, no," she said. "I'm wearing white satin. We need to match. Put something on and let's take a ride. They're taping at 5 p.m. for the broadcast tonight. We need to get you a new suit."

"Did you get a lot of sleep?"

"Hardly any," she replied. "With arranging guests for the show and people calling to congratulate me, I got about 15 minutes. The car is outside. We leave as soon as you're dressed."

Barbara headed for the limo and Michael quickly threw something on and joined her, sitting in the back of the car driven by Gary. The two men greet each other like long lost friends.

"What's that all about?" questioned Barbara. "You two are mighty giddy for having known each other for only a day."

Neither man wanted Barbara to know about Michael's near-death experience, so they avoided the question.

"So it's like that, huh? Okay, it's cool with me. I'm glad we can all get along."

Michael was sitting next to Barbara. He left the window down so they all could talk.

"How was your trip, Ms. B? Did you get a lot accomplished?" Gary asked.

"Yeah," she responded, "we're now being picked up on Channel 9 in Charlotte, North Carolina, and that means that we're moving on up in the world."

"Soon you'll be bigger than Oprah," he said with a smile.

"I hope," she replied.

"Well, you know that Oprah lost all that weight and Steadman still won't marry her," said Gary.

"That's because Steadman knows Oprah is only one donut away from being a heavyweight again."

"Not one donut," Gary protested.

"Just one," she said. "You like Oprah, Michael?"

"Well, I can't say whether I like her or not because I don't know her, but I don't like her show at all. All those male-bashing females sound like cackling hens."

"Be careful," she teased. "Don't forget, you've got a female in the car with you."

"If a man forgot you were a female, something's wrong with him," said Michael gallantly.

"Flattery will get you *everywhere,* my brother," said Barbara.

"No, what I'm saying about that is, she's a sister from the Deep South and started off doing black movies. The *Color Purple* was my joint," said Michael.

Barbara imitated Oprah. "I love Harpo, I swear I do, but I'll kill him dead before I let him beat me."

They all laughed. "Yeah, black people made Oprah, but you have to take a microscope to find a black person in her audience," declared Michael.

"Well, she'll be there tonight," Barbara informed him. "Why don't you tell her about herself?"

"Maybe I will."

"Michael, can you sing?" Barbara asked, changing the subject.

"I can carry a tune a little. What about you?"

"I thought I could sing," she said. "I actually got signed to a small record label back in the day, cut an album and everything."

"How'd it do?" he asked.

"My shit went triple plastic. I think me and my mother are the only ones that had a copy, and I got mine free."

They laughed again. Barbara put Michael totally at ease with her sense of humor.

"She's a trip, huh?" asked Gary.

"No diggity," said Michael.

"Gary, why don't we give Mr. Alexander a scenic tour of Chicago?" suggested Barbara.

"What about the clothes?" Michael questioned.

"We've got time," she replied. "G, I'm putting up the glass. I need to talk business with Michael for a moment."

"No problem," said Gary.

Barbara closed the middle window and spoke to Michael. "Sorry about the confusion," she began. "I know you were under the impression that the show was yesterday. Coretta likes to make sure her people are where they should be when they should be."

"That's alright," Michael said. "I must admit I was quite impressed with you this morning. It was lust at first sight."

"You know why I brought you here, right?"

"Yea, to escort you to the awards show."

"Not quite. I could have got anybody for that. No, I want you to show me what it is about you that would make a rich woman like Coretta call me early in the morning, singing your praises. Tell me, how spontaneous are you?"

That said, she pulled her skirt off and then took off her blouse. Barbara wore no underwear. By then, she was only wearing her pumps. Michael stared at the nude Barbara with a puzzled look in his face.

"Well," she said, "you just gonna sit there and look at it, or are you gonna do something with it?"

"Right here?" he asked, bewildered.

"Right now, unless you're scared."

Michael wondered how he could go from having a conversation with two people to having sex with one. Barbara had a beautiful body and face, a body that a 25 year old would die for. Without second thought, he dropped his trousers, pulled up his shirt and grabbed Barbara, picking her up so she could ride him. After about 5 minutes, he turned her over to do it doggy style. Michael was pumping so hard that Barbara's head banged against the door. Gary heard some of the banging, but simply turned up his music. The windows of the limo were not tinted.

On one street, the limo pulled up to an elderly couple who were in a convertible with the top down. The 70-year-old white man and his 67-year-old wife were driving around the city when suddenly, the wife noticed the sex going on in the limo. She looked on in amazement and tapped her husband on the shoulder.

"Richard, look!" she said.

The woman was disgusted, but her husband looked so hard, he almost had an accident. The man kept pace alongside the limo, getting very excited. After a while, he could no longer control himself and screamed out loud, "Work that pussy!" he yelled.

His wife reached across the seat and slapped the shit out of him, and then her husband straightened up.

After 20 minutes of sex, Barbara cracked the window and told Gary to drive directly to the store. He made a beeline to the store. Gary could smell the scent of sex wafting from the back through the cracked window.

A few moments later, they arrived at the store. Barbara Brown's hair was everywhere and Michael's pants were twisted sideways.

"Wow," said Barbara, trying to straighten up. "That was intense."

"For sure," agreed a winded Michael.

"Maybe we can try that again someday," she suggested.

"We'll see."

Barbara shopped in a specialty shop called Chicago for Men, with designer suits, tailored, but also off the rack.

Michael chose a double-breasted tuxedo with a white silk tie and white shoes, an Armani suit. He put cuffs in the trousers, and then they hurried home to change for the show. Michael needed to pack his bags because his flight would be leaving directly after the show and he was anxious to get back to Brittany.

Chapter 18

BACK IN LOS ANGELES, STEPHEN called Coretta. "Boss lady, I know for a fact that Carlos is on the take. We sold more products this month than we did all year and yet, this is our worst month numbers wise. That fool is padding his pockets. I'm going to take him out tonight."

"No," Coretta replied. "Send Manu over here with me. I'll take care of Carlos. As much as he gets paid, he has no reason to be on the take. But we need him for that thing in Miami and who knows what will come up. Besides, I have a special surprise for Mr. Carlos. Get Manu over here right away."

She hung up and called Carlos on the cell phone. "Hey, baby," she said seductively. "Come see me. I'm in the mood again."

"What time?" he replied.

"Right now. Hurry up, Big Daddy, I need you."

Carlos promised to be there shortly.

Meanwhile, the detectives received word about Coretta's tenant list. Detective Gentry called Detective Andrews, "I think I got something. Coretta James has all her places leased out except one, a piece of property signed over to a man by the name of Michael Alexander. Mr. Alexander has a five-year-old daughter named Brittany. What do you bet that she's the little girl that couldn't get into school?"

"Where do they live?" asked Detective Andrews.

"Get this, the Plaza Condominiums," said Gentry, "the four-story condo in Bel Air."

"This Michael Alexander must be loaded," replied Detective Andrews. "It takes some serious paper to live there."

"The concierge says he believes she just signed it over to him," Gentry informed him. "Says the guy never saw the place until he moved in with his daughter."

"I'll meet you over there. We need to find out what Mr. Alexander knows."

The detectives coordinated to meet at Michael's condo at the same time Carlos reached Coretta's mansion.

"Come in, baby," she said. "Take off your clothes."

Coretta was fully dressed and Carlos wondered why she didn't at least have on her robe.

"I thought you were ready," he said. "Don't tell me you had me to come over for nothing."

Coretta had a bottle of Don Perignon chilling on ice and had thrown back the covers back on her ultra king-size bed.

"Baby, I want to oil you down," she said softly, "then I want you to take my clothes off of me. Now lie back and let me massage you."

Carlos lay back obediently.

"Close your eyes, baby," Coretta whispered suggestively.

Carlos closed his eyes and relaxed while Coretta reached under the pillow and grabbed some super glue. Then she grasped Carlos' penis and pulled it to the side.

He smiled, "You want to get freaky today, huh, baby?"

"Oh, yeah, baby, I want to get *real* freaky. Just enjoy the ride."

She super glued his penis to his leg and blew it so it would dry fast. He thought it was oil and thought the blowing was to help him get more aroused. The super glue dried quickly, then Manu emerged from behind the door leading to the bathroom. Coretta rose up. Carlos still didn't know what was happening.

"Can I open my eyes now?" Seeing Coretta rising, he asked, "Where you going?"

At that point, Manu put on some sterile gloves and walked towards Carlos, reached down, and snatched his penis from his leg, tearing big plugs of skin sway from it. Carlos screamed in intense pain and yelled out at Coretta in total agony.

"You bitch! Why did you do that shit?"

"You're real lucky to be alive," she said coldly. "This better teach you not to steal from me. The next lesson you learn will be from the grave."

Carlos insisted that he never stole from Coretta. She, in turn, ordered her driver to take him to the hospital, then she prepared herself to watch the *Essence Award Show* on TV. She was anxious to see Michael and observe how he looked in one of the tuxedos she purchased. She seemed totally oblivious to what she had just done to Carlos and conducted business by phone as if nothing had happened.

Carlos screamed in terrible pain all the way to the hospital, where he had to have immediate surgery to repair his wounds. He wanted to destroy Coretta, but knew he must watch his steps and that he would be watched closely from now on. He knew Coretta was ruthless, but never had it been as obvious as it was now. He fully recognized that she would go to any extent to get her point across, including killing him or anyone else that got in her way.

→▣ →▣ →▣

MICHAEL AND BARBARA pulled up to the venue where the *Essence Show* was to be held. He had on the double-breasted white tuxedo, white silk tie, and white shoes. Barbara wore the beautiful white satin dress she spoke of, form-fitted to show off her exquisite body. As they walked on the red carpet, there was much speculation about the handsome young man on Barbara's arm. The red-carpet affair was to be broadcast tape delayed at 8:30 EST and the show itself would be broadcast at 9:00 EST. Coretta James was prepared to watch both events to see how her newest investment looked in one of the new suits she purchased for him.

At about 5:30 PST, Coretta turned on the *Pre-Essence Show* festivities being broadcast on E Entertainment Television. Also watching was Cheryl, Kenneth's wife, who never missed any black events on television. Cheryl and Kenneth were not speaking much lately because of Kenneth's strange actions toward Michael. They both watched as Barbara Brown emerged from her limo with Michael. Cheryl screamed and called out to Kenneth as soon as she saw Michael on television.

Coretta James carefully scrutinized Michael's clothing. She had seen every piece of merchandise that was sent to Michael's residence and knew she didn't buy this outfit. She was outraged. How dare he appear on national television, not wearing her clothes. Coretta turned off the broadcast and made plans for her other business endeavors, but she felt Michael had crossed her in some strange way by not wearing the clothes she picked out and purchased, and she hated to be crossed.

Meanwhile, Cheryl and Kenneth continued to watch the red-carpet program. They saw Barbara Brown interviewed and noticed how she held onto Michael tightly. Michael was doing the role reversal. He was the pretty guy holding onto the successful woman and just smiling while she carried on her business.

Ken was not amused. "If he's in Chicago, where's Brittany?" he asked. "Who's she with?"

"Remember, we spoke to her nanny the other night," said Cheryl. "From the way she spoke, I believe Brittany is in good hands."

"How do we know that for sure?" he demanded. "Michael could be neglecting that child all over again."

"Will you stop bitching?" Cheryl said frustrated. "Besides, look how good Michael looks. He has come a long way in a month."

"I know who to call," he said.

He ran out of the room to use the phone. Cheryl didn't bother to worry about Kenneth, but just continued to watch the show.

At about 8:30, Michael went to the airport with Gary driving and, of course, Barbara sitting in the seat next to him. Michael was drinking a glass of Hennessy, while Barbara drank champagne. The evening was a smashing success. Barbara had her award from the night's festivities.

"What a night," she exclaimed, "what a night." She lifted her glass to propose a toast.

"Here's to a wonderful evening," she gushed, "and wonderful company."

"I've never seen so many beautiful black people in my life," said Michael, "and of course, I was with the most beautiful woman of them all. I think we look a lot better than Oprah and Steadman."

"I've got enough time to watch the tape delay portion when I get back from dropping you off," she said. "I want to see how good we looked on TV."

"You're not going to any of the big after-parties all over the city?" he asked.

"Not without my gorgeous escort," she replied, then leaned over and whispered in his ear. "What's the chance of me getting a little 'nookie' while we ride as a good-bye gift?"

"I don't want to go through all the trouble of taking off my clothes and giving the whole city of Chicago another free show," he whispered back. "Besides, I don't want Gary to feel we're kicking him to the curb."

But Barbara didn't listen. She reached under her skirt and pulled off her thong, then unzipped Michael's pants discretely.

"Excuse me, Gary," she said, "I'm going to sit on Michael's lap. I want to feel close to him because he's about to leave."

"Do your thing," he said.

Michael's penis was rock-hard and as soon as Barbara sat on his lap, he maneuvered it right into her. His face showed immediate desire. He pumped very slightly, in his mind, not enough to draw attention, but enough for Barbara to know he's there. Gary already knew what's up, but played it off and continued to mind his business and speak only when spoken to.

"You have to come to LA soon," said Michael, "both of you. I want you guys to meet my daughter, and we all can hang out on the town."

"That's a bet," said Gary. "You down, Barbara?"

Barbara was enjoying her sexual escapade and could only smile and nod in agreement.

"I can't wait," moaned Barbara. Shortly afterwards, she got up off Michael and sighed as she sat on the seat. Michael took it in stride and zipped his pants. He realized he had a 5-hour flight to LA and would be smelling like sex.

Twenty minutes later, they pulled up to the airport. Michael grabbed his bags while Gary came around to have a last word with him and Barbara stood in the background.

"You're the realest brother I've met in a longtime," said Gary. "Here's my card. Call me, brother, and let me know what's up with you."

The two embraced.

"Thanks to you, I look at life quite differently," said Michael. "I'll never forget how you looked out for me. We're brothers for life."

Barbara was happy to see Gary and Michael get along so well, but was amazed at their closeness.

"Am I missing something?" she asked. "You guys act as if you have known each other for life, like you've been through a war or something."

"In a way, we have," said Michael. "In a way, we have."

"Don't forget," Gary reminded him, "get a gun."

Barbara wondered what had gone on between the two men, but knew Michael had a flight to catch and the baggage check situation was real tight these days. She pulled out two envelopes.

"This one is for you and Coretta, and this one is just for you. If you need anything, don't hesitate to call me and I'll be there for you, anytime, anywhere." Speaking real low, she continued, "I know I jumped your bones, but you're a very impressive black man, and I totally believe in seeing my brothers prosper. You're gonna make some woman real happy, but take your time. We need to have another one-on-one session."

With that, Barbara Brown embraced Michael tightly and gave him a big kiss. Some people there recognized her and snapped her picture, but she wasn't concerned. She just continued doing what she was doing. They finally pulled apart and Gary said a few more words, then walked away.

"Oh, Michael, I've got one more," he said, raising his voice. "Bill Clinton or George W. Bush?"

"Come on, man, Bill Clinton," replied Michael. "Bill Clinton smoked weed and loves women. George W. Bush don't have no lips. Can't be down with a man with no lips."

With that, Gary and Barbara drove off and Michael took his bags to the terminal window. He felt like he just left two friends behind, but realized that it was rare in life to run across just one true friend. By now, he was exhausted and couldn't wait to get on the plane so he could sleep the entire trip.

Back in the limo, Barbara called to thank Coretta for Michael. Coretta saw Barbara on the caller ID and didn't bother to answer. Her voicemail picked up.

"Girl, thank you so much for Michael," said Barbara. "He's everything you said, and then some. I'm already ready for our next encounter. Chow, baby."

"I bet you are," said Coretta callously, listening to the message.

Chapter 19

DETECTIVE ANDREWS AND DETECTIVE GENTRY arrived at the Plaza Condominium, where Michael lived. They walked to the Concierge Desk, where the concierge then buzzed Michael's condo. Myra informed the concierge that Michael was not in but should return that night. The detectives decided to wait. They hadn't been able to secure a search warrant yet for Coretta's place and hoped Michael could shed some light on why two women died in a 24-hour time span.

Earlier that evening, Kenneth called Michael's former in-laws, William and Susie Jackson. They hadn't seen their grandchild in over a year and although they loved Michael during the time he dated and eventually married their daughter, they now hated him, especially Susie, and blamed him for the death of their only child. They kept in touch with Kenneth since their daughter's funeral and were aware of the fact that Kenneth used a private detective to help find Michael and Brittany, but they had no idea that Kenneth had located them over a month ago. Kenneth knew the Jacksons would be upset that he not only knew of their whereabouts, but that they had actually stayed with him. However, Kenneth felt it was time to call, thinking the Jacksons might have seen Michael on TV. Kenneth called New York, where the Jacksons now resided. William Jackson answered the phone.

"Hello, Jackson residence."

"Mr. Jackson, how are you doing? This is Kenneth Bolling."

"Kenneth," he said. "Susie, it's Kenneth on the phone."

Mrs. Jackson was the dominant one of the two and motioned for her husband to hand her the phone.

"Kenneth," she said, "do you have any news about where our grandbaby is?"

"Yes, ma'am, she's right here in LA with Michael. I found them a little over a month ago."

"A month ago! Why are you just now calling us?"

The Jacksons had fought unsuccessfully to have Michael tried for murder and would have fought for custody of Brittany, but Michael fled before it even became a possibility. The Jacksons, especially Mrs. Jackson, was not going to let the opportunity slip them by this time.

"What kind of condition is Brittany in? Is the child eating right?"

"No," said Kenneth, "there's no telling what she's going through. When I found them, they were living downtown LA on Adams Avenue in a drug-filled, pissy hotel with nothing but addicts. I found them and brought them back to my home, and they stayed with me until a few days ago, but Michael met a woman at a club and moved out a few days later. I think now he is working as some kind of male prostitute. He's got Brittany living somewhere with a strange woman while he's out of town right now with one of his clients, at least, I think she's a client. I'm afraid that Michael has gone off the deep end."

"I can't believe I haven't heard from you before now," huffed Mrs. Jackson. "That bastard killed my daughter, but he's not going to do the same thing to my granddaughter. No way! She's all that I have left of Sheila."

"William, make reservations for us to fly to LA tomorrow. We're going to get our grandbaby."

"We don't have living arrangements there," interrupted Mr. Jackson.

"Make them! I want to be there tomorrow."

"I'll put you up in my house," said Kenneth. "Just call me and let me know what time your flight comes in. I'll pick you guys up, and anything you need me to do to help you get Brittany from Michael, let me know."

Kenneth was singing like a bird, telling Mrs. Jackson everything negative that he knew or felt about Michael, hoping to fuel their hatred for their son-in-law even more. He wanted to continue talking, but Mrs. Jackson wanted her husband to call and make arrangements for their trip to Los Angeles. They promised to call Kenneth back after preparations were final.

At about 10:00 p.m., Michael arrived in the terminal at LAX. He was exhausted, even having slept the whole flight. The last two days had been mentally draining. As Michael went to claim his bags, he saw Manu standing in the terminal. Then he realized that Stephen couldn't be too far behind and wasn't in the mood for another night of threats. Manu didn't say anything as he saw Michael. He simply headed for the car.

"How far away is the car, man?" Michael asked. "I'm tired as shit. I've had a busy two days."

Manu didn't say anything. He just continued to walk towards the limo parked directly outside.

"Man, can you talk at all? I know you're supposed to be a big, mean motherfucker, but you could at least say something."

Manu didn't acknowledge Michael. In truth, he wanted to crush him severely. Manu knew Coretta and although she was quite smitten by Michael, there was no one thus far that she hadn't turned against in some way. Manu believed that Michael would get on Coretta's bad side someday, and when he did, he would kill him, no matter how minor the incident. Manu was just biding his time.

They soon arrived at the limo, where a strange man was sitting in the backseat.

"Give me the envelope Barbara gave you for Coretta," he stated.

"Who are you?" asked Michael. He didn't recognize the face of the white man, but he recognized the voice.

"Stephen," Michael exclaimed. "Why are you like that?"

"Stop asking questions, punk, and give me the envelope," he demanded.

Michael reached in his bag and pulled out two envelopes, then gave one to Stephen.

"What's in the other one?" Stephen asked.

"Nothing for you," replied Michael.

"You know, you're a smart ass ole nigger," said Stephen. "Why you talk so much shit?"

"You tried to intimidate me when I first met you," Michael explained. "I'm just going with your vibes. Where are we going anyway?"

"We're going to the boss lady. You do want to get paid, don't you?"

Michael didn't check to see how much money was in the other envelope, but it felt substantial, so he didn't feel the need to get the money tonight.

"Just take me straight home. I need some sleep real bad. Tell Coretta I'll call her later."

Coretta had requested that Michael come by her mansion. Stephen knew that she liked to conduct business right away. A plan germinated in his mind to start a rift between Michael and Coretta, so he decided to tell Coretta that Michael refused to come.

"Okay," said Stephen, "take him home."

The limo changed its course and at 10:49 p.m., pulled up in front of the Plaza Condominium, where Michael exited the car. Looking back at Stephen, he said, "You know what, brother? If I had a face like yours, I'd wear a disguise, too."

Then he slammed the door and walked into the condo. In all of Stephen's days of growing up on the streets, being a hit man—no matter what his dealings—no one had ever disrespected him the way Michael routinely did. He was determined to kill Michael, even if he had to frame him to do it.

Strolling to the front of the condo, Michael waited to get buzzed in by the concierge. At the same time, the two strange figures sitting next to the Concierge Desk stood up. Detective Andrews, a 20-year veteran on the force, standing at 6 foot 1, tried to look Michael in the eyes. His partner, Detective Gentry, stood at 5 foot 7. She was a lovely cocoa brown and far too attractive to be a police officer in Michael's eyes.

"Michael Alexander?" said Detective Andrews.

"Who wants to know?" came the reply.

"I'm Detective Dana Andrews, and this is my partner," stated the detective.

"I'm Detective LaShara Gentry," said Detective Gentry. "It's a pleasure to meet you." She extended her hand, but Michael didn't accept it.

"I don't deal with police," he said with obvious hostility. "The police killed my cousin back in the day. Shot him 10 times. Said they thought he had a gun when all he had in his pocket was a comb."

The two detectives looked at each other.

"Well, Mr. Alexander," said Detective Andrews, "that doesn't have anything to do with us. We're good guys."

That statement just enraged Michael even more, but he held his tongue grudgingly.

"What do you guys want with me anyway? I haven't broken any laws. But then again, you don't have to break laws with the police. You crooks will just frame us and make a case anyway."

"Mr. Alexander, we're not here to have our integrity questioned," replied Detective Andrews. "We're here on official business. Do you know this man?"

He showed Michael the picture of Stephen. Michael barely looked at the picture before answering.

"No, I don't, and if I did, I wouldn't tell you. I won't be responsible for locking a brother up, only to be murdered in jail."

"Well, this 'brother,' as you call him, may be responsible for killing two women in the last 24 hours," said Detective Gentry. "A brother like that doesn't have any business on the streets."

Michael stared at the detective and totally ignored the statement. "How's a fine ass sister like you working for a bunch of cowards like the LAPD?" he asked. "You should be modeling or something."

She got offended at Michael's arrogance. "I don't need you to tell me what to do with my life. We believe that the women were murdered as a direct result of dealings with your daughter."

"What do you mean, dealings with my daughter? My daughter is only five."

"We know," said Detective Andrews. "We believe Coretta James may have had this man, Stephen Davis, murder Karen Atkinson because she wouldn't cooperate at a kindergarten, and they killed a potential witness named Jasmine Reese. Look at the pictures."

The detectives showed Michael pictures of Mrs. Atkinson with a broken neck and Jasmine Reese with a hole in her head.

"Now, are you sure you don't know this man?" repeated the detective.

"I'm sure," restated Michael.

At that point, Michael tried to enter the elevator, but was blocked by Detective Gentry.

"Are you gonna let one incident in your past, one that I'm sure was probably an unfortunate accident, cause you to let a murderer walk the streets?" she asked.

"You don't get shot 10 times by accident," retorted Michael. "Let me tell you something else, sister. The police are nothing but an organization of murderers. They were formed to keep blacks in line who thought they were free back in the day. For years, they have murdered, lynched, and intimidated blacks in America. If they didn't torture us on the streets, then they tortured us in jail. The police have killed tens of millions of blacks in this country, with the help and consent of the government. You guys are hired murderers, just like the man in that picture, the only difference is that you do it with the blessing of the government. Now if you don't mind, I'm going upstairs."

Michael tossed a card towards the detectives, bearing the name of one of Coretta's attorneys. "The next time you speak with me, make sure you do it through my attorney."

Finished speaking, Michael entered the elevator and headed towards his condo. The two stunned detectives just stood there.

"That man just went off the deep end," said Detective Andrews. "Nobody asked him for his version of history. I've never shot anyone that wasn't trying to shoot me first. All police are *not* crooked."

"I agree, but the man is passionate about the way he feels."

"Yeah, so passionate, he's willing to let a murderer walk the streets," said Detective Andrews in disgust. "He's just as much a criminal as the man that pulled the trigger."

"I don't agree with that," said Detective Gentry. "No matter how wrong he is, I admire a black man that takes a stand."

"Well, you ready for an old-fashioned stake out?" asked Detective Andrews. "Until we can convince a judge to give us a search warrant, I guess we have to camp out. Starting tomorrow, we stake out Coretta James' mansion until we can catch Stephen or get something concrete. Get some sleep. We'll get started in the morning."

Meanwhile, Michael had made way up the elevator to his condo. Although he made a big speech earlier, he was very shaken by the pictures of the dead women, and the thought of Stephen being the killer frightened him even more. Walking inside the apartment, he found Myra watching television.

"Hi, Myra. Where's my baby girl?"

"Asleep. She had a long day, her first day of school, and she fell asleep right here, next to me."

He went in the bedroom to see Brittany, kissed his pretty daughter on the forehead, and then put his bags away. He was tired, mentally and physically.

"Long night, huh?" she asked.

"Very long. If only you knew."

"Try me."

Michael was about to ask Myra a question when Coretta called him on his cell phone.

"I hear you had a special time with Barbara," she said, "and I guess you aren't in a hurry for your money."

"I figured I could pick it up tomorrow," he replied. "I'm beat."

"Stephen told me you got a bonus. Did she treat you right?"

"Stephen can't hold water," he replied. "I haven't even looked to see what she gave me, but you told me I get half of your fee plus all tips and bonuses."

"And I meant that," said Coretta. "Tomorrow, I need you to fly to San Francisco to see Susan Chandler. She saw you on TV with Barbara and can't wait to meet you in person."

"Coretta, I'm beat. Can we make it another day?"

"No way. Get use to it. There's a large market out there. Besides, you don't have to go out with her. She just wants to spend a little time with you, if you know what I mean. Be ready at 9 a.m."

Coretta hung up the phone, and Michael walked back towards his room, but stopped to talk to Myra first. He sat on the couch and leaned back.

"Can I get you something?" asked Myra.

"Yea, do we have any bottled water?"

"Definitely." She walked into the kitchen for the water and came back, sitting down.

"So," started Michael, "how much do you really know about Coretta?"

"I don't know her extremely well, but she's tight with my sister. She's always been kind to me. She's just so intense—she likes everything to flow in a certain order. Why do you ask?"

Michael hesitated.

"Do you think she could kill someone? Does she appear like that to you?"

"I don't know," Myra said slowly. "I guess I never thought about it."

"So you've never known her to hurt anyone?"

"I don't know anything about Coretta's business, other than the little things she asks me to do. Michael, is something wrong?"

Michael didn't want to say too much. "Nothing," he replied. "I'm going to bed."

"Michael, are you happy right now?"

"Why do you ask that?"

"Because you seem to be searching for something. Searching is fine, but searching in the wrong places can cause even more problems."

"I guess I'm trying to make up for the year I lost. I think I was dead for a year."

"Dead? How so?"

Michael had never talked about what happened to him during the time he was living in downtown LA, but he felt the need to get it off his chest.

"My wife was killed in a car accident," he said, and I was the driver. We had been to a celebration, at least, it appeared to be a celebration, but I got too drunk. I drank more before with no problem, but for some reason that night, I blacked out. The next thing I know, I wake up in the hospital, handcuffed to the rail of the bed, my wife is dead, and I'm being charged. When I beat the charges, I just grabbed Brittany and left. I had no idea where I was going, I just left.

"I wandered for days, somewhere between dead and alive—physically alive, but my spirit—my wife—was gone. I never considered suicide. I don't believe in that, but I guess I was trying to kill myself subconsciously. It was horrible. I had my daughter in the back alleys, in the slums, in the crack houses—anywhere we could go to get away.

"I tried to smoke my trouble away. I couldn't get over the fact that I, *I* had killed Sheila, the only woman I've ever loved."

Michael's eyes became red and watery as he paused. Myra simply let him talk until he was done.

"We lived on the streets for what seemed like months. I think Brittany took care of me more than I took care of her. I then started to receive welfare. I sold my car and spent all my savings and all my daughter's savings. Welfare checks and Food Stamps were our salvation, but I usually traded them for crack. We finally ended up in a hole-in-a-wall hotel. That got us off the streets, but I think that was worse," he confessed. "I had crack parties all night long. I don't have any idea how I kept Brittany. I would fall asleep, not knowing where I was, let alone, where she was. I would just wake up in the morning, and she would always be there. I can't explain it. And then Kenneth finds us and we got out of that hellhole." He sighed deeply.

"I'm sorry," said Myra. She felt a deep sense of compassion for Michael and his daughter.

"I've never shared that with anyone," he said. "Now you know my background. I went from the top of the world to the bottom of the barrel. I don't know why I'm so blessed. I lost everything except my mind and my daughter."

"Come to church with me Sunday. You and Brittany. You'll enjoy it."

Michael thought for a second, then answered, "Why not?"

He then went into his bedroom and Myra stayed watching TV. He showered, washing the residue of sex off his body that had been there for hours, set his alarm for 7, and lay down, feeling a sense of relief to get some of his past off his chest. He instantly fell asleep and dreamed. Sheila came to him in a dream.

"Come with me, Michael," she said.

"No! No! No!" he shouted, getting louder each time.

Myra heard him scream and ran into the room to find Michael in a cold sweat. She wrapped her arms around him and placed his head across her chest. Michael eventually fell back asleep.

At 6:00 a.m., she woke up and left Michael, who was looking very peaceful and attractive to her just lying there in his bed. She exited the room as he rolled over and opened his eyes briefly. Myra needed to dress Brittany for her second day in school. Brittany ran into her father's room as soon as she was dressed.

"Daddy!" she yelled, "I missed you."

"I missed you, too, baby. What's Daddy's little sweetheart been doing?"

"Daddy, I'm in school now. I'm a big girl, Daddy."

"Yes, you are. Daddy is so proud of you. Tonight, we'll go have ice cream to celebrate."

"Can Myra come too, Daddy?"

Michael looked at Myra standing in the doorway.

"Yea, baby, Myra can come to, that is, if she doesn't have anything else to do."

Myra looked back in a daze. "Nothing going on. I'd love to. Come on, Brittany, I've got to get you to school."

They left after Brittany kissed her father good-bye.

Chapter 20

OUTSIDE CORETTA JAMES' MANSION, DETECTIVES Andrews and Gentry set up a stakeout. They underestimated the size of the mansion and its distance away from the streets.

"These binoculars will come in handy," said Detective Gentry. "This woman lives in a palace."

The two of them sat back and prepared for a long day.

At 9 that morning, Coretta arrived at Michael's condo with Manu. Michael didn't pack anything but a few personal items, thinking he was only to be in San Francisco for a few hours.

Coretta knocked and Michael answered the door. She walked right in.

"Just wanted to see what the old place looked like," she said. "The decorator did a good job remodeling the place."

"Yeah," he replied, "it looks nice, but don't we have to be leaving?"

"Don't worry, we're taking my jet. We're going to leave out of Burbank Airport, where I keep it parked."

"You own a *jet* to?" he asked in amazement.

"A twin-engine Cessna. It seats up to 20, luxury all the way. You crossed that line with Myra yet?"

Michael didn't answer but just looked at Coretta in a funny way.

"Oh, by the way, here's your money. Job well done. You ready?"

Michael nodded and they walked out to the limo, where Manu was waiting to take them to the Burbank Airport for the flight to San Francisco.

After about 30 minutes in the air, they landed at a small airport outside of San Francisco near Oakland.

"So what's this Susan Chandler look like?" he asked.

"She's rich," said Coretta. "Real good for you. She's looking for a Mandingo."

"A Mandingo? Shit, I ain't no Mandingo."

"Come on," said Coretta, "Manu and I have business here so you have plenty of time to get to know Susan—very well."

Two people approached them as they disembarked from the plane, a man and a woman. The woman began speaking.

"Hi, I'm Susan. You must be Michael," she said. "It's a pleasure to meet you."

Susan was 5 feet 4, had a pretty face, nice body, and was very white. Michael excused himself and pulled Coretta off to the side to speak privately with her.

"I don't do white," he flatly stated.

"What do you mean, you don't do white?"

"I just don't do white," he repeated. "I did a couple back in the day, but it's been years."

"What's the matter? A woman is a woman. The only color that should matter to you is the green in her wallet."

"I don't do white," he persisted.

Susan noticed the conversation was getting heated and wondered what was going on. Suddenly Coretta changed and went ballistic on Michael.

"Nigger, are you crazy? What kind of backward ass hillbilly logic do you have? The only thing that should matter is that now your broke ass can pay your bills."

"No woman talks to me like that," he replied angrily. "I told you what I will and will not do. Now take it or leave it."

"Well, you better figure out how to get back to LA," Coretta snapped, "'cause you're not riding in *my* plane."

"I guess you think you have the only plane in the world," he said hotly as he walked past the plane and Manu, who looked at Coretta, seeking permission to take care of Michael. Coretta shook her head no as Michael walked into the small airport.

"I want to charter a plane and a pilot," he said to the clerk.

"Where are you going?" asked the attendant.

"LA. I'll take the next thing smoking."

Michael sat and waited on the next charter out while Coretta tried to smooth things over with Susan.

"What's the problem?" Susan asked. "Your man has cold feet?"

"No, we just had a different view about a few things. I'll get things straight and we'll be back to see you real soon."

Coretta was so upset that she instructed her pilot to turn around and return to LA. Michael waited for his charter and finally arrived in LA at 2 that afternoon. Coretta was steaming on the flight home.

"I can't believe that motherfucker embarrassed me like that, talking about he don't do white!" She was seething when suddenly the phone rang on the plane. The pilot answered.

"Coretta," said the pilot, "it's Monique Woods."

"What the fuck does she want? Tell her I'm busy and I'll call her back."

The pilot relayed the message, but Monique told him it was urgent. Coretta looked sideways at the pilot, changed her mind, and snatched the phone.

"What is it? I'm busy and can't talk now."

"Coretta, I need to know who you've got to strip for Bobby's party. It starts at 9, and we still don't have anyone."

"Monique, I haven't had time to—" Coretta stopped in mid sentence. "Monique, I've got the perfect guy."

"Is he fine?"

"*Real* fine," she answered. "Now, where is it again?"

"It's at the Golden Palace in Inglewood."

"Do they still have that levitating floor over there?"

"I think so."

"Well, how would *you* like a man coming out of a cake?"

"Oh, yeah," purred Monique. "Bobby will love that. But have him there no later than 8:45 because these girls will be wild and ready to go by 9."

Coretta disconnected the phone with Monique and instantly called Michael, who hadn't left the airport yet.

"Michael, sweetheart, can you ever forgive me?" she beseeched him. "I don't know what got into me, talking to you like that. If you have convictions, you have convictions."

"I don't know about you, woman," he yelled. "I'm seriously considering not dealing with you no more."

"Don't be that way," she pleaded. "I've got a gig for you that's easy money and you won't have to sleep with anyone. All you have to do is dance."

"Dance? What kind of dance?" he asked suspiciously.

"Only for a few girls," Coretta explained. "Come on, it'll be fun. And *very* profitable. As a special bonus, you get to keep 100 percent of the proceeds. I'll have Stephen and Manu pick you up at 8 and take you right over to the place. It's easy money, Michael, I promise you."

Michael quickly considered it and agreed to do it, but with a hint of misgiving. "Okay," he consented. "I'll be ready."

Michael didn't arrive until 2 and at 3 p.m., Kenneth drove over to LAX to pick up William and Susie Jackson, Michael's former in-laws. After picking them up from the airport, the three of them went straight to his house.

"How was your flight?" Kenneth asked.

"There was a lot of turbulence," answered Mrs. Jackson. "Planes really scare me. So are we going to see Michael?"

"I'm not exactly sure where he lives," said Kenneth. "I've got his number on caller ID. I can call the number and hopefully get directions to their house."

"I still can't believe that you are just now contacting us to let us know what's going on," Mrs. Jackson complained. "We could have gotten this process started by now had we known before. Do you have an attorney that we can use?"

"My wife works for one of the largest law firms in the city," he replied. "I'm not sure she would take the case, but I know she can refer me to someone who can handle this kind of case."

"Isn't your wife kind of loyal to Michael?" Mrs. Jackson inquired. "You think she's willing to forget about their past?"

"*We're* family, and *I* wear the pants around this house, ain't that right, Mr. Jackson?"

"That's right, son," said William Jackson compliantly.

"Shut up, Bill," said Mrs. Jackson. "You know *I* call the shots around our house. You couldn't find your nuts if I didn't tell you where they were."

Just as he had done during their entire 30-year marriage, Mr. Jackson clammed up and refused to stand up to his wife. Plain and simple, he was a "yes man." Kenneth looked at Mr. Jackson, but didn't respond. After that, he drove silently towards his house to wait for his wife to arrive and prepare the Jackson's room. Kenneth hadn't bothered to inform his wife about the Jacksons staying there.

Michael took a cab home and arrived at 3. Myra was home, preparing to pick up Brittany. Michael walked in as Myra finished preparing an after-school snack.

"Let's go see my daughter's school. We promised her some ice cream," he announced.

Myra was happy to be joining the outing with Michael and his daughter. She had grown quite attached to Brittany and Michael. In the back of her mind, she pondered the possibility of the three of them becoming a family. Myra quickly put away the snack she prepared and left with Michael. Driving in his Mercedes, they headed towards Brittany's school. He was excited to see his daughter in a school setting, and to just see her.

At 2, Coretta arrived back at her mansion and noticed an unmarked car parked outside of her gates. She had her driver pull directly beside the car and she rolled down her window, motioning for the detectives to do likewise.

"Hello, detectives," she said to Andrews and Gentry. "Interested in buying some property in this part of town are you? I hear the house down the street is for sale, but I think it's out of your price range."

"Any idea why we're having such a hard time getting a warrant?" asked Detective Andrews. "I heard you and Judge Reynolds are in business together—all kinds of business."

"Why, detective, whatever do you mean?" she smiled sweetly. "Jim—I mean Judge Reynolds—I never met the man. If you're out here this evening, I'll have my cook drop you off a snack. Donuts, is that what you people eat?"

With that, Coretta rolled up her window and her limo passed through the large gate to her mansion.

"The day we slap some cuffs on that woman will be a happy day for me," said Detective Gentry. "So, do we stay here?"

"No," her partner replied. "We need to find a way to tap her phone or get some concrete evidence to bring her down."

They took off, having accomplished nothing sitting in front of Coretta's mansion, and tried to come up with another plan to catch Coretta James and Stephen Davis.

At 5 that afternoon, Cheryl Bolling arrived home, tired from a long day in court. In her kitchen, she found Susie Jackson preparing collard greens and smothered pork chops for her husband.

Needless to say, Cheryl was very surprised.

"Hello, Cheryl," said Susie. "It's very good to see you again. I haven't seen you since the funeral."

Cheryl went and embraced Susie and kissed William, who was sitting down enjoying his chops.

"What are you guys doing here?" she asked surprised. "How long have you been here?"

"Which questions do you want us to answer first?" smiled Susie. "What are we doing here, or how long have we been here?"

"Whichever," said Cheryl.

"We got here this afternoon," said Susie. "We came here because we heard our granddaughter was here with her sorry ass daddy. We plan on taking her from that bum and bringing her back to New York with us."

"Where is my husband?" asked Cheryl. "Is he here?"

"He's in the back," volunteered William. "He said you might be willing to represent us or maybe someone from your firm will work with us."

Cheryl didn't say anything but walked straight into the den where her husband was watching television.

"Kenneth, why did you bring them here?"

"They have a right to see Brittany," he replied, "and Michael hasn't been willing to let them."

"How do you know he's not willing? Did you bother to call him?"

"Every time I try to talk to him, he goes off. I had no choice."

"You started that Ken," Cheryl accused him. "Your obsession with that man has gone too far."

"What obsession? I'm not obsessed with anyone."

"Really?" she countered. "Your whole adult life has been based around Michael—same school, same job, same shirt, same tie, same everything. Why, if Michael was walking and came to a sudden stop, you would find your head stuck up his ass. You've followed that man everywhere and now that he's about to find himself, you all of a sudden want to turn on him. I don't think you ever really cared *for* Michael. I think you want to *be* Michael."

Kenneth was seriously offended by his wife's comments. He stood up to look her in the eye and realized the Jacksons were listening.

"I don't *want* to be that drug addict," he retorted, "and why are you talking to your husband like that? Don't I deserve more respect than that?"

Cheryl calmed down.

"I'm sorry, that was harsh, but you've been so down on Michael lately. The man lost his wife and all his possessions. If he loses his daughter, it may break him."

"My main concern is that little girl," said Kenneth. "What if he gives up and decides to run away again? What will happen to Brittany then?"

"I don't think that's going to happen," she replied. "Michael seems to be finding himself."

"Yeah, but what about my grandbaby?" interrupted Mrs. Jackson. "What about what's best for her?"

"Brittany adores her father," Cheryl replied. "She always has and always will. If you take her from him, she will rebel against you all. I can't believe you, Ken. Michael has come through so many times for you, for us. You all know that Michael has a heart of gold and would do anything for anyone."

"Anyone except his daughter," said Ken, "and I'm not going to sit back and let him ruin her life."

"Neither am I," asserted Susie Jackson.

After saying that, Mrs. Jackson bumped her husband.

"Oh, neither am I," he chimed in.

"Well, I'm not going to be a party to this," Cheryl declared. "Until Michael shows me he's a detriment to that child, I'm going to stand behind him."

"You want him too, don't you?" Kenneth accused his wife. "You're just like all the rest of them. You want to be with him too. Well, you can have him."

"What are you talking about? You are *not* the man I thought you were. I don't know who you are."

Cheryl grabbed her purse and left the house, looking for a motel. She had had enough of her husband, at least for now.

At around 7 that night, Michael and Brittany and Myra were in a park having fun when he unexpectedly got a call from Michelle.

"You just disappeared," said Michelle, after Michael answered. "How is your daughter?"

"She's fine," he replied.

"How was Chicago?" asked Michelle.

"Eventful, to say the least. What's been happening with you?"

"Just work," she said. "So when am I going to see you again?"

"Maybe tonight," Michael suggested. "I've got to work, but it should only be for a short time. Maybe afterwards?"

"You must tell me more about this work you do. It sounds very interesting."

"It can be," he replied.

Myra was playing with Brittany, but was curious as to who Michael was talking to.

"You got plans for the weekend?" asked Michelle.

"None that I know of, but I need to spend some time with Brittany. I've been gone a lot lately."

"No chance another girl can hang around?" she inquired.

"You can never have enough pretty women," Michael responded gallantly. "Let's do something Sunday for sure. I know I'm not busy then."

Myra was disappointed that Michael forgot that he promised to take her to church on Sunday.

"Ah, man, I forgot," he said. "I promised Myra I would go to church with her on Sunday."

"Who's Myra?" asked Michelle. "Another admirer?"

"No, not at all. She's Brittany's nanny. Hey, I've got an idea. Why don't you go to church with us? I know Myra won't mind."

"You sure? I don't want to step on anybody's toes."

"Positive," said Michael. "We'll make a day out of it. Let me call you later, baby, because I'm in the park with my daughter. I'll call you when I'm done."

Myra was disappointed, not only at the fact that she was considered just a nanny, but also because Michael invited Michelle to church, but she didn't let that affect her attitude.

"You don't mind that I invited someone to go to church Sunday, do you?" asked Michael.

"Not at all," said Myra cheerfully. "The more, the merrier."

"Cool," said Michael. "Let's wrap it up, ladies. I've got an appointment at 9."

Michael chased Brittany as she screamed in laughter while Myra still enjoyed the company, though she felt somewhat slighted by Michael.

They arrived home at 7:30. Since Michael was to be picked up at 8, he took a quick shower and changed his clothes. Brittany was tired out and fell asleep in the car. Myra took care of Brittany and then turned her attention to Michael.

"I'm going to make dinner for you to eat later," she said, "in case you're hungry when you finish working."

"Don't go to any trouble."

"It's no trouble, it's my pleasure. I'll leave it out in case you're hungry."

"Thanks," said Michael.

Chapter 21

HE LEFT THE CONDO AT 7:57 and arrived downstairs, where Coretta was waiting outside with Stephen and Manu.

"I didn't know you were going," Michael said to Coretta.

"I'm not," she replied. "I just came to bring you your costume." Then she reached in a small bag and pulled out a pair of red silk male thongs. She snapped them in her hand and then gave them to Michael.

"What is this?" said an astonished Michael.

"That's your costume. Remember, you're a stripper tonight."

"I'm not coming out of these am I?"

"I'll leave that up to you. Just put on a good show. I've got business to take care of."

Coretta kissed Michael on the cheek and shyly smiled at Stephen. Michael looked at the tiny red thongs and wondered what he got himself into. He also remembered what the police said about Coretta and Stephen and was very leery about his trip. Coretta exited the limo and Stephen was unusually quiet.

"Never seen you guys this quiet before," said Michael. It was then that he noticed that Stephen was wearing another disguise.

"What are you gonna be tomorrow, a nurse?" he asked.

Stephen didn't acknowledge Michael but just continued to ride and look at him as if he didn't exist. As they pull up to the Golden Palace, Monique Woods meets the limo. Traffic was bad so they arrived 10 minutes late.

"You're late," said an anxious Monique. "OK, so you're the stripper? Come on, let's go."

Michael jumped out of the car, ready for his night of easy money.

Across the street, Channel 5 News was covering a high school function as a special interest event for the nightly news. It was very boring and the reporter had a hard time finding angles to report on. He and his cameraman sat outside on the hood of their news truck, waiting for something to happen.

Inside the Golden Palace, Michael was ushered in the back and through the lower level of the stage, where he climbed into a cake to make his grand entrance. He was wearing the red bikini thong, but kept his pants on to leave something to the imagination. Stephen informed Michael that he was going to Burger King and would be right back. Michael heard the cheering crowd of women and couldn't wait to get out there in front of them.

"Those ladies are hot tonight," he remarked. "They're ready for the show."

"They're *past* ready," said Monique, "now come on, let's get this party started. When the music starts, the cake will rise to the stage and then the rest is up to you."

Michael got inside the cake and Monique went upstairs to MC the festivities. As she stepped out, the crowd was at a fever pitch.

"Alright, alright, calm down, ladies!" shouted Monique. "This is the moment you've all been waiting for. May I present the one, the only—Michael!"

The cake slowly began to rise to the top of the stage. By now, Michael had taken his shirt off, but held it in his hand. As the cake fully emerged, "Nasty Girl" began playing and Michael sprung from the cake, twirling his shirt and dancing to the beat. The roar from the crowd was deafening. Bills of all denominations flew through the air—tens and twenties, fives, and hundreds—landing on the stage. Michael twirled his shirt around as Monique, the DJ, yelled, "Take that shit off!"

The crowd responded, "Take that shit off!"

After they repeated it a couple of times, Michael threw the shirt into the crowd and they went wild. Then he slowly reached down to undo his trousers and the crowd roared louder. First, he took off his belt and lowered his trousers to his knees.

"Come on, ladies," Monique shouted, "tell him to take that shit off. Take that shit off. Take that shit off, again."

After the fourth time, Michael pulled off his trousers and started to work the crowd into a frenzy. Money soared through the air and landed on the stage from all directions like confetti.

This is the easiest money ever, he thought, looking at all the money at his feet. He decided to give them a thrill and bent over to pick up some money.

It can't be this easy, he thought. *Maybe I judged Coretta too harshly.*

Michael danced around, grabbing money, and started to get close to the edge of the stage in the dark room. The crowd reached for him, but he stayed out of their grasp. He looked at the corner of the stage where a woman in blue size 14 pumps had her feet on the stage, but they burst through the side because they were so big. The beat picked up and so did Michael's dance.

"Shake it, baby," said a masculine voice.

What the fuck? Michael wondered.

As the flashing strobe light circled the room, Michael took a hard look at some of the women.

"These are a fucking bunch of dudes," he said, "fucking transvestites."

Sure enough, Monique's sister Bobbi was really a man and all the women in there screaming for Michael were men. Michael was in shock as the crowd tried to get closer to him. He didn't know what to do. The exit was not blocked, but the aisle was packed and there was only a small opening visible. Michael went to the back of the stage, took a running start, and then headed full speed for the floor, leaping transvestites, who thought it was part of the show. He landed on the floor, and they immediately went for his thong.

The thong was almost ripped off, but he managed to snatch it up and ran towards the exit. A small transsexual was standing near the door, trying to stop him. Michael's shoulder knocked the man and flattened him, making his way to the exit and busting out the door with at least 70 transsexuals following in mad pursuit.

"Come back, baby, we won't hurt you," yelled one transsexual.

"Yeah, come back, bikini red," yelled another.

The door flew open as Michael exited the building. Dashing around a corner, he caught the attention of the newsmen across the street that saw all the commotion.

"Randy," commanded the reporter, "focus your camera across the street."

Michael was running down the street as the limo passed by coming from Burger King, with Stephen laughing uproariously inside.

"Let his bitch ass run for a while," he laughed. "This is the craziest shit I've ever seen."

Michael was being chased by transsexuals, filmed by Channel 5, and Stephen refused to open the door.

"Man, open the door!" Michael screamed as the limo made no attempt to outrun him, but neither did the door open.

"Man, open the fucking door!" he yelled again. "Let me in the car."

"I figured you wanted to get in shape," Stephen chuckled, "and I thought I would help you out."

After a few more minutes, Stephen opened the door and allowed Michael to jump in. By then, Michael was totally exhausted, sweating profusely, and furious.

"Did you get all that Randy?" asked the news reporter.

"Every drop," says the cameraman. "You're not going to put this on television, are you?"

"Watch me," said the reporter. "Come on and get a close up so I can tape the segment."

"Was that a bunch of men chasing another man wearing a red thong? People will have to see this to believe it. Let's go analyze the tape for tonight's news."

Stephen was laughing loudly as Michael fumed in the car, sitting and wearing only his red bikini thong and socks. Michael saw no humor in the fiasco.

"Take me to see Coretta," he yelled. "I can't believe she set me up like that."

"Red bikini drawers," laughed Stephen. "We should have let you run for a few more minutes and see how fast those sissies were. That one on your tail was as big as a linebacker. I bet he could easily take off that dress and tackle somebody."

Michael was totally humiliated and planned to have it out with Coretta.

The limo traveled towards her mansion. Stephen continued to laugh and enjoy the Whopper with cheese he purchased from Burger King as he teased Michael. "Want some fries?" he said, still chuckling.

At 10 that evening, Detective Gentry called Detective Andrews. "I'm going back over to Ms. James' mansion around midnight. I'll park at a distance and walk up. If anything is happening, hopefully, I'll see it."

"Who going with you?"

"No one. I've got my binoculars and my high-powered camera. As soon as I see the suspect, I'll call for backup."

"Be careful. These are dangerous people, and you saw what they are capable of doing."

"I'll be careful."

Detective Gentry prepared for her late-night vigil as Michael arrived at Coretta's mansion at 11 p.m., furious at Coretta.

As soon as the limo parked, Michael rushed out, with Manu and Stephen close behind him. He stormed inside, shouting, "Coretta! Coretta! Where are you?"

"Why are you shouting, darling?" she said, sitting in her huge parlor. "Coretta is right here, baby."

"Why did you embarrass me like that?" he demanded. "What were you trying to prove, huh?"

"Well, when you're asked to do something, you do it," she answered innocently. "I don't respond well to 'no.'"

"What are you talking about? When did I tell you no?"

"You told my client no. When you told my client no, you told me no. It took years for me to establish myself with Susan Chandler. She is one of the leading cosmetic distributors in America, and you embarrassed me totally with her today. I've spent all evening smoothing it over. Imagine, a man in the 21st century still worried about black and white. I told you I see only one color, green, my brother, green. And for the record, you look cute in your red thong. I hate that I missed the show."

"Give me something to put on."

"Sorry, I'm fresh out of clothes. Your clothes and your money will get to me tonight. I'll make sure you get them tomorrow. I'm preparing another trip for you."

At that moment, Channel 5 news came on Coretta's TV, and Michael, watching it, saw himself running in red bikini thongs through Inglewood. Stephen laughed again.

"It's even funnier when you see it on TV," he snickered.

Coretta sat straight-faced, watching Michael running from the burly transsexuals. "Go home, take a shower," she said. "I've got another appointment tomorrow for you."

"You won't see me tomorrow," he replied, approaching Coretta. "I quit right now, you bitch. I don't ever want to see you again."

At that moment, Coretta nodded her head and Manu delivered a powerful punch to Michael's sternum. He hit the floor, gasping for air.

Coretta stood over him talking. "*Nobody* quits me. I own your ass. The only way you leave me is in a body bag."

She yelled to Stephen and Manu, "Pick him up and take him home."

Michael continued to gasp for air from the blow delivered by the powerful martial arts specialist.

"I'll see you tomorrow, Michael," Coretta reiterated, "and Michael, be ready to work."

Manu grabbed Michael roughly and threw him across his shoulder, carrying him to the limo, then literally threw him in the car. Michael was smarting, both physically and emotionally, and Stephen rubbed salt into the wounds by saying, "I knew you were gonna fuck up, pretty boy. It was just a matter of time. It's gonna get worse, too, before it gets better. I'm going to make sure you mess up and if you keep fucking up, boss lady is gonna give me the go-ahead, and I'm gonna take your ass out, *slowly*."

With those words of encouragement, the limo took off and Stephen kicked the already-hurt Michael several times. Michael was in far too much pain to even consider defending himself or fighting back. They arrived at condo at midnight. Manu and Stephen carried him to the Concierge's Desk.

"Michael Alexander in 435," said Stephen. "As you can see, he doesn't have his ID on him."

"What happened to him?" asked the concierge.

"He had too much to drink," Stephen replied. "He got drunk and started taking off his clothes, so we brought him home so he could get some sleep."

Several occupants of the building passed by and saw Michael in his red thongs being carried to his room. The concierge buzzed the glass door and Stephen and Manu went to the elevator for the ride to the 4th floor. They got to #435 and rang the doorbell. Myra, looking through the peephole, saw Michael being carried, so she opened the door. At that moment, Manu and Stephen threw him to the floor, then Stephen kicked Michael again for good measure.

Stephen's parting words as he exited were, "See you later, bitch."

"Michael!" screamed Myra.

Michael moaned in pain and rubbed his hand across his stomach area. Myra saw a big bruise forming.

"Oh my God," Myra said, shocked.

She quickly got a towel from the bathroom to wrap around him, then rubbed some medicine on his skin. Michael slowly and painfully began to talk.

"What is this stuff you're putting on me?"

"It's Grenada Nutmeg Oil. The Matah brothers who I know distribute it exclusively. It's supposed to heal anything instantly."

She rubbed the oil across Michael's stomach and afterwards applied a bandage across his sternum. Then she applied some ice to his head, toweled him off with a damp sponge, and offered him some aspirin, but he declined that because he tried to avoid medication.

Although still in pain, he began to feel better. But when he tried to get up, pain shot through his body, so he just lay there. Myra got a pillow and laid his head across her lap.

"I'm glad Brittany is asleep," he said. "I wouldn't want her to see me like this."

"Yea, I know. Seeing you in pain like this would have freaked her out."

"I'm not talking about that," Michael replied. "I'm glad she didn't see me with these red thongs on. That would have really scared her."

They both laughed, but Michael stiffled the laughter because it made his side hurt.

"Tomorrow, we need to get you to a doctor," Myra said.

"I'll be fine, besides, I hate doctors."

Michael shut his eyes, and Myra stroked his curly locks as he tried to relax. He fell asleep in her arms, finding comfort in her touch even though the pain remained intense.

Chapter 22

DETECTIVE GENTRY ARRIVED IN CORETTA'S neighborhood at 12:05 a.m. She parked about a half mile away and walked back. At 12:17, the limo returned from dropping Michael off and pulled up to the gate. The guard buzzed them in. Detective Gentry couldn't see through the car's tinted windows, but followed behind it through the huge gate, hid behind the guard booth, and slipped onto the grounds unnoticed. Checking her semi-automatic revolver, she cautiously walked slowly towards the front of the mansion. She saw Stephen and Manu exiting the limo, but didn't recognize Stephen because he was wearing a disguise. She immediately confronted the men.

"Alright, hands up!" she shouted.

Stephen made a move to reach for his gun, but Detective Gentry was ready. "Try it and you die. On the ground, both of you. Hands behind your head."

Searching their pockets, she found the 9mm Stephen carried, along with other miscellaneous items. As she began to dial her partner for backup, she heard an ominous voice behind her.

"Drop it!"

Slowly, she put down her gun. Manu and Stephen got off the ground and took their hardware back from the detective. Stephen looked over and saw Carlos holding a gun at Detective Gentry's head.

After all the things that Coretta had done to him, including supergluing his penis to his leg, Carlos still tried to find his way back into Coretta's good graces. Stephen pulled his gun on Detective Gentry as well and ordered her to go inside the mansion where Coretta was on a business call. Seeing them, she immediately hung up.

"Well, I see we have an uninvited guest," Coretta remarked. "Would you like some tea, my dear?"

"I saw her on the monitor and came up behind her and took her," said Carlos, brownnosing for points. "What do you want me to do with her?"

"Nothing," replied Coretta. "You're excused."

Stephen held a gun to Detective Gentry's head while Manu also watched her closely. Carlos went back to monitor the ground on the ultra modern surveillance equipment that Coretta used.

"So what can I do for you, Detective Gentry, is it? Are you looking for something or someone special?"

Detective Gentry pointed at Stephen in disguise. "I guess that's Stephen Davis," she stated matter-of-factly, "the murderer and rapist all in one."

"Does it look like him?" Coretta asked. "And why call names? You may hurt his feelings."

At that moment, Detective Andrews called Gentry on her cell phone. The phone beeped. She managed to turn it on without drawing attention to herself. Detective Andrews heard the talking in the background, but couldn't make out the voices. Stephen came from behind her with a white rag that he placed to her nose and held her as she squirmed. She fought briefly, but dropped unconscious quickly. Then he checked her pockets and found the cell phone on and panicked.

"They heard us talking, boss lady," he said.

"Get her out of here. Hurry, before we have company."

Stephen and Manu took Detective Gentry to the SUV and pulled off. Coretta stayed behind and waited for the company.

⇥⊚ ⇥⊚ ⇥⊚

DETECTIVE ANDREWS KNEW where Detective Gentry had camped out and once he had gathered up several men, drove to Coretta's mansion. However, Stephen and Manu had already taken the unconscious detective to one of Coretta's other properties and waited for instructions. Coretta braced for a visit and within minutes, she got one. Five police cars came to her mansion. They saw Detective Gentry's black Mustang parked about half a mile away. The guard at the gate refused to open the gates, but yelled out to Detective Andrews.

"You have to have a pass to get in through this gate," he informed them.

Detective Andrews aimed his 9mm gun out the window and pointed it at the guard. "This is my pass."

"Looks good to me," said the guard, who instantly opened the gate.

The 5 police cars drove quickly to Coretta's mansion, then all ten officers rushed to the front door.

"Open up! Police!" they yelled.

Coretta herself opened the door.

"Where is she?" demanded Detective Andrews, pushing Coretta slightly.

"Where is who?" replied a cool Coretta.

By then, the police had their guns drawn.

"Detective Gentry, where is she?"

"Why would she be here?" responded Coretta. "This is not her residence."

"That's odd," Detective Andrews countered. "I know she was here. I heard voices in the background."

"Oh, you heard voices in the background? Background of what?"

"I called her on her cell phone," said Detective Andrews. "I heard voices."

"Does that mean she was here?" asked Coretta. "You gentlemen are welcome to look around."

The detectives panned out to search Coretta's mansion and the other houses on the compound for any clues to the missing detective's whereabouts.

Carlos switched the tape from earlier in the evening and destroyed it so Coretta couldn't be incriminated.

After about an hour, the detectives regrouped, not having found a thing.

"Not a trace," said one police officer. "If she was here, she's not here now."

"Where is she?" yelled Detective Andrews. "What have you done to her?"

"Detective, lower your voice," said Coretta. "I have tenants."

"Her car is half a mile down the road from here," he stated. "She came to stake out your house."

"Well, maybe she's somewhere in the neighborhood. Maybe she found a *real* criminal and decided to leave innocent people alone."

"If anything happens to her, so help me, I'll kill you myself, you sick, twisted bitch."

"Detective, calm down," admonished one of the other officers. "We all want her, but we've got to go through the right channels."

"The right channels, yeah, right," said a frustrated Detective Andrews. "By the time we go through the right channels, that girl will be dead. *Dead*, Detective. Do you want that on your conscious?—Because I don't."

At that moment, a white man walked into Coretta's parlor. "I think it's time you gentlemen left," he stated.

"Who are you?" asked the Captain.

"I'm Kevin Fuller, Ms. James' attorney. Whatever you're looking for, you haven't found so I suggest you leave before I place harassment charges against you." With that, he opened the door for them.

"Good night, gentlemen," he said.

Detective Andrews stayed for a moment to express his feelings to Coretta. "I'm going to get you," he told her in front of her attorney. "I'll leave no stone unturned. I *will* follow you to the ends of the earth, if I have to. You can run, but you can't hide."

Coretta's attorney motioned the irate detective to the door, but Detective Andrews slapped his hand away.

"I know the way, punk!"

He left the house, but they continued to look outside for anything that might lead them to Detective Gentry before it was too late. They thoroughly searched outside Coretta's compound and the gate area, but found nothing, only Detective Gentry's car. Detective Andrews was very worried and blamed himself.

"I should never have let her come alone. If anything happens to her, it's all my fault."

"Why was she here by herself?" the captain asked.

"She wanted to catch Coretta so bad," Detective Andrews replied. "Her sister was raped and she said it scarred her for life. She was obsessed. I knew she was coming, but she didn't give me a chance to change her mind or come with her. I guess she felt it was something she had to do. I've got an idea, but I can't pursue it until in the morning. Meanwhile, let's keep looking."

The detectives searched throughout the night for any clues to the missing detective's whereabouts, but it was useless. They towed her car to the police station in hopes of finding something.

→═◉   →═◉   →═◉

AT 2 A.M., STEPHEN called Coretta. "Boss lady, we're at Ingles. What do you want us to do with her?"

"I'll be there," she said, hanging up the phone.

Coretta knew that her every move would be watched. Fifteen minutes later, her limo pulled away from the mansion heading toward Beverly Hills.

Sure enough, a police car followed close behind Coretta's moving limo. Coretta turned around in the rear seat and taunted the police by waving at them. They followed closely on what turned out to be a wild goose chase, because minutes later, a Mercedes convertible 320 royal blue with matching interior raced out of the complex, heading in the opposite direction, being driven by what appeared to be a man wearing a baseball cap and jeans. That man, of course, was Coretta in disguise.

Unknown to her friends, Detective Gentry was actually very close to the mansion on Ingles Street, a cottage Coretta used for special guests who wanted to be in a private, intimate setting. She checked to see if she had been followed, and then pulled onto the grounds of the beautiful cottage.

Inside, Manu and Stephen were in one room, while Detective Gentry lay on a bed, tied up in a separate room. Coretta entered the cottage where Manu and Stephen awaited her.

"Where is she?" Coretta asked. "Did she wake up yet?"

"I'm not sure," Stephen replied. "We haven't been in there since we tied her up. So what are we going to do with her, boss lady?"

"What do you *want* to do with her?" asked Coretta. "You love to have your pleasure with women, so do it."

"But she's a cop," he countered. "If anybody finds out, we're through."

"If they find out about *any* woman, we're through," Coretta corrected him. "Policewoman or not."

Coretta walked into the room and stared at a nude Detective Gentry lying on the bed, shivering in fear.

"Stephen didn't tell me he exposed all your goods," Coretta said, "but knowing Stephen, I shouldn't have expected anything less. And what a beautiful body you have. That police uniform does nothing for you. You could be one of my girls, if you weren't working for the man."

Coretta leaned over to look more closely at Detective Gentry and rubbed her face with hers and then kissed her across the lips. Detective Gentry bit her lips.

"Ouch," said Coretta, "naughty, naughty."

Then Coretta bent down and kissed Detective Gentry's nipples gently as the detective squirmed in disgust.

"Well," said Coretta, "I wish I could stay, but I've got things to do, and since you've been anxious to meet Stephen Davis, here he is in the flesh."

Coretta stepped aside to reveal a nude Stephen, the pervert of perverts, standing there erect and ready to assault another helpless victim. She grabbed Stephen by the arm before he pounced like a savage animal on the terrified woman.

"Why don't you let Manu have a little pleasure first," she suggested, "and don't forget to clean up the mess."

Detective Gentry had never been in such a totally helpless position before. Her eyes almost popped out of her head with fear as Stephen and Manu began what would be a night of endless assault and then a merciless death.

Coretta left the room, knowing what a vicious and ruthless maniac Stephen was when it came to sex. She almost felt remorseful, but didn't even bother to look back to see the pain of an innocent woman. Stephen was truly in his own element, torturing an innocent woman for his pleasure—something he was all too familiar with.

Across town, a distraught Detective Andrews, with his captain, followed Coretta's limo through the streets. The vehicle seemed to randomly be going back and forth with no apparent destination. Finally, he turned on the siren.

"What are you doing?" the captain asked. "I told you we can't harass that woman."

"Fire me," retorted Detective Andrews.

The limo stopped and the detective jumped out of his car. He verbally attacked the passenger through the rolled down rear window.

"I don't care about your punk ass attorney," he yelled. "Where is my partner?"

The terrified woman turned towards him. She was not Coretta, but had a similar hairstyle.

"She told us to just drive," said the girl. "Just drive as long as we could."

"Dammit! The longer this takes, the harder it will be to find her alive. I got a real bad feeling in the pit of my stomach."

At 3 a.m., Stephen and Manu dragged Detective Gentry's battered, dead body from the bedroom, wrapped it up in a sheet, and tossed it in the SUV.

Coretta emerged from the shadows. "Did you boys have a good time?" she said, pulling back the sheet to view Detective Gentry's body. "Ooh, you boys are brutal. Thank God that's not me."

She had been raped, sodomized, and tortured beyond belief. Coretta did not like any female to challenge her in any way—or any person at all, for that matter. And therefore, she gave Stephen permission to be especially cruel to her.

"Take the body to the beach and weight it down. But before you boys leave, torch the place. Forensic science is strong today. Burn it to the ground."

Manu and Stephen poured kerosene all over the house, and especially in the bedroom, before throwing a Molotov cocktail into the room and rushed out the door, turning the cottage into an instant inferno. Then they drove off towards the beach as Coretta traveled in the opposite direction.

At the beach, they hid the body on Coretta's boat and rode about a mile out in the ocean before throwing the weighted down body overboard. Afterward, they took the boat back to dock and wanted to catch up on some sleep, but before they did, they had a big, leisurely breakfast, not even feeling the slightest remorse over what they had just done. The detective's lifeless body lodged on a reef below the surface of the ocean, a ghastly monument to three extremely sick human beings.

Chapter 23

AT MICHAEL'S CONDO, HE TOSSED and turned all night with Myra at his side. The pain in his sternum was intense. Eventully, he got up to rub his stomach with alcohol, spread more nutmeg oil on his aches and pains, and he took Advil for the relentless pain. Then he went into his room for some shorts and a tee shirt and came back to sit on the couch next to Myra.

"You know, I'm very surprised you're still single," he said. "Women like you don't come around too often. Why don't you have a man?"

"I dated one of those basketball players at UCLA a couple of years ago, but he couldn't wait. He kept wanting me to put out, but I wasn't ready."

"What do you mean, 'put out'?" asked Michael.

"Put out, have sex. I wanted my first time to be special."

"Your first time. You mean you've never had sex—with anybody—never?"

"Never, not yet, at least, so far. But I'm looking forward to it. I guess never having done it, I don't know what I'm missing.

My friends do everything. They always brag about their freaky nights. To be honest, some of the stuff they talk about, I don't even *want* to try."

"Yeah," said Michael, "there are a lot of things I don't do. I've never, ahh, had oral sex, at least, I've never done it to anybody, but I've been asked to do it many times."

"How do you get out of it?"

"I just tell them that I don't do it. They either understand it, or they don't. Some sisters say they can't be satisfied with one thing, but I just tell them to find somebody that will do it for them, because that won't bother me any."

"What a thing to be talking about the first thing in the morning," Myra exclaimed—"sexual orientation."

"Yea, no doubt," Michael agreed. "I need to take a shower to see if the hot water will help me with this pain."

"Yeah, and I need to get your daughter ready for school. She really enjoyed the first few days of being around the other children. Now she says she wants a sister."

"Oh, boy," said Michael, "we'll see."

As Myra began walking off, Michael called her and walked towards her to express his gratitude.

"Hey, I just want to thank you for what you did for me last night. It was very embarrassing, but you treated me with respect. And I also appreciate the way you take care of my baby. Thank you."

Michael bent over and kissed Myra on the lips very passionately and then turned slowly in pain to walk back to his room. Myra truly enjoyed the kiss. It brought out feelings in her mind and body that she had never experienced before.

As he showered, the phone rang. Myra answered to find a Direct TV salesman on the line.

"Good morning, ma'am," the voice said. "Mr. Alexander ordered Direct TV to be installed, and we just wanted to verify the address."

"He's in the shower," Myra replied. "If you want, I'll get him and you can speak to him."

"No, no, no," the man responded quickly, "I just need to verify your address. Now where is that paper that I had your address on? I seem to have misplaced it. What is it again?"

"We're in #435 of the Plaza Condominium High-Rise, but I've got appointments all day and won't be home until this evening at 5."

"That's fine," he replied, "I'll be there at 5:30, in case you're running late."

Myra said OK and hung up the phone. At the same time, Kenneth hung up the phone, plotting his next strategy.

"He's staying in the Plaza," Kenneth said loudly. "How did he hook that shit up?"

In another room of the house, Mr. and Mrs. Jackson were watching the morning show on Channel 5. The woman hosting the show introduced a new morning segment.

"Today, ladies and gentlemen, we're introducing a new segment called LA's Most Embarrassing Moments. It was inspired last night by our spot reporter that thought he was covering a boring high school function when he found the action across the street to be a lot more entertaining. Take a look at this."

The next thing showing was Michael running across the lot in red thong bikini underwear.

"Look at that fool," said Mrs. Jackson. "What is that he's got on?"

Michael's butt cheeks were not seen because of computer enhancing. Kenneth entered the room to see what all the laughter was about.

"What're y'all laughing at?" he asked as he glanced at the TV.

A man was seen running across the screen. Kenneth took a second look and recognized the man's face.

"Oh my God," he said, "that's Michael."

"Michael?!" yelled Mrs. Jackson. "What the hell is he doing with those red drawers on running from those big women?"

"Actually, they don't look like women to me," Kenneth stated. "I guess Michael has been keeping a secret all these years."

At the same time in her hotel room, Kenneth's wife, Cheryl, was watching the same program. Her best girlfriend hosted the show and had called her on her cell phone, telling her to watch. She also recognized Michael.

"Oh, Michael," Cheryl murmured, "what are you doing?"

She shook her head in bewilderment, snickered a little bit, and went to work. Her husband, however, and the Jacksons continued to plot against Michael.

"See?" said Kenneth. "You see the kind of stuff he's into. We've got to get Brittany away from him."

"Damn, right," Mrs. Jackson stated adamently. "We're getting an attorney today and starting proceedings against that man so we can take our baby home."

"Okay," said Kenneth, "you work on an attorney but I've got to go."

After that, Kenneth went to the Plaza Condominium to scope out the situation. He was determined to destroy Michael, the man he supposedly went out of his way to save.

At 7 that morning, Myra and Brittany were still at the house since they were running a little late. Michael was still in pain, but able to function pretty much normally, although he winced whenever he had to bend over. He turned on the news and saw over 15 fire trucks trying to put out a fire at a cottage in Bel Air. Unfortunately, the blaze ignited several other houses in the area. Two families stood in the street as the firemen tried to control the blaze. One of the firefighters on the scene spoke to the TV reporter.

"The fire appears to have started in the middle cottage. A large kerosene can was left at the scene, so I would say it was definitely arson, but we're still investigating."

The TV reporter covering the scene then spoke to one of the victims of the other burnt house.

"We lost everything," the woman said in shock. "We smelled the smoke at about 3:15 this morning and were lucky to get out of the house. I have no idea where we go from here."

"Ah, man," said Michael, "that fire was out of control."

Myra stared at the TV and then rushed to take Brittany to school. As she opened the door, Detective Andrews was about to knock. He just invited himself in. Myra stopped.

"It's okay, Myra," Michael said. "I'll see you guys later."

As Myra and Brittany leave, Detective Andrews said, "Nice family. Is that your wife?"

"No, she just helps with my daughter," Michael explained. "What can I do for the police today?"

"Detective Gentry disappeared last night," the detective answered, "and I think you can help me find her."

"What are you talking about, man?" Michael replied quickly. "I haven't seen that woman since the other night when I talked to you both downstairs." The exertion caused him to grimace in pain.

"What happened?" asked Detective Andrews.

"I fell. I'm kinda clumsy these days."

"I bet. Look, Mr. Alexander, Detective Gentry disappeared after staking out Coretta James' mansion last night. I'm afraid that something real bad has or is gonna happen to her."

Michael seemed uninterested, but listened intensely.

"Look, this guy, Stephen Davis, I believe he is a serial rapist and a murderer. I tracked his history back from when he lived in New Orleans and San Francisco. Women seem to disappear when he's around. Some are raped and live, others never live to talk about it. He always gets off on a technicality, but the truth is, he's a sick bastard."

Michael still didn't respond.

"If Detective Gentry is with him, her life is in danger. How can you sit back and let this happen?"

Michael sighed, but still said nothing.

"Look, I'm sorry about your cousin being killed by the police," said Detective Andrews, "but how long are you gonna hold that inside of you? This woman could be killed."

Detective Andrews pulled a photo from his pocket. "How old is your daughter?"

"She's almost six," said Michael.

"Well, look at this picture. This is Detective Gentry's 7-year-old son. She's a single parent, like you. His mother is all he has. Right now, this little boy sits at the police station with people he doesn't even know because his mother didn't come home and he has no other family. Look at him. That's Paul Gentry and right now, until we find his mother, he has no one, *no one*."

Michael still didn't speak.

"If we find her dead, I'm going to see if there's some way we can try you for conspiracy, withholding evidence. Okay, you keep your little vendetta against the police while a young woman's life is on the line. You know what?" Detective Andrews added. "Even when you gave that little speech the other night and talked about bad police officers, she said she understood and respected the way you felt. You talk about the police, but you're the one that's self-righteous. You don't deserve the respect she gave you. Here—"

Detective Andrews threw another one of his cards at Michael and slammed the door shut violently on his way out. As he left the building, he received a phone call.

"Detective Andrews," the voice said, "that 4-alarm fire in Bel Air this morning happened at a cottage that belonged to Coretta James."

"I'm on my way," he replied.

Michael covered his face with his hands. He finally realized the magnitude of the treachery of the people he was dealing with. He wondered about Coretta's role in these unspeakable crimes. This time, he stored away Detective Andrews' card. Then he bowed down to say a prayer for Detective Gentry. He definitely felt the sting of Detective Andrews' words.

After he prayed, Michael called Michelle and invited her out for an early morning breakfast.

"Shelly," Michael said, "what you got going on?"

"Trying to get an early morning workout, Michael," she replied. "What's up with you?"

"You had breakfast yet?" he asked.

"Not yet."

"Meet me at Roscoe's Chicken and Waffles. I want to talk to you about some things."

"What time?"

"I can be there in an hour," Michael replied.

"See you there," she said.

Michael felt extremely close to Michelle and wanted someone to talk to. He dressed in black slacks, black shirt, and black shoes, then headed to his black Mercedes to meet Michelle.

Chapter 24

KENNETH SAT IN THE PARKING garage under the Plaza Hotel and walked to the Plaza Condominium to find a way to enter Michael's condo.

He watched from a distance as Michael exited the condo and drove off. Then he entered the front of the condominium and saw a heavyset woman by the name of Jackie Brown working the desk alone.

"Hello, how are you today?" he asked. "My name is Ken and my best friend lives here and asked me to get some things from his room."

"Well, why don't you call your friend and have him to meet you here and then you can pick up what you need?" the attendant asked.

"What's your name?" said Kenneth.

"Jackie Brown."

"Foxy Brown," he said. "I bet that's what everybody calls you. You're a sexy chocolate. I love chocolate, but sometimes chocolate can be habit forming."

"Oh," said Jackie, "you so crazy *and* so handsome."

"Thank you," he smiled. "Do you have Michael Alexander on your list?"

She looked on the list and found Michael in 435.

"Yeah, he's on the fourth floor. He has that cute little girl."

"Yeah, Brittany. I'm her godfather. You see, Michael wants me to get his barbeque grill from his apartment, but he forgot to give me the key."

"I can't let you go up there," said Jackie. "I could lose my job."

"Who's gonna know? Don't you have the key to each condo?"

"Yeah, but ..."

"Well, I just need to grab my grill," Kenneth persisted. "We're gonna have a real good time. I'll tell you what, why don't you come by? You can be my special guest, after I get the grill. I'm going to the store to get a bunch of meat. We've got about 50 guests coming over. In fact, I'll get something special just for you. What kind of meat do you like on the grill?"

"Well, I like it all, but my favorite is pigs' feet."

"Pigs' feet?" he repeated.

"Yeah, pigs' feet. They taste real good once you burn the hair off of them."

"Pigs' feet, huh?" he said snickering. "Okay, I'll pick up a bag of pigs' feet just for you. So come on, let me in."

"But I can't leave the desk," she protested. "What if I get caught?"

"By who? You're alone."

"Yeah, I guess you're right," she reluctantly admitted.

She snatched the key to the room and buzzed herself and Kenneth through the glass doors to the elevator. They rode upstairs to the 4th floor and proceeded to room 435.

"I'm not sure I should do this," Jackie said with second thoughts. "If someone comes in and they see me away from the desk, I'm done."

"Look, open the door and leave the key with me and I'll lock up," Kenneth convinced her. "It will only take a second."

"Okay, but don't take long," she pleaded.

Jackie opened the door and called out to see if anyone was home. Then she gave Kenneth the key and returned downstairs so she wouldn't get caught away from the desk. Kenneth walked in and was amazed by the décor and beauty of the condo as he went through each room.

Then he entered Michael's room and saw a closet full of designer suits and shoes and with each new item, his envy and hatred for Michael increased. He put little cameras in the lights and bugs in the phones in each room. The cameras were placed to get a full view of the bedroom and the entire living room area. Kenneth also took a letter that Michael had written to his wife and quickly left.

After he locked the door, Kenneth pulled out a clay mold and made an imprint of the key. Once downstairs, he placed the mold in his pocket and handed the key to Jackie Brown and walked out the door.

"I don't see no barbeque grill. What about my pigs' feet?"

"Well, you're a pig, so why don't you chop your feet off and grill them?"

"Fuck you with your high yellow ass," Jackie spat. "That's why you yellow niggas went out of style."

Jackie Brown sat back at the desk, put the key back, and felt stupid. She worried about what Kenneth might have done, but was afraid to say anything because of her own actions. Kenneth went to his next stop, a handwriting expert that could duplicate anyone's handwriting and began another project. His devious plan was put in motion.

—⊨◉ —⊨◉ —⊨◉

MEANWHILE, MICHAEL AND Michelle arrived at Roscoe's Chicken and Waffles at approximately 8 a.m. They embraced and sat down to breakfast.

"I can never get over how they name all these meals after entertainers," said Michael, "Smokey Robinson is my favorite. I wonder if his meals come with a free gram of cocaine. Luther Vandross' big fat Kentucky-fried breakfast."

Michelle laughed. "Stop it," she said.

"What's next? Michael Jackson's pale breakfast special?" said Michael.

"Leave Michael alone," protested Michelle. "He's still got a great voice."

"Yeah, I know. I like him." Michael moved slightly in his chair and grimaced in pain.

"Ah, baby, what's wrong?" Michelle asked. "Did you hurt yourself?"

"Did you see the news this morning?" he asked.

"No, I didn't," Michelle replied. "Why do you ask?"

Michael, of course, hoped Michelle didn't see him on the news. He became quiet and somber, and Michelle sensed that something was wrong.

"What's wrong, Michael? What's on your mind?"

"I think that I may be working with killers. I don't know what I got myself involved in. A police officer disappeared last night, and they think my employer's assistant my have hurt or killed her. I live in a house that I didn't buy, but I own. Turns out that two other women were possibly killed by my employer's assistant recently. I may be in way over my head."

Michelle paused and was not sure what to say.

"They may try to kill me if I say anything," he continued, "but that police lady that's missing has a son, a little handsome man. I've just got so much on my mind. I've just been thinking about my own little girl. If something happened to me, what would happen to her? I really feel for that little boy and that police lady also."

"So what are you going to do?" asked Michelle. "That's a lot to think about."

"Yeah, right now, I don't know what to do."

Michael paused and looked at Michelle intensely. "I want you to make love to me," he said.

"Just like that?"

"Why not? I need you to be next to me right now."

Michelle reached out her hand and Michael grasped it, and then leaned over and kissed her passionately on the lips. The waitress came over to take their order and saw them kissing.

"We've decided that were not going to have breakfast," Michael informed her. He gave the waitress a five-dollar tip, and then he and Michelle walked towards their cars.

"Follow me," he said.

Michael and Michelle drove towards his condo while Mr. and Mrs. Jackson found an attorney to start a case against Michael. They explained to the attorney that they believed Michael killed their daughter.

Attorney Hank Sanders, a white man in his mid-40s, listened to the Jacksons.

"Our ex-son-in-law got drunk last year and had an accident and killed our only daughter," Mrs. Jackson informed him. "He was up for murder, but got off on a technicality and took our granddaughter away and we didn't see or hear from them for over a year. He was living on crack-infested streets and was on crack himself, and we don't know what condition our grandchild is in."

"And this morning," she continued, "we see him running through the streets with red drawers on the TV news. I'm told he is an escort, a paid escort."

"You mean a gigolo," said Attorney Sanders. "I saw that news report this morning and didn't stop laughing until I got to work. I want you folks to understand that jurys tend to lend towards the parent and with this child having only one parent, it may come down to where this child wants to be. You folks have no problem paying my fee?"

"No, sir," said Mrs. Jackson. "In fact, we're prepared to pay a large part up front."

"Okay, I'll take a full deposition from you and then we need to put together a list of witnesses and see if we can accomplish our goals."

The Jacksons, with their new attorney, put together their case and started the ball rolling toward getting Michael into court.

Meanwhile, Michael and Michelle arrived at his condo and quickly went upstairs. Jackie Brown recognized Michael, but didn't dare tell him of the incident with Kenneth earlier.

They got off the elevator on his floor, walked inside the condo, and immediately started kissing. Michael picked Michelle up and carried her into the bedroom. Michael was in no hurry and slowly kissed Michelle. He began on her neck and slowly rubbed her body up and down. She was wearing a baby blue warm-up suit, fitted snugly to her body. He unzipped the top and kissed Michelle's breasts and ran his tongue down her stomach while she kissed his neck passionately.

"I've been wanting you since the night I met you," Michelle confessed. "I thought something was wrong with me. You spent two nights with me and hardly touched me."

"It wasn't about sex with you," Michael said. "I needed something special. I believed you were special from day one. Let's talk later."

Michael took off Michelle's sneakers and pulled off her sweat pants and stared at her beautiful body, her caramel legs, those beautiful thighs and breasts that stood straight up. Then he rose from the bed and took off all his clothes. After that, he lay back down on the bed with his legs between Michelle's. He slowly removed her undergarments and enjoyed looking at her body, then he began to kiss her all over her body. They didn't have freaky sex, but they did have intense intercourse. Michelle's body thrilled to his touch as he penetrated her.

"Oh, baby," she whispered, "oh, baby, I like it. It's so good."

Michael began to get a rhythm.

"Give it to me, baby," she moaned, "give it to me, baby."

Michael was very intense and passionate and made love with Michelle for fifteen minutes, had an orgasm and still didn't come down. His rhythm got stronger as Michael found it hard to come the second time. The second orgasm took another twenty minutes.

Little did they know as they made love, but they were being watched by a camera that was being monitored by Kenneth. Kenneth got into the sex almost as much as Michael and Michelle. He grabbed himself and masturbated, watching them make love.

While Michael and Michelle were in the throes of an orgasm, Myra came in, having left behind some important papers. Kenneth looked through a second monitor he had set up and saw her and couldn't believe how gorgeous she was.

"Damn, that's a fine babysitter," he said to himself. "Man, this nigger has got it going on."

Myra walked into the living room area looking for her papers and heard a noise. She listened intently, and Kenneth watched as Myra stuck her head into Michael's bedroom. She was shocked seeing Michael having passionate sex with Michelle and Michelle moaning in enjoyment.

Forgetting what she came in for, Myra ran out of the condo to the elevator and quickly exited the building.

"That's what you get for being nosy," laughed Kenneth as Myra exited.

Kenneth focused his attention back to the love scene and tried to again relieve himself while watching Michael and Michelle.

"Ah," said Michael, "you're trying to kill me."

"You're trying to kill *me*," Michelle responded. "That was so wonderful."

Michael fell back on the bed, breathing hard and pulled Michelle on top of him.

"You know I like you," he said, "because I want you close to me after we make love. With some women, after you come, you don't want them to touch you."

"Why is it like that? Why are men like that?"

"I can't answer that," he replied. "Once we get ours, we want to be left alone, but I got a question for you. Why do women want to talk so much after they have sex? All brothers want to do is roll over and go to sleep."

Michelle just shrugged her shoulders and lay back in exhaustion. Michael stood up, threw on his terry cloth robe, and headed to the kitchen. There he put together a big tray of fruit and juice and brought it back and fed some fruit to Michelle. She fed him in return, and they truly enjoyed the fruit of each other.

"Is it 11 o'clock?" she asked.

Michael grasped his watch. "It's 11:05."

"Turn on *The Young and the Restless*," said Michelle. "I haven't stayed home and watched it in a long time."

He turned on the TV, took off his robe, and lay back down.

"How did you get that bruise on your stomach?" asked Michelle.

"Long story. I don't want to talk about it right now."

During all this time, Kenneth watched and enjoyed Michael's sexcapade with Michelle. The show was interrupted when Kenneth got a phone call from the handwriting specialist. Although he hated to leave, he continued to record Michael escapades and left to pick up a package.

Michael watched soaps with Michelle, but eventually nodded off. At noon, Coretta called him. Michael jumped, hearing the phone ring and groaned as he answered it.

"Ah, man," he said, "hello."

"Hello, Michael," said Coretta, "I need you to be somewhere at 3 this afternoon."

Michael checked the clock and saw that it was 12. He remembered the embarrassment of last night and wanted nothing to do with Coretta, but was concerned about what might happen to him if he refused.

"Where do you need me to be?" he asked.

"Go to the Beverly Hilton Hotel. There, you will meet Laura Pinson in the lobby. I've described you to her. She's looking forward to meeting you. She's a black woman, so that should make you happy."

Michael, however, was already in a state of total contentment and didn't want to leave Michelle's side.

"We can't do this tomorrow?" he asked.

"I'm glad you're having a very nice day," replied Coretta, "but tomorrow is out of the question. She's in town on business and wants to get laid, plain and simple. She's petite but she likes her men tall, so you are perfect for her. And I'd like to apologize about last night. I think we both got a little carried away."

"That's an understatement," he said drily. "The Beverly Hilton Hotel, 3 p.m. I'll be there."

He hung up the phone and lay back down with Michelle.

"I guess you've got an appointment. How can you work for her and not trust her intentions?"

"I've got to figure out a way to get out," he replied, "but right now, I just want to rest."

Michael decided to take a nap as Michelle lay beside him. Even though she had appointments, she just blew them off, wanting to be with Michael. They both were very content at the moment.

⇥ ⇥ ⇥

MEANWHILE, KENNETH PULLED up to a local post office and dropped off a package in the day's outgoing mail and then went to his office. At that same moment, the Jacksons finished their deposition and pressed their new attorney to speed up his normal time frame and try to get out the papers to Michael as soon as possible, not only so they could quickly win custody of their granddaughter, but so they could simply see her.

The attorney filed the proper paperwork and expected that Michael would be served the papers promptly. Then the Jacksons returned to Kenneth's house to wait for news from their attorney.

Meanwhile, the detectives had a 24-hour, around-the-clock watch on Coretta's mansion, but neither she nor Stephen had been seen coming or going from the compound.

She was running her business affairs from one of her other residences.

A police captain spoke to Detective Andrews. "We've traced Detective Gentry's cell phone. She was definitely on Coretta James' property when she received the call," said Captain Murtow. Before they could talk further, the captain was summoned to his office for an urgent phone call from the Coast Guard.

After receiving the call, he returned to talk to Detective Andrews.

"I'm sorry to have to tell you this," said Captain Murtow, "but a fisherman on the Atlantic had one of his divers searching for tuna when he ran up on a body. It's definitely Detective Gentry. Apparently it wasn't weighted down enough and got tangled in some weeds."

"I'm going," said Detective Andrews.

"No," said Captain Murtow, "I've been told you definitely *don't* want to see the body. Sounds like she was terribly brutalized."

Detective Andrews threw his hands over his face and sobbed loudly. "Why?" he weeped. "I don't understand this. How could we let this happen?"

"What about Michael Alexander?" the captain asked. "You think he's involved in any way?"

"Not with what happened to Detective Gentry," replied Detective Andrews, "but he has some involvement with Coretta James. I'm just not sure what his story is with her."

"Maybe we should follow him," suggested Captain Murtow, "see where it leads us."

"Yea," said Detective Andrews, "but it's too late for LaShara, too late for LaShara. Now what is her son going to do?"

Then the detective sent a car to follow Michael and monitor his whereabouts.

◦▸▉◉ ◦▸▉◉ ◦▸▉◉

At 2:30 that afternooon, Michael prepared to leave his condo for the Beverly Hilton Hotel. Michelle was still relaxing, and Michael didn't want to uproot her.

"Just stay here," he said. "I should be back shortly. Help yourself to anything in the kitchen."

He showered, dressed, and kissed Michelle good-bye, telling her what a good day it had been. Then he drove off for his appointment at the Hilton. The Hilton was approximately 15 minutes away and he passed by Coretta's mansion.

As he drove past the bus terminal, he saw a familiar-looking face, so he stopped to call out. The person that he saw was a tall, Panamanian woman with severe bruises on her face and a black eye and was extremely frightened. Michael got closer and couldn't believe his eyes.

"Bernadette!" he said. "Bernadette, what happened?"

"Michael, don't look at me. I hate for you to see me like this."

"Bernie, what happened? What happened to you?"

"Oh, Michael," she said in terror, "get away from me while you can. You don't want to be seen with me."

Bernadette was standing at the Greyhound Bus Terminal, frantically waiting for her bus to leave.

"Bernadette, tell me what's wrong. Tell me how I can help you."

"It all started the night of the party, the night you and I slept together. Coretta at first told us to be with you, but she changed her mind and wanted you for herself that night. I told you, you were off-limits, but you said she had changed her mind again. Why did you tell me that, Michael?"

He didn't answer. He just sat there, stunned. Bernadette stared at Michael, waiting for an answer.

"I was drunk," he finally said, "and you were so fine. I lied. I shouldn't have."

"Coretta doesn't like to be crossed by anyone," Bernadette continued, "especially people she employs. And to top it off, Stephen has a thing for me. I never wanted him. I thought he was crazy, but he never stopped chasing me. And then when he found out I slept with you, he was furious. That night, he beat and raped me all night. I've been a prisoner in that house ever since the party. I haven't eaten. I've barely slept. The other night Coretta didn't come home, and I sneaked out of the side of the compound."

"Well, do you need anything?" Michael asked. "Money, food? Here, takes this." He handed her seven hundred dollars. "This will help some. Did you go to the police?"

"No, Coretta has half the police force over for personal pleasure, and besides, they would kill me, I know it."

There was no question that Bernadette was completely terrified as she frantically awaited for the 3 o'clock bus. As it pulled up, she rushed to give her ticket to the driver.

"Bernadette! Tell me where you'll be."

"No," she screamed. "They're going to kill you, Michael. Stephen hates you. They'll find an excuse."

With those words, Bernadette jumped on the bus and curled up on the seat so she wouldn't be seen. Michael watched the bus leave and then continued his journey to the Beverly Hilton Hotel, but for the first time in a long time, fear crept into his heart. He was ten minutes late pulling into the parking lot, he noticed, giving the valet his car.

"You're late Mr. 6 foot 4," said Lorna. "Hi, I'm Lorna Pinson, and you must be Michael Alexander."

"Yes, I am."

Lorna was petite. She weighed less than 100 lbs, was barely 5 feet tall, wore glasses with bags under her eyes, and had a small cut across her lip from some kind of surgery. On top of that, she had an attitude. She had nothing that Michael liked physically.

"Coretta speaks very highly of you, sir. She's right, too. You are fine. You ever thought about being a supermodel?"

"Never, that's not my thing. A little too superficial for me."

"Well, what is your thing?"

"Just enjoying my little girl," he replied.

"Oh? How old is she?"

"She's five." Michael paused.

"Well," said Lorna matter-of-factly, "I don't mean to be forward, but I've got a 6 o'clock flight to D.C. that I don't want to miss, so follow me."

Michael followed Lorna, an architect from D.C., to her suite in the hotel. They exited the elevator on the top floor and entered into the luxurious penthouse suite.

"Wouldn't you rather do this when you have more time?" he asked. "Or maybe when you come back to town?"

"No way. I don't know when I'm coming back, and I don't have a man in D.C. Brothers up there don't appreciate a beautiful woman."

"What beautiful woman?" he replied.

"Me, of course," she stated.

Michael didn't make a move so Lorna did all the work.

"Here is your envelope for Coretta," she said, "now let's get started."

She removed Michael's pants and grabbed his penis. However, since he had just had passionate sex with Michelle, he was totally drained. His penis did not even attempt to rise, and he didn't have even the slightest attraction to Lorna.

"Little wee-wee is asleep," Lorna remarked. "Lets' see if we can wake it up."

She kneeled down to give Michael oral sex, but it still didn't respond. She did all she could, but Michael only got a slight erection. Then she immediately put a condom on Michael, dropped her pants, and lay back, but Michael made no move so she pulled him down on top of her. Even though his penis was still not erect, she tried to force it into her. Since Michael didn't want to touch her, she thrust her pelvis back and forth.

After about two minutes, Lorna yelled out, "Oh, I'm about to come!"

Shortly after that, Michael pulled his penis out and pulled up his pants. Lorna was disappointed in him, but didn't want to hurt him, although Michael could care less.

"That was good," she said. Putting her panties on, she walked towards the shower. "Are you gonna shower?" she asked.

"No," he answered, "I'll shower at home."

As he started to leave, she pulled out a second envelope for Michael with four thousand dollars in it. He refused the money, knowing he didn't really perform, but she forced it on him.

"Go ahead," she exhorted him, "consider it a loan, if you like, but take it."

Lorna used the money as an incentive for a future encounter as Michael took it. She gave Michael her card with her personal number, as well as business number on it, and then he left, very happy the experience was over. He went home, and Lorna immediately called Coretta.

"Coretta, I thought you said this nigger could fuck. Not only can he *not* fuck, but he has a little dick. That was a waste of my time and money."

"I'm sorry," Coretta said sympathetically, "maybe he was having a bad day."

"With the equipment he was working with, he's gonna have a lot of bad days, but I still paid him and gave him a four thousand dollar tip. At least I found a way to get myself off."

"Again, I apologize," Coretta said. "I'll speak to my man."

"You do that."

Coretta got off the phone with Lorna and without hesitation, called Michael. "Well, that's twice," she said. "Three strikes and you're out."

"What are you talking about?" he asked.

"Lorna Pinson just called me. She said you can't fuck and have a little dick."

"*WHAT?* No, she didn't."

"Yes, she did," Coretta said bluntly. "I don't know, maybe the night we were together, I just needed some. Maybe it wasn't as good as I remembered."

"She didn't *really* say that, did she?" he asked again.

"Well, you got a four thousand dollar tip, didn't you? How do you think I know about that?"

"I'll call you back," he said, hanging up the phone, then searching for Lorna's number, he called.

"Why you got to talk about me like that?" he asked. "Now, that wasn't necessary."

"Well," she responded, "I didn't want to bruise your ego or hurt your feelings."

"First of all," Michael lectured, "only a fool would have his ego or his self-esteem based on sex. Just for the record, I got some pussy just before I got there."

"Oh, you're sick," she said. "Why'd you do something like that?"

"Because I didn't know. Coretta called me at the last minute and told me about meeting you."

"You're lying. You're just trying to make an excuse because I embarrassed you. Maybe you can get an enlargement or something."

"Let me tell you something," he said loudly, "I don't have to lie to you or anyone. I did get down right before I saw you.

But even if I hadn't had sex with someone else, my dick still wouldn't get hard for you. You see, sex is about chemistry and you and I don't have any. You don't have no face, no body, no personality—nothing. You've got to have at least one of the three, and you have none. You barely weigh 100 lbs soaking wet, fresh out of a shower, and you look just like Tweety Bird."

"Fuck you!" she said, hanging up the phone to call Coretta to complain of Michael's insults. Coretta had her phone on voicemail at the time, so Lorna left a long, hateful message on her answering machine, and then called Michael back.

"Michael, this is Lorna again. I want my four thousand dollars back."

"What?" he said.

"I want my money back. I considered it a loan, but now I want it back."

"Please," he responded, "I didn't ask for it, but I'm definitely keeping it now."

"I'm gonna have a friend of mine pay you a visit," she threatened. "I *am* gonna get my money back. You're an ole sorry motherfucker anyway."

She hung up the phone before Michael could reply and got ready to catch her flight. Michael was shocked because it seemed that he had trouble every day and it came at him like the plague. No matter what he did, he couldn't seem to avoid it. He went home, but first, he stopped at a pawn shop and pur-chased an all silver 380 semi-automatic handgun. Michael filled out the necessary paperwork and had to wait 48 hours before he could pick it up. He had a gut feeling that something was going to come to a head, he just didn't know what or when.

BACK AT HIS CONDO, MICHELLE has had a wonderful day and took a leisurely shower after lying around. After showering, she reached into Michael's closet and took one of his dress shirts and put it on, then went into the kitchen to get some food. As she closed the refrigerator, the front door opened and Myra and Brittany walked in.

Myra looked at Michelle walking around almost nude in Michael's button-down dress shirt.

"Hi, I'm Michelle. You must be Myra, Brittany's nanny."

"Hi, Brittany," said Michelle, "remember me? I came to dinner over at Ken and Cheryl's house. How are you, sweetheart?"

"Fine," Brittany answered.

"Don't you think you should put some clothes on?" suggested Myra, "At least while Brittany's around."

"Yea, you're right. I only dressed like this because no one was here, and I wanted to go into the kitchen and get some food."

Michelle walked off, and Myra looked at her from behind. Although they were both women and Myra was definitely straight, women definitely noticed beauty in other women. Even though Myra herself was gorgeous, she could easily see that Michelle was beautiful and classy. Myra herself was attracted to Michael, but didn't try to antagonize or disrespect Michelle in any way.

The two women sat around the living room area and talked and enjoyed Brittany like they'd been friends for life.

Chapter 25

MICHAEL CALLED CORETTA AGAIN AND offered to meet her to give her the payment from Lorna. She instructed Michael to meet her on her boat parked at the Redondo Beach pier and gave him directions. As he drove towards the ocean, he thought about all the things he had heard about Coretta and Stephen in the last few days. He didn't know what to expect once he arrived.

Arriving at the pier, he parked and walked to her boat where he found his three favorite people, Stephen, Manu, and Coretta. He was still sore from Manu's punch the night before, which caused him to walk very gingerly as he boarded the boat.

"Michael, my boy, how's your stomach feel today?" Stephen asked. "You're lucky. I've seen him almost take guys out with one shot. Oh, I hear your dick is not working too well these days. Maybe you need something to give yourself a boost," he laughed.

Michael realized the Coretta had talked to Stephen about what Lorna had said.

"Why don't you ask Bernadette how good it was? I heard through the grapevine that you had a thing for her. Ask her how good it was."

Michael knew that Bernadette had left and was in no danger from Stephen anymore.

"You little bitch," Stephen said. "I ought to—"

"Boys," Coretta scolded, "boys, you two argue more than women. Where is my package, Michael?"

Michael handed her the envelope and waited for her to give him his portion.

"You know, my dear, the secret to being successful in business is rising to the occasion," Coretta explained, "and I mean rising. You can't discriminate. You have to get up for everyone."

"I need a little more than a couple of hours' notice, and I need to see what they look like, at least a picture of them. That girl was too skinny, and then she's got the audacity to talk stuff."

Michael jumped a little bit when he realized the boat was moving.

"Fix yourself a drink. I just want to talk to you for a moment."

Coretta had Stephen pilot the boat out to sea while she talked to Michael.

"Carlos is going to France," said Coretta. "I want you to go with him. I have someone over there that I want you to see, and Carlos will attend to business for me."

"France? For how long?" he inquired.

"Only for a day. Carlos only has to be there for a couple of hours, but he is to stay there until your work is finished."

"When? When are you talking about?"

"Tonight."

"No way," he replied. "I've been running around ever since I met you, and I need some time to breathe, to spend some time with my little girl."

"You have thousands in your pockets right now because of this 'running around,' as you call it," she rebuked him mildly. "Don't run away now."

"I don't really like this," he protested. "The money is good, but I've gone through more in the last few days than I have ever been through. I've almost been killed twice and I've been threatened again today. Enough is enough. I need to get out."

"Really? Well, I can't let you get out. I'm just beginning to enjoy our little arrangement."

"Well, I'm not enjoying it. I have no idea what to expect from day to day. Now I know you gave me the condo and the car, so you can have it all back. I don't care about that stuff. I want peace right now."

"Actually, I never gave you the condo. I simply leased it to you. Take a look at the document you signed. Also, can you swim, Michael?"

Michael looked overboard and realized he was surrounded by water and far from shore.

"No, I can't."

"Really? How can a man grow up in California and not know how to swim? Well, maybe if something happens to you, you will be able to find Flipper underwater and he can give you a ride to shore."

Michael looked over at the water again.

"Don't worry, Michael. I'm not going to push you over. No, I wouldn't do that. Besides, I've got a better idea. You know that beautiful daughter of yours—what's her name— Brittany, right? I would hate to see something happen to her."

Michael stared at Coretta.

"Stephen likes girls of all ages," she said calmly. "Maybe I'll let her meet Stephen one day."

"You sick bitch. Don't threaten my daughter."

"One thing you will find out about me, Mr. Alexander," said Coretta coldly, "I don't make idle threats. Now, you *will* be on that flight with Carlos tonight, and you will do what you do best when you get there. I don't want to have another client tell me about your inadequacies. All I want to hear about are your sparkling performances."

Coretta gestured to Stephen to turn the boat around and head for home. Then she walked away, leaving Michael to sit back and think about his messed up life right now and how he could change it. Stephen came down to where Michael was and fixed himself a drink from the bar.

"You want one?" asked Stephen.

Michael shook his head no.

"I hear your little girl is real pretty," he volunteered. "A bit young for me, but I *can* make an exception. And don't think we don't know where she is. We've got one of our best people watching her at all times, so don't even consider running. And our people at the condo tell me the police have been by to see you. I don't know what they've been asking you, but I'm sure you didn't tell anything, right?"

Stephen patted Michael across the face, not hard at all, just enough to antagonize him. Soon the boat pulled back to the dock. Michael jumped off, and Coretta spoke to him.

"Here is your itinerary. Your passport is inside that package, too. I know I'm a miracle worker. Don't thank me. It's a gift."

Without a word, Michael turned and went to his car to drive home. He realized that Coretta had plans for him and that her plans were definitely not good and those plans currently revolved around the trip to France. He drove home in a daze when suddenly his phone rang and a pleasant voice spoke at the other end.

⇀⊨⊙ ⇀⊨⊙ ⇀⊨⊙

"HI, MICHAEL, HOW ARE YOU?" the voice said.

"Cheryl, is that you?"

"Yes, it's me. So you're running around on TV in red bikini drawers nowadays."

"Believe me, that's one of the worst moments of my life. How did you get my cell phone number?"

"Myra gave it to me. I got your home number from the caller ID when she called the other night. Why, you don't want me to have your number?"

"Of course, I do. To what do I owe the pleasure of this call?"

"Well, Michael, I think you should know your in-laws are in town. Kenneth called them, and they're staying at the house."

"Bill and Susie Jackson," he said sadly. "I guess I should have called them by now, but they were just so bitter when their daughter died. But they have a right to see Brittany."

"Well, they're still bitter, and Ken is fueling the fire."

"What's up with him anyway? What's his problem with me?"

"I think his problem is that he can't be you," said Cheryl. "That man has been obsessed with you ever since I've known him and it only seems to be getting worse. You're the only person that I know that can elicit that kind of reaction out of people. They either absolutely love you, or absolutely hate you. There is no middle ground."

"Well, where does Ken stand?" asked Michael. "His position towards me is strange."

"I hate to say this about my husband, but I believe he has always hated you. I just believe there was no one better for him to be around than you. You were a great athlete, the life of every party, and very good at anything you put your mind to. Kenneth just rode your coattail. I left him the other night, Michael. He wants me to help the Jacksons take Brit from you. I can't do that."

"Take Brit! You're joking, right?"

"I wish I was," said Cheryl remorsely. "I don't know what steps they'll take, but I know they will try something with Kenneth's help."

Michael paused in silence, not believing what he was hearing.

"I love you, Michael, and I love Brittany. I know you're a good man, and that's why Brittany clings to you like she does. Anything I can do to help you I will."

"Thank you, Cheryl. For the record, I love you too. Take care."

Michael hung up the phone and continued to drive home. He needed to see a pleasant face right now and none was more pleasant than Brittany, along with Michelle and Myra. He arrived home at 7:30 and found the three of them playing around and watching TV. Brittany rushed to hug her father. Michael grabbed his daughter and hugged her real tight.

"So what's my baby been doing?" he asked.

"Daddy, we've been watching TV and playing games and having girl talk," said Brittany.

"Girl talk, huh? What kind of girl talk?"

"We've just been doing some female bonding," said Michelle. "You know, three ladies talking about the man in their life. In this case, all three women are talking about the same man—*you*."

"Uh-huh, I'm afraid of this conversation. I hope there was no male bashing going on."

"Of course not," said Myra. "We all had nothing but good things to say about you."

"Sorry, Myra," he said. "I should have called you and told you that Michelle was going to be here, but I've got so much on my mind right now that I just forgot to call."

"That's okay," Myra said. "I've been enjoying her. She's very nice. I see why you like her."

"What did you guys cook? I'm starving," Michael announced. "I could eat a horse."

"Yea, we didn't cook one of those," said Michelle.

Myra prepared Michael some food and he sat down to enjoy it, along with some pleasant conversation and laughter with the three beautiful ladies.

"Michael, you know your daughter's birthday is this weekend," whispered Myra in Michael ear. "We want to throw her a surprise party here and invite a bunch of kids and parents from the school. What do you think?"

Michael had been running so much that he had forgotten his daughter's birthday and definitely had no plans for it.

"That's a good idea," he replied. "What time Saturday?"

"Around 3 o'clock," she said. "I'll print up the invitations and get the cake and make all the arrangements, but *you* have to be here."

Michael knew he was scheduled to fly out of the country, but didn't want to spoil Brittany's birthday plans. At that moment, Carlos called Michael on the cell phone.

"Be ready, I'm picking you up in 15 minutes," he said, then immediately hung up, not giving Michael a chance to respond. Michael simply left the table and went into his room to pack a bag for Paris, France. Michelle followed him into the room and saw him packing.

"Where are you going?" she asked.

"Paris. I'm leaving in about 15 minutes."

"When were you going to tell us?"

"I just found out about 2 hours ago myself. I didn't have any choice but to go. Look, Michelle, if I don't make it back, please watch out for my daughter."

"What do you mean, 'if you don't make it back'? What's happening with you? It's that woman you work for, isn't it?"

"Just promise you'll look out for Brit," he pleaded.

"I promise," she said. "I'll do what I can. Paris is a 15-hour flight from LAX. How you gonna be back by Saturday?"

"I don't know," he confessed. "I don't know. But I really enjoyed you today. That's the first time I made love since I was with my wife. It was all good."

"It was all good for me, too," said Michelle.

Michelle and Michael kissed passionately as he prepared to leave the country.

Chapter 26

CARLOS AND STEPHEN TALKED SECRETLY as they prepared for Carlos' trip to France. "You know what to do, don't you?" asked Stephen.

"I know what to do," answered Carlos.

"Just make sure Michael has the bag when he leaves the plane," said Stephen.

Carlos took off and arrived at 7:45 to pick up Michael, who had finished packing.

"You can sleep in my bed tonight," he told Michelle. "From this point on, we should spend our nights together whenever we're in the same city."

"I'm with that," she agreed. "I'll leave in the morning with Myra and Brittany."

Michelle embraced Michael, then he said good-bye to Myra and hugged his daughter, who couldn't understand why her father had to suddenly leave and why, lately, he was always gone. But he had no time to explain. There was only time for hugs and kisses, then he rushed downstairs.

Coretta called on his way out. "Once you arrive in Paris, you and Carlos will go your separate ways. A driver will be there to take you to your hotel. You will attend the International Music Awards with supermodel Daphne Irie. This is more of a promotional thing than a date, but if you talk right, who knows what might happen. Don't forget, Michael, when you work for me, you make every performance seem like it's your last. Your attire will be provided for you upon arrival."

Stephen and Carlos had a plan in progress for Michael unbeknownst to Coretta. Stephen had heard stories of the cruelty of the French prison system and wanted to see Michael locked up there for life. He liked that thought much more than merely killing him.

Carlos picked him up for their 9 p.m. flight. The two said very little on the way to the airport. Michael was caught up in his own world of troubles. As they arrived at LAX and entered the Continental terminal, all their bags were thoroughly checked, including the black briefcase that Carlos had at his side. Once they got on the plane, Michael buckled in for the long flight, with only one stop in Houston. They had adjoining seats, but Michael ignored Carlos and just watched movies and drank.

Meanwhile, Detective Andrews continued searching for Stephen. He hadn't slept very much in the last couple of days. He believed that Stephen was responsible for the murders of the two women at the condo and for the murder of Detective Gentry. The 24-hour surveillance of Coretta's home hadn't produced any solid evidence and Coretta had not been seen at the mansion since the night Detective Gentry disappeared. The detectives believed they had enough circumstantial evidence at this time and obtained arrest warrants for Coretta and Stephen. Finding them was the next task. The two fugitives maintained a very low profile, but were not completely out of sight.

Meanwhile, that night as Michael traveled to France, three people had him on their mind exclusively. Brittany missed her father and struggled to understand why he stayed gone. Myra, who had secretly fallen for Michael, hoped one day they would be together, and Michelle, after an afternoon of passionate love, could not get him out of her mind. Michelle slept in his bed, wearing his boxer shorts and one of his tee shirts, cuddled up with his pillow still bearing his scent on it. She held onto the pillow all night, at times thinking that the pillow was actually Michael. Michelle considered Michael dangerous, but couldn't help wanting to spend time with him, no matter what the cost. She, like many others, was in love with Michael and devoted to him.

***

The next day, the flight to Paris International Airport arrived on time at 12 p.m. Michael had crazy jet lag from the trip. Neither Carlos nor Michael spoke to each other the whole trip, but suddenly, Carlos wanted to be chummy.

"Enjoy the ride?" he asked. "That was a hell of a long trip."

Michael didn't say anything. He just looked despondent.

"Do me a favor, man," Carlos said. "Carry my briefcase for me."

"Something wrong with your hands?"

"Yea, my hands hurt from an accident I had, and I've got this other bag to carry."

"Okay," Michael agreed, "I'll carry it until I get to baggage check and then you're on your own."

He took the briefcase as they exited the plane and walked towards the baggage pickup. Carlos slowed down behind him and quickly went in the other direction as Michael was accosted by the French police. They detained him and took him to a police station inside the terminal to be interrogated. Meanwhile, Carlos disappeared out of the airport. Michael was taken to a room with a desk and no windows and a French police officer who spoke fluent English came in to talk to him. Michael was terrified and had no idea what he was being held for.

"Monsieur Alexander, I am Detective Francois Consteau, captain of the French Brigade," he began.

"How did you know my name?" asked Michael.

"We checked the briefcase, and it had all your vital information," said Consteau.

"That's not my case," Michael replied. "That briefcase belongs to a man named Carlos. He asked me to carry it for him as he got off the plane."

"How long have you been delivering drugs over here? Who is your contact in France?"

"Drugs? What drugs?" asked Michael.

Detective Consteau ordered a member of his police brigade to bring in the case. He popped the secret compartment on the briefcase and it opened, revealing four large bags of cocaine.

"So you're trying to tell me that you don't know anything about this?" asked Consteau. "Who is your contact?"

"Oh, shit. That motherfucker set me up." Michael paused. "Man, I came over here for the International Music Festival," he explained. "Carlos asked me to carry his briefcase because he hurt his hand or something."

"Someone has been smuggling drugs through Paris on a regular basis," said Detective Consteau. "According to our contacts, we also received a call earlier that a tall, black, American man would be carrying a briefcase full of goods—and there you were."

"I'm telling you, I don't know anything about that stuff. Please listen to what I'm trying to tell you. If I was a drug dealer, I wouldn't be a big enough fool to bring it through the airport the way they check all the bags after the 9-11 attacks."

"Maybe you're a fence for your government," suggested Detective Consteau. "Maybe this is payback for us not being in the war."

"Man, I wasn't for the war either," Michael said. "I'd be the last person they would send over here. There's *got* to be a way I can prove my innocence."

The two men went back and forth. Michael had never felt so helpless in his life. After a few moments, a television was rolled into the room and a tape put inside the recorder.

"We had you under surveillance once you hit the terminal," explained Detective Consteau. "Let's see what we got here. You have a chance to confess now."

"Man, I'm telling you, I don't know anything about this stuff," Michael protested. "Carlos gave me the bag as soon as we got off the plane."

"Well, where is this Carlos?"

"I don't know," Michael said, sobbing slightly, "I don't know."

As the detectives looked at the tape, Michael is seen walking up through the airport towards the baggage department. Carlos is seen in the video clearly running away from him.

"I guess that's Carlos running," said Consteau. "He didn't waste any time."

Michael raised his head and looked. "Yeah, that's the sucker. That's why he wanted me to carry his case. He had the whole thing planned."

"How do I know you two weren't in it together and he ran because he saw us coming?" Consteau probbed.

Michael didn't answer but looked scared and sad.

"You need to find better friends," Consteau told him. "Friends like that will get you killed or put away for life."

With those words, Detective Consteau stood up and walked outside to talk. "I'll be right back. Don't you go anywhere."

He took the briefcase full of cocaine and conferred with his colleagues. Michael was left to sweat alone with his thoughts for about an hour before they came back into the isolated room.

"Monsieur Alexander, we're going to allow you to leave. But you are *never* to come back to our country again. If we see you at the airport, we will instantly lock you up—no questions asked. Our police will escort you back through the terminal and put you on the first flight out of Paris. Good day, Monsieur Alexander."

Michael was taken back through the terminal where he had almost lost his mind. At 3 that afternoon, he boarded an airplane headed to Los Angeles, seriously shaken by the experience he just went through.

"I could have been locked up for life in a foreign country and never seen my child again," he said quietly to himself. He wiped his face and rested his head on the tray in front of him. He felt like when his wife died, all alone in the world. Then he began to cry, not knowing what to do next. He was feeling really sorry for himself and had 15 more hours to sit there and dwell on it.

"What did I do to deserve all the things I'm going through?" he asked himself aloud. "God is punishing me for something."

Finally a stewardess came over. "Sir, are you okay?"

"No I'm *not*," he answered emphatically. "I almost got locked up permanently in France. I couldn't have called nobody—nobody. I would have rotted in that jail and died without ever seeing my child again."

"Sir, you're disturbing the other passengers. Please pull yourself together."

Michael looked around to see all eyes on him. He decided to recline his seat and say nothing more for the moment—a broken man.

Chapter 27

AT 6 A.M., MICHAEL ARRIVED IN Los Angeles after a very restless flight. It was Saturday morning. He hadn't slept very much in the last 34 hours and wasn't about to sleep now. He found a cab, but instead of going to his Bel Air condo, he went downtown. His driver's first stop was a liquor store, where he bought a gallon of Hennessey. The second stop was the Downtowner Hotel. The cab fare was thirty dollars, and Michael gave the cab driver a fifty and told him to keep the change.

Going to room #130 on the first floor, he knocked on the door, but no one answered.

"Dr. Cook?"

Dr. Donald Cook was Michael's partner in crime and together, they were a hard team to beat—the life of any party.

"Who the fuck is it?" asked Donald Cook.

"It's Michael, man. Open up."

"Michael?"

He opened the door and hugged Michael tightly, shaking him around. Then he saw the gallon of Hennessey.

"Michael, man, where you been? And where did you get all that Hennessey?"

"I bought it."

Donald had a woman in the room with him and ordered her to leave. "Get lost, bitch. I'll see you later." He turned back to Michael, "Crack open that Hindu."

"I knew I could count on you to hang with me," Michael replied. "Man, blaze up a joint or something."

"I got one rock, that's it," replied Donald.

Michael reached in his pocket and pulled out wads of money. "Fire that up and we'll get plenty more. By the way, what day is it?"

"It's Saturday, man. Where have you been?" Donald asked.

"To Paris," said Michael, hitting on the pipe, "but I don't even want to talk about that."

"Where did you get all that cheese from?" Donald asked while drinking a shot of Henessey.

"I worked for it. Believe it or not, I get paid to fuck. I'm a gigolo."

"Right," Donald retorted, "and I'm the king of Egypt."

"For real. I met this billionaire bitch in a club and she let me fuck her and I socked it to her and she's been paying me to sleep with women since then. But she's a ruthless so-and-so and I don't know what's next with her. That's why I came down here. If I'm going out, I'm going out having a ball. Man, wake up some of your boys and let them drink some of this Hindu."

Michael and his friend party all morning as Myra and Michelle organized Brittany's party.

Around noon, Michelle was still decorating and Brittany wanted to know where her father was.

"Where's Daddy? Will he be here for the party?"

"I hope so, baby," Michelle said. "I want to see him too."

"Did you call that woman, Cheryl?" Michelle asked Myra.

"Yes," Myra replied. "She said she wouldn't miss it for the world. She will be here around 1 o'clock to help out."

By this time, Michael and Donald were plastered, walking up and down the street of LA, smoking crack. Michael was flashing his money, and they had been drinking and smoking all day.

"Let's go buy some pussy," Donald suggested.

"I don't want no pussy," Michael replied. "I told you, I get paid to fuck."

"I still can't believe that shit. Any of them fine?"

"All of them were fine but one. This real skinny one named Lorna. She might have weighed 100 lbs with a sack of bricks strapped to her leg. Now Barbara Brown, she was fine, in her 40s with a body like a 20 year old."

"Oh, yeah?"

"Yea, she was fine and rich and living in a mansion on Lake Shore Drive in Chicago."

"What about the lady you work for? Is she fine?"

"She looks just like that girl Dawn from En Vogue," said Michael. "I mean, she's a pretty, sexy, chocolate sister, but the bitch is sick in the head."

"Let's get another hit," said Donald. "My high is about to come down."

"Man, you know I've spent five hundred dollars on your ass already today," Michael said, "but okay, let's get another one."

⤛⤜ ⤛⤜ ⤛⤜

MICHAEL AND DONALD continued their binge as guests started to arrive at Brittany's party. Myra, Michelle, and Cheryl prepared for the party's events. Myra called Coretta to inquire about Michael.

"Coretta, do you have any idea when Michael is coming back? We're having a birthday party for Brittany, and she's constantly asking for her father."

"I know for a fact he won't be back today. The International Festival of Music isn't until tonight, and that's the event he will be attending.

"A birthday party, huh?" Coretta said.

"Yeah, the guests are arriving with their children now. Let me call you back later, OK? I've got to handle the guests."

Myra hung up the phone and Coretta decided to make a surprise visit to the party to check things out.

"Aunt Cheryl, where's my daddy?" Brittany asked. "What time will he be here?"

Cheryl looked at Myra and didn't know what to tell Brittany. "I hope soon, baby. I hope soon."

Myra took Brittany over to greet some children as Cheryl and Michelle talked. "That little girl loves her father," said Cheryl.

"Okay, girl," said Michelle, "has she always been like that?"

"Let's put it this way," said Cheryl. "Her daddy can't do no wrong in her sight."

As the party progressed, the children played games and had fun singing. The party turned into a merry event. However, one little child, little Eva Reese, was constantly disrupting the party, starting trouble with the other children and picking her nose while all the other children were playing and enjoying themselves. Her parents, Sylvia and John Reese, were just as obnoxious and John was obsessed with a fantasy that everyone wanted his wife.

"Are you fixing the plates?" John Reese asked Cheryl, "'cause if you are, I could use some more chicken wings and some more baby back ribs on my plate."

"No, I'm not fixing the plates, but you are welcome to help yourself."

Cheryl walked off and talked to Michelle and Myra. "The nerve of that man," she said. "His whole family has been acting crazy all day."

"And look at his wife working on those ribs," said Michelle. "She acts like she hasn't eaten in days."

"You mean *months*," said Cheryl.

Sylvia and John Reese were both heavyset, dark-skinned black people with a passion for food.

"Well, you know it's not days," said Michelle. "Look at that waistline. She ain't missing no meals."

The girls shared a laugh at the Reeses' expense.

The party was still in full swing at 4 when a knock came at the door. About 40 people were still present, even though it came about at such a short notice and Brittany was new to the school. Black people love to socialize.

Myra made her way to the door and opened it. She was very surprised to see Coretta standing there.

"Thought I'd come by and check things out," Coretta said. "It's been a long time since I've been in the old place."

"What a surprise," Myra exclaimed. "I didn't expect you to come over."

"I always like to know what's going on," said Coretta. Then she saw a little girl with a birthday crown on her head.

"You must be Miss Brittany," said Coretta. She saw that Brittany was wearing a very pretty outfit and assumed it was her birthday. Brittany answered Coretta by nodding her head like any 5 year old and looked shy.

"Ah, you're so pretty," said Coretta, "and that outfit looks so good on you. The best outfit my money could buy."

Coretta let everyone know that she paid for Brittany's clothes and that she owned the condo. She was in her usual, self-aggrandizing mode.

"Hi, I'm Coretta James," she said to Cheryl.

"I recognize you," said Cheryl. "We've been at a couple of functions together. You're into real estate, right?"

"That and a lot more," Coretta replied. "I try not to limit myself to just one area. You don't become as rich and powerful as I am by limiting yourself."

Coretta walked off and Cheryl thought to herself what a bitch she appeared to be. After that, Coretta went around the party and made herself and her status known to everyone.

John Reese saw Coretta coming through and began to talk loudly in front of his wife. "Damn, she's fine. That's the kind of woman I used to be with before I met you. I settled for you because I thought you were a good woman."

"In your dreams," responded Sylvia. "You didn't settle for me. *I* settled for you. I was dating a fine attorney and he asked me to marry him, but I told him no. I wanted you."

"Now that's my baby," said John.

John and Sylvia continued to do damage to the barbeque while the party flowed with children having a good time and acting more mature than many of the adults. Coretta posted Manu outside the door and continued her cameo appearance, boasting about herself until she recognized and approached Michelle.

"Well," said Coretta, "I thought you wouldn't even want to know Michael after that night at the Beverly Club. Just for the record, he took me home that night and gave me some of that good dick of his. The man can definitely handle his business."

Several people heard Coretta.

"I know he can handle his business," said Michelle. "I just got some all day Thursday, and you're right, it was good."

Coretta recalled on that Thursday, Michael met with Lorna and couldn't perform. "Really? Well, I guess we have one thing in common. You do realize he's in Paris right now spreading himself around. I'm sure you don't want to continue to get sloppy seconds."

Michelle was hurt by Coretta's words, but didn't want to let her know that. "Maybe I like sloppy seconds," she snapped. "Yea, maybe I like that. Eventually he'll realize what he has in me and not want to be with women so desperate for sex that they have to pay for it from a strange man, no matter how fine he is."

"These are wealthy women just having a little fun," came back Coretta. "They're not desperate. I told them how fine Michael was. If they were desperate, they would lay around a man's house while he was out of town, waiting for him to come home from having sex with another woman."

Coretta had hit Michelle below the belt, but if it's a fight she wanted, she chose the right one.

"Listen, Ms. James, you're walking your sidity ass around here, bragging about you own this and you own that, boasting about material things, just showing everybody that you have no class. You would think that a woman with so many material possessions would be humble, at least a little. So Ms. Rich Materialistic Bitch, do yourself a favor. Act like you had something before. Oh, and as far as Michael is concerned, he asked me to stay here in his bed until he comes back. You see, he wants some more of this when he returns, and I'm going to give him all he can handle."

Coretta stepped closer to Michelle and gave her a cold stare in the face, a look that could cut her in half. "If I were you, I would be very careful what I said. I would hate for you to end up six feet deep. I could put you down so easily, so easily."

While the two of them were in the middle of the floor arguing, Cheryl stepped in between them.

"Ladies," she said, "not here at Brittany's party, please."

"You're right," said Michelle. "We have a lot of invited guests. It's the uninvited one who is causing all the problems."

"I promise you," Coretta seethed, "you *will* regret the day that you spoke this way to Coretta James, I promise."

With those words, Coretta stormed out of the party and didn't bother to close the door. She and Manu left the building, and she was very upset. John Reese watched the scene from a distance with a drumstick in his hands, talking, eating, and spitting on people at the same time.

"Damn," he said, referring to Coretta, "she was hot. I wouldn't want to be around her tonight. Hey, anybody here know where the hot sauce is?"

Chapter 28

ON THE OTHER SIDE OF town, Michael and Donald made their way to the mall and were as high as a kit and girl-watching.

"Damn, she's fine with all that ass," said Donald.

"Yeah," Michael remarked, "looks like she's got two basketballs in her pants."

"You'll stick that?" asked Donald.

"Hell, yea," Michael answered.

They continued to walk through the mall talking loudly. A girl walked by and they talked loud enough to make sure she heard them. "Man, that sister got a ton of ass," said Donald.

"No shit," said Michael.

"Man, it looks like somebody took two sticks of dynamite and exploded that big ass out," Donald crudely remarked. "Let me give you a call, baby. Come on, you'll never regret it."

The woman gave Donald a dirty look and kept walking.

"Man, she shot you down," Michael told his friend.

"Would you stick that?" asked Donald.

"Yes, but why you keep asking me that crazy shit? You pick the finest woman in the mall and ask me that, and you already know the answer. Look, I'll fuck a snake if I can hold his head where he won't bite me."

The two laughed loudly.

"Come on," said Donald.

The two men continued through the mall, still talking loudly and bumping into people until the mall security walked up to them.

"Excuse me," said the security guard, "people have been complaining that you two have been harassing them. I'm gonna have to ask you to leave the mall." As he was talking, his partner stood back and watched.

"I ain't going nowhere," Donald said loudly. "You flashlight cops can't tell nobody what to do. What you gonna do, shine that light in our face until we give up?"

"Well, you know I have nightmares about flashlights," Michael said sarcastically. "The light might be too bright and mess up my eyes."

Michael and Donald laughed and tried to walk off.

"Gentlemen," said the security guard firmly, but politely, "I'm asking you nicely to leave the mall. The next step is to call the police and from the looks of you two, you both would be on your way to jail, now please leave the mall."

"Fuck you," Donald said belligerently. "I'm not going nowhere, Barney Fife."

The security guard immediately got on his radio and called the police, which had a precinct right outside the mall.

"Okay," the guard replied. "The police are on their way."

"Let's roll," Michael said. "Let's go somewhere else." He took Donald by the arm and led him to the mall exit while Donald continued to talk loudly and obnoxiously on the way out.

"I could whup both your punk asses," he said. "You wannabe fake ass niggers with your tight ass pants on. I don't see you breathe with those nut huggers on. Y'all ain't nothing but fagg bait."

With that parting shot, they exited the mall and wondered what they would do next.

"I don't feel like waiting on that bus," said Michael. "I wish I had my Benz. We could roll around the city in style."

"I'm tired of you talking about what you have. You got a million dollar condo, a new Benz, all this good shit."

As Michael and Donald talked, a police car passed by. They looked away so as not to be seen.

"We can go to my place, right now," said Michael. "You can see everything I have."

"Well, let's take the bus up there," suggested Donald.

"Fuck the bus. Let's go over here to the cab stop and take the cab."

Michael walked over to the yellow cab stop an asked the cab driver to take him to the Plaza Condominium in Bel Air. Donald also came over. The cab driver told Michael the price. He was a foreign man of Middle Eastern descent and had an accent.

"You know that trip will be at least sixty dollars," the driver said. "You guys don't look like you can afford that."

Michael had on the nice outfit that he flew to Paris in, but hadn't changed clothes since Thursday so the outfit was very wrinkled and he smelled like liquor and desperately needed to brush his teeth. He pulled a wad of money out of his pocket. Even though they had already spent a couple of thousand dollars getting high and hanging out, Michael still had several more thousand in his pocket.

"You see this, Saddam?" he said flaunting the money, "I've got enough money in my pocket to pay cab fare to Florida."

"Yea, Osama Bin Laden," chipped in Donald, "I knew we would find your ass. You finally decided to move out of them caves. I should turn your ass in for that 25 million."

Michael and Donald laughed, then Donald tried to light a cigarette.

"There's no smoking in my cab," said the driver. "This is a smoke-free cab."

"Alright, Yasser Arafat," said Donald, "you don't have to get an attitude."

"My name is not Saddam or Yasser Arafat. It's Addullah Akbar."

"Abdullah Akbar," mocked Michael. "I like Saddam better. Well, anyway, Abdullah, take us up to Bel Air and make it fast."

"Hey, man, stop by the Golden Bird," stated Donald. "I'm hungry and could use some of that yard bird."

"I stopped eating chicken," said Michael, "but I'll eat a couple of pieces for old time's sake."

"You stopped eating chicken?" asked Donald. "How can a black man not eat chicken? You got to be the only black man in America that don't eat chicken."

Michael didn't respond. He and Donald headed for the Golden Bird as the party for Brittany was still going strong. Everyone was having fun, especially the Reeses, who were trying to eat up the whole birthday cake. Brittany enjoyed the party, but was constantly asking for her father.

"Poor child," said Michelle. "No matter how much fun that child has, she can't get her daddy out of her mind."

Myra gathered all the children together to play a game and to sing happy birthday to Brittany just as Michael and Donald reached the Golden Bird.

"Give me a twenty-piece set with hot sauce," Michael ordered. "You want any side orders?"

"Red beans and rice," said Donald. "Hey, Akbar, can I grab you some soda from the store?"

The driver said okay. Michael gave Donald a twenty dollar bill and paid for the chicken as Donald went into the store.

But instead of soda, Donald bought a six-pack of Red Stripe beer and some beef jerky, then came back to the car.

"Man, Akbar's gonna trip when he sees that beer," said Michael, "and you still eating that beef jerky."

They drove on toward Bel Air with the chicken, hot sauce, red beans, rice, and jalepenos. Michael and Donald ate as if they hadn't eaten in years. Riding up Wilshire Boulevard, all they did was scarf down chicken and talk about people.

"Look at that old white woman in that Cadillac with that dog hanging out the window," said Donald. "They treat dogs better than people. You know why that is? 'Cause they smell like dogs, and they have dog hair."

Michael just looked at him and smirked and rolled his eyes. "I thought I was prejudiced, but you got me beat."

"Man, white folks kiss their dogs in the mouth," said Donald, "and pay for expensive grooming. They feed them better than people. Then if a homeless person comes up, they run in fear, yet they baby those animals. You know that ain't right."

"Man, talk about something else," Michael suggested. "Hey, Abdul, you want some of this Golden Bird?"

"No, thank you. I don't eat chicken."

"You don't know what you're missing," said Donald. "What we gonna do with these bones?"

"Put them in the bag," said Michael.

"I've got an idea." Donald leaned out of the window and threw the bones on the hood of the cab. Michael did the same thing, and they laughed loudly.

"What are you doing?" demanded Akbar. "You cannot throw those bones on my car. What's wrong with you black men?"

"Watch your mouth, Abdul," Michael threatened. "Don't make me put my foot in your Iraqi ass."

"Yeah, we'll send some more bombs over there and wipe out your whole country next time," Donald quipped.

"First of all, I'm not from Iraq," he said. "Second, why do black people fight in wars for this country anyway? Your people have been the most persecuted and tortured race in the history of the world."

"Abdul got a point," Michael agreed. "The white man robbed us of our history, raped our women, murdered most of the black men, and locked the rest of them in jail. We're fools for fighting in that fake war. Weapons of mass destruction, ha! They ain't found no weapons yet."

"They make sure there's no good jobs so your people have no choice but to go into the military," said Akbar.

"And besides, George W. Bush don't have no lips," Michael stated.

"Okay, Malcolm Farrakhan," Donald said, "pass me another one of those red stripes."

"Why you drink beer in my cab?" said Abdul. "I could lose my license."

"Come on, Golda Meir," Donald declared, "we gonna give you a big fat tip."

"Yeah," said Michael, "don't walk home by yourself."

"That was corny," Donald stated.

They continued to throw chicken bones out the car as they pulled up to Michael's condo. When they stopped out front, Donald almost lost it.

"Damn, man, is this where you live?"

Michael nodded.

"This shit is *super* fat," Donald exclaimed.

"See that car parked right there?" Michael asked. "That's my Benz."

"Man, you got it going on," Donald said in admiration. "And you just met this chick in the club, and she hooked you up like that?"

"For sho," Michael replied.

The two men, still drinking Red Stripe, exited the cab and left the greasy chicken bag in the backseat, but the cab driver blew the horn.

"You forgot to pay your fare," Akbar stated.

"Oh, yeah," Michael said, "what do I owe you?"

"Forty dollars."

"Hey, Michael, remember when we would jump out of the cab and run and not pay?" Donald recalled.

The cab driver took a hard look at Michael and Donald.

"He's just joking, man," Michael said. "Here's eighty dollars. Keep the change."

"Are you going to get that chicken bag outta my car?" asked Akbar.

"Man, we gone," said Michael.

They stumble into the lobby, talking loudly, and Donald was in awe as he spoke. "Man, this shit is sweet," he exclaimed. "This is more my style. This fits a man of my stature."

Donald was only about 5 foot 5 inches tall, but had a big stomach and was dressed in blue jeans and tennis shoes. His front tooth was about to rot out, but he had endless energy and always seemed to have something to say. He talked to the concierge working the desk. "Man, y'all got any vacancies? I need to move from downtown to up here. What's the rent like?"

"The average mortgage is about twenty-five hundred dollars a month," said the concierge. "Can you afford that?"

"Hell, no," he replied. "If it was fifty dollars a month, I couldn't afford it."

"Is he with you, Mr. Alexander?"

"Yeah, man, buzz us in," said Michael.

They took the elevator up to the fourth floor. Donald was amazed all the way up at the luxury of the building.

⇢⊨◎ ⇢⊨◎ ⇢⊨◎

It was 5:30 at Brittany's party, and some people were about ready to go, but the Reeses were still there with their daughter, little Eva Reese. Her parents were still talking loud and gobbling up all the food. Then the door opened and Michael and Donald hit the party like a bomb.

"Awe, man, it's a party going on," yelled Donald. "We walked in right on time."

All eyes at the party turned to the door and looked at Michael and Donald.

"Awe, man, I forgot all about Brittany's party, but better late than never," said an inebriated Michael.

Brittany spotted her father and rushed over to hug him. "Daddy," she yelled, "you like the presents that I have?"

She proudly showed Michael her presents and he hugged his daughter tightly. He smelled like alcohol and needed a shower, but Donald looked and smelled even worse. The smell of alcohol was easily recognized by anyone close by.

Cheryl, Myra, and Michelle looked at the men and couldn't believe they came to the party drunk. Brittany didn't care how her daddy looked or smelled as long as he was there.

"Remember Uncle Donald, Britt, from the hotel we lived in?"

"Hi, Uncle Donald," she said. "How are you?"

"Hi, sweet pea," he replied. "As you can see, uncle is doing very well. I'm as fine as ever."

Donald looked over and spotted Cheryl and instantly tried to flirt. "Damn, girl, you fine. Where you been all my life?"

She ignored Donald, but he was relentless towards her.

"Them jeans are hugging that ass," he said. "You need a brother like me to show you how it's done."

"I don't think so," she said drily.

"Who are those loud-ass niggers?" huffed John Reese. "How did they get invited to the party?"

"I don't know, but that tall one is sure fine," replied his wife.

"Yeah, if you like the skinny type," he retorted.

Sylvia picked her nose as she stood and looked at Michael. Michael noticed her looking at him and picking her nose, so he just looked away. Donald's eyes strayed from Cheryl for the moment and noticed Sylvia examining Michael.

"I see that big tub over there is checking you out. Maybe you need to make your move," he suggested.

"Please," Michael responded.

Michelle approached Michael and smelled him and the alcohol. "Thought you were in Paris," she said. "Ms. Coretta James came by the party, throwing her weight around."

Michael's eyes were bloodshot and he looked very tired from not sleeping the last couple of days.

"I was in France, but I turned around and came right back. Long story. I'll tell you about it later."

"You need to take a shower and brush your teeth," she said. "You look real run-down."

"It's nice to see you too."

"I'm sorry," she replied, then kissed him on the lips, no matter how bad his breath smelled.

"The air in here is cold," Cheryl said. "Can we turn it up a little?"

"We don't need to turn it up," Donald volunteered. "Why don't you come over here and get some of this body heat?"

"No, thank you."

"Who is that man with you?" asked Michelle.

"That's my boy, Donald."

"He's loud," Michelle complained, "and he keeps following Cheryl around the room."

At that moment, Sylvia made her way over to Michael at the punch bowl, and Michelle walked over to Myra for a second. Sylvia tried talking to Michael.

"How are you doing?" she asked. "I'm Sylvia Reese. Our daughters go to school together. That's my daughter, Eva, over there."

"That's nice," he replied.

"I don't usually do this, but I'll give you some loving," Sylvia said.

"Isn't that your husband over there?" asked Michael.

"Yeah, but we have an understanding. Here's my card. You can just call me on my cell phone."

"No thanks," said Michael, "you're not my type, plus I don't mess with nobody's wife."

"Well, forget you then," she huffed. "You should feel privileged to get some of this good stuff."

Michael just stared as Sylvia walked off in disgust. While they were talking, John Reese grabbed Donald as he walked by.

"Hey, man," John said, "is that your friend over there?"

"Yeah, that's my boy, Michael. This is his place."

"Well, I don't care whose place this is," stated John firmly. "You tell Mr. Gigolo if I catch him messing with my wife, I'm gonna kill him."

"Hold that thought," said Donald, who ran over to tell Michael what John Reese had said. Michael was talking to Michelle and Cheryl.

"Hey, man, I've got a message for you from John Reese."

"Who is John Reese?"

"He's that fat, greasy guy over there that can't stop eating," pointed out Donald, "and that was his wife you were talking to you in the yellow hot pants."

"So?"

"Well, he gave me a message to give to you. He said if he catches you messing with his wife, he's going to kill you."

"What?" said Michael in disbelief. He stormed off directly towards John and Sylvia Reese as Cheryl and Michelle tried to stop him. But he rushed past them and started talking directly to John as Donald looked on closely.

"Hey, man," he said, "I wouldn't mess with your ugly ass wife no way."

"Who you calling ugly?" said Sylvia Reese.

"You," he said, holding back no punches. "You're ugly, nasty, and fat. What would I look like messing with you in the first place?"

Donald laughed loudly, and Cheryl and Michelle also snickered.

"Honey, you gonna sit there and let this man talk to your wife like that?" said a livid Sylvia Reese.

Her husband stood up but didn't say anything out of fear.

"You damn right he ain't gonna say nothing," said Michael. "He's got two rings around his eyes now. I'll put two more there if he tries something."

Sylvia looked at her scared husband in disgust. "Come on, let's go," she said. "I don't have to take this."

"Yea, leave," said Donald. "If you bend that big ass of yours over outside in that yellow outfit, some guys might jump on your back, thinking you're a yellow cab."

"Yea," Michael added, "or a school bus."

The Reeses stormed towards the door in disgust. Eva, their daughter, still stood by the food with a chicken leg in her hand.

"And don't forget to take this piglet with you," Michael added.

Sylvia Reese took her daughter's hand and headed towards the door. Michael grabbed the drumstick from the child's hand on her way out. Meanwhile, Donald rolled on the floor in laughter as Myra came up to talk to Michael.

"You didn't have to do them like that did you," she pointed out. "Eva does go to school with your daughter."

Michelle and Cheryl hid their laughter.

"You need a shower," Michelle said. "Come on." She pulled Michael into his room, but first, Michael instructed Myra to give Donald a towel so he could shower. Donald then went to the guest shower, but continued to flirt with Cheryl.

"I need somebody to wash my back," he hinted to Cheryl. "You know anybody with those skills?"

Cheryl thought Donald was funny and liked him, but not in a romantic way.

"No, I don't know anybody that can wash your little back," she replied. "Hopefully, there's a brush in the bathroom you can use."

Michael asked the rest of the guests to stay as he wanted to get to know some of the parents. Michelle turned on the shower and helped Michael take off his clothes.

"Whew, you stink!" she said. "Where do you keep your toiletries?"

Michael jumped in the shower completely nude and even brushed his teeth while there. Michelle handed him his scented soap to match his cologne. Playfully, he grabbed her and pulled her into the shower as she screamed, "Oh no, I just had my hair done."

"You ever made love in the shower?" he asked.

They began to kiss and Michael removed her clothes. He threw the wet clothes on the bathroom floor, and they made love in the shower. In the other bathroom, Donald was truly amazed by its size and the rich décor. He had lived downtown LA for two years, having moved from Kansas City looking for fulfillment, but instead, got caught up in drugs and the streets. He ended up giving up on his dreams and just lived day by day, trying to survive and still have as much fun as he could.

He admired the nice towels that were in the bathroom, the cleanliness of everything, and it reminded him of what he didn't have in life, and wanted.

Finally, Michael and Michelle finished their freaky time in the shower and she exited the shower first.

"I hate you," she said playfully. "Now what am I going to put on?"

"Put on some of my stuff."

"What stuff? I can sleep in some of your stuff, but I can't fit in your clothes."

When he dried off, Michael looked through his closet and handed Michelle a tee shirt and a pair of long, LA Lakers shorts. She put her sneakers on and left the room. Then Michael called Myra to the door and gave her one of his tee shirts and some shorts for Donald. The shorts fit okay, but his stomach stuck out of the tee shirt.

Everyone noticed Michelle's change of clothes when she came out. "What happened?" Cheryl asked Michelle. "You look a little different than when you went in."

"He pulled me into the shower, and my clothes got wet."

"What else got wet?" said Myra, out of character. She tried to giggle it off, but in her heart she meant it. Donald came out and flirted with Cheryl, his stomach sticking out of the tee shirt but with no lack of confidence.

"Alright, baby, I'm fresh and clean now," he said. "I'm ready to show you how I let my hair down."

Cheryl just laughed, thinking how cute he was in a funny kind of way. When Michael came out, he went around the room meeting people, apologizing for his rude entrance, and just being a charming salesman.

He came up with the idea to switch the party by telling Myra to set all the children up in one of the rooms and then he switched the CD player to an adult party mix. They broke out some alcohol and the kiddie party turns into a full-blast party.

Several people jumped onto the dance floor. Michael and Michelle danced, and Donald kept talking to Cheryl and finally got her onto the dance floor after she initially brushed him off. R. Kelly remix to ignition kicked in.

"Come on, baby," Donald implored, "can't you see yourself next to this powerful body?"

"Oh, yeah," she said, snickering, "that's my kind of body."

"Oh, you trying to clown a brother?"

Cheryl rubbed his stomach. "I wouldn't do that, baby," she said. "I wouldn't mess with the playground."

Usher's song "Yeah!" came on and the crowd of responsible adults started to really party and chant and cheer, and the party got stronger.

Myra kept an eye on the children in their room and an eye on Michael and Michelle on the dance floor. The parents partied for a couple of hours, then the guests started leaving to get their children ready for bed.

Everybody had a great time and truly enjoyed the quickly thrown-together party, especially Donald. Cheryl had also had a long day and wanted to go back to her hotel room and sleep. She talked to Michael.

"You and Ken are not hooking back up?" Michael asked. "You're not going to give up everything, are you?"

"I don't know what I'm going to do," she answered. "We've had our problems before, but he is so totally obsessed with your life, and always has been."

"It can't be that serious," he replied. "He's done very well on his own."

"He wants to be *you*," said Cheryl. "The man is so fascinated and consumed by your life. I don't know how far he's willing to go to become you. It's scary."

"I think you're exaggerating a bit. I know he followed me around a bit, but I schooled him. He was kind of a nerd and people picked on him, but we all had our heartaches growing up. That doesn't make you go over the deep end."

"Look, Michael," said Cheryl, "I slept with that man every night. He married me because I reminded him of your wife. I know things about him that no one else knows. Nothing he does towards you would surprise me—nothing—so protect yourself."

Their conversation was interrupted by Donald still chasing after Cheryl. "Come on, baby," Donald said, "let a brother get a hug before you go."

"What brother?" she asked.

"Me," he replied.

Cheryl gave Donald a slight hug, then went and hugged Michael, kissing him on the cheek. After that, she left. Brittany had fallen asleep from exhaustion so Myra put her to bed. Everyone had left and Donald began to set up on the sofa in the living room. Of course, Michelle was still there, devoted to Michael and his every need.

"Hey, man," said Donald "what's up with your assistant, you know, that dime piece that takes care of Brittany?"

"Don't even think about it," said Michael. "That girl is a sweetheart, and she's in the process of getting her master's degree from UCLA, and we want to keep her on the straight and narrow."

Myra overheard Michael talking to Donald and realized that Michael viewed her as a girl and not the fully grown woman that she was. She was determined to make Michael see her as a woman.

"Well, since I can't mess with your assistant, how about we take another hit," Donald suggested. "I'm still wired."

"No more for me and definitely not in here. If you want to do that, go out on the balcony because I don't ever want to do that in here."

"Oh, this place is too good, huh?" Donald remarked. "We would do it all night in our rooms when we were in the hotel."

"Well, not here," said Michael. "I'm going to bed. I'm two days behind in my sleep, and I need to help clean this place up sometime tomorrow. Help yourself to anything you need."

Michael needed his old friend, Donald, when he first came back from France, but this big binge had not turned him into a crack addict again. Michael knew he was blessed and didn't want to go back to where he came from. He closed the door to his room and found Michelle already in bed. He undressed and climbed into bed and after only a few moments, fell soundly asleep and began to snore. She tried to bear it, realizing he must be exhausted. Michael looked like an innocent child sleeping. Michelle realized that he had great qualities with many character flaws, but that he was still worth putting her energy into. Besides, she didn't give her body up easily and once she did, she tried to be devoted to that man.

Early Sunday morning, Michael's cell phone rang. He was still knocked out, and Michelle ignored it. Myra rose early that morning and knocked on Michael's door. Michelle told her to come in.

"He's asleep, huh?" she asked.

"Out like a light," said Michelle. "I don't see him waking up no time soon."

"We were supposed to go to church. I guess I should go ahead and take Brittany anyway."

"It shouldn't be a problem and anyway, by the time you return, he'll probably still be out."

"You want to see something funny?" Myra asked. "Come check this out."

Michelle was nude under the covers, but grabbed Michael's robe and followed Myra out front. Donald was sound asleep. His big stomach made him look as big around as he was tall. He had fallen off the sofa onto the floor, his big stomach fully visible, and his hands stuck in his pants. The girls laughed. Myra threw a cover over him so Brittany wouldn't see him.

"Could you imagine having all that gut wrapped around you while you sleep?" said Michelle. "He's a little butterball."

She went back into the room, and Myra got Brittany ready for church. Michael's phone continued to ring.

Michael was completely out, and Michelle, for the most part, ignored the phone. It was Coretta calling Michael. She had received word that he never showed up for his appointment. Coretta was worried. She had also been calling Carlos with no answer. Carlos, of course, had no idea that Michael preceded him in coming back to the States. He arrived Sunday morning and met Stephen at the airport.

Chapter 29

"DID IT WORK?" ASKED STEPHEN.

"Yeah, it worked," Carlos replied. "When I saw them coming towards us, I went in the other direction. Michael never saw me."

"Did they grab him?"

"Yeah, they snatched him up quick. That shit definitely worked. But what do I tell Coretta? She's been calling all morning, but I wanted to speak to you first."

Carlos, Manu, and Stephen approached the SUV parked at LAX. Entering the car, Manu drove off.

"Do you think you were seen at all?" Stephen inquired.

"If they saw me, I wouldn't be here," Carlos answered.

"Good," said Stephen, who put a silencer on his gun and shot Carlos point-blank through the skull.

"You won't have to worry about what to tell the boss lady now," said Stephen without any emotion. "You won't tell her anything."

Stephen and Manu drove off to an isolated area to dump Carlos' body in the ocean as his cell phone steadily rang.

Coretta grew increasingly frustrated as neither Carlos nor Michael answered their phone. Carlos was dead and Michael was dead asleep.

"Well, we killed two birds with one stone," said Stephen. "We got rid of Carlos, who was robbing us the whole time, and we got rid of the pretty boy Michael. To be honest with you, I would rather be dumping Michael in the water than Carlos, but at least we won't have to deal with either one of them again."

⊶⊷ ⊶⊷ ⊶⊷

MICHAEL SLEPT THE day away as Kenneth and the Jacksons finalized their plans to take Brittany from him. They secured the right to have an emergency hearing on Tuesday. Kenneth had been monitoring the video system at Michael's and edited the tape to show Michael having sex and doing perverted things in Brittany's presence. Kenneth had a state-of-the-art editing system that was almost undetectable.

The Jacksons, along with Kenneth and their attorney, solicited Judge Rudy Johnson to have Michael come down for the custody hearing on Tuesday to award temporary custody to someone else until a formal hearing could be held. Michael was sent a certified letter stating that he must show up in court at 8 a.m. on Tuesday morning or relinquish all custody of his daughter until the formal hearing. He had not seen the certified letter because he had been out of town and had not checked his mailbox. The special Sunday session with the judge showed the determination of the Jacksons, going to Judge Johnson's home to show what they believed to be the urgency of the matter. The Jacksons want to show the judge the doctored up tape, along with a letter supposedly sent to Kenneth by Michael.

This is how the events happened. Attorney Sanders and Judge Rudy Johnson were college buddies. Attorney Sanders, along with the Jacksons and Kenneth, arrived at Judge Johnson's house at 9 a.m. Sunday.

"Good morning, Rudy," said Attorney Sanders, "what a fine Sunday morning it is."

"Hank, we go back a long way," Judge Johnson greeted him. "This had better be good."

"It is," he replied. "This is Mr. and Mrs. William Jackson and this is Kenneth Bolling. We need to draw your attention to this matter immediately because we believe the Jackson's grandchild could be in danger and she is also being exposed to pornography in her home by her father. We have evidence today of the said pornography, and we believe that the child should be turned over to her grandparents pending a formal hearing."

"Yes," affirmed Mrs. Jackson, "and not only that, our former son-in-law is a crack cocaine addict who took our grandchild to live on skid row for over a year. He is now a professional escort who gets paid to have sex and has admitted to sleeping with his clients without protection. Just the other day, he was photographed on television almost nude running across the TV screen."

"And you say you have evidence of this behavior?" asked Judge Johnson. "What evidence?"

"I have a letter that he wrote me just the other day boasting about his actions," said Kenneth, "and I have a tape he gave me showing his escapades in his daughter's presence."

"Why would this man write a letter to you and send you a tape of himself doing such foul things when he knows they could incriminate him?" asked the judge.

"Because we've been friends since we were five," Kenneth replied. "He doesn't think I would ever do anything to hurt him in any way. But I can't sit back and watch this beautiful little girl be violated."

Kenneth had paid a handwriting expert to forge the letter and he edited the tape himself with his sophisticated equipment. By pressuring the Jacksons to call for an immediate hearing, Michael would have no chance to have the tape authenticated. Judge Johnson read the letter with its sordid tales of perversion and viewed the tape which appeared to show Michael having sex in Brittany's presence. The phony evidence was concocted with the knowledge of Mrs. Jackson, but not her husband.

"This is an outrage," said the judge. "Why hasn't this man been arrested? I want him arrested immediately."

Judge Johnson himself called down to the police precinct and had a warrant drawn up and he signed it himself. The police immediately executed the warrant after they received it that evening.

⇥ ⇥ ⇥

THE PEOPLE AT Michael's house had no idea of impending trouble. Michael was still asleep, and Myra and Brittany returned from church but stayed in the back because Donald was still on the couch passing gas and scratching his butt while he slept.

At 4 o'clock that afternoon, Coretta called Michael again. He was still sleeping. Michelle checked the caller ID and saw Coretta's name. She decided to answer the phone to antagonize her.

"Hello," said Michelle.

"Who is this?" asked Coretta.

"Who is this?" Michelle asked in return.

"Did Michael leave his phone here, or is this someone in France?" Coretta asked.

"This is definitely not France. Michael is right here in bed with me."

Coretta recognized Michelle's voice and went off. "You better find you a toy, little wench. Now put Michael on the phone immediately."

"Michael's asleep, and if I did wake him up, it wouldn't be to talk to you. And I got your wench."

"You know, I pay for that phone you're on," Coretta snapped, "and that bed you're lying on and everything around you."

"You made that clear yesterday," Michelle said drily.

"Well, one thing I obviously didn't make clear, bitch, is that I'll kill you so fast, you won't even know you're dead. I've had hundreds of people taken out, tough people, killers and thugs, so what makes you think you can get away with talking to me like that?"

Michelle heard the absolute evil in Coretta's voice and realized in her spirit that she was serious. She also recalled Michael's thoughts about Coretta's ability to commit crimes. Michelle stopped antagonizing Coretta anymore.

"You're quiet now, bitch, but it's too late. I'm coming for you personally and, believe me, from this point on, I'll always know where you are."

Coretta hung up the phone, and Michelle worried about their conversation. But she didn't have long to think about it. The police were on the way. The Bel Air Police Department had a signed warrant for Michael's arrest. The Jacksons and Kenneth followed the police cars. The police arrived at the front and showed the concierge their warrant. They were immediately escorted to the fourth floor.

FOUR POLICEMEN KNOCKED at the door. Myra answered it.

"We have an arrest warrant for Michael Alexander," said the lead officer. "Is he here?"

Myra knew that Michael was in the bedroom sleeping and reluctantly pointed to the bedroom door. Michael was still asleep and Michelle lay next to him. Both of them were nude.

Donald awoke and jumped up when he saw the police. Brittany came from her room and Mr. and Mrs. Jackson instantly approached her.

"Brittany," said Mrs. Jackson, "it's Paw-Paw and Granny. It's good to see you."

Brittany didn't remember the Jacksons well and besides, she was more concerned with what the police were up to.

The four policemen opened Michael's bedroom door as Donald looked in fear, knowing that he had two outstanding warrants for traffic violations himself. The police looked into Michael's room and found both of them sleeping. The police nudged Michael, and Michelle awoke to see not only the police, but everyone else in the house watching them.

"What are you doing in the room?" she asked, stunned.

The police didn't respond but continued to nudge Michael awake.

"Uh?" he said, rolling over.

This time, the policeman nudged him harder with his billy club.

"Man, who keeps poking me?" he said in a fog.

"Michael, Michael," Michelle said urgently, "Michael, wake up."

He finally lifted his head and looked at Michelle, who pointed to the police. He rolled over to see the police standing over him.

"Michael Alexander, we have a warrant for your arrest."

"For what?" he said dumbfounded.

"Child pornography. You have the right to remain silent." As the officer read him his rights, Michael felt this had to be a bad dream.

"Child pornography? What do you mean, 'child pornography'?"

"You know what child pornography is," said Mr. Jackson. "We saw your own child in this mess."

Michael was totally unaware of what is going on.

"Mr. Alexander, are you wearing anything?" asked the police officer.

He looked under the cover. "No," he replied.

An officer went to his closet and grabbed a jogging suit and sneakers and handed them to Michael to put on, then he closed the door on everybody else but the police and Michelle. Michael had a total disdain for the police and jumped from his bed and started to go off.

"Man, what the fuck y'all doing in my house? I'm not involved in no child pornography."

The police ordered him to put on his clothes, but he refused.

"Put them on him," said the lead police officer.

The three other police officers seized Michael, and he fought back. Michelle jumped from the bed as the other officer grabbed Michael around the neck. He felt the pain of the lock, but continued to kick. The officers forcefully put Michael's clothes on him, lifted him from the bed, cuffed him and led him out the door.

"Michelle," yelled Michael, "look in my drawer. I have a card with Barbara Brown's home and cell number. Call her for me and tell her what happened."

As Michael was led from the room, he saw Kenneth and the Jacksons standing over by the door.

"So that's what this is all about?" he demanded. "You three have made something up on me."

"This is nothing made up," said Mr. Jackson. "We saw the tape, and we read the letter. You're a sick man."

Mr. Jackson attempted to go after Michael, but was restrained by Kenneth.

"What's your part in this?" Michael yelled to Kenneth. "I know you have something to do with this."

As he was taken out the door, Brittany yelled and screamed for her father and Michelle and Myra cried. The police placed Michael in their car.

"We have an order from the judge saying that Brittany is to go with us," stated Mrs. Jackson. "We're going to take her out of this hellhole. Come on, baby."

Brittany didn't want to go with the Jacksons, but they insisted on her coming and finally Kenneth picked her up as she kicked and screamed.

The Jacksons were stunned by Brittany putting up such a fight. Michelle and Myra covered their eyes and continued to cry. Michael was struggling as he was forced into the police car, especially when he saw Brittany being forced into a car by Kenneth and the Jacksons.

"Give me my baby!" he yelled from the police car.

"Daddy! Daddy!" screamed Brittany.

After Brittany was placed into the car, Kenneth drove off.

Michael sobbed in the police car, then kicked the glass with his feet while still handcuffed. One of the police officers shocked him with a stun gun and subdued him until they arrived at the police station.

Meanwhile, back upstairs, Michelle and Myra still sobbed.

"Michael ain't no pervert by no stretch of the imagination. That's some made-up shit," said an angry Donald.

Michelle still cried loudly. Donald took charge and said, "Find that number Michael told you to locate and call that woman. Tell her what happened. She's got to be somebody that can help."

Michael was taken to the Los Angeles County Jail to be booked.

The booking agent looked at the papers containing Michael's charges and said aloud, "They're going to love you in the county when you get there. They don't take kindly to child molesters and perverts."

"I ain't no child molester," Michael protested. "All this stuff is made up."

"That's what they all say," replied the officer.

The officer obtained Michael's vital information, then put him in a holding cell with about 40 other men of every nationality. It was so crowded that they were almost lying on top of each other, and they smelled terrible. Some of the men found a corner to sleep in while others tried to find a way to call collect to anyone who could get them out of jail. Michael just stood in the corner and looked at the paperwork with his criminal charges on them. He spoke to no one.

After a few minutes, Michael was called with several others to be fingerprinted, then afterwards, he was put into a different cell. Trustees brought sandwiches and frozen juice to the cell and passed them out to the inmates. Michael just looked at the food.

"You ain't gonna eat that, man?" asked an inmate.

He said nothing and passed the sandwich to the inmate.

After a few more moments, Michael was called from his cell and an officer read his charges.

"You have been charged with child pornography and lewd behavior on a minor, and you haven't been given any bail."

"No bail?" he exclaimed. "What the fuck is up with you people? I didn't do anything."

Michael continued to talk loudly, so finally two deputies placed him in a cold cell all alone, with no attention given to him at all, and no cover. He was forced to sit and sleep on the hard, freezing cold floor. He balled up in a corner and tried to stay warm, and his misery was accented by the conditions around him.

⇥ ⇥ ⇥

AT MICHAEL'S HOUSE, Michelle called Barbara and left a message. Soon, Barbara returned the call. Donald, Michelle, and Myra were in the condo when the call came and Myra answered the phone.

"This is Barbara Brown. I'm returning a call."

"Mrs. Brown, I'm Myra Irvin. I work for Michael Alexander."

"Oh, yeah," Barbara said, "where is Michael? Put him on the phone and let me thank him again for the lovely evening we had."

Myra paused so Michelle took the phone.

"Michael's in jail," said Michelle. "He was locked up this evening."

"For what?"

"I'd rather not go into details," Michelle replied. "He told us to find your number and give you a call."

"Where is he?"

"LA County Jail," Michelle informed her. "We've been calling. He doesn't have bail, but he will be in court in the morning."

"Get him an attorney," Barbara ordered. "I'll be there tonight and see what I can do for him when I arrive. Give me your address and I'll be over there as soon as I arrive."

Michelle gave Barbara the address, then Barbara made arrangements for the trip. She called Gary.

"Pack a bag. I want you to go to LA with me. Michael's in trouble, and we need to go see what we can do."

Gary put his stuff in a bag and hurried to the mansion to pick up Barbara then drive to O'Hare Airport to take an emergency flight to LA.

Myra and Michelle talked and decided to call Cheryl and explain what happened. After Cheryl received the call, she rushed over to Michael's, arriving approximately a half hour later. She was full of questions.

"You said that Michael was arrested for child pornography? That's so not Michael. He would never put his child in that kind of situation."

"Well, he needs an attorney," said Michelle, "and you're the only person I could think of."

"Tell me what happened," said Cheryl.

"The police came in and arrested Michael," said a distressed Michelle. "They had Michael's former in-laws and your husband, Kenneth, with them."

"Kenneth?! Why was he here?"

"I don't know," Michelle answered, "but they had a document giving them authority to take Brittany. She really didn't want to go, poor child. She kicked and screamed all the way."

Cheryl called the jail and was informed that Michael had no bail and would be in Judge Johnson's courthouse in the morning. She realized that she must get Michael out on bail and review the evidence against him.

"I've got to go," she said. "I've got only 9 hours to prepare. I'll see you guys in the morning."

Although most of the people in Michael's circle hadn't known him long, they all had one thing in common: complete faith in Michael and his integrity. Although he had his faults, he inspired those close to him to be completely loyal.

⇥ ⇥ ⇥

MEANWHILE, AT KENNETH's house, Brittany refused to cooperate with anyone and cried and called for her father all night. Finally at midnight, Kenneth called over to the condo to speak to Myra.

"Hello, Myra," he said, "this is Kenneth Bolling."

"You've got a lot of nerve calling me. What do you want?"

"Brittany won't stop crying. We were wondering if you could come over to be with her. Maybe then she'll stop crying. We can't get her to go to sleep."

Myra hesitated for a second, but realized that Brittany was more important than any hatred she felt for the situation. She got directions to his house, then hung up the phone and picked up her purse to leave.

"Where are you going?" asked Michelle.

"That was Kenneth on the phone."

"Kenneth?" Michelle asked angrily. "What did he want?"

"Brittany won't stop crying," Myra answered. "I've got to go to her."

Michelle thought about it for a moment and agreed that Myra should definitely go and be with Brittany.

⇥ ⇥ ⇥

MEANWHILE, AS THE night progressed, the cell that Michael was in got colder and more uncomfortable. The pain of being in jail was terrible; the pain of the lies being told about him was worse. He tried to get a little sleep, but he was in so much discomfort that he couldn't even close his eyes. He had a miserable night, but tried to maintain focus because he had been through enough to push him over the edge.

At Kenneth's house, Myra arrived and Brittany rushed over to her for comfort. Myra wiped the child's eyes and sat down in a chair with her, then began singing to her until Brittany fell asleep in Myra's arms. Myra knew the charges against Michael were trumped up.

"Can I get you anything, Myra?" asked Kenneth.

"I don't want anything from you," she said. "I can look in your eyes and tell you're behind all this."

"Michael should not expose his child to perversion," said Kenneth. "He's only getting what he deserves."

"One day soon," said Myra, "you're going to get what you deserve, count on it."

She cuddled with Brittany in the chair and finally went to sleep, at least for a little while.

At 6:30 a.m, Barbara Brown arrived at Michael's condo. She and Gary were invited in by Michelle. They introduced themselves to each other and talked about what was going on.

At 7, Cheryl called from jail. She was about to see Michael for moral support. He had been brought to the courthouse by deputies that morning at 6:30 and had to wait in a holding cell to be called into court.

Cheryl saw him shortly after 7 in the part of the courtroom where the lawyers can visit their clients. Michael came in wearing handcuffs, looking like a beaten man, still with the jogging suit on.

"Oh, Michael, I'm *so* sorry," she said. "You look like you had a long night."

His eyes were red from lack of sleep, and he sneezed, coming down with a cold from the holding cell. He could barely hold his head up from the pain of lying on the concrete and steel all night.

"I slept in a freezing cell all night," he complained. "This has been the worst night of my life, and I think I'm sick."

"Well, I've been reviewing the evidence they say they have," said Cheryl. "They said you wrote a letter to Kenneth, confessing, and they have a tape showing you having sex with your daughter watching."

"Never!" he exclaimed. "I would never expose her to that. I'd rather die first."

"I believe you. We need to get a physical copy of the evidence and take a look at it and go from there. I know it's cold in that holding cell, so I'm going to try to keep you in here with me until they call your case, so bear with me."

Kenneth and the Jacksons arrived at the courtroom together while Michelle, Donald, Gary, and Barbara arrived shortly thereafter and prepared for the hearing. Michael walked into the courtroom with his attorney, Cheryl. He looked tired, but ready for business. As he looked across the courtroom, he saw Kenneth and the Jacksons. Myra stayed behind at Kenneth's place to care for Brittany, who was still sleeping when everyone left.

"All rise," said the clerk. "The Honorable Judge Rudy Johnson is presiding."

"Be seated," said Judge Johnson. "This hearing is to decide if Michael Alexander is to have bail and if so, the amount."

"Your Honor," said Attorney Sanders, "we are opposed to bail because of Mr. Alexander's past as a drug user. We feel that he is a flight risk and due to the sordid nature of the crime, we don't want him to have freedom to soil the minds of any other children."

Kenneth looked across the room and was shocked to see his wife defending Michael.

"Your Honor," said Cheryl, "we would like for the court to consider that my client hasn't been convicted of any crime and he has never been accused of such a crime before. We contend that he isn't a risk to run and needs to be free to prepare his case properly."

Judge Johnson considered both points and tried to come up with a solution for both parties.

"Considering the serious nature of the crime and the implications of them, I will agree to set bail, considering that Mr. Alexander has no prior criminal record of any kind. Bail is set at fifty thousand dollars. This will be a cash-only bail. If Mr. Alexander makes bail, he is to have no contact with his daughter at all until we return to court one month from today. Custody will remain with Mr. and Mrs. Jackson until the dynamics of this case have been litigated."

"Your Honor," said Cheryl, "my client doesn't have fifty thousand dollars cash to put up for bail."

"That's not my problem," he responded. "He needs to come up with it if he wants to get out of jail."

At that moment, Barbara Brown walked outside the courtroom to make a call.

"Your Honor," said Cheryl, "we would like to review the evidence for ourselves so we can prepare our case."

"Of course," said Attorney Sanders. "We will provide the defense with copies of both pieces of evidence."

"Very well," said Judge Johnson, "we will be back here on the 10th of next month for the trial of Mr. Alexander. This court is adjourned."

Michael looked at Kenneth and the Jacksons with disgust and was led back to the holding cell inside the courtroom. Donald, Michelle, Cheryl, and Gary talked.

"Where is Barbara?" asked Michelle.

"She went outside to use the phone," Gary replied.

Moments later, Barbara returned. "He'll be out in 20 minutes," she said. "That's how long it takes for that money to be wired to me. My business partner is in the process of getting it here right now."

"That's wonderful," said Cheryl. "Now we can go home and look at this stuff and see what's really going on."

Michelle and Barbara drove off to the bank where the money had been wired and then hurried back to pay the cash bond. At 10:30, Michael was released.

Everyone was there waiting for him when he came out of the jail. Michelle hugged him tightly.

"Ah, baby," she said, "it's so good to see you, to touch you. Are you alright?"

"About as alright as I can be, considering the circumstances," he replied. "I need a cup of hot tea. How did you get the money so fast?"

"You have to thank Ms. Brown for that," Cheryl said. "She was on it as soon as she heard the amount."

Michael hadn't seen Gary and Barbara in the courtroom and rushed to hug them as soon as he spotted them.

"I can't believe you're here," he said to them. "I knew you guys would be there for me."

"We said that we were true friends," Gary smiled. "True friends are always there for each other."

"Yeah," said Barbara, "and besides, I figured you probably didn't want to spend another night in there. Some birds shouldn't be caged, and you are definitely one of them."

"I'll get you the money back as soon as possible," Michael promised. "I'll get it to you as soon as I get it."

"Don't worry about it," said Barbara. "Just get yourself out of this mess. Now can we go eat? I'm starved. Breakfast— or lunch—is on me."

"I'm with that," Donald quipped.

"I'll bet you are," Cheryl teased.

They all went off to eat and tried to make the best of a terrible situation.

⇥ ⇥ ⇥

MEANWHILE, AT KENNETH'S place, the Jacksons are preparing to go back to New York right away. Kenneth and Mrs. Jackson talked.

"Do you think that they can find out that we edited that tape the way we did?" asked Mrs. Jackson. "That would be a real disaster for us if they did."

"It's possible, I guess," he replied, "but you have to be an expert."

"What about the letter?" she asked.

"What about it? My handwriting expert gets paid a lot for his service. You've got to know for sure that Michael didn't write it and nobody knows that but us and him. We're not going to tell, and nobody will believe him."

"Well, we'll be on our way shortly," said Mrs. Jackson. "We're going to take Brittany back to New York until we have to be back for trial. Now that I think about it, we've got a beach house in the Bahamas. I think we'll go there instead."

"Okay," Kenneth remarked. "Just let me know where you are, and I'll keep everything together on this end."

The Jacksons prepared to leave town. They had to make Brittany go without trying to force her. Myra was still there and didn't realize that the Jacksons were about to leave.

"Brittany," said Mrs. Jackson, "how would you like to go on a little vacation?"

"No, I just want to be with my daddy."

"Your daddy is coming," said Mrs. Jackson, "and Myra is coming too. You and me and Paw-Paw are going first, and they will be coming later on."

Myra looked at Mrs. Jackson and spoke. "What are you doing? I'm not going along with this. I'm not going to lie to her."

Mrs. Jackson called Myra off to the side, away from Brittany. "We've got custody of her," said Mrs. Jackson, "and we're gonna take her one way or the other. Her father has a fifty thousand dollars all-cash bail. What do you think the chances are he will come up with fifty thousand dollars? Now you don't want her to spend the rest of her nights like last night do you? I'm sure you want her to have some peace until she gets used to us, because like it or not, she belongs to us now and I'm gonna do everything in my power to make it a permanent situation."

Myra thought about it and decided that under the circumstances, it might be best for Brittany, so she went along with Mrs. Jackson's lie.

"Yes, Brittany," she said, "your dad and I will be coming soon, and we will all be together."

"And Michelle too," said Brittany.

Myra felt terrible about her lie, but thought it was the right thing to do, not knowing how long Michael would be in jail. She had no idea he had been released on bail. After that, she walked out of the house with her head down and returned to Michael's condo.

Chapter 30

AFTER EATING, MICHAEL USED CHERYL'S cell phone to call and check his messages. The gun shop where he went to purchase the gun left a message that he could pick up his gun immediately. He had Michelle stop by the gun shop on the way to the condo. Michael, Donald, and Gary went in while Michelle and Barbara remained in the car. Cheryl followed closely behind in her car. Michael finished the paperwork and the silver 380 semi-automatic handgun was his. He purchased two boxes of ammunition and was given the registration to put in his car.

"That's a nice gun," said Gary. "With all that's going on in your life, you need that."

"That's for real," said Donald. "It seems like a bunch of people have it out for you."

They left the store, got back into the car, and headed back to Michael's condo to view the tape and read the supposedly incriminating letter.

Once they reached the condo, Barbara was anxious to go. "I've got to be getting back to Chicago," she said. "I've got some appointments tonight. I can make it if I take the red-eye. Gary, why don't you stay for a couple of days? Maybe you can help in some way. At least, you'll be around your friend."

"Yea," said Gary, "if you're sure you can get along without me."

"I think I can manage," she smiled. "I got this extra cash from the wire. You take it and stay as long as it takes."

"Michael?" said Barbara, "tell Coretta that I hate I missed her, but I've got to get back out of town."

When they arrived at the condo, Barbara insisted on taking a cab to the airport. She knew that it was important to get started on Michael's case and everyone's help might be needed.

Donald, Michelle, Michael, Gary, and Cheryl went upstairs to Michael's place to view the tape. Myra was already there, having left Kenneth's house. She was very surprised and excited to see Michael walk through the door. She grabbed Michael as soon as she saw him.

"Michael, I didn't think I would see you this soon." She held on tightly to Michael's neck and pulled his head down, hanging on.

"Okay," he laughed, "you're going to break my neck."

"I'm just so glad to see you," she exclaimed. "How did you get out?"

"First, Cheryl got me bail and then Barbara paid the bail. Oh, Myra, this is my friend, Gary. We became friends in Chicago. He and Barbara came down from Chicago to help get me out of this mess. We were just about to view this so-called incriminating tape. You want to watch?"

"Sure, if you don't mind," she replied.

Michael was so confident in his innocence that he didn't hesitate to invite everyone to watch. He put the tape into a VCR and everyone watched the contents. The tape showed Michelle rubbing Michael's nude body with Brittany standing by and watching.

Later in the tape, Michael and Michelle were making love with Brittany right there in the bed. Everybody was appalled at the picture and stared at Michael and Michelle.

"I see why they locked me up after they looked at this mess," he declared, "but that's impossible. That day when Michelle and I made love, Brittany wasn't even here."

"Well, it looks like she was here to me," said Donald. "Michael, I never thought you would do this."

"I didn't, fool," he replied.

They continued to look at the tape. In everything Michael had done in the house sexually, Brittany was in the picture.

"Somebody filmed all this and then transposed the picture of Brittany," he said. "As wild as we were having sex, we would have at least knocked her off the bed, and as you can see, she doesn't even move or look stressed in any way. And besides, I've never filmed myself having sex in my life."

Michael began looking around the room. His eyes roamed up to the light, and he unscrewed the bulb. Fully exposed was a tiny camera that was being monitored by Kenneth at that time.

"Aha," he said. "The jig is up."

Michael found cameras in every room. "Well," he said, "I see how we were recorded. I'm guessing Kenneth did this. He was always so good with computer equipment. He must have figured out a way to get in here and planted these cameras, and some of my mail is missing. I bet he doctored up that letter too. I would never write no mess like that."

"I don't believe that he would go to this much trouble," said Cheryl. "This goes beyond sick—he's lost it."

"Yea, he's lost it," Michael agreed, "and Brittany's over there. Cheryl, can you get an expert to analyze these two phony pieces of evidence? Your husband and my ex-in-laws are in for a big surprise."

"I'm sure it won't be a problem getting them analyzed," she said. "How did the judge miss this?"

"Maybe he just rushed to judgment and didn't thoroughly analyze them," Michael suggested.

"I still can't believe this," Cheryl replied.

"Myra," Michael said, "have the locks changed immediately."

Myra looked strange as Michael spoke to her.

"What's wrong, Myra?" he asked. "What's up?"

"I don't know how to tell you this, but the Jacksons took Brittany and went back to New York."

"What? When did this happen?" he asked.

"Not long ago. They left right after they came from the courthouse. I guess they knew they would be caught and wanted to have their granddaughter with them, away from here at all costs."

"No!" he yelled.

Michael rushed out of the room, followed by Gary and Donald. He ran to his car and fired up the engine, taking off before Gary and Donald could get in it, then he flew out of the parking lot and headed straight for Kenneth's house. Donald and Gary went back upstairs.

"He took off," said Gary. "I think he's going to see Kenneth. And he's got his gun."

"Oh, no," said Cheryl, who ran out the door to her car, followed by everyone.

MICHAEL STOPPED TO load the gun and then continued to Ken's house. He knew the gate code and pulled into Ken's driveway, getting out and slamming the door. With the gun in his hand, he rang the doorbell, but Ken had already gone to his office. No one answered the door.

Michael's next stop was Kenneth's office.

About 5 minutes after Michael left the house, Cheryl pulled up. She didn't see Michael's car. She also went to the door, but realized no one was home.

"Damn, no one's home," she said. "I bet he went to Ken's job."

At that exact moment, Michael pulled up to Progress Insurance, where Ken worked. Cheryl dialed Kenneth on his cell phone. When he saw her number, he hesitated before answering.

"So do you want to come back?" he asked. "If you beg, I might think about it."

"You better think about getting out of that building," she said brusquely. "We found the cameras, and we see where you superimposed Brittany into the film. Michael's on his way, and he is packing some serious heat."

Kenneth immediately hung up the phone. He knew what he had done and truly believed Michael would kill him. He was on the 3rd floor, which had a fire escape outside of his office. Without a word to anyone, he quickly moved towards it just as Michael came to the front desk where the secretary sat. She remembered Michael from his days of working there.

"Hello, Michael," she said politely.

He didn't stop or speak. He just rushed into Kenneth's office.

"You can't just go in there," she yelled.

Michael burst through the door and looked out the window, only to see Kenneth jump in his car and take off. Michael calmly walked to Kenneth's desk, knocked over a picture of him and Ken, and stomped on it. Ken's secretary tried to call for security, but Michael was not in the mood to face any more authority. He pulled his gun and showed it to the woman.

"Bitch, I advise you to drop that phone if you know what's good for you," he said angrily.

The secretary immediately dropped the phone in fear and Michael calmly walked back to his car and returned to his condo. Ken disappeared, not to be seen for days.

After Michael parked at the condo and exited his car, a stranger greeted him. "Michael Alexander?" the stranger inquired.

Michael was in a daze and simply nodded in acknowledgment.

"Loren Pinson told me to give you this," continued the stranger.

The man pulled an iron rod from inside his coat and cracked Michael across the leg. Michael screamed and fell back onto his car. The man started to hit Michael again, this time across his head, but Michael pulled the gun from his waist and pointed it directly at the man's head. The stranger stopped in his tracks and dropped the iron rod. Michael stood up and began to limp closer, putting the gun directly against the man's head.

"You know, I've had a real fucked-up day," said Michael. "In fact, I've had a real fucked-up life, and I could very easily blow your head off, so if I were you, I'd get away from here quickly."

The man ran to his car, jumped in, and drove off. Michael limped towards the condo as Cheryl pulled up with the rest of the group. They noticed Michael limping.

"What happened, Michael?" asked Gary, bounding from Cheryl's car.

"You don't want to know," came the reply. "I'm going inside before the building falls on me."

He hobbled upstairs and collapsed on the couch. Then he checked his cell phone. At least 20 calls were from Coretta, along with his other calls. Michelle quietly walked up behind him and massaged his shoulders.

"It should be very easy to prove these documents were doctored," Cheryl said. "Barbara will have to return to get her fifty thousand dollars bail money back."

Michael didn't say anything as Cheryl spoke. Gary and Cheryl had been making eye contact all afternoon, but ignored the building chemistry, considering the situation.

"How long will you be here, Gary?" Cheryl asked.

"I'll be here for however long it takes to get my boy, Michael, straight."

After that, Cheryl left to handle some legal matters and Donald took a bottle of Hennessey XO that was on the bar and poured Michael a large glass.

"It shouldn't be hard to find the Jacksons," Michael stated. "I'll hire a private investigator. I have to get my baby back." Then he drank some of the cognac and just held his head down.

"Michael, can I get you anything?" asked Myra.

"No, I've got what I need here in my hands." With that, he took another drink of the Hennessey.

"Pour me some more," he said.

"Take it easy," Michelle said softly. "We're all here for you." Then she got up to leave.

"I've got to go get some clothes," Michelle said.

"Don't go, baby," Michael pleaded.

"I won't be gone an hour," she answered. "All your friends will be here with you until I get back."

She kissed him on the lips and made a quick run to her hotel suite to gather up clothes and other necessities.

Chapter 31

FOR THE LAST COUPLE OF days, Coretta had been busy getting passports for her employees and herself and transferring her funds to undisclosed accounts. She had been totally incognito on those few occasions that she went out in public. The police had been searching frantically to find her and Stephen. She used her cell phone, but never from where she was staying so it couldn't be traced. She stayed in hotel rooms under assumed names and still was unaware of Carlos' death, knew nothing of the plot against Michael in France, and couldn't understand why Michael wouldn't return her phone calls. Stephen and Manu had been living on one of Coretta's boats and also kept a real low profile.

The police searched all of Coretta's houses, but had yet to come up with a clue to where any of them were. With everyone lying low, Detective Andrews paid Michael a courtesy visit. He knocked on Michael's door.

"Oh, no," Michael groaned, "don't open it. The way things are going for me, it may be the Grim Reaper."

"I doubt very seriously if the Grim Reaper would be knocking on your door while your friends are here," Gary assured him.

"Maybe he wants to torture me before putting me out of my misery," Michael replied.

Myra answered the door. Detective Andrews stood there with a child. He entered and looked at Michael, who appeared to be extremely stressed out.

"Had a few problems today, huh, Michael?" he asked.

"I guess you still got that tail on me," Michael replied. "You didn't think I knew about that, huh? Well, he doesn't keep up too well anyway. Who's the kid?"

"This is Paul Gentry," said Detective Andrews, "Detective Gentry's son. I'm trying to adopt him."

"That's good," said Michael, "but today is not a good day for a social call."

"Just checking to see if you can put me in contact with Ms. James. I wouldn't want this child's mother's life to be in vain. We just came from her funeral."

Michael paused, "Sorry, Detective, I haven't seen her and besides, I've got major problems of my own with my own child."

"Sorry to hear that," said Detective Andrews, "if you think of anything—"

Michael cut him off "You'll be the first to know. It's been nice to meet you, Paul."

Michael opened the door so Detective Andrews could leave, then closed the door and sat back down. Paul Gentry was a handsome young man with a sad face that touched Michael even through his own problems and left a deep impression on Michael's heart.

That evening, Cheryl took her experts to see Judge Johnson and the tape and the letter were quickly revealed to be a fraud. She told the judge of the Jacksons leaving town with Brittany and reminded him that it was his ruling that allowed the Jacksons to take Michael's child. She also reluctantly revealed that it was her husband, Kenneth, who was probably the mastermind behind the whole thing. A federal warrant was issued for the Jacksons for kidnapping, and a warrant was issued for Kenneth Bolling for falsifying evidence.

After Cheryl left the judge, she went back to Michael's condo to update him on the situation. She arrived at the same time that Michelle did, pulling two bags. All eyes were upon her as she walked through the door.

"I'm a model," she explained. "My bags are always packed."

Everyone laughed.

"There's a warrant out for the Jacksons," Cheryl said, "and for Kenneth." She paused. "They won't get away."

Michael continued to throw back Hennesseys and was joined by Gary and Donald.

"This stuff is smooth," Gary remarked. "I see why it costs so much."

At that time, Cheryl took some, and so did Michelle.

"I don't drink," said Myra.

"Well, pour yourself a fruit punch and join the party," said Donald merrily, "and fix me a bologna sandwich."

"We don't have any bologna," said Myra, pouring herself a glass of juice and joining the group as Gary proposed a toast.

"Here's to friendship," said Gary, "to always being there for each other, no matter what."

They all toasted to friendship. Michael kept a straight face but continued to think about Brittany. He raised his glass alone.

"Here's to Brittany," he said. "Be safe 'till Daddy sees you again."

Everyone was somber, thinking about Brittany, but happy to be among friends, *real* friends.

At midnight, Michael and Michelle went to bed, and Donald continued to flirt with Cheryl, but she had eyes for Gary.

Gary, Donald, and Cheryl all bunked up in the living room, and Myra went to her room. No one slept in Brittany's room. Donald had been wearing his old sneakers all day with no socks. He took off his shoes to lay down on the floor and went to sleep.

"Man, you stink," Cheryl grumbled.

"Really," Gary chimed in. "Man, wash your feet or something."

Donald was too tired to get up. "I don't smell nothing."

After a few moments, Gary cracked, "Hey, if I give you four or five dollars, will you wash those feet?"

Cheryl and Gary laughed loudly. Even Donald joined in. Eventually they ignored the smell and fell asleep. It had been a mentally draining day for everyone, and they all slept soundly.

⇥⊚ ⇥⊚ ⇥⊚

AFTER A LONG night of flying, Susie and William Jackson, along with Brittany, woke up in their cottage in the Bahamas. Mrs. Jackson had wanted to fly to the Bahamas to get away for a while, but secretly, she was really fleeing from the law.

Brittany was getting impatient and wanted to see her father and Myra and Michelle.

"When is Daddy coming?"

"Soon," said Mrs. Jackson.

Brittany walked off to play with some toys.

"When are you going to tell her that they won't be coming" asked her husband, "and that she won't see them until the trial?"

Mrs. Jackson paused for a moment. "Bill, I need to tell you something," she said. "I doubt if there's going to be a trial."

"Why? We've got to see what happens to Michael after what he did to Brittany."

"Kenneth made it up."

"Made what up?" he asked, confused.

"All of it. The letter, the tape, everything. The letter was written by one of Ken's friends, who is a handwriting expert, and the tape Kenneth edited himself using some new, expensive equipment to make it seem as if Brittany witnessed all of Michael's sexual encounters."

"You mean, Michael didn't do any of that stuff?" a shocked William Jackson said. "No pornography and no perverted letter?"

"That doesn't take away the fact that he killed our daughter," Mrs. Jackson stated, "our *only* daughter. She was all we had."

"Shut up!" Mr. Jackson said loudly. "You mean to tell me we had that man locked up and took his daughter under *false* pretences?"

"She's our granddaughter," Mrs. Jackson emphasized. "We need her too."

"Yes," but she is *his daughter*," Mr. Jackson stated, "and *he* has all the rights. Now we don't have a leg to stand on. Not only did you blow our chances to win a custody hearing, but you also may have locked us up for the rest of our lives. I'm too old to go to prison."

"Prison?! For *what?*"

"Kidnapping, fraud, falsifying evidence. Oh, Susie, what have you done?"

"It wasn't me. It was Kenneth," Mrs. Jackson declared. "He has such a hatred for Michael that he was willing to do anything to bring him down, and I wanted Brittany so bad that I just didn't think. I'm sorry."

"Yes, you are sorry. *Now* what are we going to do?"

Mr. Jackson walked out of the room in disgust. He had never stood up to his wife before and realized things would have been different if he had been stronger. Mrs. Jackson was out front with Brittany, sobbing slightly as Brittany continued to ask the same question.

"Where's my daddy?" Brittany whined.

⇥⊕ ⇥⊕ ⇥⊕

AT 10 TUESDAY morning, Myra prepared breakfast for everyone. Cheryl's cell phone rang. After speaking for a few moments, she hung up the phone. Gary was sitting close to her on the living room floor, and Donald was sleeping not far away from the two of them.

"That was Judge Johnson," she said. "He will allow Gary or Michael to pick up Barbara's money so she won't have to come back to town to pick it up unless she wants to."

"We'll call her today and see how she feels," said Gary. "Whatever she decides, we'll go with."

"Something smells good," said Donald, waking up, smelling Myra's cooking.

"I bet it ain't your feet," smiled Cheryl.

"Definitely can't be his feet," laughed Gary.

"Y'all want to play tag team on me first thing in the morning," pouted Donald playfully, "but it's cool."

He put his shoes back on and went to the restroom to clean up, but he kept wearing the sneakers with no socks. Michelle emerged from Michael's room with long pajamas on, followed by Michael with a tee shirt and pants. Michael poured some juice. Myra finished cooking eggs, grits, and turkey bacon, and Michael was ready to eat. Cheryl skipped breakfast because she needed to leave. She had work awaiting her at her office, but wanted to return to her hotel room to change first. Gary offered to walk her downstairs and she gladly accepted.

Michelle also had business to take care of, but only after breakfast.

Even Donald was anxious to get back downtown, to take care of his business. Michael thought Donald probably wanted to get more crack. He called a cab for his friend. They walked to the front of the condo, past Jackie Brown, who was working the front desk. The cab was waiting so Michael paid his cab fare.

"You want to come with me and get a toot-toot?" Donald asked.

"I can't even think about that," Michael replied. "I've got to get my daughter back. I need to hang around until that happens. Every time something happens, I run away. I can't run away this time. Brittany needs me."

"Well, a toot-toot will help you forget all this mess," Donald suggested.

"I don't want to forget this time," Michael said, giving Donald some money to spend.

"Tell Cheryl I'm coming back for her," Donald said with a sly smile. "I want them hips in my life."

"Why don't you take Jackie Brown at the front desk? She's got big hips, and she's chocolate."

"Yea, elephant hips," said Donald "I don't need no woman bigger than me. There's only so much room in the bed."

Michael laughed. "You really helped me make it through the last few days. You've kept me laughing when I needed it."

"What are friends for?" said Donald.

"Alright, my brother, head downtown," Donald said to the cabbie.

Michael said, "Don't forget, if you need anything, I'm here."

"Yeah, man," said Donald, "you're getting too emotional. You know I'm a free spirit. I can't take all this lovey-dovey stuff. Come back downtown when you want to have some fun. Later, brother."

The cab took off with Donald waving good-bye as he headed downtown. Michael went back upstairs just as Michelle was preparing to leave. The locksmith had arrived to change the locks and Myra made a suggestion.

"We've got revival at church this week. Why don't we all go tonight?"

"I don't think so," Michael answered. "I don't really feel like being around a crowd."

"This is not the time to worry about crowds," said Myra. "You've tried everything else, why not try God? You promised me that you would go Sunday, and I realize a lot has happened since Sunday, but you have nothing to lose and maybe *everything* to gain."

"I'm game if you are," said Michelle. "What about you, Gary?"

"Why not?" he replied. "Let's ask Cheryl to go. We all could use some spirit right now."

"Well, Michael, that leaves only you," Myra pointed out. "Why not go for it?"

"Alright, I'm with it."

"Good," said Myra, "I'll drive. I've got enough room for everybody. Church starts at 7. Just be ready to have a hallelulah good time." Then she left to run some errands and Michelle prepared to leave.

"Michael, what are you going to do the rest of the day?" asked Michelle.

"I'm going to stay here in case someone calls about Brittany, and I have to wait for the man to finish the locks."

"Well, I'll be back around 5 p.m. Stay out of trouble, OK?"

"You too," he said.

Michelle kissed him and left for her appointments.

"That's a sweet girl," said Gary, "and not bad to look at, either."

"Definitely not bad to look at," Michael repeated.

"How do you do it?"

"Do what?" Michael asked.

"How do you stay so calm around women that all have feelings for you? I mean, Michelle is devoted to you, and that girl, Myra, can't even hide her emotions. And yesterday, I know a lot was going on, but including Barbara, there were three women in direct contact with each other that would jump your bones at any moment. When I grow up, I want to be you."

"Yeah, right," Michael chuckled. "You know what? I haven't even thought about it. I just try to be myself at all times. What about you? I can see you've got an eye for Cheryl. What about that?"

"Yeah, but she's still married."

"How long do you think that will that be?" Michael asked. "Kenneth is looking at a couple of felonies, and I don't think they would have stuck it out anyway."

"We'll see how it goes," Gary said. "I'm just going to take it slow."

They continued to talk and although Brittany was still missing, Michael had something he hadn't had in a while— an *un*eventful day.

The day went by with no call from Brittany, no calls from Coretta, and nothing negative happening.

At 6:00 that evening, everyone dressed for the trip to Yorba Linda and Friendship Baptist Church. Myra drove an Infinite Q45 and all five people were comfortably seated for the ride to Orange County. Michael wore a black suit, blue shirt, and a canary-yellow tie. Myra wore a blue dress, as did Michelle. Cheryl had on a biege dress, and Gary wore a gray suit, blue tie, and white shirt.

They arrived at the church at 7:05 and found the choir already singing.

"Glory, glory, hallelujah, since I laid my burden down, glory, glory, hallelujah, since I laid my burden down."

The church was filled to capacity, and the five of them finally found a seat in the middle of the pew on the far right side of the church. The church was a modern building holding a capacity of 7,000 people. The choir rocked and the congregation was on its feet, singing praises. Myra instantly started clapping and singing. After two songs, the deacon said a long, emotional prayer and got the congregation even more into the service.

After the scripture reading, the ushers took the first offering of the evening.

"You know, church don't get started until you pass the first offering plate," said Michael. "I heard there was a church in Kansas City that had a metal detector at the door to make sure no one brought change to the church."

He and Gary laughed.

"Y'all better stop that," Cheryl said disapprovingly.

"Myra, what kind of car does this preacher drive?" asked Michael. "Rolls, Bentley, what?"

"His name is Pastor Simmons, and he drives a Caprice Classic," she said. "He's not like that."

"Maybe he drives his Caprice here and his Bentley when he handles his other business," Gary hinted.

As the collection plate went by, they all placed money in the plate that was filled to the top. The ushers stopped to pour money out and then started over.

"Man, I'm in the wrong business," Michael said. "Look at all the money they're raking in."

"Friendship Baptist has many programs," Myra explained. "We feed the homeless, provide shelters for the battered and exploited, provide scholarships for our young people to go to school. The money doesn't go into the pastor's pocket."

Michael realized that Myra was serious about her convictions and stopped trying to antagonize her. They all tried to enjoy the service.

After the collection came the altar call, a time to lay all your burdens at the foot of the Cross. The whole congregation held hands and went to the altar for prayer. Pastor Simmons prayed for the burdens of all and told the congregation that this night, all of their sins could be washed away. Michael began to find a peace concerning his daughter and felt that Brittany would soon come back to him. A huge weight was lifted off his mind and he felt a contentment like never before.

After the altar call, the choir sang another selection before the sermon began. After the choir selection, Pastor Simmons stood up to introduce the guest speaker.

"Is the Lord in this house tonight?" Pastor Simmons shouted.

The congregation shouted *yes* in unison. People were shouting and praising God, and Michael truly enjoyed the service.

"Our guest minister is from Greater Macedonia Baptist Church in Kansas City, Missouri," said Pastor Simmons. "He is a powerful man of God, and you are truly in for a treat because he can really bring the word of God. After another selection from the choir, the next voice you will hear is from Pastor C. Dennis Edwards."

Pastor Simmons sat down and the choir stood to sing "Lord, Remember Me" and as was the case all night, the whole congregation joined in and sang along as one. The church was truly rocking as Pastor Edwards spoke.

"Praise the Lord, saints," said Pastor Edwards, "praise the Lord."

The congregation repeated his statements.

"It is truly a blessing to be in your midst," he continued. "That introduction by Pastor Simmons was so sweet that I felt like a pancake that has just been loaded with syrup."

Everyone laughed.

"Turn with me if you will to Psalms Chapter 1, verses 1–6 and everyone say 'Amen' when you find it. It reads as follows:

[1]Blessed is the man that walketh not in the counsel of the ungodly, nor standeth in the way of sinners, nor sitteth in the seat of the scornful [2]But his delight is in the laws of the Lord and on his law doeth he meditate day and night [3]And he shall be like a tree planted by the rivers of water that brings forth fruit in its season and whose leaf also shall not wither, and whatsoever he doeth shall prosper. [4]The ungodly are not so, but

are like the chaff which the wind driveth away.
⁵Therefore the ungodly shall not stand in the
judgement, nor sinners in the congregation of the
righteous. ⁶For God knoweth the way of the righteous:
but the way of the ungodly shall perish.

"Ladies and gentlemen, I'd like to speak on the subject of
the Word of Life, the Word of Life. Have you ever met people
who had every reason to be depressed and sullen, but who
are perpetually joyful and full of life? Their lives seem to
consist of an endless series of tragedies. Some of them are
imprisoned in bodies ravished by disease and deteriorated
by injury. Others endure family turmoil, economic
hardships, or personal misfortune. Yet, in spite of numerous
reasons for feeling discouraged, there seems to be a continual
revival within them. They have learned how to survive.

"The secret of this authentic, victorious living is found
in Psalm 1. A life of unfailing joy grows when we are rooted
in delighting in and meditating on the word. Jesus said in
John 6:63, 'The words that I speak unto you they are spirit
and they are life.' In the word of God, one can find renewed
joy, renewed hope, renewed strength, and renewed passion
for life. God's word is a deep well and a refreshing stream.
The person whose life is planted like a tree by this 'stream of
water' shall be constantly revitalized and motivated, finding
satisfaction in serving others.

"Let us pray. Lord, grant that I be planted more deeply in
Your word. May I be refreshed and nourished that my life
will be fruitful and that I may glorify You. Amen."

As Pastor Edwards spoke, the whole congregation
repeated almost every word. The church was spiritually
uplifted, but Michael felt the message was meant for him.
He felt that because he knew that the way he had lived his

life caused him to lose his daughter. He had turned his back on God.

The pastor preached for another half hour and then opened the church up to anyone who wanted to come forth.

Michael quickly stood up and stepped between the people in his aisle to go sit in one of the chairs that had been set up front. The invitation got about 20 people to come forth. Although some were families, everyone was allowed to speak. Single mothers came forth with their children and spoke for themselves and their children, husbands spoke for their families. Michael was the first to come forth, but the last one to speak. 7,000 people watched as he spoke.

"And now coming with Christian experience is Michael Alexander," said the preacher.

Michael took the microphone, paused, and tried to keep from shedding a tear. "I accepted God at an early age," he said, "but as soon as things went bad, I turned my back on God. I started doing drugs, sleeping with all kinds of women, doing everything I knew I shouldn't do. And to top it off, I ran around so much that I lost my daughter. But I come forth today, believing that if I rededicate my life, maybe God will see fit to give me my daughter back, and I can get my life back."

He cried openly, and Pastor Simmons said a special prayer, and promised Michael that he would get his daughter back. Michelle, Gary, Myra, and Cheryl cried openly for their friend, whom they had come to love very much. Pastor Edwards took Michael's number and promised to call and check on Michael and, of course, offer up prayers on his behalf.

As they left the church and Myra drove home, everyone was upbeat and truly energized by what just happened.

"That was a great service," said Cheryl. "It makes me want to get myself back into the church."

"Yeah," said Gary, "I've got a real good feeling to. Myra, I'm glad you made this suggestion."

They all conversed casually as they made their way up the freeway back to the condo, then everyone piled out of the car. By then, it was about 11 p.m. and everyone was tired, but not ready to go to sleep.

"Hey, Cheryl," Gary said, "let's go have a converstaion. Maybe we can be friends."

"Why not?" she replied. "I'll show you around LA and give you the late-night tour."

The two of them left in Cheryl's car as Michael, Myra, and Michelle walked into the condo.

Myra felt a little out of place as Michelle and Michael decided that they wanted to watch a movie, but Michelle made Myra feel at ease.

"Myra," she said, "come watch this movie with us. Don't be in there by yourself."

Myra came over to the sofa. Michelle sat on one side and Michael sat in the middle of the two women.

"I'm truly blessed," Michael said fondly. "I get to sit between two beautiful women and watch a movie. What a blessing."

Michael and girls watched the movie and afterwards, Michael and Michelle went to bed and Myra went to her room.

Michelle took off her dress and put on a very short nightgown. Michael was enticed, but didn't want to kill the spirit of the night.

"Let's pray together," he suggested.

They prayed together and afterwards, they talked. "I've got a surprise for you tomorrow," he said. "It's something I think you'll love."

"What is it?"

"If I tell you what it is, then it won't be a surprise," he said, "but again, I think you'll love it."

They went to the bed and even though he wanted to make love all night, he fought the feeling.

Chapter 32

THE NEXT MORNING, MICHELLE LEFT early for an appointment. Michael went through the clothes that she brought over and found a formal dress, then he called David's Bridal and made an appointment to come over. He talked to Stephanie at the bridal shop and asked if they could make a white chiffon wedding gown the right size.

First they had to find the right gown. Stephanie and Michael found the perfect gown that Michael was looking for and he had the dress immediately altered to the same dimensions of the dress Michael brought in. Then he took Michelle's dress and went home at 1 in the afternoon and called Michelle.

"Come home right away," he said. "I want to give you your surprise."

"Michael, I can't leave now," she protested.

"I need you now," he urged, "right away."

Michelle told the photographer that she had to leave and she took off, arriving at Michael's condo at 1:45 p.m.

Gary arrived at the condo at 1:30 p.m. after a night with Cheryl and he and Michael began to talk.

"Out all night, huh?" he asked. "So how'd it go?"

"We just talked," Gary replied, "but we found out that we have a lot in common. I'll see her again tonight."

"Nothing happened, huh?" Michael said.

"Not even a kiss," Gary replied, "but she did allow me to sleep next to her. Oh my God, what a body."

"Don't let Donald beat you to her," Michael advised.

They both laughed as Michelle entered.

"Michael, you're going to cause me to lose this job," Michelle complained, "now what's this urgent surprise?"

"We're all going to take a trip," he said, "me, you, Gary, and Myra."

"A trip? Where?" she asked.

"I'll tell you when we get there," he promised.

"Myra," yelled Michael, "stop what you're doing. You're going with us."

Myra looked at Gary, who just shrugged his shoulders.

Everyone dropped what they're doing, jumped into Michael's Mercedes, and headed toward Burbank Airport.

Coretta's plane was there and her pilot stayed on or near the plane in case of an emergency. Michael and crew pulled up to the airport. The pilot recognized him from the trip to San Francisco. Michael stepped on the plane.

"Is the plane all fueled up?" Michael asked the pilot.

"Yeah, it's ready to go," the pilot replied.

Michael told the others to come aboard. Then he said, "Good, let's take off."

"Ms. James didn't tell me we're going on a trip," the pilot remarked.

"Oh, she didn't?" Michael said. "It must have slipped her mind. Hurry, we need to be in Altanta by 8 this evening."

"Let me call Ms. James to verify everything," said the pilot, picking up the phone.

"That won't be necessary," Michael replied. "I'll take responsibility for the trip."

The pilot reluctantly called the tower for clearance to go to Atlanta and after receiving clearance, he taxied the runway and flew off to Atlanta.

"What's in Altanta?" asked Michelle.

"You'll see when you get there," he replied.

Michael, Myra, Gary, and Michelle sat back and enjoyed the trip on Coretta's private jet. The pilot got acquainted with all onboard and they arrived at 7:45 p.m.

Michael's friend, Audran Johnson, owned the revolving restaurant on top of the Westin Hotel in downtown Atlanta. He also owned Ultimate Limousine Service. He had a limo waiting to pick up Michael full of champagne. They all entered the limo, having no idea of what Michael was up to.

As the limo headed downtown, Michael popped the cork and made a toast: "to everlasting love," he said.

They all drank but Myra, who simply clanged an empty glass against the others.

As they arrived at the Sundial Restaurant on top of the Westin, Audran Johnson greeted the group and presented Michelle with a large bouquet of beautiful red roses with a card from Michael. Michelle kissed Michael and looked at the beautiful restaurant full of guests as Michael and his friends were escorted to the best table in the house.

In the small silk pillow sitting on the table was a three-carat diamond ring. A violinist came over to serenade the table and another bottle of champagne sat on the table. Michael picked up the ring and kneeled down on the floor in front of Michelle as the whole restaurant moaned. Myra and Gary were stunned. Michael held Michelle's hand.

"Last night while we were in church, I realized how much you meant to me," said Michael, "and although we haven't known each other long, the last several nights that we've spent together have shown me that I don't want to share my bed with anyone else. So Michelle Davis, will you be my wife?"

Michelle was in tears and could barely speak as she answered. "Yes," she answered, "yes, yes, yes, yes, yes."

The whole restaurant cheered.

An older couple sitting next to the table truly enjoyed the moment. "Why can't you be that romantic with me?" she asked her campanion.

The man just shrugged his shoulders. Michael pulled out a bag that he carried from LA and gave it to Michelle.

"Go get dressed," he said.

"You want to get married right now?" asked Michelle.

"When we're together tonight, it will be as husband and wife," he said. "Myra, help her out."

Myra loved Michael herself but truly wanted him to be happy, so she swallowed her feelings and helped Michelle get dressed. Michael packed a white tuxedo for himself and went to change also.

"If you don't mind," said Michael to Gary, "I want you to be my best man."

"It would be an honor, my brother," Gary replied, "an honor."

Michael had arranged with his friend, Audran, to set up the restaurant for a quick wedding. Everything was together and all that was needed was the bride and groom. Even the minister was in place. Michael emerged from the bathroom looking handsome in his tux with Gary in regular clothes.

"You could have told me so I could have dressed for the occasion," said Gary.

"I just came up with this last night," Michael told him, "but I wanted to surprise everyone. There's been so much bad stuff going on that we need something to celebrate. Besides, you look fine."

Myra exited the ladies' room and walked down by herself and stood at the front across from Michael and Gary. The violinist played the wedding song as Michelle walked down alone with a huge smile on her face. A man from the crowd in the restaurant stood up and extended his arm and walked Michelle down the aisle where Michael was waiting for her. They joined hands as the minister spoke.

"As we gather together today for a most unusual service, we come to join a man truly in love with his woman and not wanting to live in sin any longer. Marriage is something that God ordained when He said, 'those who I have brought together let no man put asunder.' Do you, Michael Alexander, take Michelle Davis as your wedded wife?"

"I do," said Michael.

"Do you, Michelle Davis, take Michael Alexander to be your lawful wedded husband?" asked the minister.

Michelle had tears pouring down her eyes. "I do," she sniffled.

"I see you already have the ring," says the pastor, "so by the power vested in me by God and by the state of Georgia, I now pronounce you man and wife. Michael, you may kiss your bride."

Michael paused to look at his new wife and then stepped up her and gave her a big, passionate kiss as everyone in the restaurant applauded, including Myra.

"Ladies and gentlemen, may I present to you Mr. and Mrs. Michael Alexander," said the DJ as Michael and Michelle headed for the dance floor. "The groom has requested that we play the old Patti Labelle song, 'If only You Knew,' for their wedding song," he said.

As the song began to play, Michael and Michelle danced to a standing ovation from the guests in the restaurant. The new husband and wife stared into each other's eyes as they grasped each other very tightly on the dance floor.

"I'm so happy," said Michelle. "This was beautiful and such a surprise. I promise you our love will know no boundaries."

Michael hesitated and then said to Michelle, "You know when my first wife died, I didn't think I could ever love another, but then I saw you and I knew I could love again. Before today, I was only half a man. Now I'm whole again. And I just want to thank you for that."

Michael was very emotional and tears streamed down from his eyes. Michelle wiped his tears away and squeezed her new husband tighter. The patrons of the restaurant celebrated as if they had known Michael and Michelle.

After a few moments, other couples joined in and danced to the song and tried to help celebrate Michael and Michelle's day.

After the song, Michael informed Audran that he needed to get back to the airplane and return to California.

As the new couple headed towards the exit to the limo, the restaurant was out of the traditional rice to throw, so Audran opened a bag of grits and everyone threw grits at the new couple.

"Everything was first class until they threw those grits," laughed Gary. "If they threw some bacon and eggs, I could make myself a nice breakfast."

Myra laughed although the man she wanted to lose her virginity to, the man she hoped to someday marry, just married someone else. She had a crazy thought in her head that she would one day be with Michael, but she wondered if that meant that she would break her most sacred rule, which was to never sleep with a married man.

As Michael and Michelle went back to the limo along with Myra and Gary, Coretta called her pilot to routinely see what the condition of the plane was.

"Quiet night, huh, Derrick?" she asked. "I bet you wished I flew out more than I do."

"Well, if I keep flying these side trips like tonight," he said, "I won't have to sit around and be bored."

"What side trip? Aren't you in Burbank?"

"No," the pilot answered.

"Then where are you?" Coretta asked.

"I'm in Atlanta."

"Atlanta!" she yelled. "What are you doing in Atlanta?"

The pilot realized that Michael had tricked him, and he also knew that Coretta hated surprises.

"Michael said you knew," the pilot said in fear. "I tried to call you to confirm, but he said there was no need."

"You know to consult with me before ever moving that plane," she said coldly. "Where is Michael now?"

"I don't know. A limo picked him up and his friends. Do you want me to take off and come back now?"

"No, I need to know what they're up to. Is Michelle with him?"

"Yes," the pilot replied. "They seem to be pretty close."

"Okay, hit me on my two-way and let me know what time you'll arrive. I'll make sure we welcome them back to California."

Coretta hung up the the phone and called Stephen. "We need to take a ride. I'll be down to the pier in three hours. Meet me, and then we'll need to go to Burbank."

Meanwhile, in the limo, the merry group toasted and laughed, all except Myra, who had mixed emotions.

At 10:30, they arrived back at the plane. After everyone boarded, the pilot took off headed back to LA. He looked at Michelle's dress and Michael's tuxedo.

"You came to Atlanta to get married, I see. Congratulations. You make a beautiful couple."

Michelle sat on Michael's lap during the trip back to Los Angeles. The pilot contacted Coretta, informing her of their arrival around 12:30 a.m. Coretta, Manu, and Stephen planned to welcome them back.

Michael rarely answered his cell phone calls, trying to avoid Coretta. Cheryl called Michael on his cell phone and when he recognized her number, he handed the phone to Michelle to answer.

"This is Mrs. Michael Alexander," she said. "How can I help you?"

"Michelle, is that you? What do you mean, 'Mrs. Michael Alexander'?"

"Michael and I just got married. Michael flew us to Atlanta, proposed to me there, and we got married, all at the same time. He bought me this beautiful gown, and we rode in a limo, and we were married in a beautiful restaurant. It was so exciting."

"Who is 'us'?"

"Gary and Myra are here too," Michelle answered. "We're on our way back to LA now."

"Congratulations," Cheryl responded. "Michael never ceases to amaze me. What time are you guys coming in?"

"I don't know. Let me ask the pilot."

"Sir, what time will we arrive?"

"Probably around 1 a.m," he said.

"About 1 a.m. we'll be coming into Burbank," Michelle told Cheryl.

"Okay, I'll meet you guys there. Tell Gary I said hi."

"Okay," Michelle replied.

They hung up the phone, and the plane continued its ascent toward Burbank Airport.

At 12:17 a.m., Coretta's jet taxied down the runway at Burbank Airport and came to a final stop a few minutes later. The new bride and groom, along with their friends, began to get off the jet. Michael emerged from the jet behind Gary and Myra, who stopped in their tracks after seeing Coretta, Manu, and Stephen waiting at the side of the plane.

"Funny, I don't remember telling anyone to use my plane," said Coretta. "I wish someone had invited me to the party."

No one said anything.

"Looks like two of you went to a formal party and the other two went to a cookout," she continued. "Somebody want to explain?"

Michael spoke up. "I did all this. Nobody else knew where they were going. I decided to do this at the last minute."

"Do what, pretty boy?" Stephen asked.

"Get married. This is my new wife."

"Myra, I employ you," Coretta said. "Why didn't you let me know what was going on?"

"Because she didn't know," Michael stated. "I told you, this was my idea. No one knew."

"So how are you gonna work for me with a wife, Michael?" Coretta demanded. "She would have to be real understanding to accept your line of work."

"I don't work for you anymore," Michael said matter-of-factly. "I quit."

"When were you gonna let me know?"

"I just thought you would figure it out."

"Well, if you don't work for me anymore, then you owe me for a trip to Atlanta and many other things," Coretta said. "I'm also going to have to evict you from your condo and then take back my car. You stand to lose so much."

"I've got a house," said Michelle, "and a car and all the money we will ever need."

"Nobody quits on me!" Coretta screamed. "I either dismiss them, or they leave on a stretcher."

Stephen reached in his pocket, but a light shined on him, so he stopped in his tracks.

Cheryl suddenly emerged from her car, but left the lights on.

"Michael!" she yelled. "Michelle, Gary, is that you guys?"

"Over here, Cheryl," Gary yelled.

"What's going on?" she asked.

Cheryl remembered Coretta from the party and knew something wasn't right. Thinking quickly, she said, "Let's go, guys. The police are on their way."

Stephen looked around, then he, Coretta, and Manu rushed to their car and left.

Gary and Myra climbed into Cheryl's car, while Michael and Michelle got into Michael's Mercedes, which had been parked at the airport all day.

As soon as Michael drove off, his phone rang.

"Hello, Coretta," he said.

"You won't get away from me that easy, and you will regret the day you met Coretta James."

"I already regret that day. Do you know that the police are looking for you and that rapist, Stephen? I think I'll give them a call as soon as I get off the phone with you, and tell them they should follow us around, and maybe they will find you."

"You know, Michael, when you play with fire, you *always* get burned."

She hung up the phone, and Michael and Michelle headed over to Michelle's hotel suite, followed by Myra, Gary, and Cheryl. As they parked, Cheryl got out of her car, jittery.

"You think they followed us?" she asked.

"I hope not," Michelle answered.

"That's a scary woman," Cheryl said. "I think she has bad intentions for you, Michael."

"She has bad intentions for anyone who doesn't do what she wants," said Michael. "I chose the wrong person to try to do business with. This woman doesn't even hide the fact that she is a killer."

"We've got to be extremely careful," Cheryl stated. "She is very dangerous and can't be trusted."

Meanwhile, across town, Coretta, Stephen, and Manu arrived at the pier where Coretta's yacht was docked.

"I told you, boss lady, that bitch, Michael, was weak," Stephen grumbled. "He takes your plane and flies to Atlanta, trying to impress that winch."

"That's the woman he met the same night he met me," Coretta mused. "That's also the woman that loudmouthed me at the party Saturday. Stephen, we need to speed up our trip. Make sure our passports are ready. We're leaving town as soon as I take of a little business. That bitch, Michelle, will die. I'm not leaving town until that happens."

"What about Michael?" Stephen asked. "Just the thought of killing him makes my dick hard."

"If we get one, we should get the other," Coretta said. "They are husband and wife now."

"But what about the police? Michael threatened to call the police," he reminded her.

"Fuck the police," she replied. "The first thing we have to do is find out where they are. Let's go over to the condo and see if we can find something to tell us where they are."

Coretta knew that they were wanted all over the city, but she refused to be told what she can or cannot do or where she can go. She was totally obsessed with finding Michael and teaching him and Michelle a lesson.

The three of them drove over to Michael's condo, fully armed and with a car full of ammunition. They planned to go out with a bang, if they go out.

Cheryl, Myra, Michael, Michelle, and Gary had gathered in Michelle's suite at the hotel, not knowing what to do next.

"I think you should call the police, Michael," Cheryl said. "You definitely want to protect your new wife."

Michael didn' t hesistate to follow her advice and found Detective Andrews' card and informed him that he had seen Coretta and that she threatened to kill him and his new wife.

Detective Andrews reminded Michael of his hypocrisy, that he was a man that hated the police so much that he wouldn't cooperate with them, but he didn't hesistate to call them for protection. However, he immediately arranged for a police officer to stand guard at Michelle's hotel suite and a police car with Stephen and Coretta's picture in it to patrol the hotel grounds.

Upon arriving at the hotel, the police officer alerted them that he was there and and would guard the door for the rest of the night.

Michael and Michelle wanted to spend their wedding night alone, but were willing to share the suite with everyone. Myra felt akward. This was the first time she witnessed some of Coretta's wrath, and she was also the odd person out in the group of five. On top of that, she still had feelings for Michael. She didn't know what to do under the circumstances.

Cheryl decided to go to her home and asked Gary and Myra to spend the night with her, but Myra wanted to be dropped off at the condo.

⇥⊚ ⇥⊚ ⇥⊚

OVER AT THE condo, Coretta was still recognized as being the condo's owner so she was quickly buzzed in through the glass doors, along with Stephen and Manu. They immediately went upstairs.

She pulled her key from her purse and tried to unlock the door, but it wouldn't turn.

"This key doesn't work anymore," Coretta exclaimed in dismay. "They must have changed the locks. Stephen, go downstairs and tell them to send the keys up here."

Stephen went back downstairs to ask the concierge for the keys.

"I'm sorry," the concierge said, "but you're not on the lease so I can't give you the keys."

"Really?" said Stephen.

"Really," said the concierge.

At that moment, Stephen pulled out his 9mm and pointed it at the concierge's head.

"You sure I'm not on the lease?" he asked.

The concierge was working alone and had no one to back him up, so he immediately handed Stephen the keys.

Stephen cracked him over the head with his gun, knocking the man unconscious.

He went back upstairs with the keys, throwing caution to the wind. They entered the condo and started to look around for any information on where Michael and Michelle might be.

In the closet in Michael's bedroom, they saw the bags that Michelle brought over. A tag on one of her bags had her address in Louisiana and a receipt for her hotel in town.

"Hey," Stephen yelled, "here it is, Hotel Nikko. It gives her suite number and everything."

"Let's go," Coretta said. The three of them took the elevator downstairs and saw the concierge still knocked out.

"Should I shoot him?" Stephen asked.

"Somebody might hear it," Coretta said. "We'll be out of town after tonight, so we won't have to worry about him identifying us. Let's get out of here."

⇥ ⇥ ⇥

MOMENTS AFTER THEY leave, Myra was dropped off at the condo by Cheryl and Gary and entered the building.

She saw the concierge in a daze, just waking up from a meeting with a 9mm.

"Are you okay?" Myra asked.

The man didn't respond, so she took the phone at the desk and called the police. She knew what had happened and called Michael, who had his phone turned off. Myra left him a frantic message.

The police guard outside the door of their suite made Michael and Michelle feel safe. Although they felt the threat of danger, they wanted to make their wedding night as special as possible. Michelle wore a sheer red negligee and Michael looked forward to making love to his new wife. He finally felt that he was living right.

He wrote something special for his wife and had her sit her down as he read it to her.

"Michelle," he said, "I wrote this for you to let you know how I feel. It's called "Love.""

LOVE

I told God how I felt about you and He heard my feeble voice

I prayed that He would guide my life, that He would make the choice

I believe that you were sent from on high, a gift from heaven above

From this moment and for the rest of my life, I pledge to you my love

I'll love you when your hair turns grey, I'll love you when you're old

I'll love you on sunny days or when the days are cold

I'll love you when you're feeling down, I'll stand and hold your hand

I'll let it be known all over town, boldly proclaiming that I am your man

The night I met you, my dreams came true. I truly was set free

I never understood the power of the word, the awesome power of l-o-v-e

So to you, my wife, I give my all and promise that I'll be true

The only thing that I'm trying to say is that I'm deeply in love with you

Michelle grabbed her husband and kissed him passionately. "That was so beautiful," she said. "I am going to have this framed." She wanted to consummate their marriage, but Michael stopped her at the moment. He took a shower first, and then came out and wanted to have a drink. By then, it was about 3 a.m. and they wanted to enjoy the whole night.

Outside, the police car with the two officers stopped along the side of the hotel. The officers talked about their personal lives, then one had to use the restroom.

As he stepped towards the building, Manu emerged from the shadows and grabbed him, breaking his neck with one quick twist.

Stephen pulled right in front of the police car and shot the other officer right between the eyes.

They then walked right into the hotel and went upstairs to Michelle's suite. Inside the suite, Michelle was about to take a shower. Michael, however, noticed that they were out of ice.

"Michelle, I'm going to get some ice," he said. "I'll be right back."

Michael put on his robe and went outside, leaving the door cracked, thinking that he would walk right back in. He told the officer that he was going for some ice. As he turned the corner to go to the balcony, Coretta, Manu, and Stephen arrived on the floor.

Stephen looked around the corner and saw the policeman at the door. He motioned for Coretta to go around the other side of the floor.

As she does, she came out in the open. The police officer recognized her as being wanted and pulled his gun, ordering her to stop.

However, as he turned his back to one side, Stephen came from behind with the silencer on his gun and shot the officer in the back of the head.

The three of them entered Michelle's room.

"She's mine," said Coretta.

"I want that pretty boy," said Stephen.

Coretta pulled her gun and walked into the shower when she heard the water running. Michelle was about to exit the shower and wait for her new husband.

Outside, Michael had just found the ice machine and filled up the bucket.

Stephen looked around the room and saw no one, so he thought that they both were in the shower.

Coretta stood right at the base of the shower as Michelle emerged from the tub, brushing her hair. She immediately dropped the brush when she saw Coretta standing there with her gun cocked. She was terrified.

"I told you I was gonna get you," Coretta said as she shot Michelle at point-blank range twice. "This has to be the shortest marriage in history," she said to a dying Michelle. "I guess you're marriage is annuled.

"Let's get out of here," Coretta said.

"I want that pretty boy," yelled Stephen.

"Let's go now," Coretta insisted. "There are two bodies on the outside and two bodies inside. We need to move."

As they left, Michael turned the corner, coming back with the bucket of ice, looking happy and singing.

Stephen spotted him and yelled. "Pretty boy!" Then he shot at Michael three times, but he missed.

Michael ran back outside to the balcony and hid.

"Let's go," yelled Coretta.

The three of them ran outside and left the hotel as fast as possible.

Michael hid, not knowing whether to come back and not knowing where Stephen was with his gun.

He heard the sirens coming towards the motel and felt safe enough to go back inside. Then he saw the officer at their suite dead with a bullet through the back of his head. He slowly walked back into the room and saw the blood tracked through the front. When he entered the bathroom area, he saw his wife dead right in front of the shower.

"Michelle! Michelle!" he screamed.

Michael slumped to the floor in the pool of blood and wrapped his arms around his wife, cradling her head against his chest and rocking back and forth.

Several policemen ran upstairs to the room and rushed in to see Michael holding his dead wife in his arms, covered with her blood.

Michelle's body was nude. Michael sobbed. "They didn't even give her a chance to put her clothes. I can't believe this. We were just married tonight. We wanted to be married so we could live our lives right. She never hurt anyone."

Michael was not very coherent, and at times, did not make much sense. He was filled with an uncontrollable sense of remorse. He believed that he had killed Michelle just as much as he killed his first wife, and that if he had not met her and brought Coretta into her life, she would still be alive.

The police were finally able to talk Michael into letting his wife go. He was covered with his wife's blood and needed someone to come and assist him.

At that moment, Detective Andrews arrived at the scene because he was the one who ordered the officers to guard the hotel. As he entered the room, he saw Michael covered with blood.

Detective Andrews offered to take Michael home to the condo. The medical examiner at the scene gave Michael some medication to take once he arrived home to help him sleep. Michael whispered to Detective Andrews that Coretta, Stephen, and Manu were responsible for his wife's death and Stephen was the one who took shots at him. The police were sure that they were also responsible for the deaths of the three police officers.

Michael was very fragile at this point. Detective Andrews covered him with a blanket from the room and drove him home. Michael didn't say a word on the way home, he just stared in space.

Michelle had less than 24 hours to be Mrs. Alexander.

Detective Andrews assisted the bloody Michael to his condo. He walked him upstairs to his door. Myra hadn't yet fallen asleep and reacted nervously to the sound of the doorbell. She looked through the peephole and saw Detective Andrews holding up Michael. Quickly she opened the door and saw Michael with his wife's blood all over him. He was in a daze and couldn't even speak.

Myra screamed immediately at the sight which greeted her eyes.

"Oh my God, Michael. What happened?" she asked.

The detective escorted Michael to the sofa in the living room, where he crumbled down as if he died himself.

Myra continued to cry uncontrollably and asked Michael what happened. Detective Andrews left the dazed Michael on the sofa and went to comfort Myra.

"Honey, calm down. Michael's girlfriend was just killed."

"Michelle? No, she was such a sweetheart. Coretta. It was Coretta who killed her, wasn't it?"

"Yea, it seems like it," said Detective Andrews. "Michael says there were three of them."

"They just got married," Myra said bewildered. "Only hours ago we were at their wedding in Atlanta. Now she's dead."

"Michael's in real bad shape," Detective Andrews told her. "He needs to take the sedative that the EMS man gave him so maybe he can get some sleep."

Myra got some water and tried to coax Michael into taking the pill. He opened his mouth, swallowed the pill, and sat back on the couch in a state of shock.

Shortly afterward, the pill took effect, and he fell asleep.

"What happened?" asked Myra.

"Looks like they killed the three police officers that I sent to protect Michael after he called me," said Detective Andrews. "They made their way to the room, where I guess she was alone. Michael mumbled something about getting some ice. I guess he's fortunate he wasn't there. I've never in my years on the force seen anyone as bold as Coretta and this guy Stephen. They kill while the police are right there. They are extremely dangerous."

"Oh, no," sobbed Myra, "poor Michelle."

"Look, it' a little after 5 a.m., said Detective Andrews. "I'll be back later to check on him. Just make sure you keep an eye on him, especially after he wakes. There is no telling how he's going to respond when he wakes up."

"Yeah," said Myra, "this is his 2nd dead wife."

Detective Andrews left Myra and went about the task of calling Cheryl and everyone else in their inner circle to let them know of Michelle's death.

Chapter 33

BACK AT CORETTA'S, THEY GATHERED up everything to make a quick exit out of the country. Coretta had already deposited millions of dollars in unmarked accounts across the world and had over one hundred million dollars in cash on her person.

Manu and Stephen, along with about 10 members of Coretta's entourage, prepared to make the trip to Kingston, Jamaica, where Stephen was well connected. They finished up their packing and rushed towards Coretta's plane.

"You gonna love Jamaica, boss lady," Stephen told her. "We can really come up over there, and protection will be the last thing you have to worry about. My brother pretty much runs Kingston. But, boss lady, we need to make one more attempt to get that pretty boy, Michael. I would smile all the way to Jamaica, knowing I put him out of his misery."

"We don't have time for that," said Coretta. "We need to leave here now, right now, so let's go."

Meanwhile, Detective Andrews had tirelessy stalked Coretta and finally found where her yacht was docked. He took several police officers over to the boat to try to apprehend her and her associates.

The police SWAT team surrounded the boat and rushed at it with heavy artillery. They kicked in the door, only to find an empty yacht with nothing to tell them of Coretta's or her associates' whereabouts. They combed every inch of the boat, but found nothing.

Detective Andrews called back to Michael's condo to see if he were awake. All Michael's friends had gathered at his home, and Donald had called to check in and after hearing the news about Michelle's death. He was on a bus from downtown and on his way to the condo at that very moment.

Detective Andrews was looking for any information that might help to locate Coretta and Stephen. Myra was talking to him.

"Michael is still out, but Coretta parks her jet at Burbank Airport. Maybe she is going there now or she will be there soon."

Detective Andrews hung up the phone and took off on his own for Burbank Airport in an effort to find anything to take Coretta and her accomplices off the street. He turned on the siren on his car as he zoomed towards the airport. Once he arrived at the small airport, which had about 40 jets parked, he hurried into the building to speak with the controller and ask about Coretta.

"Excuse me, sir, I'm Detective Dana Andrews from the North Hollywood Police Department. I'm looking for Coretta James. I heard that her jet is parked here all the time."

"Yes, it was here," said the controller.

"What do you mean 'was'?" asked the detective.

"They left, a couple of hours ago," he replied. "Seemed to be in a real big hurry."

"They had to file a flight plan, right? When are they coming back?"

"Never," the controller said. "They're gone for good. They loaded up all their personal things and said they wouldn't be back."

"When did they go? Do you know where they went?"

The controller paused for a moment as if he didn't want to reveal their destination. "I don't know. I just know they're leaving the country."

The controller was a large white male, blond, and somewhat muscular.

"These people are killers," Detective Andrews informed him. "They just killed a woman this morning. They killed my partner and who knows how many others, and I'm going to find them, now where did they go?"

"I've known Coretta James for years, and I would never betray her trust," said the controller, "so I plead the fifth."

Detective Andrews ran out of patience and slammed the controller's head into the desk and then stuck his gun to his head.

"I've already asked you nicely," said the detective. "Now I must insist that you tell me all you know about where Coretta James is going. And you don't have much time to think about it."

"She's going to Jamaica," yelled the controller in distress, "to Kingston, Jamaica."

"Where in Kingston?" said Detective Andrews, applying pressure to the controller's neck.

"I don't know," yelled the distraught controller. "The pilot said Jamaica so we could plan the trip and see how busy the airways were going to be. I never even spoke to Coretta. Now come on, man, let me go."

Detective Andrews released the man and walked towards his car while the controller rubbed his neck. He immediately reported Detective Andrews as he headed back toward his office.

Once Detective Andrews arrived at Police Headquarters, he had a message to see Captain Lewis. He hesitated and first asked a fellow detective to find him the quickest flight to Kingston, Jamaica.

"What's in Jamaica?"

"I'm going to bring back a murderer," Detective Andrews said grimly.

Then Detective Andrews went about his business as Captain Lewis yelled for him to come into his office.

"Get that information," Andrews told his co-worker as he walked into Captain Lewis' office and closed the door.

"I had a man call me and say you slammed his head into a desk," Captain Lewis said, "and that you also put a gun to his head. Is there any truth to that?"

Detective Andrews didn't respond.

"I guess that means yes," the captain said. "Dana, what's gotten into you?"

"While we've been procrastinating, getting search warrants and holding our nuts, Coretta James and Stephen Davis continue to murder innocent people," Detective Andrews explained, "and now they are out of the country. How long will it take to get some people down to Jamaica to find these killers and bring them back to justice?"

"We don't know for sure that they are in Jamaica," the captain stated. "We've got to use intelligence to find out where they are."

"Are you on her payroll too, Captain Lewis, or are you one of her clients that solicits her girls for service?"

"Fuck you, you asshole," Captain Lewis retorted.

"Well, I know where they are," Detective Andrews said, "and I'm going to find them, and I'm going *today*."

"I'm not sending you to Jamaica."

"You don't have to send me," said Detective Andrews, taking off his badge. "I'm going on my own. I've got to look in the face of a 7 year old every day, a child that is sick with grief over his mother's death, and I've dragged my feet long enough. I'm going to Jamaica, and I'm going today."

Detective Andrews left the captain's office and walked back over to his desk. There he talked to his fellow detective.

"I'll need two passports," he told him, "one for myself and the other for Michael Alexander."

The other detective gave him a crazy stare at the mention of Michael Alexander's name.

"Don't worry about it," Detective Andrews said. "Just *do* it. I'll get you his vitals shortly."

Detective Andrews walked out and drove over to Michael's condo.

Back in Michael's condo, it was mid-morning and Michael was taking a long shower. He gazed intently at his wife's blood as it washed off him down the drain.

Cheryl, Gary, Myra, and Donald, who had arrived by city bus, sat in the living room.

Donald was high on crack and telling jokes, thinking that might lift Michael's spirits as he walked out of the shower.

"Yeah," Donald said, "I met this chick in a club in Miami. We went back to her house, and I talked my way up on the pussy."

As Donald spoke, everybody frowned but Michael. He continued, "So once I started hitting the pussy, she told me to slap her across her ass, so I did. *Pow! Pow!* I slapped her about three times across the ass. After that, she told me to lick that pussy for her and I told the bitch she was crazy, that

I don't eat no hairy hamburger. I don't eat nothing that gets up and walks away.

"So she starts asking crazy questions. She goes, 'Whose pussy is this?' I said, 'This is my pussy.' She said, 'No, this is Elaine's pussy.' Her name was Elaine, and then she says, 'Whose pussy is this?' And I said, 'This is Elaine's pussy,' and she said, 'No, this is your pussy.' Then, 'Whose pussy is this?' And I said, 'This is my pussy,' and she said, 'No, this is Elaine's pussy.' So she asked me that that a couple of more times and finally I said, 'Hell, you tell me whose pussy it is. I'm hitting it right now, so I guess it's mine. I guess the next nigger that hits it, it'll be his.'"

Donald laughed hard, and Michael smiled, but the women in the room failed to see the humor.

"That was disgusting," said Cheryl. "Michael, can we get you anything?"

Michael was still quite dazed, but was speaking now and declined the offer of food, but he did ask for a shot of Hennessey or Remy, whatever was in the house.

"Michael, you don't need to drink now," Cheryl said. "Alcohol will only make you more depressed."

"I need a drink," he replied, "I need a drink."

No one got up to pour it, so he poured it himself. As he did so, Detective Andrews knocked on his door.

Myra answered the door with the detective following her in and walking right up to Michael.

"How you feeling, man?" he asked Michael.

Michael merely took a drink and looked at him. "In a minute, I'm not going to feel anything."

"I need you to go to Jamaica with me," said Detective Andrews. "Coretta went there. We need to find out where they are."

"Man, I've got to bury my wife," Michael replied, standing up to pour another drink. "What would I look like going to Jamaica?"

"We've got to stop these bastards," the detective stated firmly. "There's no way we can let them get away with this. They killed your wife the same night you got married. They raped and killed my partner and then threw her body in the water and left her son an orphan. We can't let them get away with this."

"I'm not a police officer," Michael protested. "I can't do police work."

"I'm no longer an officer either. I gave them my badge this morning. I'm going to Jamaica to bring them back dead or alive."

Michael didn't say anything, but just continued to drink. Detective Andrews got angry and slapped the glass from Michael's hands violently.

"Put this shit down. Man, you had your wife's blood all over you last night. You just got married, and you didn't even get to spend the night with your new wife. They came into your honeymoon suite and murdered your wife, and all you can do is drink?! Stand up and be a man."

"Leave him alone," shouted Myra.

"I am a man," shouted Michael, "I've been through more the last week than most people go through in a lifetime. I don't know how much more I can take. I lost my daughter and both of my wives. How much is a man supposed to take?"

"Your first wife was an accident," the detective said. "Yeah, I know about your first wife. But this wife, this beautiful woman who had everything to live for, was killed for no reason, and if you had not stepped out of the room, you would be dead, too. Who will they kill next?"

Detective Andrews looked across the room. "The next time, it could be one of you. Michael, I know you've got some heart. I'm asking you to find it. I'll be back in an hour. I'm going to Jamaica—with or without you."

"Revenge is mine, saith the Lord. I shall repay," quoted Myra.

Detective Andrews made no comment but continued out the door as Michael sat back and thought about what he had just said.

"He's right," Michael said. "I was violated beyond belief. For them to kill my wife on her wedding night is inexcusable, and I have to avenge her life."

"Michael, you need to let the police handle this," Cheryl exhorted him. "Besides, you don't know anything about guns and stuff like that, and you've got to make arrangements for Michelle."

"You do it for me. I've got all her contact numbers. You could set up everything for me, and I promise I'll be back before she's buried."

"Give it some thought, Mike," Gary urged him. "Those people are killers for real, and who knows what you'll be walking into over there. If they chose to go to Jamaica, I'm sure they have themselves in a situation that's very favorable to them. You might be walking into a hornets' nest."

"I wonder why he wants you to go to Jamaica instead of someone from law enforcement," Cheryl said. "He must know you can't back him up if he gets in trouble."

"Thanks," Michael replied sarcastically.

"I don't mean it like that," said Cheryl quickly, "but you need to be aware of the fact that there could be extreme danger."

"Well," Michael said, "at some point in your life, you have to stand up for something. Michelle knew all my baggage and still accepted me in spite of it, never once saying anything negative about me or what I did. I don't know why Detective Andrews wants me to go, but it was my wife, and I can't let her death be in vain. Who was it that said that if a man hasn't found something he's willing to die for, he isn't fit to live?"

"That was Martin Luther King," Myra stated.

"Yea, man," Donald added, "the way you're talking almost got me motivated. Hell, maybe I should go over there with y'all and kick some ass."

"Short as you are, how you gonna kick anybody's ass?" Gary laughed. "You can't reach high enough to kick nobody's ass. You so short, you can tie your shoes without bending over."

"Oh, you wanna joke?" Donald replied. "Well, your mama so ugly that a Peeping Tom peeped into her window and then broke into the house and pulled down the shade. He said he don't peep at no shit like this."

"See, I didn't say nothing about your mama," Gary said.

"Boys," Cheryl interjected, "cut it out, please. This is serious."

"I'm going," Michael stated flatly. "End of discussion." He got up from his seat and went into his room to dress and pack some clothes.

Barbara Brown had given Michael the money that was used for his bail. He gave a portion of it to Cheryl for Michelle's funeral arrangements and kept the rest, along with the money he already had from his gigolo work to take to Jamaica in case they need a lump sum of money.

Michael prepared as a man on a mission, but also as a man who had no idea what tomorrow might bring. As he packed, the reality that he was serious started to dawn on everyone, including the high Donald. They all gathered together in Michael's room and he spoke.

"You know, for the last year or so since my first wife died, I've always had to be ready to move at the drop of a hat. I've been mentally and physically unstable. Now I don't have my child or either of my wives, and I don't know if this is my last time seeing you, my friends. Cheryl, if I don't come back, please find my daughter. You know the true story, and she is going to need family. I will be gone and her grandparents will be locked up. And you guys stick together, no matter what your differences. Right now, we are all we have. Myra, when Brittany comes back, stand by her. Let her know you will be there for her."

"Michael, you don't have to do this," Myra implored him. "You can change your mind and when that detective comes back, you can just tell him you decided not to go."

"I can't," he replied. "I'm responsible. Coretta would not have met Michelle had it not been for me, that teacher would not have died either, and that female detective would be here. The only connection between Coretta and those people was me. A lot of tears are being shed because of me."

"Brother, I don't agree with you putting your life on the line like this," said Gary, "but I truly respect the reason why you're doing it."

"Yea, man," Donald added, "there are a lot of fine women in Jamaica. Maybe I should go pick up a few."

"Shut up, fool," Cheryl rebuked him. "Get serious."

Michael pointed at Donald, "Y'all take care of that boy."

They continued to talk as Michael puts together a few things. "I don't know what to take. I better pack some shorts."

He packed enough clothes for a few days, not knowing how long he would be gone. Then he carried his bags to the living room and sat down with his friends. Cheryl and Myra held his hand and Gary and Donald sat close by, not knowing if this was the last time they would ever see him.

They all sat and waited, watching as time passed by and hoping that Detective Andrews was just blowing off steam. But like clockwork, one hour almost to the second, Detective Andrews knocked on the door. Everyone looked at the door but no one moved to open it. Michael, himself, stood up to open the door.

Detective Andrews was surprised to see Michael standing there. "So, what did you decide?"

"Let's get my bags," came the answer.

Michael looked at his friends as he was about to leave.

"Take care of yourself," Gary said. "You've got an angel watching over you and don't you ever forget it." Then Gary embraced him.

"Yeah, man," Donald said, "hurry back so so we can hang out. We can get some more of that Golden Bird Chicken."

"For sho," Michael smiled. Then he and Donald hugged.

"You promise me that you'll come back," Cheryl said, "that you'll be here for your wife's funeral, and that you will be there for Brittany, and that you will be there for all of us because we all love you." Then she started to cry as she hugged him.

"I can't imagine life without you being around," Cheryl told him. "You've got a lot to live for."

Myra just stared at Michael and hugged him aggressively. She planted a big kiss on him and didn't want to let him go. She whispered in his ear, "I love you Michael. Please come back to me."

"I will," he promised. Then, turning to Detective Andrews, he said, "Let's go. Let's get out of here, Detective."

The two men left the apartment and took the elevator downstairs.

"We've got to make a quick stop to take a photo for our passports and then we're off to Kingston, Jamaica," said Detective Andrews. "We're set up in the the Kingston Villa, an all-inclusive hotel in the heart of Kingston."

"You police have all the connections, don't you? Anywhere, anytime."

"I wouldn't know, I'm no longer with the police. But I got a couple of fake badges. They may come in handy."

"So what's your plan?" asked Michael. "How we gonna catch Coretta James?"

"I don't know, but I'll come up with something when I get there."

"When you *get* there? What do you mean, 'when you get there'? Man, I'm going back home."

Michael turned to to walk off, but Detective Andrews grabbed him. "I've got a plan, but I can't put it into effect until I get there."

However, Detective Andrews had no plan, but he really wanted Michael to come. He believed Michael was the ultimate survivor because no matter what happened, he always survived.

Chapter 34

AFTER GETTING THEIR PASSPORTS, THEY boarded a plane bound for Jamaica, scheduled to arrive that afternoon.

"You don't really have a plan do you?" Michael asked him. "You just told me that so I wouldn't go back."

"I don't exactly have a plan," the detective replied honestly. "I just plan to use you. See, I believe this whole thing is about you. I believe you and Coretta have a lot in common and you being with me will be my ace in the hole."

"What do you mean, 'we have a lot in common.' I'm not capeable of going around killing innocent people. I'm not like that."

"Not the killing part, but I just believe you and Coretta think alike. And I believe you can find Coretta just by being you."

"Whatever, man," Michael replied. "I'm tired."

"You get some rest."

Michael lay back and tried to sleep from another unbelieveable night and finally after much tossing and turning, fell off to sleep.

As Michael slept, he started to dream, where he was taken to a graveyard and two black caskets were waiting to be lowered into the ground. The caskets opened and the faces of his two dead wives were revealed, made up and prepared for burial. At that instant, they both opened their eyes.

Michael screamed and woke up, sweating from his dream. He looked over and saw Detective Andrews sound asleep. He lay back and tried to rest in comfort as he continued his flight to Jamaica.

At 3 that afternoon on Friday, they arrived in Kingston. The third world country was in exact contrast to Los Angeles—underdeveloped landscape, poverty in the midst of pure beauty. Crystal clear water that allowed you to see exotic marine life—picturesque beauty in a land so impoverished, it was a truly unbelieveable setting.

The cab driver pulled up in an old, unmarked car. As they rode from the airport to the hotel, they admired the landscape surrounding them.

"This is a beautiful country," Michael exclaimed. "I truly feel as if I'm in another world."

"Yea, it's a different vibe for sure," Detective Andrews remarked.

It was a long, 40-minute ride from the airport to their all-inclusive villa. The beauty of the villa was in stark contrast to the poverty-stricken landscape.

"I need to get a drink," Michael said. "I'm coming back down to buy a couple of shots after I put my bags up."

"It's all-inclusive," the detective reminded him. "All you can eat, and all you can drink at no extra cost."

"That's sweet," Michael said. "I'm definitely coming right back down."

The bellhop approached the two men and offered to take their bags. The hotel was packed with people in town for the

Caribbean festival. Michael and Detective Andrews bumped into various people trying to make it to their rooms.

Michael was still down from the events of the last several days and was not as excited as he normally would be in the midst of such a crowd.

As they walked towards the room, Detective Andrews gave him a pep talk. "I know you've been through a lot, man, but I need you to do what you do best."

"And what is that?"

"Well, you were paid to be a gigolo. I need you to *be* a gigolo. I need you to meet and greet and find out what's going on in the city. Coretta James, Stephen—they're gonna be where the action is. I need you to get us there."

"Why don't you get in the mix?" Michael asked. "You know, meet and greet."

"I'm a square. I don't know how to mingle."

"You need to learn," Michael informed him.

The bellhop stopped at a room and put Michael's stuff inside. Michael went to close the door, but the bellhop also brought in Detective Andrews' bags.

"Man, where you going? What room are you in?"

"I'm in this room too," the detective answered.

Michael looked around and saw one queen-size bed, a sofa, and a bathroom.

"No, hell, you ain't," he yelled. "I'm not into that gay shit. If you brought me all the way to Jamaica to come out of the closet, we're gonna be some fighting asses."

Detective Andrews tipped the bellhop and spoke to Michael. "Man, I'm *not* gay. I was able to get us over here, but with the festival going on, I was lucky to get this one room. You can have the bed."

"Okay, but if I see your hands coming anywhere near me, you're through."

Detective Andrews laughed. "Michael, you're homophobic."

"Whatever."

Michael went into the bathroom and threw on some long jean shorts, a tank top, and some sandals, then headed for the bar. "I'm going downstairs to have a few."

"Okay, I'll be down shortly."

Michael went downstairs to the bar.

"Hey, brother," he said to the bartender, "give me one of your favorite mixed drinks and make it taste good."

"Do you like pineapple?" the bartender asked.

"Love it," answered Michael.

"I've got you covered, man," said the bartender, a tall Jamacian with a dark complexion, wearing dreads and having a strong island accent.

"Hey," Michael continued, "where can I get me a bag of smoke?"

The bartender called another brother out on the beach and pointed to Michael. Michael motioned towards his lips as if he were smoking. The Jamaican nodded his head and extended his hands. Michael reached into his pocket and handed him a ten dollar bill. The man took off.

"Where's he going?" asked Michael.

"He'll be back, man."

The bartender handed Michael his drink and then Detective Andrews came down, wearing some checkered shorts, white sneakers, and a polo shirt.

"You'll never blend in looking like Tiger Woods," Michael told him. "Man, look around at all these fine sisters. They're *not* looking for Tiger Woods."

"Why not?" said Detective Andrews. "He's a black man ruling a sport we once couldn't even play."

"When did Tiger Woods become a black man?" Michael asked.

"He's always been a black man. You're just a hater."

"I ain't no hater," Michael replied. "Tiger Woods said himself he wasn't a black man. He said he was a mutt. But when he was playing golf in college, before he became rich, he was a black man. But once he made his millions, he wasn't a color. That's how entertainers are—they're only black when it's convenient."

"Is there anybody that you like?" Detective Andrews asked him. "You have no respect for authority."

"I love black people. I'm hoping one day to move to Africa."

"Africa? Michael, America is the best country in the world. I wouldn't want to live anywhere else. And besides, look at all the AIDS in Africa. They're lucky the United States passed that bill to send that fifteen billion dollars over there to help fight that disease."

"They should send more than that," Michael said, gulping down his drink. "They're the ones that put it over there. AIDS is a man-made disease.

"Man, this drink is good. Give me another one."

"Why are you a police officer anyway?"

"I graduated from Long Beach State University," Detective Andrews told him. "I couldn't find a job and I had a clean record, so I joined the academy. After a few close calls on the street, I decided I better learn my craft like an ordinary employee and so I did, and here I am, a career officer. What about you? How did you become a gigolo?"

"I fuck real good," Michael laughed. "Man, where is that nigger with my weed?"

"Say what?" said a surprised Detective Andrews.

"Oh, nothing," Michael answered, polishing off another drink and continuing to talk politics.

"You know what, Detective? Man, what is your first name again?"

"Dana."

"Dana? That's a woman's name," said Michael. "OK, Dana, you talk about America being the best country in the world, but you can only judge a country by the way it treats its elderly and its poor. The elderly people in this country can't afford health care or the basic necessities of life, and the poor are treated like slop thrown in a pen for the hogs to consume."

"Well, if you're so concerned, why don't you help them out?" asked Detective Andrews.

"I plan on it. I'm just waiting on my change to come."
***

As the two men talked, two women emerged from the pool area, wearing bathing suits. One woman sat next to Michael, and the other woman sat next to the detective.

"Let's get the kids some food and go upstairs to change," one of the woman said. "You don't mind if I sit next to you, do you?" she asked Michael.

"Not at all," he answered.

"Give us two Mai Tais," she said to the bartender. "My name is Shelly, and this is my friend, Violet."

"Nice to meet you. My name is Michael, and this is Dana."

"That's my son, Marvin, swimming in the pool," Shelly said, "and my niece, Keidra, beside him. We're here for the festival."

"What are the children going to do while y'all enjoy the night life?" asked Michael.

"My son is sixteen years old," Shelly said. "He can take care of things. He's in the theatre and an honor student. I'm so proud of my baby."

"No sports, huh?" Michael asked.

"We gave him a choice to play sports, but he chose theatre instead," answered Shelly.

"And this is my daughter, Jaden," said Violet, showing a picture to Michael then Detective Andrews. "She's the prettiest little girl in the world, and she is so smart. She is only two but she reads at a first-grade level."

"Yea, she is cute," agreed Shelly, "and so smart. She's my godbaby. We have some beautiful kids."

Shelly was 5 foot 4 inches and very light with freckles. She had a lazy left eye that was hardly noticeable with makeup. Violet was 5 foot 6 and somewhat heavyset.

"Excuse me for a moment," said Violet, who walked off towards the gift shop to buy souveniers.

"So where you guys from?" asked Michael.

"Baltimore," Shelly replied. "You have to excuse my girl. She is always showing that picture of her daughter and talking about how cute she is, but her daughter is not cute."

"Why you wanna bust your girl like that as soon as she walks off?" asked Michael. "As long as she thinks her daughter is cute, that's all that matters. What kind of two-faced friend are you?"

"I'm from Edmundson village in B-more," Shelly replied, "and where I come from, a punk like you will get slapped. Don't no nigger talk to me like that."

Michael stood up and looked at the woman in amazement, not believing what she just said. "You slap me and you will regret it for the rest of your life," he said matter-of-factly.

Detective Andrews stood up and tried to calm the tension between the two.

"Your tall weak ass won't do nothing," Shelly remarked. "I'll chop your tall ass down to size where your moma won't even know you."

"You can chop these nuts," Michael responded. "You better sit your cock-eyed ass down and take your faggity-looking son back to Baltimore."

The woman reached around Detective Andrews and slapped Michael across the face. Michael reached back and slapped her a lot harder and her face turned red from the vicious slap.

"Ain't no woman suppose to hit a man," Michael said. "If you hit a man, your ass should expect to get hit back. Brothers always get locked up for fighting women when y'all start all the fights."

At that moment, Violet came back, challenging Michael and pushing him from behind.

"You should push her," Michael said. "I was getting on her because as soon as you walked off, she said your daughter was really ugly. You need to dump her as a friend."

"That nigger's lying," huffed Shelly. "You know I wouldn't say that about my godchild. I love Jaden."

"Actually," countered Detective Andrews, "she did say it as soon as you walked off."

Violet immediately went upstairs, and Shelly followed, trying to explain what happened.

"I'm not for hitting women," said Detective Andrews, "but she had it coming."

⋅►▐═◉   ⋅►▐═◉   ⋅►▐═◉

MICHAEL SAT BACK down, and the man he gave the ten dollars to for the weed finally showed up.

"Man, you've been gone so long, you must have had to grow this weed today," Michael said sarcastically.

Although he had given the man ten dollars, the man brought Michael back enough marijuana to smoke for a month.

"Damn," Michael said, "you get all this weed for ten dollars? I would be rich if I could get some of this weed back to the States. If you would have come ten minutes earlier, you would have saved me from getting slapped."

He put the weed in his pocket and sat back down at the bar and talked again to the bartender.

"So where's the happenings at tonight?" he asked. "Where's the hot spot?"

"You're at the hot spot," said the bartender.

"Yea, I can see that," he replied, "but where do the regulars hang out?"

"There's a lot of clubs," said the bartender. "You looking for naked women? Trying to buy some sex?"

"Nothing like that," Michael replied, "but where do the high rollers hang out?"

"The Kilminjara. That's where all the action is. But …"

"But what?"

"It's run by the society," said the bartender, "the Jamacian Mafia. A lot of people go in, but some don't come out. It takes a real man to be a high roller in there. You slap a woman in there, and they will cut your arm off."

"What time does it start kicking?" asked Michael.

"It's packed now, but the night crowd brings the real action in."

"Sounds like a good place to start," said Detective Andrews. "I'll bet we can find something there."

"Yea," Michael agreed, "but what? I'm going to the beach to smoke me a king-size joint, then I'm going to the room to take me a nap. I think I'm going to need it."

"Yea," said Detective Andrews, "I'm going to take me a power nap too."

"Don't forget," Michael reminded him, "you take the couch."

Michael went to the beach to fire up a big spliff while Detective Andrews went for a nap. But first, he asked the bartender another question.

"Where can we get some guns, some we can leave behind when we finish with them?"

"I'm off in two hours," replied the bartender. "I can take you to a man I know. Two hours sharp. I won't wait."

"I'll be here on time," Detective Andrews told him.

Michael smoked weed on the beach while Detective Andrews napped, preparing for what could be a very long night. Michael lay around the beach for an hour and a half and then headed for the room to take a nap. There he found Detective Andrews already dressed.

"Get dressed," the detective said. "It's time to go."

"Yea," Michael replied, "it's time to go to sleep."

"We've got to be downstairs in thirty minutes," said Detective Andrews. "I laid your gear out. Put it on."

"Steel toe boots, black pants, long sleeve black shirt," said Michael. "It's 90 degrees outside!"

"You've also got to wear this vest. It's the only protection we have. Get dressed, we've gotta go."

"We're trying to go incognito," Michael said. "Don't you think we'll stand out with all this gear on?"

"We'll have to take our chances," said Detective Andrews. "Let's go."

Michael threw on his clothes and the vest and followed Detective Andrews. They arrived on time and the bartender drove them off to a small shack in the midst of what looked like a farm. Goats and other animals walked around openly and the two men couldn't understand where they could get guns in a place like this. The bartender talked to a man who waved Michael and Detective Andrews inside.

Inside the shack towards the back was a bunch of older handguns and a few shotguns, none that appeared to be in great condition.

"Man, we don't know what we might be walking into," Michael stated, "and all they got is some .38 specials and some old rifles."

"Before semi-automatic guns came about, this is all they had," Detective Andrews replied. "We just have to make them work."

The bartender stood around as Michael and Detective Andrews discussed the merchandise.

"Give me six of those pistols and two knives," Detective Andrews requested. "We don't know what kind of combat we may get into."

"What's your name, brother?" Michael asked the bartender.

"My name is Desmond," he replied with an accent.

"Ask him how much for the guns," Detective Andrews said.

"It will be fifty of your American dollars," Desmond answered.

"Damn," Michael exclaimed, "six guns and two knives for fifty bucks. That's cheap even for these raggedy ass guns."

"Tell him we need ammo," the detective said. "I also want to test them out."

The man provided the ammunition and Michael and Detective Andrews went out back and fired off their guns.

"They all seem to work pretty well," Detective Andrews said. "Here, take this." He gave Michael a leg holster and a shoulder holster for the guns.

"Stash the knife in your sock and put the other gun in the back of your pants. Make sure you put the safety on the one you put in the back of your pants."

"Why?" Michael asked.

"Because if you jump up too soon, the gun might go off and blow half your ass off. Then you'll be the only brother in the club missing one ass cheek."

"Yea," Michael smiled, "I can't dance to this reggae with only half my ass."

They both laughed out loud and and shared their first friendly moment. Detective Andrews paid the man for the guns and gave Desmond twenty dollars for the trip.

"How would you like to make a lot more?" the detective asked.

Desmond thought for a second and nodded yes.

"Take us to the club and wait around for us. I'll give you one hundred dollars."

Desmond quickly agreed.

"It doesn't take much money to bribe people, does it?" stated Michael.

"On the contrary, the American dollar is worth far more than their money. To him, he's getting over on us."

The three men got strapped down and headed for Club Kilminjara. It was a 25-mile ride from where the gun shack was located and through some very rough terrain.

"So what do you men seek?" asked Desmond. "Club Kilminjara can be a very treacherous place."

Detective Andrews pulled out a picture of Stephen Davis and Coretta James. Desmond looked at the picture of Coretta and didn't respond, but recognized the picture of Stephen.

"I have seen this man before," Desmond said. "It has been a long time, but he looks like X-Warrior. His brother, who is the leader of the Jamaican Mafia, is known as God to his people. They worship his every move. These people are known for torture. X-Warrior's mother disowned him. She did not care for him and just left him on the streets to fend for himself.

"When he was 10, he was assaulted by several boys at a foster home. He blamed it on his mother and since then, he has hated women, especially those that bear any resemblance to his mother. He has killed many women, including his own mother, and many men."

"How do you know so much?" Michael inquired.

"My brother would frequent the club. One night, he crossed the wrong woman and X had him beheaded. Before that, they had been friends. X didn't even hesitate to kill him."

Michael and the detective looked at each other in shock.

"What about this God?" asked Detective Andrews.

"He is far more brutal than his brother," Desmond stated, "if that's possible. If you cross him in any way, he has no mercy."

"Man, what the hell am I doing over here?" yelled Michael. "I should be at home with my family, burying my wife." He held his head down as they continued to drive.

"Another thing," Desmond added, "you have to be a member to carry a gun in the club. The guard at the door will check you to see if you're carrying a weapon."

"That's it," Michael exclaimed. "There's no way we're getting in."

"How do they know who's a member and who isn't?" Detective Andrews wanted to know.

"I don't know," Desmond replied. "They all wear a symbol, but they change it on a regular basis. You never know what it's gonna be."

After 40 minutes of driving, they arrived at the entrance of Club Kilminjara. The club looked like a large country jook joint. It was one level, a very large club, with one road in and one road out. The three men sat back off from the club and watched to see if they could figure out what was happening. They saw many people going in and a select few just walked past the bouncer.

"Look at the size of the doorman!" Michael said, agitated. "He's taller than I am, and he looks like he weighs 350 lbs. Oh my God, what a monster ..."

"The bigger they are, the harder they fall," said Detective Andrews. "I can take his big ass."

"Yea, right," Michael retorted.

"It's the hat," said Desmond.

"What the hell do you mean, 'the hat'?" asked Michael.

"Their hats," Detective Andrews enlightened him. "Don't tell me your militant ass don't recognize those hats. A lot of the Muslim brothers wear them."

"I know," Michael replied, "I was just testing you."

"They've got the exact same hats on," Detective Andrews observed. "Come on, Michael."

Detective Andrews handed Desmond a one hundred dollar bill and told him to wait for them.

"Where are we going and why did you pay him already?" asked Michael. "He's going to leave us."

"No, he won't," the detective replied, "and besides, he's done his job."

The two men walked behind the club and sat back, waiting by the garbage dumpster.

"Why are we sitting by this funky ass garbage?" asked Michael.

"Shhhh."

After a while, a couple of members of the Jamaican Mafia came around the back to smoke and take a leak.

"Nasty sucker taking a leak outside," whispered Michael.

The rear of the club was somewhat isolated. Suddenly, Michael and Detective Andrews jumped from behind the dumpster with guns drawn. They forced the two men behind the dumpster where they hit both men across the head and knocked them unconscious. Detective Andrews and his partner took their socks off and tied them around the men's mouths and wrists and took their hats. They lifted up both men and threw them in the dumpster.

"That funk from your socks should keep them knocked out for a while," laughed Michael.

"Did anybody ever tell you that you were a comedian?" asked Detective Andrews. "Well, if they did, they lied. Martin Lawrence's job is safe."

They really had to strain to throw the second man in the dumpster. "This is a heavy ass Rastafarian," said Michael, "and he's got a big ass head. This hat is swallowing my head. That doorman is gonna know something is up."

"Just don't make eye contact with him, and keep your hand on your gun because if he suspects something, we need to move fast. Let's go."

Chapter 35

MICHAEL AND DETECTIVE ANDREWS WALKED to the entrance
of the club as other members were walking in. As they
approached the entrance, they both made a concerted effort
to look away from the doorman, not knowing if he could
recognize the members by their faces. They stumbled over
each other as they rushed in the club to see what they could
find. The first thing they found was a trash can, where they
immediately dumped their headgear, then continued their
walk through the club.

The club was packed and the dance floor was full. Reggae
music blared from the loudspeakers. Although the club was
only one level, it had three parts. The first part had exotic
dancers and Michael noticed one.

"Man, that chick's got a big ass," he said. "This shit's on
like popcorn."

In the middle was traditional reggae.

"Man, these Jamaican girls dance freaky," he observed.

And in the back was American music, R&B, rap, and
other types.

"Now this is the nicest hole-in-the-wall club I've ever seen," he said. "I could really get my groove on here."

"Okay," said Detective Andrews, "here's a picture of Stephen. Show it around and see if anyone has seen him. You go back to the middle, and I'll just float around."

"Okay," Michael agreed. He went back to where the reggae was playing and walked up to the bar to try and order a drink, but had to yell above the music to give his order. A song by Sean Paul came on called "Shake that Thang" and one young lady danced on the floor alone as everyone stood and watched.

Detective Andrews walked over to Michael at the bar. Michael had his back turned, trying to order a beer.

"Give me a Red Stripe," he yelled.

"Whew-ee," said Detective Andrews, "that's one of the sexiest sisters I've ever seen."

Michael looked at the woman dancing by herself as everybody else watched. "Somebody needs to get on that," he remarked.

"Why don't you get on it?" countered Detective Andrews. "Mr. Gigolo."

Detective Andrews was just joking, but Michael loved a challenge and although they were trying to blend in, he rushed to the dance floor.

The detective tried to grab him, but he was too late. Michael reached the dance floor and the woman gyrating alone. He grabbed her boldly from behind and put his hand between her legs and pressed his face against her and gyrated in tune with her. The song was half over. The woman reached over her head and grabbed Michael around the neck and pulled him closer.

The two continued to grind to the music as everyone watched and wondered about who the new dancer was. Detective Andrews looked in amazement at Michael and the intensity at which he and the woman danced together.

As the song ended, some people clapped. The woman turned and kissed Michael on the lips and walked away. Michael returned to the bar. All eyes were on him.

"I didn't know you had it in you," Detective Andrews said, admiringly. "You were freaking her. I'm gonna keep moving."

Michael wiped the sweat from his brow and drank some of his beer. The dance floor filled up again and the freaky dancing continued.

People were openly doing cocaine in the club and smoking marijuana. Michael continued to look around and noticed a large black male with dreadlocks staring at him. He drank his beer and walked around, and he noticed that the man continued to stare at him. Michael looked away again and went to sit at the crowded bar. The man still stared and started to approach him.

Michael glanced around again and tried to ignore the man, slowly sipping his beer as the man fought his way through the thick crowd towards him. As the man got closer, Michael put his hand on one of his guns.

Detective Andrews casually searched the room for Stephen. The crowd was so loud and the flow of the music so good that it was hard to see or hear anything. But he did see the man approaching Michael from a distance and made a beeline in that direction as the man reached Michael and stared him in the eyes. He was not wearing the Muslim hat, so he was not a member of the Mafia. He began to speak.

"American black man weak man. American black man ruled by woman. American black man stands for nothing, but falls for anything."

Michael looked at the man who was almost eye to eye with him, but far more muscular, Detective Andrews observed, watching closely.

"Black American man a slave. Jamaicans overthrow their slave masters. American black man still bow down to their white slave owner."

Detective Andrews did not intervene and one of the bartenders watched closely. Some Jamaicans had been known to dislike American blacks, believing them to be phony and weak. Michael continued sipping on his beer and looking around. The man looked at Michael's hair.

"American black man like woman, with processed hair, fake, want to be white man."

Michael looked back at the man and sniffed. "Jamaican man funky," he said, "and if he don't leave me alone, he is about to get an ass whupping."

The Jamaican had deep red eyes and a scowling disposition and reached for Michael, who pointed his Saturday Night Special at the Jamaican's head.

"Jamaican man 'bout to get his head blowed off," said Michael.

Three of the Jamaican's friends stood up as Michael pointed the gun to the aggressor's head. Detective Andrews showed his weapon and the three men retreated. Detective Andrews walked up to Michael.

"Is it my imagination or do people just like to fuck with you?" he said. "I hope none of those Mafia people saw you pull your gun. They're the only ones that are supposed to be armed in here."

The bartender who was watching spoke, "That man is a wannabe. He is always in here, looking for trouble, trying to become a member of the Mafia."

"Have you seen this guy?" Michael asked, holding up a picture of Stephen.

"You're looking for even more trouble," he replied.

With that, the bartender just walked away and didn't even answer. Michael and Detective Andrews walked back through the club together, intent on finding information on Stephen or Coretta immediately. The club itself was a distraction. It offered everything in entertainment, from people playing cards to those openly doing drugs. The party seemed to be getting stronger.

The two men walked back to the part of the club where the strippers were. Detective Andrews noticed a man over by the strippers, yelling and screaming at the girls and touching them as they danced.

"Look at that fool," said Michael. "He's all over those girls. Where I come from, you can't touch the strippers."

"I thought I heard you say you didn't like strip clubs," remarked Detective Andrews. "Now you know their code of conduct."

"I just heard you can't touch them," Michael replied.

"Yeah, right."

The man near the strippers was making such a spectacle of himself that Michael and Detective Andrews continued to look at the way he was carrying on. Michael noticed the large men nearby with their Mafia gear on and took an even harder look at the man.

"Why are you staring at that man?" Detective Andrews asked. "Keep your eyes open."

The man turned to the side as he interacted with one of the strippers. "I don't believe it," said Michael. "That's the bastard right there."

"Stephen? Are you sure that's him?"

"Positive," Michael replied. "I could never forget that face." He took off towards the stage without thinking.

"Michael, wait!" said Detective Andrews, "Wait, man!"

Michael walked slowly past the two Mafia members, right up to Stephen and stuck the gun to the back of his head as the two men watched, but couldn't see the exposed gun.

"Michelle," said Michael with the gun centered to the back of Stephen's head.

"Michelle?" repeated Stephen. "What is Michelle?"

"Michelle is all you better say. Anything else comes out of your mouth, and I will blow your brains out."

Stephen looked over his shoulder to see Michael. "Pretty bitch," Stephen said. "I underestimated you. You got balls, but you gonna die tonight."

The two Mafia members started towards Michael and at that point, Detective Andrews stuck his gun in their faces. They stopped in their tracks. The detective relieved them of their semi-automatic weapons and followed Michael's example of looking around the club with his gun drawn.

"You'll never get out of here, pretty boy," Stephen informed him. "They're all around, and they will die for me."

As Michael and Detective Andrews headed towards the exit, the man that Michael had the argument with came from the side to hit Michael with a stick and knocked the gun from his hand. Michael fell to the floor.

Stephen ran out of the club as several people converged on Michael and Detective Andrews. The man tried to hit

Michael again, but Michael grabbed the gun in his sock and shot the man twice in the chest. Detective Andrews helped Michael up.

"I didn't know you could shoot like that," Detective Andrews said, impressed.

"Neither did I," Michael responded, "but we got to get the hell out of here."

Immediately, gunfire exploded towards Michael and Detective Andrews and everyone panicked. Innocent people were hit by gunfire, but not Michael or Detective Andrews.

"Let's go," Detective Andrews said tersely.

They ran towards the door, chased by several Mafia members firing at them.

As they reached the front door, the big doorman grabbed Michael. At the same moment, Detective Andrews reached into his pocket and pulled a vial and sprayed a substance into the doorman's face. He released Michael instantly, screaming in pain and rubbing his eyes, then the two men ran toward the road where Desmond was supposed to be waiting for them, but the car was gone.

"I told you not to pay him before we got back," Michael complained. "Now we're up shit creek."

"You better run and stop talking," the detective urged.

They ran through the wooded area and all of a sudden, the shooting stopped. The two looked back and noticed that the Mafia had not only stopped shooting, but stopped chasing them as well.

"Well, we can't go back that way," Michael said. "We better see what's through these woods."

"Let's just walk," Detective Andrews said, "and see what we find."

"Why do I feel like we just walked out of the frying pan and into the fire?" Michael asked. "I got a real bad feeling."

"You're paranoid."

"We're in the woods in a third world country, being chased by many men with guns," Michael stated. "And we have no idea what's on the other side of the woods. I think that goes beyond paranoia, don't you?"

They walked through the wooded area over a mile in the dark and came upon an opening in the woods. A large compound was in the midst of the woods and a tall fence protected the compound from the outside world. The compound was made of marble with a beautiful design and was at least 15,000 square feet.

"All I've seen since I've been here is slums," Michael said in bewilderment, "but in the midst of these woods stands this magnificent building. That's amazing to me."

As they looked through the fence, Michael heard a snarl and fell to the ground in fear. A *huge* Rottweiler ran towards the fence with two other attack dogs on its heels.

"I've been around dogs all my life," said Detective Andrews, "but I've *never* seen dogs that big or that vicious before."

The dogs snarled with foam spraying from their mouths as they tried to work their way through the thick fence.

"These dogs are as big as horses," Michael said, trembling. "That's why those people stopped chasing us. They knew we had nowhere to go. We're trapped. Whoever is in that building probably already knows we're here."

Michael sat back and pulled out a joint and tried to light it, but Detective Andrews grabbed it and threw it to the ground.

"You need a clear head. You don't need to smoke that mess now."

"Smoking weed gives me a fresh prospective," he protested. "It helps me think better."

Michael picked up the joint and tried to light it again and this time, got hit in the head by the barrel of a shotgun, knocking him out instantly. Detective Andrews threw up his hands as several men held guns on him.

Chapter 36

MICHAEL WOKE UP AN HOUR later, tied up in a dungeon-like area without his shirt on and stripped of his guns and knife. About a foot away, Detective Andrews was tied up in the same manner. Michael had a headache and sore lumps on his head.

"You're gonna wish you were still out," said Detective Andrews as Michael came to.

"Aw, my head," he moaned. "My head hurts bad." He tried to focus and look around.

"Oh, shit," he screamed.

Directly across from the men was a 27-ft crocodile, chained to the wall, but not for long as it strained and pulled the cement blocks from the wall.

"That wall is not going to last long," the detective observed. "I guess we're gonna be dinner for that big croc."

The two men were terrified as the croc continued to pull the cement from the wall while their hands were tied securely and they wiggled about, trying to free themselves.

"We've been testing a new product," announced a voice

from above, "which makes our animals bigger and stronger. You are about to meet Hercules, our prize pupil. You see, we don't like uninvited guests on our private sanctuary."

Standing above Michael and Detective Andrews were Stephen, another man holding a rifle, and Stephen's brother, known as God.

"My brother, X, tells me many things about you, Michael," said God. "It seems your reputation proceeds you."

"I'm flattered," Michael responded. "Are you the one they call God?"

"I am."

"Well, you're just as crazy as your brother. No man can be God. Only a fool believes he's God."

"I am God on this island. If I say a man dies, he dies. Right now, I'm God in your life. If I say you become dinner for a crocodile, you become dinner—unless you bow down and worship me like my subjects do."

"I'll never worship you or any other man," said Michael. "The God I know raises men from the dead. He can walk on water."

"The secret to walking on water is knowing where the rocks are," sneered God.

As they talked, the crocodile was very close to demolishing the wall.

"Your time is short," Stephen proclaimed. "Bow down and save yourself."

"If it isn't the rapist," Michael said with disgust. "Rape any women today?"

Stephen scowled because Michael was so close to death and *still* wouldn't show him any respect.

"I was hoping we'd get the chance to see who the best man was," Michael said, "but since I'm the only man between the two of us, I guess there's no question. You're a rapist and your brother thinks he's God. What kind of bloodline do y'all come from?"

As Michael finished, the crocodile finally broke free and headed directly for him and Detective Andrews. Stephen grabbed the gun from the guard and shot the crocodile point-blank in the head. The force of the shot split open the gigantic beast's head.

"Untie them and bring them to me," God said. "We're gonna have a little fun with them, especially, you, Michael. When I'm done with you, you *will* call me God."

"You really know how to make people mad," Detective Andrews said, "but you probably bought us a few more minutes."

They were untied and led to a room upstairs and tied up with their hands above their heads so they couldn't fall down and their stomachs were completely exposed.

Stephen and two large men walked in with their stun guns and other objects. Stephen walked up to Michael and punched him in the stomach. Michael tried to double over, but couldn't because of the way he was tied. He couldn't breathe and slobbered at the mouth as he tried to catch his breath. Michael finally got a few words out.

"You hit like the bitch you are," he spat.

Stephen came close to Michael and looked him in the eye. "When I'm done with you, you will wish you had shown me some respect."

He then kissed Michael on the lips, and Michael spit directly into his face.

"I knew you were a faggot."

Michael and Detective Andrews were about to be tortured when Stephen's cell phone rang. After talking on the phone for a moment, he ordered his companions, "Cut him down," pointing to Michael. "Take him to the main room."

"What about him?" Michael said, nodding at Detective Andrews.

"If I were you, I'd be worried about myself," Stephen replied. "I'll be seeing you real soon."

Detective Andrews remained tied up as Michael was led to what was called the main room. There he saw a very familiar face inside.

"Michael," said Coretta, "I just heard you were here, and I thought you might like it better in here with me, especially with what they plan on doing to you."

She was in the bed with four women as Manu stood guard over her as usual, and he had his usual frown for Michael.

"I thought maybe you would like a little pleasure instead of being with those mean boys," she smiled seductively. "Everything your heart desires is in this room."

On the table across the room was all the cocaine a man could ever ask for, ounces and ounces of it, all at Michael's disposal.

At that moment, the man known as God came into the room, disrobed, and jumped into the huge bed.

"I thought you could try something familiar and something new," Coretta laughed. "You can say you slept with God."

"I don't sleep with men," Michael said coldly. "I'd rather be dead first."

"Well, technically, you have slept with a man," Coretta explained. "You see, I was my daddy's man. My father wanted a boy so bad that he taught me all the ways of a man. I played sports at first, but my father wanted me to learn the business world. He taught me to think like a man in the business world, and that's how I made my fortune. He started me out with a nice lump sum, and I turned it into billions. You see, I have a man's mind with a woman's features, and you must admit that my features are quite nice."

Michael didn't comment.

"You see, Michael," Coretta explained, "men are so weak. They won't help each other, but they will give a woman anything because this hole we have between our legs is a powerful weapon. I didn't even have to sleep with men to get what I wanted. If men even think they have a chance to get some, they will give you the world. So I just flirted my way to super wealth. Men would give me all their money, tell me all their secrets, all for the possibility of having sex—that's a powerful thing.

"But not you, Michael. That's the thing I like about you. You're your own man. You won't even buy a woman a drink. You're tall, dark, and handsome, and you don't care if anyone likes you or not. When that woman said you weren't good to her in bed, it never bothered you. Most men would have tried to kill the woman, but you took it in stride. I've kept you alive this long, but there is no more I can do. You can get in this bed and show God how thankful you are that he spared you, or Manu over there can't wait to show you how much he dislikes you."

On cue, Manu stepped towards Michael and waited for him to give an answer. As they talked, Stephen walked in through the side door and waited for Michael to make a decision.

The setup of the room was classical with paintings and beautiful vases, as well as machetes from Egypt. It was class in every way. Michael looked for a weapon, but the machetes were too far away.

"Can I get a toot of that cocaine?" he asked. "I need to be ready for this."

"Help yourself," Coretta replied sweetly.

Michael approached the cocaine, but had no intention of snorting it. He reached down to grab the tray with the cocaine in it and threw the substance into Manu's face, burning his eyes.

Then he rushed across the room as Manu lashed into the air and grabbed a machete, returning and slicing Manu's face in half. The burly Chinese man fell dead to the floor as Coretta screamed.

Stephen quickly dashed across the room and commanded Michael to put the weapon down. Instead, Michael approached the bed and with a mighty swing, cut off the head of the man everyone called God while he was pointing at Michael, as if he were casting a spell.

"Ronald!" screamed Stephen. "You killed my brother."

"I thought you said he was God," Michael said calmly. "I never knew God's name was Ronald."

"I'll kill you!" yelled Stephen.

Michael stood near the bed and watched as Ronald's blood ran everywhere. The three other women in the bed were so high that they hadn't yet reacted to what's going on. Michael started to lift the machete towards Coretta, but she had a gun stashed in the bed and fired at Michael, hitting him in a shoulder. He took the machete and ran from the room, down the hall, and entered into the room where Detective Andrews was.

Detective Andrews was hanging by his arms, stretched out in pain, but he had not been touched yet. Michael quickly cut him down and helped him to his feet.

"You're shot, man."

"We'll worry about that later," Michael said urgently, "but we're getting out of this place, first. Let's go."

Michael and Detective Andrews rushed out of the room and were greeted by gunfire as they ran down the hall. They rushed into the room where the gas incinerators were kept that provided fuel throughout the large building. The room contained some tables and furnishings, along with some chairs.

"Well, we could light this furnace if we had a match," the detective said. He barricaded the door to slow down the oncoming men.

"I don't have a match, but I have a lighter," Michael informed him, "and they left this joint in my pocket. I ought to fire it up."

"Boy, give me that lighter," Detective Andrews told him. "Fire that up later."

As the men banged on the door, Detective Andrews prepared to ignite the furnace. "We may not survive this, so pull that sofa over your head because there's gonna be an explosion."

Michael pulled the sofa over his head and Detective Andrews found cover and lit the inferno just as the men forced their way through the door. The incinerator exploded, sending fire directly out the door in a huge fireball and knocking Detective Andrews across the room. The fire engulfed the room as the men that chased Michael and Detective Andrews lay dead.

Detective Andrews rose up and went over to lift up Michael. "Boy, you alright?" he asked.

"Where am I?" Michael joked.

"Do you ever stop?" Detective Andrews asked him. "Come on, let's get out of here because the place is about to burn up."

"How did we survive that and they didn't?" asked Michael.

"Because we saw it coming and they didn't."

They exited the room and grabbed two guns off the dead men, then headed out of the building. Michael was running fast. Suddenly, he heard a yell as he neared the exit.

Out of nowhere, Stephen appeared and grabbed Michael, tackling him to the ground and kicking him in the midst of the inferno. Michael dropped his gun into the fire after being tackled by Stephen. Detective Andrews continued to run, unaware of Michael's predicament as Michael was trapped in a battle with Stephen.

"You killed my brother, bitch," yelled Stephen. "I'm going to kill you!"

Stephen tried to kick Michael again, but he rolled away and got to his feet. Michael wanted Stephen just as badly and they fought fiercely as the fire blazed all around them and spread out of control. Then Detective Andrews looked back and saw Stephen and Michael fighting. Stephen grabbed Michael by the throat and tried to force his head into the blaze. Michael strained to keep his face away from the flames. Next, Stephen dropped Michael with a punch to his gut. He spotted the gun that Michael had dropped.

"You about to swim with the fishes, just like Carlos," he gloated as he reached down to pick up the gun, but the heat from the fire had made the gun scorching hot. He screamed as his flesh burnt from the pain and instantly dropped the hot gun. At that instant, Michael grabbed a burning board from the floor and rammed it directly through Stephen's abdomen with all his might and he fell to the floor dead.

"That's for everybody you ever raped and murdered, bitch," Michael said coldly as the fire blazed fiercely around him.

Detective Andrews ran back to help Michael. He took him by the arm, and they rushed towards the exit. As they reached the front of the building and ran into the yard, the big Rottweilers immediately saw them and attacked.

"Oh, shit,"shrieked Michael. "I forgot about those big ass dogs."

"Run," shouted Detective Andrews.

They both reached the fence, but Michael was slow as Detective Andrews scaled the fence quickly. Michael was only halfway up the fence when he was bitten in the buttocks by one of the overgrown beasts, but he freed himself and reached the top of the fence, then fell over all the way to the ground and landed with a thump.

"Oh my God," yelled Michael.

"You alright, man?"

"Yea, but I believe I left one of my butt cheeks in that dog's mouth," Michael painfully exclaimed.

They laughed loudly and looked back at the burning building as day broke.

"Did you get Coretta?" asked the detective.

"No, but I got Stephen and his brother, God, whose real name was Ronald. He's given his last commandment. You don't think Coretta could have survived that fire do you?"

"Hell, no," Detective Andrews replied. "I still don't know how *we* survived it."

The fire around the compound had spread into the woods and Michael and Detective Andrews walked back towards the club as people from the club, including Mafia members, stood outside, staring in wonder at the orange sky.

"How we gonna get back to town?" asked Michael.

"I guess we walk," came the reply.

As they walked up the road, the beauty of the sunrise hit their eyes and they heard a horn.

"Come on, get in," yelled a familiar voice.

"Desmond, where you been?" Michael yelled back.

"I was with you the whole time, man, but I had to hide in case the Mafia members saw me and asked me questions."

"Yeah," Michael replied. "You hid so good, you even hid from us."

"Yea," said Detective Andrews, "don't expect another tip."

The two exhausted men jumped into the car with Desmond, who took them back to the hotel, where they made immediate arrangements to leave the island.

In the room as they packed, Detective Andrews made an observation. "I admire you, man. Even in the midst of all that drama, you kept joking. How do you do that?"

"I've had so much happen to me lately," Michael explained, "that I have to laugh to keep from crying. Now, I've got to go home and bury my wife, and then I have to find my daughter."

As they finished packing and started to leave, they stopped by the bar first to speak to Desmond.

"Desmond did not show up today," said the bartender. "I have not heard from him or seen him today."

"Probably tired from last night," suggested Detective Andrews.

"Yeah, all that hiding can really wear you out," Michael said sarcastically. "Well, let's go."

Michael and Detective Andrews left the hotel for the airport and later that day, some members of the Jamaican Mafia came to the hotel searching for them. By then, they were safely gone, but definitely not forgotten.

The two men boarded the evening flight and with connections, and would arrive in LA at 9 a.m. Sunday. They both slept the entire flight, but were wide awake as they landed.

Detective Andrews had parked his car at the airport. He gave Michael a ride to his condo.

"What are you gonna do now that you are no longer with the police?" Michael asked.

"I'm not sure. I need a vacation."

"I hear Jamaica is nice this time of year," he snickered.

"Funny," the detective said. "I'm sure Coretta died, but in case she didn't, she is still on the most wanted list. Stephen, too, even though I'm sure he's dead."

"I hate to admit this, but I realize that all police aren't bad," said Michael. "You're actually pretty cool. But get rid of those Tiger Woods shorts. They make you look even more square."

As Detective Andrews dropped Michael off at the condo, Michael embraced him.

"Alright, brother," Michael said.

"Take care and God bless," replied the detective.

Chapter 37

MICHAEL WALKED UPSTAIRS WITH A flesh wound to the shoulder, cuts and burns, and a dog bite, but very much alive.

Myra was very excited to see him. She hugged him around the neck as he walked through the door.

"Michael!" she screamed, wearing a black dress. "You made it back!" Then she kissed him.

"You made it just in time," she told him, calming down. "Michelle's service is at 11. Her parents are having a service here and will fly her back for a service and burial in Louisiana. The cemetery is placing a headstone with Michelle's name on it at Forest Lawn. Get dressed. We've got less than an hour. Gary, Cheryl, and even Donald are going. Cheryl took care of everything."

"Gary is still here?"

"Yea," said Myra. "He and Cheryl are kind of sweet on each other."

Michael didn't have any time to regroup. He quickly showered and threw on his dark suit after medicating his wounds and headed towards the door with Myra. They drove to the chapel and arrived on time for the service. He sat on the left side near the family he never met and felt the vibes of dislike.

After the minister delivered the sermon and eulogy and the body was being viewed, Michael, Cheryl, Myra, Gary, and Donald gathered together as people somberly walked around the casket to view Michelle's body. Michael had bandaged cuts and wore dark sunglasses. He looked as if he had been in a battle.

As Michael looked at the crowd going around to view Michelle's body, he saw someone he couldn't believe was present—Kenneth Bolling. Kenneth made eye contact with Michael as he passed by the casket. Michael was enraged at the sight of Kenneth, but didn't want to cause a scene at the funeral.

When Michael viewed the body, he caught a glimpse of Michelle's mother and father crying, then he went back to his seat to sit down. The casket was then taken from the church to the Hertz, where it would be driven to the airport to be loaded for the flight to Louisiana for burial. Michael followed the coffin to where Michelle's parents were standing.

He silently approached Michelle's parents as everyone from the funeral procession looked on.

"Mr. and Mrs. Davis, I'm very sorry about your daughter. She was a very special person with a beautiful spirit, who I wanted to share the rest of my life with. She will truly be missed."

Michelle's mother approached him and took off her glasses and looked Michael deep in the eyes, then she slapped him violently across the face.

"It's because of you that my daughter is dead," said the distraught woman. "My baby is dead because of *you*."

She started to scream violently and hit Michael in the chest as her husband grabbed her and put her in the Hertz. Then he got in and looked at Michael.

"I'm sorry, son," he said.

As the Hertz departed, Michael sobbed uncontrollably. Cheryl and Myra put their arms around him. Kenneth looked on from a distance and smiled. Michael continued to sob as his friends tried to comfort him.

"It's okay," said Cheryl. "It's not your fault what happened. It's not your fault." Then she walked off and approached Ken as Myra and Gary stayed with Michael.

"What are you doing here, Kenneth? How did you hear about this?"

"It's been all over the news," he replied. "I thought I would come by and pay my respects."

"Well, I wonder what the police would think if they knew you were here. I'm sure you realize that you are still wanted."

"You're still my wife. I hoped we could talk civilly. We can still work things out."

"How?" asked Cheryl. "You doctored a tape to make Michael look like a pervert and because of that, his daughter was kidnapped. And now, his second wife is dead. How much is this poor man supposed to take?"

"Fuck, Michael," retorted Kenneth, cussing outside the church. "Why is everything about Michael? And I see that girl's parents weren't too happy to meet him."

"Because I was married to you, I won't call the police," Cheryl stated.

"*Was?*" Kenneth said.

"Was," she repeated. "I don't want to see you again until divorce court, because I definitely don't know you."

That said, she walked away from him and went over to Michael, where Myra, Gary, and Donald were trying to calm him down.

"Come on, Michael," Cheryl encouraged him, "let's go look at the headstone they put in the cemetery."

Michael and Cheryl walked over to view the headstone that had been placed in the cemetery while Myra, Donald, and Gary wandered off.

"In memory of Michelle Davis," read the headstone. It had her birth date and the date she passed, and also said, "in memory of a beautiful spirit."

"I think they should have put her new last name on there," Michael remarked, "even though we were only married for a half a night. But it's a beautiful headstone."

Michael still had tears in his eyes as he talked about Michelle. Cheryl continued to hug Michael as Kenneth came from out of nowhere and whispered something in Michael's ear.

"You know," he said, "everything you touch dies."

Michael turned and looked Kenneth in his gloating face, pulled off his glasses, and hit him with a crushing right blow. Kenneth dropped like a sack of potatoes and landed across the headstone of a nearby grave. The impact cracked the headstone and Kenneth was knocked unconscious.

"Come on, Michael, let's go," Cheryl urged him.

They left the cemetery with no concern for Kenneth, who lay sprawled across the grave as if dead. Other people in the cemetery came to help him, but Cheryl walked off as if he were a stranger.

⋯⊫◉ ⋯⊫◉ ⋯⊫◉

MICHAEL RODE HOME with Myra, and his friends came over to be with him. As Michael entered into the condo, he didn't want to eat anything. He just went into his room and closed the door, then fell across the bed in mental pain and exhaustion from the trip to Jamaica.

Cheryl, Gary, Myra, and Donald talked. "That man really needs something good to happen to him," Cheryl said. "There's only so much the human mind can take."

"Yea," Gary agreed. "My man, Michael, has got to be the strongest brother I've ever seen."

Donald was unusually quiet. He just sat back and took everything in.

"I'm gonna have me a drink," Gary said. "You want one, Donald?"

"No, man, I'm trying to get my head together. I need to quit getting high so much."

"What?" Cheryl exclaimed. "I'm proud of you, Donald. You got to start somewhere."

"Well, if you're chilling, I'm chilling," said Gary, who puts the glass back down. "Myra, is there anything around here to eat?"

"I'm sure I can find something," she replied.

Meanwhile, Michael lay across the bed and fell asleep in his suit as friends stayed close by in case he needed them. He slept most of the day away as his friends watched television and sat around, pretty much doing nothing.

At about 8 that evening, Michael arose to take a shower and afterwards emerged from his room, ready to eat and ready for the next step. He went to the refrigerator and poured some juice, then sat down on the sofa.

"I've got to find my daughter. I really need my baby right now. I need to know she's okay. Cheryl, they still don't know where the Jacksons are, right?"

"They haven't been using their credit cards," she replied, "and no one has reported seeing them. It's just a matter of time before they turn up."

"Well, tomorrow I hire a private detective," Michael said. "If it takes my last dime, I'm going to find her."

As he started back towards the refrigerator to get more juice, the doorbell rang. Michael didn't hesitate, but immediately opened the door.

"Daddy!" yelled Brittany as she grabbed her father and wouldn't let go.

"Brittany," Michael yelled in joy. "Oh, my baby girl, you came back to me. I can't believe it! How I've prayed for this moment."

Michael cried tears of joy as did everyone else in the room, including Donald, who pretended that he had something in his eye.

Standing in the doorway was William Jackson. Michael looked at him. Mr. Jackson asked permission to come in and talk for a moment. Michael didn't think he would be able to hold his peace and as everyone hugged Brittany, Michael told Myra to take her to the back for a moment.

"No, Daddy, I want to stay here with you."

Michael hugged her again.

"Look, baby," Michael said, "I'll never let you out of my sight again, but I need you to go into your room and get one of your dolls so we can play."

"Yea, come on, Brittany," said Myra, "let's get some cookies and then you and Daddy can comb her hair."

Myra took Brittany to the room and Michael invited William Jackson in. When he entered the room, Michael tried to attack William, but was restrained by Gary and Donald.

"Call the police," Michael said angrily. "I want this kidnapper arrested."

Cheryl went to dial the phone, but Mr. Jackson stopped her.

"Please," Mr. Jackson requested, "let me explain. I never knew about the plot that my wife and Kenneth put together. They didn't involve me because they knew I wouldn't go for it. I only found out a few nights ago in the Bahamas. I was shocked."

"Well, why did it take you so long to bring her back?" Michael demanded.

"I had to send my wife back home. She said she couldn't spend the rest of her days in jail. She committed suicide."

"I'm sorry," said Michael.

"Don't worry," said William, "Brittany doesn't know. She was asleep. You know, for so long I've blamed you for my daughter's death and hated you. But Brittany worships the ground you walk on. She couldn't sleep, and she would barely eat. For her to love you so much means that you had to do something right. But I promise you, I didn't know. I was caught up in my hatred, and I didn't allow myself to see. Now if you don't mind, I need to go to New York and bury my wife, and then I'll come back and face the music."

As he finished speaking, William Jackson slowly walked towards the door with a solemn look on his face.

"Hey, man," Michael said as he wrote something down, "This is my phone number, home and cell. Your granddaughter needs to see you sometime."

"You don't know what this means to me," he said soberly.

"Yes, I do," said Michael. "Take care, man."

William Jackson left and Michael rushed to play with his daughter and enjoy his friends. He didn't allow Brittany out of his sight for the rest of the night. Again, all the friends decided to stay over and laugh and joke all night and enjoy the fact that something real good had finally happened to Michael.

Michael slept on the living room floor next to Brittany with Myra next to him. Gary and Cheryl were on the sofa, and Donald under the television.

The next morning, Michael rose early and as everybody else slept, he had a long phone conversation. He was so excited that he cooked breakfast for everyone and was in the best mood he had been in for a long time and he let it be known. Michael was singing a lot of old songs as he prepared the food, and Donald woke to the singing.

"Please don't quit your day job," Donald smiled. "Man, what smells so good?"

"Eggs, turkey bacon, grits. You name it, I cooked it. I was so happy last night that I could barely sleep."

"I was happy for you, man," said Donald. "No one deserves to be happy like you do right now. By the way, brother, what happened in Jamaica?"

"If I told you, you wouldn't believe it. It was like something from a movie. We were very blessed to make it home, very blessed."

Donald stuck his hand in the food as Michael talked.

"Hey, man, wash your hands first," Michael scolded him.

"I thought I heard you on the phone," Donald remarked. "Who were you talking to so happily?"

"Believe it or not, I was talking to my mother. I'm going to live in Alabama, in the country. I need to get out of LA, and I definitely need to get out of this condo. Nothing good has happened to me since I've been here. I need a change."

"Yea, but Alabama?" Donald asked. "Those backwoods country bumpkins will be too slow for a city boy like you."

"I need slow," Michael said. "I've been living the fast life, and I need to slow it down. My mother lives in a place called Letohatchee, in Lowndes County. I'm going to try to teach at the local school called Calhoun High. They just won the state basketball championship."

"Let-o-hat-chee," said Donald. "I bet that place ain't even on the map."

"I hope not. I want to get as far away from LA as I can."

"Well, you can't get much farther than Letohatchee, Alabama," Donald concurred. "Isn't that where Jed and Elly Mae Clampett came from?"

"I'm not gonna comment," Michael replied. "My mother has a furnished cottage there that she says is in a perfect location and it has three bedrooms and 2½ baths, and you can hear the crickets chirping and see the leaves change in the winter and they have the four seasons."

"The Four Seasons Hotel?" said Donald. "All the way down there?"

"No, winter, spring, summer, and fall."

As Michael and Donald talked, the rest of the crowd woke up and smelled the food and heard some of Michael's conversation with Donald.

"Alabama?" said Gary. "I don't know if Alabama is ready for you, Mike. Those country girls won't know what hit them when you get there."

"Brittany is the only girl I'm worried about," Michael said. "I'm giving up women for a while."

"What about Myra?" asked Donald. "What is she going to do?"

"I guess whatever she wants," Michael replied. "I know she's tired of being burdened by us."

414 The Black Gigolo

Myra listened as Michael talked, but she didn't say much.

By then, everyone got up to enjoy breakfast and then go their separate ways. Gary wanted to get back to Chicago to check in with Barbara. Donald wanted to go back downtown, and Cheryl needed to get to work.

Michael made up his mind to get out of the condo as soon as possible. Cheryl returned Michael's money to him for Michelle's funeral because Michelle's parents paid for everything.

"I'll check on the agreement you signed for this place," Cheryl said, "and let you know if you own it or not. If you do, you can sell it and pull out a lot of cash. There probably isn't much owed on it."

After breakfast, Gary asked Cheryl to take him to the airport, but said good-bye first to Michael and Brittany in case they didn't see each other for a while. Michael told Gary that they were friends for life, brothers. Gary had saved Michael's life once, and he had been there all the way through his latest troubles.

"I hope all your endeavors come to pass," Gary said. "I hope you find peace in your decisions and in your life, and I hope you find love."

"I appreciate the way you've been there," Michael said. "If it wasn't for you and Barbara Brown, I wouldn't be here."

"Okay," Cheryl called out, "you're gonna miss your flight."

"Okay," Michael said, "well, I love you, brother."

"Likewise," said Gary. "One last question, Michael Alexander or Denzel Washington?"

"Funny," said Michael, "Michael Alexander, of course. Denzil Washington is far too short."

They laughed as Gary left the condo for Chicago, but he yelled back another question for Michael from the elevator.

"Beyonce or Ashanti?"

"Now, that's a good question," answered Michael. "Ashanti's got that ooh wee, ooh wee."

The elevator closed on Gary and he was gone. They promised to always keep in touch and to always be friends.

Donald decided to hang around the condo until Michael left that afternoon. Michael was so anxious to leave that he started to gather Brittany's clothes as soon as everyone left. As he was rushing and packing, Myra pulled him to the side and wanted to have a heart to heart.

"You're gonna leave me behind? I no longer have a life that doesn't include you and Brittany."

"What about your church, your family?"

"I can find another church. You and Brittany are my family."

"You mean, you want to give up your whole life for us? Everything you've always worked for?"

"I just want to be happy," she replied. "And taking care of you and Brittany makes me happy."

"Good," said Michael, "we need you now more than ever."

Michael hugged Myra and continued packing his clothes, wanting to rush out of town to put the nightmare of Los Angeles behind him.

"You going too, Donald," Michael said. "You're moving to Alabama with us too."

"Hell, no," Donald replied. "I'm a big-city boy, and I'm *staying* in the city."

"Well, if you change your mind, let me know. You're always welcome. What are you going to do, go back to the Downtowner?"

"Yea," said Donald, "that's my home."

Michael packed his clothes next, and Myra gathered her stuff and Brittany's and by the time the afternoon came, they had gathered all their possessions together and Michael was anxious to take off.

"So you're gonna leave, just like that?" said Donald. "Just take off?"

"I'm out," said Michael. "When I make up my mind, I don't like to second-guess myself."

Michael was desperate to find peace in his life and a fresh start from LA. The country was all he could think about. He packed up his Mercedes, and then rented a small U-Haul to carry as much stuff as possible.

Myra and Brittany helped Michael, then he called Donald over to speak to him.

"So you gonna do it, huh?" Donald said. "You're gonna move to Alabama?"

"Right now," Michael replied. "I'm all packed. We'll drive my car and send for Myra's later."

"How long does it take?" asked Donald.

"It's supposed to be a two-day drive, but I'm not exactly sure. You know, man, we've been through a lot together. You're just plain fun to be around, and I hate to leave you behind. Like me, you have lived a tough life, but I think all you need is a break so this is what I'm gonna do."

Michael gave Donald some keys and an envelope.

"What's this?" asked Donald.

"It's the keys to your new condo," said Michael. "Once we get the ownership thing straight, I'm going to refinance it, but I'll pay it up for you for two years to give you time to get it together. There's enough money in this envelope to take care of you until you find a job and to buy you some new clothes. We've done drugs together, and I know you can take this money and get high and sell all the stuff in this house, but the only person you'll be hurting is yourself. We both need a change. This can be yours. I've set it up downstairs. They already know you live here now."

Donald was so overwhelmed that he didn't know what to say. No one had ever done anything for him like this before. For once, Donald, the constant jokester, was without a punch line.

"Remember, you can't sell nothing from the home now, no drugs," Michael said.

"I heard you the first time," Donald replied. "I'll never forget this or you. Michael, we have had more adventures than people in the movies. We have laughed and cried together, got drunk together, munched at the Golden Bird, we've been friends. I just want you to know I love you, brother, and I hope you find whatever it is you're searching for "

"Likewise," said Michael, "likewise."

"We've got everything," said Myra. "Let's put this nightmare behind us. I'll drive first. I should be able to make it to Phoenix, and you can take it from there."

"Cool," said Michael, "I'm gonna sleep until we get to Phoenix. Alright, my brother, Donald, we're out. We'll call as soon as we get there."

Michael walked towards the elevator as Brittany and Myra embraced Donald. Then the three of them climbed into Michael's Mercedes and buckled up, heading towards the Freeway 10.

"We're gonna go through Phoenix and San Antonio and Houston and New Orleans," said Michael. When we stop, I'm gonna get a disposable camera so I can take some pictures of the best skylines."

"Daddy, can I take pictures too?" asked Brittany.

"You know it, baby," her father responded.

As Michael, Myra, and Brittany drove on the freeway, Michael's cell phone rang.

"Where are you at, Michael?" the voice asked.

"On my way out of town, and to whom am I speaking?" Michael said.

"This is Dana, Detective Andrews."

"Oh, man, I'm on my way to Alabama. I'm on my way down there to be a farmer."

"Alabama? I hate to see you go, man. I kind of got used to your militant way of looking at everything. I still can't believe what happened to us in Jamaica. It seems like a movie."

"No doubt," Michael agreed. "I guess all police officers aren't assholes like I thought. You burst my bubble, man."

"So you're already on the road? Man, you don't waste no time do you?"

"I had to get away. Too many ghosts in LA for me."

"Well, keep in touch," the detective said. "I consider you to be a friend."

"You're a friend too. By the way, what did you decide you were going to do with yourself?"

"I'm thinking about being a gigolo," he laughed. "Maybe I can take your job."

"Well, you can have it," Michael said. "I'm hanging up my late-night rendevous. You can have it all."

"Drive safely," Detective Andrews said. "Me and my son, Paul, are going to make a life of it."

"That's wonderful. That young man deserves to be happy and so do you, brother. Peace."

Michael and the detective hung up, then Michael relaxed and enjoyed the ride, believing that peace was sure to follow him.

Chapter 38

AFTER 3 DAYS OF SIGHTSEEING and travel, Michael, Myra, and Brittany arrived in Alabama and drove down I-65 to the Letohatchee exit.

"Wow!" Michael said, "This is the sticks. I've never seen so many trees. My mother said to go left off the freeway and then go over a small bridge and take another left."

They traveled down the small road and watched carefully since there were no street signs at all.

"Look out!" Myra said.

Crossing the road were two deer. The city slickers were amazed to see wild animals running around.

After several more minutes of travel, Michael and crew finally pulled into his mother's house. It had been more than a year since they were together, so she was very excited. She invited many other members of the family over, and they had prepared food and drinks as if a prodigal son had returned home.

Michael was overwhelmed at the reception as at least 40 people came over to his mother's nice 4-bedroom house to welcome him and Brittany and their surprise guest, Myra.

Michael pulled into the driveway to see barbeque grills with all kinds of meat cooking—deer, goat, hog, and, of course, beef. Many beers and bottles of liquor were available and unknown members of the family were ready to greet them.

The first person to greet Michael was his uncle, his mother's brother. "Hey, boy," said his uncle. "My name is Raymond, but they call me Jimbo. I'm the coolest cat to ever come through these parts."

"And the most modest, I see," Michael smiled.

Brittany exited the backseat and Myra came from the passenger side. Michael's mother rushed over to embrace her son and to hug and kiss Brittany. Michael wanted to embrace his mother longer, but his uncle wanted to be the star of the show.

"Hey, boy," Uncle Jimbo continued, "let me introduce you to some more of your relatives. This is your cousin Rodney, your cousin Alfred, but we call him Speedy, for Speedy Gonzales, your cousin Florida, and your cousin Al. You need to know your female cousins cause they are all fine, and we don't need no insects."

"That's *incest*, fool," said Michael's mother. "Shut up and let somebody else talk."

"Ain't no rednecks down here, right?" Michael asked. "The Klan don't still march, do they?"

"There are a few rednecks left," Cousin Alfred replied, "but there better not be any Klan down here. They'll get some buckshot in their ass."

As the men talked, Myra emerged from the side of the car.

"Oh," Michael said, "Myra, this is my family, family this is my friend, Myra."

"Hello," Myra said, smiling.

"Hello," answered Uncle Jimbo. "Damn, boy, this girl is fine. You definitely an Alexander 'cause you know how to pick the fine women."

"Myra takes care of Brittany," Michael said.

"And you too, I hope," Uncle Jimbo replied.

Michael didn't say anything, but just smiled.

The sun was beaming, and the food was good. Brittany walked around with her grandmother while Myra talked with women at the cookout. Michael, on the other hand, was telling stories to Uncle Jimbo, Speedy, Rodney, and Al.

"And that's how I got out of Jamaica," he said, finishing the story. Then he looked under the hood of his car to check his transmission and had a bottle of fluid in his hands.

"That's a high-performance car," Speedy said. "You don't change the fluids yourself."

"I know, just thought I'd check."

"So let me get this straight," said Uncle Jimbo, "you were a gigolo who got paid thousands of dollars to fuck beautiful women; you went to Jamaica to avenge the death of a beautiful woman; while there, you got kidnapped by the Jamaican Mafia; you were tied up in a dungeon with a 27-foot crocodile that was chained to a wall, but pulled a concrete block from the wall only to be shot by a madman. Then you're tied up, beaten, and go into a secret room where four women enticed you into the bed, but you say no and kill a huge Chinese bodyguard and free your friend.

"Then you cause a huge explosion and kill the man that killed your woman on the way out of the door, only to be attacked by Rottweilers as big as Shetland ponies, but you escape them also."

"Yea," said Michael, "that pretty much sums it up."

They all looked at each other.

"I know it's hot out here, but you're having hallucinations," Uncle Jimbo announced. "Beautiful black women and adventures on exotic islands. Hell, you must be drinking that transmission fluid. Shit, give me a hit of that."

"Yea, give me a shot, too," said Speedy.

"Shit, I'll take a nip," smiled Rodney.

They all laughed at Michael and wondered if their cousin was a little off.

"What about that girl, Myra?" asked Speedy. "I know you're climbing that mountain."

"Nah, man, we're just friends. There's nothing going on."

"Just friends?" said Uncle Jimbo. "A friend is a buddy you watch the ballgame with, not gorgeous females that worship the ground you walk on. Boy, you ain't got no sugar in your tank, do you? We don't need you down here embarrassing the family chasing hairy booties."

"Hell, no," Michael said. "I'm not like that. We're just not on that level, and what do you mean, 'worship the ground I walk on'?"

"Anybody can see that girl has got love in her eyes," Uncle Jimbo informed Michael. "You think she gonna give up her life to come all the way to Alabama just to take care of your daughter? Boy, you sure your elevator goes all the way to the top floor?"

Cousin Speedy weighed about 150 lbs, but stepped up to the plate. "If you don't want her, let me know. I'll take her off your hands. I can handle them ham hocks."

"Go for it," Michael said. "Shoot your best shot."

"So what's up with the neighbors around here?" Michael asked. "Eeverybody go to the store and leave their doors open?"

"You leave your door open, and you'll come back to an empty house. These boys across the street are robbing everybody blind. Niggers on crack don't want to go to work."

"Crack is down here?" asked Michael.

"Man, please," said Rodney. "This is crackville. There still ain't no jobs around here and all people do is drink, smoke crack, and rob people. But there are far more good people than bad. There are just a few bad apples that need to be weeded out."

At that moment, a white woman walked by that had been invited to the cookout by one of the distant family members and Uncle Jimbo was running his mouth as usual.

"That white girl got some ass," he said. "These white girls got ass like sisters nowadays."

Then he yelled at the white woman as she walked by. "Hey, gal, you got any black in you?" When she didn't respond, he said, "Well, would you like to have some black in you?"

"Man, y'all talk to white women like that in the South nowadays?" Michael asked. "I thought there were nothing but Southern gentlemen around."

"Boy, you act like this is 1940," Uncle Jimbo responded. "We ain't no Emmitt Till. We can say whatever the hell we want."

Michael and his cousins talked and had a good time. This was Michael's first totally pleasant day in quite a while.

THE COOKOUT WENT into the evening, and Brittany fell asleep in her grandmother's arms. Michael, Myra, and Brittany stayed at his mother's house that night and would go to see the cottage the first thing in the morning.

The next day, they woke up to a big breakfast prepared by Michael's mother. After breakfast, Michael and Myra drove over to the cottage and were greeted by Uncle Jimbo, Speedy, Rodney, and Al, who were ready to help unload the car and help with the cottage.

The cottage was very beautiful and roomy, an older place with a real homey feel. As they walked inside, they saw that the place was nice, but very dusty. Everybody pitched in to help with the cleanup, hang curtains, and clean the bath. Everyone had a good time helping out.

Uncle Jimbo, of course, talked all day and was the life of the party, keeping everyone smiling and making their workday a little easier.

Late that afternoon, a 1989 Lincoln Continental pulled up to the cottage and a heavyset woman missing two front teeth came over with food and walked up and gave Uncle Jimbo a big kiss, then set the food on the table.

"Hey, Martha," said Michael's mother. "Michael, this is your Uncle Jimbo's wife, Martha."

"How are you?" Michael asked.

"Fine," she answered.

Martha was very pleasant and had been married to Michael's uncle for a few years after the death of his first wife. Michael set up a TV stand and Uncle Jimbo came over.

"Before you say anything, I already know she's ugly," he said, "but I love me an ugly woman. Pretty women are too high maintenance. I work hard and come home to a good meal. I go out to the club and she don't say nothing. Whatever I do is fine with her, and I treat her like a queen. Plus, she got some good coochie."

Michael's mother just stared at her brother.

"I wasn't gonna say a word," Michael said. "A good woman is hard to come by. I respect the fact that you know when you have something good."

"Yeah, man," Uncle Jimbo replied, "I have so much respect for the black female. I admit they fly off the handle sometimes, and sometimes they talk too much, but there is no other woman I would rather be with than a sister. They nurture our children. Half the time they raise them by themselves, and yet they still prosper."

"Yea," said Michael, "but they always want to fight, they want to take the role of a man, be a man. They can't be a man, no matter how hard they try."

"Sometimes they don't have a choice," Michael's mother said. "The black man won't stand up and take his rightful place in the world."

"Well, all I know is that we can't make it without each other," Michael replied. "If we don't come together, we will never truly prosper as a people."

They continued to debate the point and after a hard day's work, the cottage was livable. Everyone left except Michael, Myra, Brittany, and Michael's mother. They just sat around and relaxed.

"So Myra," said Michael's mother, "what are you gonna do in these country woods to keep yourself occupied?"

"Well, I know Montgomery is the closest city," she replied. "I'll enroll at Alabama State University and get my master's degree, and I'm certified to teach, so I'll try to get on with the school system. It shouldn't be a problem."

"Oh, okay, and what about you, son? What's your plan?"

"For a while, I'm not going to do anything, Mom. I'm just going to take it easy. I've got money and some real estate that set me up for life. My job will be making sure Brittany is secure."

"We will all see to that," his mother replied. "Well, I'm going to bed. I'll catch you cats tomorrow."

⇥ ⇥ ⇥

MICHAEL'S MOTHER WENT home, and Myra offered to fix
Michael some food, but he was exhausted and just wanted to
go to sleep. The crickets chirping loudly outside and the
pitch-black darkness gave him a sense of peace.

"You don't think there are any bears in these woods, do
you?" Myra asked.

"If there are, I'll protect you," he replied. "I'm like
superman. No bear can handle me."

"Yeah, you're my hero," said the always complimentary
Myra.

Myra was finally in a position where there were no other
women around Michael. She went about the task of making
Michael notice her as a woman. First, she put Brittany to
bed as Michael dressed for bed, then she came back to ask
Michael a question, wearing the skimpiest short set that she
had.

Michael had always noticed Myra's features, but managed to stay away from her. As she entered the room,
Michael was spellbound by the incredible body she had and
her beauty with her hair let down.

"Michael, do you want me to make breakfast in the
morning?"

He just stared for a moment and then caught himself.
"Yea, that will be fine. I mean, that will be okay," he stuttered.

Myra said OK, then turned to walk away so Michael could
see the other side. He just stared at Myra's rear end and wiped
his face with a cold towel as he tried to go to sleep.

As Myra and Michael slept that night, they had no idea
that someone had been watching their every move.

After two weeks of being in Alabama, not a single
incident happened. The family had gotten together to take

good care of Michael and his family. Then Myra noticed that little things around the house started coming up missing and brought it to Michael's attention, but he just brushed it off because things had been going so good.

Myra's plans to entice Michael were successful. Michael was becoming very weak and definitely began to look at her differently. Myra planned to take it to the next level tonight.

It was a quiet Thursday evening as Michael came home with a bottle of Hennessey.

"Michael," Myra said, "I thought you had stopped drinking."

"I have. It's just a souvenir, kind of a reminder of what I've been through. Besides, I want to stock the bar because we get so much company. I've stopped drinking, but it's still good to have on hand."

"Yea," she replied, "but it can also be a temptation."

"Yeah, I guess you're right. Where's Brittany?"

"Your mother came by and Brittany wanted to go, so I guess it's just me and you tonight."

"Oh," said Michael.

He went into the room and closed the door. It's not that he was not extremely attracted to Myra, but he had lost two wives in the last year and a half and thought that he was bad news for any female. But Myra had her own agenda.

Michael went into his closet to check the safety on his gun and to kill time. After that, his door opened.

Myra stood in the doorway with a see-through negligee on, and no bra or panties.

Michael dropped the gun on the floor, looked at Myra for a second, and then walked over, picked her up in the air, and started to kiss her all over.

Myra's nipples were straight and erect, and Michael's penis stood up like a pole. He pulled the gown over her head and lay back on the bed, and Myra climbed on for the ride. She rode him real hard as Michael pumped up and down. Then she screamed out in pleasure as she had an orgasm. Michael came at the same time.

Although it lasted only a few minutes, it was very intense and Michael and Myra lay on the bed, exhausted. Michael looked at the beautiful woman at his side and began to speak, never realizing that they were being watched.

"Didn't you want your first time to be more special than that?" he asked.

"I wanted my first time to be with *you*," Myra said, "and it *was* special, *very* special."

Michael had pulled his pants off but never removed his shirt. He just lay there, drained, as the phone rang. Myra went to the bathroom as Michael dug in his pants to find his cell phone and answered the phone, blowing hard.

"Hello," he said, out of breath.

"Why are you blowing so hard?" said the voice belonging to Cheryl. "I've got Gary on three-way. You turned into a farmer down there yet?"

"How y'all doing?" asked Michael. "To what do I owe the pleasure of this phone call?"

"We haven't heard from you, and we wondered how things were going," she continued. "How are Brittany and Myra?"

"Fine," Michael replied with a smile as Myra lay back down beside him, "real fine."

"So what's going on in Alabama?" asked Gary. "You ready to go back to LA yet?"

"Naw, man, this is the best move I've ever made. I'm a country boy for the rest of my life."

"Well, I just wanted to let you know what's happening," Cheryl said. "They dropped the charges against William

Jackson. They realized he didn't know what was going on."

"Good," said Michael, "I'm going to call him so he can get to see his granddaughter."

"I've examined the deed that you signed on the condo, and it was an agreement that signed the property over to you," Cheryl told him. "I guess Coretta didn't cover all her bases like she thought. I have already talked to a mortgage person. He said he would call you this weekend.

"Oh, I went by the condo. Why did you give Donald all that money?"

"What happened?" Michael asked.

"Liquor bottles all over the place," she said. "Crack pipes too, and he had a couple of his crack buddies staying there with him. You need to get over there and get it straight for the appraiser."

"Boy, I hate to hear that," Michael said. "I'll make arrangements to fly out there next week after I speak to your mortgage guy.

"What about Kenneth? They ever catch up with him?"

"No," said Cheryl, "but it's only a matter of time. He can't just disappear off the face of the earth."

"I guess not," Michael replied. "Gary, how's Barbara Brown?"

"Great," he said enthusiastically. "You haven't been watching her show?"

"No, I'll check it out tomorrow."

"Well, Michael, we gotta go," Cheryl said. "You're eating up my anytime minutes. Just wanted to touch base and let you know how much we love you."

"Yea, I love you guys to," he said. "Go by the condo and tell Donald he better straighten up before I get there."

"I'll let you surprise him," Cheryl said.

"Okay. Later."

They hung up the phone and Michael turned over to embrace Myra. They fell asleep in each other's arms under the watchful eye of an intruder.

Chapter 39

THE NEXT DAY WAS FRIDAY, and Michael and Myra spent all day in Montgomery while Brittany was with her grandmother. Michael had planned to go to a high school basketball game that night and take Myra and Brittany. They would meet Uncle Jimbo and his cousins.

At 7:30 p.m., they arrived at the Calhoun High School gymnasium, home of the Calhoun Tigers. The crowd was wild and the gym was packed as Calhoun played Lanier High School from Montgomery.

"Man, these country boys can jump out of the gym," said Michael.

"Yeah," Uncle Jimbo responded, "three state championships and one runner-up. They can hoop in Calhoun."

"Ah, I'll take all of these young boys to the hoop," said Michael. "They don't want none of this."

"Yeah, right," said Uncle Jimbo. "Oh, nephew, I meant to tell you to be careful around your property at night. There's an old well over there, and all the boards are cracked and rotten. If you fall in, you're in big trouble."

As they talked, Michael's cell phone rang. "Hello, I can barely hear you," he said.

"It's Dana," said the voice, "how are you?"

"Fine," answered Michael, "I'm at a basketball game and as you can hear, the crowd is wild."

"Remember Desmond, that bartender in Jamaica that helped us find the club and picked us up that morning as we left that compound?" asked Detective Andrews. "They found him the other day with his head cut off. That's the trademark of the Jamaican Mafia. Apparently, they came to the hotel the night after we left, looking for us. They said they won't stop looking for us until they find us and kill us."

"Well," said Michael, "you better get out of LA. They won't be able to find me because I'm not even on the map. Man, I'm sorry about the bartender. All he did was help us, and he died for it."

"I know," the detective said, "but remember, Michael, it doesn't matter where you are. These people have their ways, so be careful. You would be surprised how easy it is to find someone these days. Even down there. Take care."

Michael hung up the phone and Uncle Jimbo talked to him. "You know, your friend, Myra, told my sister that she kinda feels like she's being watched. She says small things have been missing around the house."

"She's just paranoid," said Michael.

"Well, you know how jumpy women can be," Uncle Jimbo said. "I've got a dog. He's a mutt, but he barks at everything. Anybody gets close to your house, you'll know it. After the game, I'll bring him over. I've got several of them."

"Okay," Michael agreed.

They continued to watch the game and have fun. At 11:00 p.m., they arrived home from the game with Brittany sleeping and Myra and Michael tired from a long day.

A car pulled up in front of driveway and Uncle Jimbo exited with a dog.

"You said he was a mutt," Michael said. "You weren't kidding. I'm scared for you to leave him over here because he might have fleas all up and down the place."

"Well, he ain't much to look at, but he won't let anybody come up to your house," said Uncle Jimbo.

"He got mange or something?" Michael asked. "What's his name?"

"D-O-G," Uncle Jimbo replied. "This is a good dog. You're so into appearances."

"You're right," said Michael, "I'm sorry. Thanks, Uncle Jimbo."

"Okay, nephew. I'm going home to my ugly wife."

Michael laughed at his uncle's sense of humor. As he jumped back into his car to head home, Michael tied the dog up to a post and walked back inside.

"Is Brittany asleep, Myra?" he asked.

"She just dozed off."

Myra went into the room and came out with a short nightie on. She and Michael began to have sex on the sofa, and then they moved into the bedroom. At midnight, they were both sound asleep.

At about 12:30, the dog started to bark excessively and the noise woke Myra.

"Michael," she said, "listen to how that dog is barking. Maybe someone is out there."

"Probably just a rabbit," he said sleepily, "or he's homesick already."

The dog continued to bark and Michael sat up and took notice. Suddenly, the dog yelped out loud and stopped barking. Michael and Myra heard the noise, then Michael went to his closet looking for his pistol, but couldn't find it, so he put on some pants and shoes and quietly went outside to where the dog was tied up.

The dog had been shot, and his head had been severed.

Michael immediately thought of the Jamaican Mafia and that they had somehow found his family. At that moment, Myra screamed out real loud.

"Michael," she yelled.

Michael rushed back into the house to see Myra and Brittany and a third party, covered with the dog's blood, standing in the living room.

"Man, what the fuck you doing here?" said Michael.

"You shouldn't leave your window unlocked," Kenneth replied. "I've been watching you guys ever since you moved here. Oh, sorry about that mutt. I tapped your cell phone and heard you talking about the Jamaican Mafia. Just thought I'd cut the dog's head off for effect."

Kenneth had awakened Brittany from her bedroom, holding a 9mm to her head. He also had a tight grip around her neck, his hands dripping with the dog's blood.

Michael made a move towards Kenneth.

"Don't try it, Michael," said Kenneth. "I don't have a problem killing her."

"Daddy," moaned Brittany, "Daddy."

"Here, baby," said Michael.

"You want Daddy?" yelled Ken. "Uncle Ken is here."

Kenneth licked Brittany across the face and turned up the bottle of Hennessey that Michael bought the other night. Michael moved again.

"Michael," Kenneth said menacingly, holding the gun to Brittany's head, "try that again and somebody's gonna die. I got a few secrets to tell. You know all those little girls that were missing in LA? That's the work of yours truly. I like 'em young. As soon as I kill you, Brittany, Myra, and I, we're gonna have some fun."

Kenneth turned up the Hennessey again. "I only started drinking this because of *you*," he said. "In fact, my whole life has been built around you."

Kenneth pulled out some paper and showed Michael a large amount of cocaine. "Look, Michael, I've got your favorite," he said, "but you probably only like it in crack form."

Kenneth threw his whole head in the cocaine, snorting it violently, leaving powder all over his face.

"Tony Montana," said Kenneth. "Remember how we used to watch all those Scarface movies, i.e., Tony Montana, who said you fucked up, then you fucked up and you had to die? Well, you fucked up, Michael."

Myra stood there in her robe, sobbing.

"You fucked up, Michael," said Kenneth again.

"Fucked up how?" asked Michael.

"Shut up!" yelled Kenneth, pointing the gun at Michael. "Shut the fuck up. It was always Michael this and Michael that. Everybody wanted to be around Michael. All the women wanted Michael, the great athlete, the great student. We were never friends when we were children. You pitied me. I would hear you talk about me and laugh when I was not around. Do you know how that feels, do you? Of course not. You're Michael, you don't feel pain.

"Remember when you told me it was a sin to worry. Well, I wanted to see if you were true to the game. I wanted you to feel pain. I wanted to see how much you could bear. So I chose a special night—your night—to make my move. You see, I had to take a backseat to you again. You were being promoted to the top of the hill, the first black president of a major insurance company, president of Progress Insurance. I just snapped. I couldn't take it any more. I had to do something. So I spiked your Hennessey, you know, the date rape drug. Never thought I'd use it on a man. That's why I wanted to toast you. I put just enough in to make you groggy. I knew it would eventually put you out. And I loosened one of your tires. I'm surprised the police didn't see that. I guess since they thought you were drunk, for them, it was an open-and-shut case.

"But I didn't plan for Sheila to die, just you. I offered to give her a lift, but of course, she didn't want to leave you. Nobody wants to leave Michael."

"You mean that you deliberately poisoned me and loosened the nuts on my tire so I would crash?" Michael asked in disbelief. "You killed my wife and robbed my daughter of her mother, and you killed my unborn son? And because of you, other people have died, all because you've got this sick jealousy thing going on about me, you perverted bastard."

Michael stepped forward again.

"Stop!" yelled Kenneth, "I won't tell you again. I never meant to kill your wife—just *you*. It just happened that she died. It was her time to go. After you died, I was gonna win Sheila over and then Brittany would be my daughter. You see, I can't have children and since we were supposed to be best friends since five, I figured you wouldn't mind if I had yours. And now, well, Myra will have to do—Kenneth, Myra, and Brittany. I saw you guys making love the other night. Don't worry, Myra, I can do much better than that."

Kenneth blew Myra a kiss.

"You'll never touch me," Myra stated adamantly. "I'd rather be dead first."

"Really?" said Kenneth. "Well, we can make that happen."

Michael kept looking for an opening and Brittany continued to cry as Kenneth stood there drinking Hennessey.

"And then, to top it off," said Kenneth, "you're a crack fiend and I get you back into the club scene and you meet Coretta James who offers to pay you to have sex with women, sets you up in a condo, and pays you thousands of dollars. I even see you on TV. That was the last straw. I knew I would eventually have to kill you myself.

"I thought a cat had nine lives until I met you. I tried putting a camera in your house, but that only got me in trouble. Anyway, enough of this confession. I need to get rid of you so my new family and I can have a late dinner."

Kenneth turned up the Hennessey again and then fired quickly at Michael, striking him in the shoulder. Michael ran from the house, and Kenneth pushed Brittany down, then ran out the door after Michael. Myra picked Brittany up, who was crying hysterically, and made sure she was alright.

"Brittany, Brittany, are you alright?" Myra asked. "Stay here."

Myra ran into Michael's bedroom and looked into the box where he kept his gun, but it was not there. Searching for it, she threw stuff from the closet, but the gun was nowhere to be found. Then she remembered that Michael had dropped the gun on the floor the other night and looked under the bed, to see the gun lying at the edge. She grabbed it and took the safety off, then rushed out of the house.

Michael ran in the dark, having no idea where he was running as Kenneth pursued him, firing the gun at him.

"I've got 16 in the clip and 1 in the hole," said Kenneth. "I'll get you in a minute."

Michael ran into the old well area and a board broke, trapping him in the well as he yelled out in pain. Kenneth slowly walked towards Michael, ready to kill him.

"I can't believe it's this easy," Kenneth said. "No long speeches. When I kill you, then I'm going back and have me some of Myra and then Miss Brittany, and then I'm going over to your mama's house. Mrs. Alexander is still looking good. I always wanted some of that growing up."

Michael moaned in pain as Myra arrived and shot at Kenneth, but missed him by a long way. Kenneth turned and shot, striking Myra right on the hand. She dropped the gun and yelled in pain.

"Don't worry, baby," said Ken, "I'll fix you up as soon as I'm done. Michael, as much as I enjoy hearing you squeal like a little bitch in pain, I've got things to do. Me, Myra, and Brittany have got some work to do."

Kenneth raised the gun to shoot Michael and a loud shot rang out. Kenneth was shot in the head. He stumbled across Michael and fell in the well, dying instantly. Standing over the well holding the gun was Uncle Jimbo.

"That motherfucker killed my dog," he said. "I couldn't let him get away with that."

Myra was in pain but got off the ground as Uncle Jimbo pulled Michael from the well. Michael had severe cuts and possibly a broken leg. He groaned loudly as Uncle Jimbo pulled him from the broken wood. Although he was in pain, he was very glad to see his uncle.

"I could kiss you, Unc," he said.

"I know you're happy to be alive, but an Alexander doesn't get gay, no matter how happy he is. Come on, let's go home," he said.

"How did you know what was going on?" asked Michael.

"Well, at first I heard the dog," he said, "and then I heard the shots. That's one advantage of living in the country. You can hear everything. Nobody comes on our property and hurts a member of our family."

⊷⊷ ⊷⊷ ⊷⊷

TWO WEEKS LATER, Michael, on crutches, closed the sale on his LA condo. "Mr. Alexander, here is your check for seven hundred fifty thousand dollars," said the attorney. "Congratulations."

"Thank you, sir," Michael said. "This is going to take care of me and my family quite nicely."

Cheryl and Gary were in the attorney's office, along with Myra and Brittany, and waited to greet Michael as he finished up his transaction.

"Well," said Michael, "that's over with. Let's go get something to eat."

"How long is Donald going to be in rehab?" asked Cheryl.

"I'm not sure," said Michael. "As long as it takes, I hope. I'm just blessed that I didn't have to go myself. My family really looked out for me."

"Well," Cheryl smiled, "Gary and I are getting married."

"Congratulations," smiled Myra, "maybe we can have a double wedding."

Myra looked at Michael, and Michael looked away.

"We'll see," he said.

"We're going to get the car," said Gary and Cheryl.

Michael leaned against a pole. "Myra, you and Brittany go with them. I'll lean here against this pole until you guys come back and pick me up."

"You sure?" asked Myra.

"Definitely. It's a little chilly," he said. "I don't want Brittany to catch a cold."

"Okay," said Myra.

As everyone walked off, a woman walked up to Michael with a black dress on and a shawl over her. As she got next to Michael, she uncovered her head.

"Hello, Michael," said Coretta. "I never meant to hurt you. You're an incredible man, Michael. I will always hold a place for you in my heart."

Michael was stunned and then the car approached. Coretta pulled the shawl back over her head and walked away as the car pulled up.

"Who was that woman, Michael?" Cheryl asked.

Michael just stared into space. "Nobody," he said. "Family, let's go get something to eat."

THE END

Dedication

I DEDICATE THIS MANUSCRIPT TO my son, Troy, and my daughter, Taylor, the two most beautiful gifts I have ever been blessed with. I also dedicate it to my mother, Joan Andrews, and my seven brothers and sisters, Cheryl, Carl, Erica, Joyce, Derrry, Sharon, and Dana. Most importantly, I dedicate it to the memory of Willie Lee Andrews, our grandmother who raised us all with a firm hand, and who made sure we had a chance to prosper in this world.

Only Jah knows how much I have believed in myself and how many gifts I have been blessed with, and I am very thankful for all the blessings that I have been given. Most of all, thanks to everyone that talked about me, lied about me, and did all kinds of things that they thought would hurt me. I don't believe in allowing anyone to dictate my strengths and weaknesses. I'm far too secure in who I am. Thank you. I would like to end this with a poem called "Ode to a Hoe."

ODE TO A HOE

There is an interesting task when you live in this
world
If you're a man that can pull plenty of girls
You have to be careful of the decisions you make
And be totally conscious of the chances you take
If "pounding the honeys" is part of your plan
And you think that makes you a man
There are a few things that you need to know
If you decide that you want to be a hoe
Sometimes when you're getting and the getting
gets good
You don't protect yourself in the way that you
should
When you get in the mood, I guess you don't care
All you think about is their legs in the air
You struggle with yourself but you don't know
There're dire consequences to being a hoe
You're not lookin' for a woman or a wife
You're looking to mess up somebody's life
To be a hoe you cannot be led
And you have to get used to many different beds
Being a hoe is like losing a bet
It's kinda like a person playing Russian roulette
If you don't wear a condom, that's the chance you
take
If you do wear a condom then it may break
The coochie may be good, my brother, as you blast
it
A tisket a tasket a condom or a casket
I'm a gigga high, I'm a gigga low
I sometimes brag about being a gigolo

Think about all the people that you have to please
Who can you please if you have a disease?
You can give it to her sista and make her holler
She may even give you that almighty dollar
You're the life of the party and you have many
friends
One day that party is gonna come to an end
When you're a hoe you just make people cry
And if you're not careful you can make people die
If you're gonna be a hoe you can't live right
And you're gonna have a lot of sleepless nights
You might be out of one bed by 2
When 4 comes around you gotta do what you do
Can you be a hoe and be part of the plan?
You're taking your life right out of your hands
So give it some thought if you like to get down
If you believe in spreading yourself around
If you have an ear then hear what I said
That may not be the only thing that you spread
You can spread contempt, it can knock you to your
knees
You can share your body, you can spread disease
Be careful of the things that you choose to do
The choices you make can come back to haunt you.

CPSIA information can be obtained
at www.ICGtesting.com
Printed in the USA
BVHW081656300921
617726BV00001B/1